FIC
Andrews
Gideon

BKM

DATE DUE

MAR 3 0 2010 7A			

GAYLORD MG

gideon

gideon

RUSSELL ANDREWS

BALLANTINE BOOKS

NEW YORK

A Ballantine Book
Published by The Ballantine Publishing Group

Copyright © 1999 by Peter Gethers and David Handler

http://www.randomhouse.com/BB/

Library of Congress Cataloging-in-Publication Data
Andrews, Russell.
Gideon / Russell Andrews. — 1st ed.
p.   cm.
ISBN 0-345-42346-1 (alk. paper)
I. Title.
PS3551.N4525G53   1999
813'.54—dc21   98-47422
                                                      CIP

Text design by Ann Gold

Manufactured in the United States of America

First Edition: June 1999

10   9   8   7   6   5   4   3   2   1

To Bill Goldman, who deserves many things,
but two above all: total credit for this novel
and a Knicks championship season

ACKNOWLEDGMENTS

Thanks to John Alderman and his colleagues at Merrill Lynch for their financial expertise; Elaine M. Pagliaro of the Connecticut State Police Forensic Science Laboratory for her demolition expertise; and Jon Katz for his Internet expertise. Janice Herbert did diligent and wonderfully thorough research, and Marv Donnaud is a pilot and long-distance flying instructor extraordinaire. Thanks must also go to Dominick Abel, Jack Dytman, and Esther Newberg for believing in this from the very beginning; Lorenzo Carcaterra, William Diehl, and Stan Pottinger for their early readings and advice; and Linda Grey and Leona Nevler for their confidence, support, and superb editorial direction. And, of course, thanks as always to Janis Donnaud, for her ruined weekends and evenings, and Diana Drake, who asks only for fertile soil and happy endings.

The past isn't dead. It isn't even past.
—William Faulkner

prologue

July 8

Washington, D.C.

O nce again he woke up screaming.

It was the dream, of course. The same dream. The same overwhelming, inescapable dream.

But there was something different this time. There was no distance to it, no feeling of safety. It had crossed over and crystallized and become stiflingly, palpably, claustrophobically real. The colors were bright and the sound was crisp. He could see the faces, hear the voices. Feel the pain.

And he had to listen to the crying.

When he realized he was awake, that the sound he heard was real, was actually coming from inside him, he bit the scream off and the physical effort hurt his throat, as if the noise were being ripped out of him. He had to force himself to think about where he was, who he was, to stop himself from screaming again. And then he had to bite down on his lip so hard he drew blood. Otherwise he knew he could have howled and wept for minutes, for hours. Forever.

He was drenched in sweat, the sheets so damp beneath him he thought he'd wet the bed. But none of that was new. He was used to that. No, it was the *end* of the dream that left him weak and trembling. That's what was different.

This time he dreamed that he talked.

And because he believed in the veracity of dreams, he woke up terrified.

The reasons for his terror had dominated his thoughts ever since the moment she had come to him, the woman he loved so absolutely, shaken and subdued, ever since she had told him she had to talk to him in private. It had been sunny that afternoon, and he remembered the warm glow he'd felt, basking in the realization that everything was going perfectly, all their plans were coming together so smoothly. When she leaned over and whispered to him, he had never seen her look like that. So frightened. Pale and trembling. He couldn't imagine what had done this to her. Then she told him about the package that had arrived. What was in it. And what the instructions were that came with it.

They had sat together, holding each other, for a long time after that. Saying nothing because there was nothing to say. Because everything he had worked for, *they* had worked for, was crumbling now. No, not crumbling. Exploding.

He had canceled all meetings, shut off all phone calls. They had locked themselves behind closed doors. Then she spoke, examining their options, going over every choice rationally and calmly. Analyzing. Probing. Until finally she had put her hand over his, her skin cool and soft. Her softness was all that kept him from bursting into tears.

"There's only one thing you can do," she said.

"That's the one thing I *can't* do," he said sadly.

"There's no other choice. Anything else is too risky, too terrible for you." She touched his cheek. "What if they find out? Think what would happen."

He didn't have to ask who "they" were. And he didn't have to think. He knew what would happen. He knew exactly what would happen.

He also knew that he could never accept the way out she was urging him to take. She could propose it only because she didn't truly understand his power, didn't know what she was really asking him to give up.

After all her rational explanations, after eliminating choice after choice, ultimately it was still impossible, what she was asking him to do.

So he'd thought of another solution. A far better one.

The latest dream showed him that it was right. And just. He knew better than anyone that it was just.

He sat up suddenly in the bed, as if the quickness of his movement could shed the fear like an unwanted layer of skin. He blinked furiously, willing the nightmare—and the night's solitude—to disappear.

It was just getting light outside, the sun's first rays filtering down so passively they didn't seem to have the strength to make it all the way through the windows of the bedroom. But neither the shadows of the dawn outside nor the icy air-conditioning inside—the best system money could buy—were able to disguise the brutal humidity of this Washington summer. His rapid breathing slowed somewhat, and he uncurled the clenched fingers of both hands. He tried to force himself to be still, to relax. To come back to life. But he could not.

He glanced to his left, where his wife slept soundly. He wondered how she could possibly sleep, and yet he was glad she did. For the first time since he'd known her, he didn't think he could face her, couldn't talk to her, tell her what he was thinking. Yet despite everything it pleased him to hear her gentle, rhythmic breathing, so comfortably familiar to him, soft and delicate. And there was another marvel: In twenty-seven years of marriage she had never been anything but a comfort to him. Never anything but a tower of strength.

He swung his legs out of bed. They were not yet steady. Still sitting, his bare feet planted in the pastel Aubusson carpet, he ran his left hand over the smooth, hollowed-out top of the bedpost. He loved their four-poster bed. Built in 1782, dated and signed by Nathaniel Dolgers, the greatest of colonial carpenters. It was too short for them, really, and not all that comfortable. But he insisted they sleep in it. He looked at his wife, curled up in the sheets, and smiled. She thought his affection for the bed was because he'd always loved working with his hands, had always, above all, worshiped craftsmanship. But that wasn't it at all. The real reason was that the bed had cost $175,000. A bed! And every single night before he slept—if he slept—he thought about what his mother had done when he'd told her he was sleeping in a $175,000 bed.

She'd laughed. She'd thrown her head back and laughed and laughed until tears of wonderment flowed down her leather-tough cheeks.

His legs were steadier now, his heart no longer pounding. He stood slowly, padded over to the window. Directly before him he could see the square, deserted and still. To the right, below him, at the eastern side of the house, he could make out the garden, the silhouettes of her flowers. He glanced back at the sleeping woman and had to shake his head. They always referred to them as "her" flowers. And when she talked about them, she might have been talking about the children they'd never had. Put her before a Grant Thomas rose or a *Campanula lactiflora* and her face would soften, her eyes would glisten, her voice would coo in that tender, musical tone of hers. And when she *touched* those petals—what caresses, what love. Whenever he passed one of the arrangements she'd cut for the house, he couldn't help but reach out and stroke the petals himself. He always felt as if he were touching her. And she were touching him.

He turned away now from the garden, walked quietly to the bathroom. He stared at his face in the mirror above the marble sink counter. He looked good for fifty-five. Damn good. His face had served him well. The jaw was square, the eyes blue and confident. Sure, his hair had gotten grayer, particularly over the past three years. But he'd maintained his weight, maybe ten pounds above what he'd weighed in college, certainly no more. There were a few lines, particularly around his eyes; what the hell, he was entitled. And everyone said they made him look distinguished.

Now there was a description he'd never envisioned about himself when he was young.

It was time to shave his distinguished face, he decided. He picked up the electric shaver, wishing as he did every morning for an old-fashioned razor. But she would not allow him one. It was too unpredictable, she said. What if he cut himself? What if he showed up for his first meeting of the day with a bloody little wad of toilet paper stuck to his chin? He sometimes wondered if anyone would say anything. Well, he would never know. He was incapable of doing anything as unpredictable as using an old-fashioned razor.

When he was done shaving, unsatisfied as always with the result, he lay down on the cold tile floor and began to do his back exercises. He slowly brought his knees up to his chest, hugging them toward him. Then he rocked back and forth, stretching, feeling his muscles loosen up.

There was a gym in the house, of course. Being the perfect wife, she had converted one of the bedrooms on the second floor, put in all the latest equipment. He would use it sometimes, hop onto the treadmill for a ten-minute mile, even do some bench-pressing. But for morning stretching, he liked the bathroom. He was comfortable in there. It was quiet.

And, best of all, he could be alone.

The dream had begun to fade now. As it always did, morning brought him some relief. And today, a new clarity. For, in some sense, the dream had not ended with the sunrise. One part of it lingered, beckoned, seduced. The part that held the promise of relief. And of truth.

If there was anything that terrified him more than the dream itself, it was finding out that truth. What he was beginning to suspect *must* be the truth. Yet he knew it had to be done. And he knew exactly how to do it.

There was a phone mounted on the wall to the right of the beveled, gold-framed mirror. He picked up the receiver, hesitated, drumming his fingers on the rose-colored marble counter that held the double porcelain sink. It was a call he made all the time, one that always brought laughter or caused him to glow with long-forgotten pride. But today he didn't want to dial. He'd had a long time to think about what he needed to say and what he was likely to hear in return. He was fairly certain it would not make him laugh or glow.

He placed the call, and the voice on the other end cackled with humor and quivered with age and sounded as if it were being filtered through seventy years of gin, hand-rolled cigarettes, and ragged love affairs.

"Mother," he said, keeping his voice low and even.

The old woman's voice replied with enormous pleasure. "I'll be a son of a bitch if this isn't early even for you. Don't tell me they're keepin' you busy up there."

"No busier than usual."

"Talk to me, lovey."

"I'm talking, Mother."

"No, *talk* to me. I hear that tone in your voice. It's way too early for bullshit."

"Have you looked in your safe lately, Mother?"

"My safe? Why in the world would I—"

She stopped. He waited for her to understand. It didn't take long.

"Darlin'," she said, "I haven't opened that safe in a long, long time. The arthritis, damn it, it just makes everything so—"

"I'd like you to open it now."

She didn't ask why. She just put the phone down, kept him holding for perhaps five minutes. When she came back on the line, she told him what she had seen.

And now he was face-to-face with the truth. There it was, inescapable and undeniable, and it took his breath away, doubled him over with pain. It not only left him speechless, it left him empty inside.

His mother knew him well enough to know she didn't need to say very much more. She told him she loved him. She told him he shouldn't worry too much. She told him that she would do whatever he needed her to do.

She told him she was sorry.

He hung up the phone and stood there, leaning on the marble counter for support. It was a full minute before he had the strength to step into the shower, where he let the hot spray sting his chest and then his back, let the steam swirl around him, fogging up the stall and the mirror. For a moment he felt as if he were back in the nightmare, he couldn't breathe, so he yanked the handle and turned the water off. He slumped against the glass stall, breathing hard until the air began to cool back down and his head began to clear.

That's when it came to him. A plan.

He stepped out of the shower, dried himself in a thick, white towel, put on deodorant, and splashed himself with cologne. All he was thinking about was the simplicity and ease of the plan.

And he began to wonder: Could he really do it?

In his dressing room, his outfit was already laid out. Dark blue suit, white shirt, red and blue striped tie. His black socks were thin, mid-calf length. Wing-tip shoes, polished to a marine-quality sheen. Next to his clothes was his day's agenda, neatly typed up. He had four morning meetings followed by a lunch with Wall Streeters. The lunch would be no problem. All they wanted was money. That was all anyone seemed to want these days. That had never been his motivation, not really. Money was not what drove him.

He had always been driven by fear.

Six-fifteen now. He had time before he started his workday. But he had to hurry.

He called for his driver and told him to get moving. He wanted to leave right now.

He raced downstairs. Suddenly every second seemed to count. He had many things to say. So many things.

Six-seventeen A.M.

And now he knew what he was going to do. He was going to make the dream go away.

Forever.

The sixth largest cathedral in the world.

Every time Father Patrick Jennings stood at the pulpit, he couldn't believe that he was spreading the gospel at the sixth largest cathedral in the world.

He also couldn't help thinking: *I don't deserve this. When they find out about me, they're going to take it all away from me.*

Father Patrick chewed at the cuticle of his right thumb. The skin was raw and broken, and now a thin trickle of blood appeared. He watched the blood seep toward his knuckle, and he shook his head sadly. Sadness was now a way of life for him.

Father Patrick was losing his faith, and he didn't know what to do about it.

It was eating away at him. Tearing him up inside.

After six years at the seminary at Marquette, he'd graduated with the highest honors. Quickly gained a reputation as a forward-thinking theologian—able to argue logically and brilliantly for the strictest doctrines handed down from Rome, yet never alienating that great majority of modern-day believers, those seeking the comfort of the church but not the inconvenience. Most important, word spread that he was also a charismatic orator. He could hold his flock spellbound for even his longest and most intricate sermons. A baritone voice that rang out with strength and fervor, a soothing manner that rivaled the most solicitous doctor's, and a face as handsome as the most appealing television actor's. He didn't smoke. He didn't drink. He'd been scrupulously celibate. Well, since he'd decided to become a priest he'd been scrupulously celibate. It was not long before word reached even the cardinal about his potential, and soon after that he'd been seized upon by both the archbishop and the bishop. They couldn't wait to wine and dine him, transfer him to the nation's capital, and quickly make him pastor.

Of the sixth largest cathedral in the world.

Several of the priests weren't happy to have been passed over for the position. The bishop was getting on in years, and it wouldn't be long before the time came to pick a successor. The young pastor was now clearly the front-runner and there was a certain amount of jealousy and bickering, but Father Patrick confronted it head-on and it didn't take long for the petty grousing to stop. He was, after all, wonderful at his job. And he loved it so.

St. Stephen's Cathedral—even Father Patrick thought of it as such, though its official appellation was Washington's St. Stephen's Cathedral Church of the Apostles—was a magnificent Gothic church, rivaling its fourteenth-century counterparts anywhere in Italy, England, or France. The nave, flying buttresses, transepts, and vaults had been built stone by stone, and one had only to stand before them to feel the pride that had gone into the construction, the power that emanated from the structure itself.

When he'd first arrived, Father Patrick Jennings had felt his Savior to be in its very walls.

But lately he had not felt his Savior at all.

Six months earlier, Father Patrick's younger sister had been killed by a drunk driver.

Sweet Eileen. Twenty-four years old, ten years his junior. So beautiful. So full of promise, with so much love to give.

She used to laugh at him for becoming a priest, for she had known him in his less holy days. She was never one to limit herself and never understood why he would not only accept such limitations but willingly place them there. He would explain that he was throwing off the shackles. She would insist he was putting the padlock on and tossing away the key. But she recognized in him the desire to attain purity—a desire she greatly admired. He recognized in her an already pure spirit—a state he could only pray to attain. And underneath their difference was a layer of support and love that neither of them could equal elsewhere.

It was bright and sunny the day she died. She was meeting Father Patrick for lunch. A flat tire forced her over to the side of the road by the Washington basin. Father Patrick could picture her standing on the road's shoulder, her hands on her hips, her lips pursed in annoyance, shaking her head, which was what she did whenever she got angry. He was told that she had reached through the open window on the driver's side, to grab her cell phone. He didn't know whom she was calling—perhaps the restaurant to say she'd be late, perhaps AAA to come help her. But she never got to make the call. A station wagon veered across two lanes and hit her straight on, knocking her high in the air, up over the roof of her Honda. She landed facedown on the pavement some thirty-five feet away. It could not have been a more deadly attack if it had been deliberate. Which it wasn't. But the driver, who'd had thirteen citations and was driving without a license, was blind drunk and out of control. And Eileen just happened to be in the way.

At least she was out of pain. That's what he told himself. But Father Patrick was alive and suffering. He was being tested. And he was forced to admit that he was failing the test.

Soon after the accident, he began to drink. Soon after that, he began to drink a lot.

He'd had a stiff vodka already this morning, minutes after he'd awakened.

Before the accident, he'd loved to come to the cathedral early, when all was quiet and he could hear his footsteps echo on the stone floor, could look up at the fanciful gargoyles, the most faithful—if silent—members of his congregation. Before the accident, he'd liked to sit in silence and revel in his faith. He still came early. Still sat in silence. But now he sat and prayed for that faith to return.

There were priests to take confession, but at this hour penitents tended to remain in bed. Father Patrick had begun to encourage his priests to begin their day later than the archbishop would have demanded. He needed to be alone, hoping, praying that God might appear and speak to him. He would sit in the confessional during this quiet time, thankful for the solitude and the peace, which was interrupted only occasionally by the sins of an early riser.

This morning there was such a sinner.

Father Patrick heard footsteps before he saw the man. He immediately popped a breath mint into his mouth to help disguise the odor of alcohol. But when the man sat in the booth, Father Patrick swallowed the mint in a gasp of surprise.

And thought: *Oh, yes, I am being tested.*

"Forgive me, Father, for I have sinned. A terrible, terrible sin."

"God will be the judge of that, my son," the pastor said quietly. And thought: *The same God who judged that Eileen should no longer have life.*

"Sometimes man must judge himself."

"And sometimes," Father Patrick said, "man is a much harsher judge than God."

"Not this time, Father. Not this time. I've done things . . . and this morning I learned things . . . and for all of it, for all of us, there is no judgment that can be harsh enough."

The priest looked at the familiar gray hair, the determined jaw, the piercing blue eyes that could charm one minute and turn brutally cold and immovable the next. The man with those blue eyes hesitated, as if gathering strength.

"I have a secret, Father. One I've kept even from you."

Father Patrick was suddenly very, very sad. *Who among us does not need help?* he thought. *Who among us does not have a secret strong enough to destroy us?* His own secret was that he knew he could help no one, least of all himself. Certainly not the man kneeling before him. What kind of sins had he committed? What kind of guilt was stored up? What kind of penance could possibly be paid? It made little difference. For what could he, Father Patrick, a man whose weakness was slowly devouring him, possibly do for such a man?

The man in the confessional began to talk now, softly, urgently. His pleasing southern accent gave the sentences meter and a soothing, singsong rhythm. But the words themselves were anything but soothing.

"My sin goes back a long time, Father. To when I was very, very young. I wish I could say that I was so young I didn't know the difference between right and wrong. But that would be another sin, for it would be a lie. . . ."

The man never hesitated, never stumbled, as if this was a confession he had been rehearsing, perfecting, for years and years. Listening, Father Patrick began to sweat. First his palms, then his neck. Then he felt the back of his shirt soak through. And as the words poured out, as the years of sin were revealed, Patrick Jennings was no longer filled with sadness. Or curiosity. Or self-pity.

He was filled with terror.

July 13

E ver since he'd finished his confession and walked out of the cathedral, an eerie serenity had taken hold. His physical surroundings had seemed vague and cloudy. His mind felt clear, but his thoughts were unstructured and jumbled, leaping almost randomly from past to present, from person to person and idea to idea. He was still pleased with himself for going to the priest that morning five days ago. It had been a long time since he'd done something so spontaneous. And even longer since he'd made such a crucial move with no wifely input.

For years she had made him feel safe. For so long he had wondered what he'd done to deserve such a wonderful woman. She had protected him fiercely, resolutely, not just from his enemies but from himself. But no one was strong enough to protect him any longer. Safety was now a fantasy. Power was meaningless. The future was . . . nonexistent.

His eyes were closed now. There was a roaring noise; at first he couldn't tell where it was coming from, then he understood it was coming from inside his head. That wasn't all. There were other noises, and he realized that people were talking to him. Jabbering, carping, asking questions, shouting out answers. Where was he? He opened his eyes, stunned to find he was in a meeting. How had he gotten there? And why was everyone arguing?

Then he remembered. It was a budget meeting. He had left her an hour ago. She had pressed him relentlessly: Was he all right? Was he sure he could manage his regular schedule? He had only nodded and smiled sadly. She kissed him gently, on the lips, then again on the cheek. She said he had to keep going. Act as if nothing were wrong. They would find a solution, she said.

He almost felt guilty. Yet at the same time he was giddy. For he had a real, honest-to-goodness secret he was keeping from her: He already *had* a solution.

He looked around the room, at all the familiar people. Why did they all think they had the right answer? They didn't. He knew that much. They were bean counters. Every single one of them. They were small. Insignificant. And he realized now, with genuine surprise, that he hated them.

He sat there, watching their mouths move, hearing nothing except the roaring noise that was inside his own head. He reached for the glass of water in front of him and his hands shook. He wondered if anyone noticed, but of course they did not. They were too small to notice.

He was no bean counter. Never had been. He was an idea man. That's what he was good at. "I like to think of myself as an idea man"—he'd said that at his very first job interview. How long ago had that been? A hundred years? Two hundred? A million? Yes, a million years ago, when it was all going to be okay. Only it wasn't going to be okay. Not ever.

Unless he made it okay.

That's what he finally understood.

He stood up from the table, startling everyone, and left the room without a word, heading down the corridor to his office. The hallway felt tilted; he was bouncing off the walls. His legs were rubber, and yet he had never felt this strong. This big. This powerful.

His secretary smiled at him, confused. What was he doing out of the meeting? It was too early. She spoke to him, but he couldn't hear what she said. The roaring drowned out everything.

He was in his office now, and he sat at his desk. He looked around, tried to make some kind of connection to what he saw surrounding him, but he couldn't. He hated this room and everything in it. This room had always felt as though it belonged to someone else. To someone better.

For the moment, however, the room belonged to him. And in a strange way, he realized, from this point on it would belong to him forever. He was alone now, but that wouldn't last long. One of the little people would be there soon. Someone with papers to sign and problems to solve and statements to issue.

He liked being alone.

It was time for him to be alone.

It was time for his solution.

He reached into the drawer of the desk and pulled out the second secret he'd been keeping: the .45 revolver he'd put there the day she had told him about the package. The day he'd first known it all had to come to an end.

It was his old service revolver. He had almost thrown it away many times in the past. Always he changed his mind and kept it. Now, it was clear, there'd been a reason.

He put the barrel of the revolver into his mouth, all the way until he felt it touch the back of his throat. He had to be thorough. This was one time he could not afford to make an error.

He sat at his desk and tried desperately to think of something he was going to miss. It was important to him. Maybe it was the roaring in his head, it was so damn distracting, but he couldn't think of anything. Not one thing. It made him overwhelmingly sad. There had to be something.

He heard the footsteps then. They were coming. The bean counters. The little people. And suddenly he thought of something. Yes, there *was* something he would actually miss: her flowers. He smiled, satisfied. Those goddamn flowers. The roaring inside his head stopped. He felt happy. He felt lucky. And he was. Because he didn't feel the back of his head explode. He didn't see the blood and hair and bone that splattered all over the wall of the office he so detested. He didn't hear the door crash open and someone say, no louder than a whisper, "Jesus Christ!" and he didn't hear the voice that tried to say, "Call his wife," but couldn't get the words out without crying. He didn't hear any of the words that were now being screamed or the hysteria that was erupting outside the door as people began rushing up, demanding to know what had happened. And he didn't hear the weeping or the wailing or feel the shock of pain that swept through the hallway when they learned the answer to their frantic questions.

He didn't know or care or think about anything. Not after his one final thought, which raced through his brain moments before the bullet destroyed it, and provided him with a surprising amount of glee and then sadness and then regret.

It's a great and terrible thing I'm doing, he thought. *And no one knows why.*

And God help anyone who ever finds out.

book one

June 18–July 9

chapter 1

It had not been one of Carl Granville's better weeks.

For starters, in his weekly pickup game at the Chelsea Piers, he had been taken to the hoop and dunked on by a spindly high-school kid. Then *New York Magazine* gave the Nathan Lane profile they'd promised him to another freelancer—the editor's sister-in-law. Then his dad called from Pompano Beach to tell him he thought Carl was wasting his precious Ivy League degree and his life, not necessarily in that order. Plus the Mets had lost three in a row, Nick at Nite had cleared out *The Odd Couple* and *Taxi* to make way for *I Dream of Jeannie* and *Bewitched*, and now, just to round things out, he found himself in a room with the only two people left in the world who believed in his talent, in his future, in him. Unfortunately, one of those people was dead and the other one hated his guts.

No, it had definitely not been one of Carl's better weeks.

He was standing next to an open casket in the Frank E. Campbell funeral parlor on Madison Avenue and Eighty-first Street, where Betty Slater, the legendary literary agent and even more legendary alcoholic, was laid out, looking as rosy and lifelike as a basket of wax fruit. At least she was not glowering at him with undisguised hostility, the way Amanda Mays, standing on the other side of the casket, was. Amanda was still angry over a slight misunderstanding. Something to do with a certain plum job in Washington, marriage, and living happily ever after. Carl had to admit to himself that some of the misunderstanding was his fault.

Actually, Carl had to admit that all of the misunderstanding was his fault.

The turnout for Betty's funeral was huge, considering just how cranky Betty had gotten toward the end of her life, when she'd managed to offend just about every publisher, critic, and author in town. It was her brutal honesty, mostly. Throwing out words like *stinks*, and *phony*, and—one of her favorite combinations—*pseudointellectual crap*. Nonetheless, this was an event and people had dutifully turned out in droves for it, clustering around her open casket in solemn tribute. Norman Mailer was there. And John Irving. Maya Angelou was there. So were Sonny Mehta, Tina Brown, Judith Regan, and a number of prominent editors and literary agents. All to pay their respects. To mingle. And, Carl was horrified to observe, to work the room. Because Betty had still had a few money clients in her stable, and now they were on the loose. Most notably Norm Pincus, the balding, splayfooted little shlub known to the reading public as Esmeralda Wilding, author of eleven straight best-selling bodice rippers. Agents were hovering around the tubby little gold mine like vultures, waiting to swoop down on him. It was, Carl reflected, in terrible taste.

Especially because not one of the vultures was paying the least bit of attention to *him*.

Hey, wasn't he talented? Didn't he have the potential to write best-sellers? *Quality* best-sellers? Couldn't he go on *Oprah* and charm the hell out of America?

And wasn't that Maggie Peterson staring at him from across the room? It was.

Holy shit. *The* Maggie Peterson. Staring at him. And not only that. Now coming toward him. Smiling and sticking her hand out. The most famous, the most visible, the most flamboyant, and by far the hottest editor in New York publishing was speaking to him. She'd had three number-one best-sellers in a row. Her own imprint at Apex, the international multimedia conglomerate. She was a star. And Carl Granville knew that what he could use more than anything else right now was just a little bit of stardust. He was twenty-eight years old and burning to write the next great American novel. He had just delivered the first draft of his most recent attempt to Betty Slater, but she had died before she could tell him what she thought of it. And now he had no agent, no money to pay this month's rent, and no reason whatsoever to believe that his next payday would arrive any sooner than the twenty-fourth of never. But suddenly there was hope. Maggie Peterson was saying something to him.

She was saying: "I don't know whether to hire you or fuck you."

Carl had to admit, she got his attention.

Everything about Maggie Peterson was calculated to get attention. The severe blue-black pageboy hairdo that had been cropped sharply at the chin, with what looked to be a hatchet. The wide slash of bright red lipstick. The matching skintight black leather jacket and trousers. This was a highly charged woman, most likely forty, a lean, tightly coiled whippet who exuded energy and sexual challenge. This was a very sexy predator. A meat eater. And right now she was eyeballing him up and down as if he were a T-bone steak, medium rare.

Carl glanced around just to make absolutely, positively sure that he was the person Maggie had said those words to. He was. So he cleared his throat and took his shot. "If I have a choice," he said, smiling, "I need the job more."

Maggie didn't smile back. He got the feeling that smiling was not usually on her agenda.

"I read those murder mysteries you ghosted for Kathie Lee," she said, gazing up at him. "I liked them. I liked them a lot."

That would be Kathie Lee Gifford. Not his proudest creative moment. But a job was a job.

"Betty got that for me," he said, and modestly shrugged his broad shoulders at Maggie, feeling the twinge in the left one that was always there. A Penn power forward who was now playing over in Greece had given that to him under the boards his senior year. Carl had started at point guard for Cornell for three years, a smart, determined floor leader, a good passer, an accurate shooter. He was the complete basketball package. He had it all—everything except the height, the vertical leap, and the foot speed. He was an inch and three-eighths over six feet tall and his weight hadn't changed, it was still 185. Although fifteen of those pounds kept wanting to drift south. He had to work out regularly to prevent that.

"Betty sent me your novel, you know."

"No, I didn't know." He couldn't help it; his pulse was definitely quickening.

"It was the most dazzling prose I've read in two, possibly three years. Parts of it were even brilliant."

There it was, the *b* word. The word every writer hungered to hear. And it wasn't just anybody saying it to Carl. It was Maggie Peterson, who could actually *do* something about it.

"We need to talk," she was saying now.

Carl stood there a moment, grinning. He looked no more than eighteen when he grinned. He looked, Amanda once told him with a disgusted look in her eye, like an overgrown Campbell's Soup kid, with his shiny blue eyes and apple cheeks and unruly dirty blond hair that was forever tumbling down into his eyes. He was so wholesome and innocent-looking that bartenders still asked him for his ID.

"Well, sure," he said. "Let's talk."

Maggie glanced abruptly at her watch. "Meet me at three o'clock."

"Your office?"

"I have a lunch date on the East Side. It'll be easier to meet at my apartment. Four twenty-five East Sixty-third. We can be alone there. Have a nice little talk in my garden."

"It's pouring rain outside."

"I'll see you at three, Mr. Granville."

"It's Carl."

"I thought people called you Granny."

"Some do," he allowed. Although precious few, and it had to be his idea, not theirs, and . . .

And how the hell did she know that?

"I do my homework," she said, as if reading his mind. Her eyes were already elsewhere, flicking around the crowded room, restlessly searching. When they came to rest, she was looking down at the waxen body in the casket. "This really is the end of an era, isn't it?" The realization seemed to please her. She turned her gaze back to him. "Don't disappoint me, Carl. I can't stand to be disappointed."

And with that she vanished back into the crowd of mourners.

It was Amanda Mays who offered Carl the ride home in the rain.

Her same old dented, rusted-out wreckage of a Subaru station wagon was parked illegally out front in the loading zone that was reserved exclusively for hearses. The interior, as always, was littered with collapsed Starbucks containers, an assortment of coats and sweaters and shoes, notepads, file folders. Neat the woman never was. He stood there on the curb with the rain pouring down the back of his neck while she unlocked the door and threw the shit that was on the front passenger seat on top of the shit that was in the backseat so that he could get in.

Once inside, he folded his long legs so that his knees almost touched his chin. Other than offering him a ride, Amanda still hadn't said a word to him. He realized it was up to him to be mature and civil. "When are you heading back to—"

"Washington? Right now. We're in the middle of a huge team investigation of the D.C. school board. I'm quarterbacking and I don't want anyone else mucking it up. Besides, there's no reason to stay around, is there?" she said pointedly.

"Amanda, can't we at least be—"

"Friends? Sure, Carl, we can be friends." She was forever cutting in on him like this, never letting him finish a sentence. Their conversations were always fast, sometimes furious, rarely linear. It was the way her mind worked—in overdrive.

"Well, do you want to get—"

"A cup of coffee? No, thanks. I just don't think I can handle that much friendship today."

The Subaru didn't particularly want to start. The engine was balky and reluctant. And when Amanda finally pulled away from the curb, it started clanking, regularly and loudly.

"You're not going to drive this thing all the way back to D.C. sounding like that, are you?"

"It's *fine*, Carl." The day they'd broken up was the day she'd stopped calling him Granny. "It's been making that noise for the last seven thousand miles."

"But—"

"It's nothing. So just shut up about it, will you?" She floored it, just to prove her point. He closed his eyes and held on for dear life, remembering.

Remembering *them*.

They'd met at a pub party for a mutual friend's book. And for eighteen months, two weeks, and four days after that, they had been inseparable. She liked the Velvet Underground, the Knicks, and cold pizza for breakfast. She was pleasantly round in all of the places she should be and enviably taut in all of the others. She possessed great masses of rust-colored hair that tumbled every which way, impish green eyes, a smattering of freckles, and the most kissable mouth he had ever personally kissed.

Remembering their nights together. Making love, talking into the dawn, making love again. And again.

Remembering how she made him feel: warm and excited, exhilarated and insecure, always so alive. Amanda was tremendously warm and passionate and even more tremendously opinionated. She was also a pain in the ass. Not easy to get along with. Intense, spiky, and stubborn. She was the smartest person he had ever met and, sitting next to her now, Carl realized with a touch of regret that her approval and respect still meant everything to him.

Remembering how it had ended between them.

Badly, that's how.

Mostly, she'd said, she wanted him to get real. Like she had. After years of scratching around as a freelancer, living month to month in a crummy studio apartment, she had decided that what she really wanted more than anything else in the world was a life. A good job. A nice place to live. Commitment. Him. She had found the good job—deputy metro editor of the *Washington Journal*. And D.C. was the perfect place for her. She loved politics, it was her passion. That was where they were different. Numbers were his. As in 30.1 and 22.9, which were Wilt Chamberlain's scoring and rebounding averages per game for his career. Or .325—Dick Groat's batting average in 1960, when he beat out Norm Larker for the National League batting title on the last day of the season. Still, there was a good job waiting there in D.C. for him, too. Hell, a great job. The *Journal* was looking for someone to cover sports as a form of popular culture, not a game. Profiles. Think pieces. It might even lead to a column. But he had turned it down. The job would have been all-consuming, and he refused to abandon his book. He also refused to abandon New York, so, furious, she had gone without him. She had not understood. How could she? She was thirty then. He was twenty-seven—which, in gender evolution, meant she was somewhere between nine and twelve years ahead of him on the maturity scale. He knew he was giving up something special. But he could not change how he felt.

He just plain was not ready to get real yet.

That had been almost a year ago. And now they were hurtling through the rain-slick streets of New York in her car and they had nothing much to say to each other. She took Madison up to Ninety-sixth and shot across Central Park on the Ninety-seventh Street Transverse. Carl lived on 103rd between Broadway and Amsterdam, one of the only blocks on the entire Upper West Side that had somehow managed to elude gentrification. It was a street of scruffy, grimy tenements where unemployed Latino men sat on stoops all day drinking cans of Colt 45 they bought from the bodega on the corner.

"Since when are you and Maggie Peterson so tight?" she asked.

"She read my novel. She liked it."

He waited for her to be happy for him. Or even impressed. But there was nothing. She gave him nothing.

"I wonder if the gossip about her is true," Amanda said.

"I doubt it." He glanced over at her. He hated it when she sucked him in like this. "Okay, what gossip?"

"When she was editor of the *Daily Mirror* in Chicago, she broke up her top columnist's marriage."

"What, she was having an affair with him?"

"She was having an affair with him *and* his wife."

"No way."

"Way. Believe me, way."

"She just wants to talk," he said as casually as he could.

"She wants a lot of things. Including her own talk show on the Apex network. She'll probably get it, too. She and Augmon are totally tight." Augmon being Lord Lindsay Augmon, the reclusive British-born billionaire who had personally built the Apex empire, piece by piece: the TV network, the movie studio, newspapers in London, New York, Chicago, and Sydney, magazines all over the world, book publishing houses in New York and London, international cable franchises. Lindsay Augmon cast a wide and powerful net, and Maggie Peterson was his biggest, hungriest shark. His miracle worker. She was the woman with the sizzle. The *Mirror* had been failing when she took it over, and she raised its circulation by 25 percent in six months. From there she took two of his moribund monthly magazines and turned them into must-read trendsetters. And now she had put his publishing house on top.

"She never likes to stay anywhere for very long," Amanda added. "She doesn't like to manage. Her job is to come in and make a big splash."

Carl nodded, wondering just what sort of splash Maggie Peterson had in mind for him.

"Have you met anyone?" he asked her over the clanking of the engine.

"Tom Cruise," she answered. "It's hot and heavy. But keep it to yourself, okay? We don't want Nicole to find out." She pulled a cigarette out and lit it from her lighter, filling the car with smoke. "And I swore I'd never get mixed up with a married man."

Carl rolled down the window so that he could breathe, the rain pelting him. "When did you start smoking again?"

"Guess," she said sharply. Too sharply, and she knew it. She softened. "How about you?"

"Never. Nasty habit. Bad for the wind."

"I meant—"

"I know what you meant. And the answer is no. Starving artists aren't very popular these days."

"Starving artists were never popular."

"Now you tell me," he said, grinning at her.

"Uh-uh," she said, shaking her head. "It won't work, so don't even try it."

"What won't work?"

"The Granny grin. I'm wearing a Kevlar shield now. It bounces right off me."

"Look, Amanda . . ." He reached over and took her hand.

She pulled away. "Please don't," she said quietly. "Don't tell me you're confused and you don't know how you feel. Because I'll tell you how you feel, Carl. You feel relieved."

He fell silent after that. They both did.

"I guess it was too soon," she said finally. "It still hurts too much. Maybe . . . maybe we can try again next year."

"I will if you will," he said gamely.

"Done," she said, stubbing out her cigarette.

Carl's street was largely deserted. Thanks to the rain, the idlers had been driven inside. She pulled up with a screech in front of the beat-up brownstone Carl had lived in since he first moved to New York. He had the front apartment on the fourth floor, a studio that was hot in the summer, cold in the winter, and noisy all year round. The waterbugs and the mice didn't mind, and neither did he, but Amanda had despised it. They had always stayed at her place, which had heat and hot water and other such luxury amenities.

A very attractive young blonde was trying to wrestle an old overstuffed chair in through the front door of his building. She wasn't having much luck. The chair was getting all wet and so was she. The T-shirt and tight jeans she was wearing were thoroughly soaked.

"New neighbor?" Amanda asked with a raised eyebrow.

"Upstairs." He nodded. "She moved in last week."

"She's not," Amanda said.

"Not what?"

"Wearing a bra. That *is* what you were thinking, isn't it?"

He turned to stare at Amanda. "It might surprise you to learn that I'm not always thinking what you think I'm thinking."

Her eyes searched his face carefully, as if she was trying to memorize how it looked. "You're absolutely right," she said gravely. "That would surprise me."

"Watch out for the pothole," he warned her as he climbed out. It was a broad, deep one in the middle of the block. It was really more of a crater. And, of course, she accelerated right into it. Would have lost a hubcap, too, if she'd had any hubcaps left to lose. Carl watched her cross Broadway and disappear down the street, feeling rueful and glum and dissatisfied and lonely. He shook it off and started inside. But the chair and the very wet blonde were in his way.

"You're not planning to carry that thing all the way up to the fifth floor by yourself, are you?" Carl asked his new neighbor.

"I sure am," she replied. She possessed a soft, cotton-candy voice and the biggest, bluest, most arresting eyes that Carl had ever seen. Her silky blond hair glistened with moisture. She wore hot pink lipstick and matching nail polish. She was a tall girl, nearly six feet in her steel-toed Doc Martens. "I found it around the corner on the street. Can you believe someone was throwing it out?"

The chair was covered in green vinyl. And huge. Not to mention hideous.

"I can't believe anyone bought it in the first place," he said.

"Well, I think it's perfect. Particularly because I don't have a chair and I need one. Only it won't fit through the damned door." She began chewing fretfully on her luscious lower lip.

Carl stood there thinking that it had been a long time since he'd dated a woman who wore hot pink nail polish. Come to think of it, he had never dated a woman who wore hot pink nail polish. Amanda's nails were unpainted and bitten to the quick.

"Sure it will," he said bravely. "We just have to angle it, that's all." He bent down and grabbed an end, trying as hard as he could not to stare at her nipples, which protruded right through her wet T-shirt, large and rosy and in his face.

"This is very nice of you."

"No problem," he grunted. "Neighbors do these things for each other. That's what holds this cruel, dirty city together. Besides, if I don't help, I can't get in out of the rain."

Together they angled it through the vestibule and wrestled it to the bottom of the stairs, where they dumped it. It was heavy and ungainly.

"I'm the Granville whose buzzer is right below yours, by the way. Carl goes with it. What goes with Cloninger?"

"Toni. With an _i_."

"Nice to meet you, Toni with an _i_. You new to the city?"

"Just moved from Pennsylvania. I'm an actress. Oh, God, that sounds so funny to say out loud, doesn't it? I want to be an actress. Mostly I've just done some modeling and stuff. And taken a ton of classes. How about you? Do you model, too?"

"Keep talking to me like that and I'll curl right up on your welcome mat and never leave."

"There's another thing I have to do—get a welcome mat," she said, smiling at him.

She had a wonderful smile. It made the entire lower half of his body feel like it was suspended in warm Jell-O. He took a deep breath, sizing up the logistics of chair and stairs and banister. "Okay, I'll push, you pull. On three. Ready?"

"Ready. Did I remember to say this was real nice of you?"

"You did. But feel free to keep right on saying it."

He pushed, she pulled, and somehow they managed to force the big, horrible, overstuffed thing all the way up to the second-floor landing, where they rested. Only three more flights to go.

"Can I ask you something personal?" she said, huffing and puffing. "I keep hearing this *ba-boom, ba-boom* noise coming from your apartment every morning. What exactly are you doing?"

"Banging my head against the wall. I'm a writer."

She let out a laugh, which was just as wonderful as her smile. It was big and easy and genuine. "I've never lived over a writer before. This may take some getting used to."

"Oh, you'll learn to love it. In fact, pretty soon you'll wonder how you ever got along without me."

She eyed him with flirty amusement. "Seriously, what *are* you doing?"

"It's my heavy bag. A sixty-pound Everlast. I work out on it every morning." He picked up his end of the chair. "You never know what might come up."

His lower back was in spasms by the time they reached the fourth floor. "I'm feeling uncommonly generous. Why don't you just leave this at my place? You can come visit it anytime you want."

"One more flight, Charles."

"Carl."

Her place was a studio like his, but the ceiling was lower and it felt even more cramped. She had very little in the way of possessions: a bed, a dresser, a TV, a cactus that looked dead, although Carl wasn't exactly sure how you could tell with cactus plants. There was still some stuff in cartons. The chair went in an empty corner, facing the TV.

"The least I can do is offer you a beer," she said gratefully.

"The least I can do is accept," he replied, waiting for her to move toward the refrigerator. But she made no move toward anything. "I don't actually have any beer," she admitted.

"Do you always make such empty offers?"

"It's not empty. You know Son House?"

"The blues bar down on Ninth Avenue?"

She nodded. "I wait tables there most nights, eight to two. Stop by and I'll treat you to a brewski. Deal?"

"I don't know. I'll have to think about it," he said. He looked at this gorgeous creature not two feet away from him. Then he pictured Amanda, angry as ever, hurtling through the pothole. "Okay, I thought about it," he said. "It's a deal, Toni with an *i*."

chapter 2

The twin-engine Cessna touched down on runway thirty-one at Nashville International Airport exactly, to the minute, on time. No one seemed to notice. Certainly not the ground-controller in the tower, who kept the plane sitting there for thirteen minutes, until the pilot called in for the second time, saying, "This is Cessna November Sixty Golf Charlie. How many times do I have to tell you that I need to go to Mercury Air Service?" "Sorry, Charlie," the operator responded. "Busy day today. I forgot all about you." And certainly not the line service attendant at Mercury, the fixed-base operator, who, after the Cessna had finally been given clearance to taxi over there, took seven and a half minutes before coming out to marshal the plane into its parking space. And most definitely not the painfully thin man behind the desk in the FBO terminal, who kept the pilot waiting another four minutes before taking the order for twenty-five gallons of fuel in each wing tank.

No one seemed to care except for the Cessna's pilot and sole passenger, H. Harrison Wagner, who was traveling today under the name of Laurence Engle.

Harry Wagner believed in punctuality. It greatly bothered him that no one else in the whole wide world apparently gave a shit whether anything arrived on time or left late, was real or fake, was done well or poorly or, for that matter, was done at all. To Harry, that was intolerable. But there was much about the world that H. Harrison Wagner found intolerable.

Not the least of which was the job he was about to perform.

Harry was not particularly proud of the life he'd led up to this point. He loved his work—the excitement it provided, the freedom it gave him, the respect it could engender. And he was thrilled by the erotic world he'd managed to enter through the bars and clubs he frequented at night—the games he played, the bodies he touched, the lust he caused and felt. But his entire existence was dependent on deceit. For too many years, each day had been but another lie to survive. If there was anything he felt good about, it was his strength. He had learned to live with his lies and learned to live with them alone, separate and always distant from the world around him.

Until now. Now he was no longer alone. Now he was vulnerable. He was no longer strong. That's why he was about to cross the only line he'd so far managed to avoid crossing.

That's why, for the first time in his life, Harry Wagner was about to kill another human being.

It would have been easier to fly into the Oxford airport. But Harry was not interested in easy. Even in these circumstances, he was interested in *right*. That's why he'd flown to Nashville. The Oxford airport was closer to his real destination, but it was small. In case anything went wrong, he would need anonymity. And distance. And then, of course, some things were done right in Nashville. The Loveless Cafe had the best breakfast anywhere in the country. The music played by the true pickers late at night down in Printers Alley was still real and heartfelt. He loved genuine country music, the sentiments, the lyrics, the emotion. Loretta Lynn was his favorite. And he owned everything George Jones had ever recorded. Hell, he even had Conway Twitty magnets on his refrigerator back home. His ex-wife once told him that the real reason she'd left him was those damn magnets. But he knew that wasn't true. There were many other reasons. Too many.

Unfortunately, the city was merely a stopping-off point today. Fly in. Change mode of transportation. Reach destination. Find target. No time for even a quick layover. Perhaps on the way back. He could go to that little bar he'd discovered during his last trip. The place where he'd fallen in love. If twenty-four hours of passion could constitute love.

And in the world he lived in, who would possibly say that it couldn't?

When he arrived at the rent-a-car office, the fat, pimply woman behind the counter was gossiping on the phone, paying no attention to him, throwing him even further behind schedule. When she finally deigned to hang up and do her job, he glared at her, hoping to arouse some sense of shame, of duty. But, of course, there was none. She merely glanced at his driver's license and handed it back to him with a smile. A big, friendly, open and extraordinarily stupid smile.

She asked all the usual questions: what time would he be returning the car, did he want the additional insurance, would he use their automatic refill system or put gas in the car himself. She might as well have been a machine. Until he gave the name of his company and his business phone number—a phony company and equally phony number with a Philadelphia area code.

"I'm *from* Philadelphia," she said, showing him that same stupid smile again. "What kind of business are you in?"

"Commercial real estate," he answered, and saw she was impressed. Harry had to admit, he did look impressive. At 6'3", 225 pounds, he was physically imposing. Harry enjoyed his physicality: his thick, meaty hands, his broad chest and shoulders. He knew that in clothes he could look blocky, like a retired football player gone slightly to seed. But he also knew what happened when he took those clothes off. He'd gotten more than one gasp at the hardness of his body, the flatness of his stomach, the taut muscles that rippled up and down his arms and legs. And he loved it. God, how he loved it.

He didn't consider vanity a major flaw, just a minor indulgence. Today he was indulging himself in a perfectly tailored Armani suit, dark gray and conservative. A white shirt. Black and white polka-dot tie. Quite dashing, but not his usual taste. He preferred something a little flashier. Pastels. Brightly colored ties. But today he looked exactly like what he was pretending to be, a rich white businessman, the kind who'd rent a car and nod distractedly when the fat, pimply girl at the rental counter said, "Have a nice day, Mr. Engle."

It was a five-hour-and-thirty-five-minute drive in his rented Buick Skylark. That included a half-hour stop at the Loveless Cafe for a taste of his beloved biscuits with gravy and a side of country ham. He'd be damned if he'd stop at a McDonald's on the road. It was no wonder America was in such trouble, Harry Wagner thought. Everyone in it lived on cardboard and grease. A second ten-minute interlude came at a rest stop on the side of the highway, just outside of Corinth on the Tennessee-Mississippi border. He had allowed time in his schedule for such a break, and he knew this place was spotlessly clean. Harry Wagner did not frequent anyplace—even if it was just to urinate—that wasn't clean.

Driving out of Nashville was much like driving out of any other booming American city these days. The downtown skyline was small and pristine. He could make out the new glass-and-steel football arena. And, of course, the usual lineup found in any up-and-coming metropolis: Blockbuster Video, Planet Hollywood, and the Hard Rock Cafe. Once out of the city limits, the terrain turned New South suburban, with mall after mall, and gated communities, subdivision after subdivision that had gone up seemingly overnight. It was only a few more miles before the highway was cutting through pure country—mile after mile of kudzu, gas stations, and fast-food joints. Welcome to the real South.

He was well versed in the history of his final destination. Harry Wagner believed in preparation. He did not like surprises. He also liked to know things. It was part of his theory of minutiae: There was nothing in life that was so big it could not be broken down into tiny pieces, analyzed, and understood. The more minutiae he had stored in his mind, the broader the base it gave him. His job had many different demands, both physical and mental, but above all he considered himself an analyst. For any problem that might arise, he was being paid to figure out the solution.

The solution to this particular problem lay in the small town he was heading toward in Mississippi, a gray, gritty, early-twentieth-century pit on the banks of the Mississippi River that had been born in the wake of the Industrial Revolution and slowly dying for the past forty years. The white side of town was clean, orderly, and well run. People walked on sidewalks, shopped in nice, quiet stores, bought whatever they needed from polite salespeople. Their pleasant-looking houses sat on carefully tended lawns, adjacent to a well-groomed golf course. The black side of town had rather different, if just as distinctive, features. Instead of sidewalks, there were muddy ditches deep and wide enough to bury a car. Ripped mattresses were strewn by the roadside, a nice complement to the clumps of abandoned tires. A large factory loomed over the rows of cinder-block cottages. It no longer spewed out its foul-smelling smoke, having been closed down nearly twenty-five years earlier. There were more rusty swings than there were stores.

When Harry Wagner pulled into town, his suit was still immaculate despite the heat, his shirt looked as if it had been ironed only minutes before, and his tie was knotted perfectly. From the looks of things, he was the only person in town wearing a proper suit. But that was all right. He had certain standards to maintain. Without standards, you were nothing.

Without standards, you were just like everyone else.

He found what he was looking for almost immediately. It wasn't hard to find the town hall in a place with a population of two thousand. It was not quite fifty yards from the abandoned train station. Which was maybe another fifty yards from what once must have been an attractive town square but now was a slab of cracked concrete dotted with weeds. The woman at the desk reminded him of the girl at the car rental counter. She had the same dumb smile, the same vacant eyes—just twenty years older.

"Can I help you?" she asked.

"I hope so," he said politely. "I represent a law firm based in Hartford." When her eyes seemed to register a vague look of noncomprehension, he added, "Connecticut." He then reached into his wallet and pulled out a business card. It read: *Laurence Engle, Associate, Broadhurst, Fairburn, and March, Law Offices.* He handed her the card and said, "We're looking for someone in connection with an estate settlement. She's come into some money, and our client very much wants to make sure she receives it."

"Well, isn't she the lucky one," the woman said back to him. She seemed to be genuinely pleased that someone else had fallen into such good fortune. It surprised Harry, went against his general view of human nature. "What's her name and I'll see what I can do."

"There's the rub," he told her, with an embarrassed shrug. "We know her only by her nickname."

"Well, gosh," the woman said. "Who'd leave money to someone without knowin' their name?"

Without knowing *her* name, Harry thought. Not *their* name. He hated the mixing of singular and plural. It was so imprecise. "We felt the same way when we heard about the bequest," he said, and rolled his eyes conspiratorially. "But you know how rich people are."

The look on the woman's face said she did indeed know. She knew exactly how they were.

"It's someone our client knew as a child, someone who was very kind to him. She was his nanny, did work for the family. Our client is recently deceased, and his will specified that if she's still alive, he wants to reciprocate. But he never knew her legal name. He knew her only as Momma One-Eye."

The woman shook her head in astonishment. "Now, that *is* a strange one. Don't believe I ever heard it." She hesitated, lowering her voice. "She a black woman?"

"I believe she is," Harry said graciously.

The woman nodded knowingly. Without another word, she turned on her heel and disappeared into the small room behind her desk. Harry heard voices. Then a black man came out of the office. He was tall and lean with sprinkles of white in his hair, perhaps fifty-five years old, maybe as old as sixty.

"I'm Alderman Heller," the black man said. "Luther Heller. How can I help you?"

Harry pulled out another card from his wallet and repeated his story, almost word for word. When he said the words "Momma One-Eye," Luther's eyes twitched. Just a tad, but nonetheless, there it was. Harry was not the type to ever miss a twitch.

"I know her," the alderman said. "Or rather, I knew her. I'm afraid she's passed on."

He was lying. His face was an easy one to read. Harry went along with the lie, sighed, and shook his head sadly. "I'm sorry to hear that," he said. "Has it been long?"

"Three weeks," Luther said. "Maybe a little more."

"That recent," Harry said quite mournfully. Then he pulled out a pad and pen. "What was her name? I'll need it for when we file the final estate settlement in probate court."

"Clarissa May Wynn," the alderman told him. "She was an old, old woman. In her nineties, I believe."

"Buried locally, is she?"

"Why, no," Luther said tightly, narrowing his eyes at Wagner. "She was cremated."

"Ah," Harry said. "Then may I bother you for a copy of her death certificate? We may need it."

"In a few weeks—that's the best I can do. Our records are all being converted to computer right now. I'm afraid our little town's coming into the twentieth century just as the twenty-first's about to start."

"What about an official notice of death?"

Alderman Heller stared at Harry Wagner for quite a long time before answering. "The *Gazette*'s about half a mile down the road," he said.

"What a shame," Harry said as he started for the door. "She'll never know how well she was remembered."

"Momma's in a better world," Luther Heller said. "I'm sure if it's worth knowin', they'll tell her up there."

It took Harry only five minutes to reach the local newspaper office, but by the time he got there he was certain Luther Heller had called ahead. The black clerk couldn't find any issues from the previous month. He said it would take him several days to locate what Harry was looking for. As much as Harry hated inefficiency, he hated even more being treated like some kind of fool. The black man did let him use their phone book—*that* he could find—but there were no Wynns listed.

But he did find a listing for Luther Heller.

Harry drove out to the black side of town, past the tires and mattresses and patches of dead grass covered with discarded beer cans and whiskey bottles. He found Luther's cinder-block house, slightly larger than some of the others but certainly not much in the scheme of things. A small front yard, a fenced-in vegetable garden off to the side, an American flag hanging over the front door. Because the air was so still, the flag seemed shriveled, unmoving.

Several feet in front of the door to Luther Heller's house, under the shade of a tall maple tree, an attractive black woman was sitting in a beach chair. She was reading a paperback book. From time to time she sipped from a pink plastic glass, which rested on the burnt, brown grass by her right arm when she wasn't drinking. She was perhaps thirty years old, but she looked tired, worn out. Playing jacks on the hard, sun-baked earth near her was a young girl, maybe six or seven years old, humming to herself as she expertly scooped up the tiny pieces. Luther's daughter and granddaughter, Harry decided. They had his eyes.

He introduced himself and smiled politely. Said that he was looking for Momma One-Eye. Said that he had some money for her. Luther had told him to come by. Luther had tried to describe the route himself but it was too complicated, decided it was easier if someone who knew the way would just take him. Luther said his daughter could do it if she was around. The woman on the beach chair didn't say a word, simply stared at him. Harry felt himself getting angry. He was being polite. He was perfectly friendly. This woman should have the decency to respond to him.

From the neighboring porch, two black men also stared, saying nothing. Their shirts were off and the sweat on their hard bodies caught the sun just right and glistened.

Harry Wagner tried again.

"I'm looking for Momma One-Eye," he said patiently. "She's come into some money and I'm here to make sure she gets it. Your father said that you would be kind enough to show me the way to her house."

Still the woman said nothing. And at the end of his explanation, one of the men from the neighbor's porch came over into Luther's yard. He stood a foot away from Harry and leaned over so his face was maybe three inches away.

"Can I help you?" Harry asked him.

"Yeah," the man said. "You can help me by gettin' the fuck outta here."

"Perhaps you're not understanding me," Harry said, holding both hands up to show that he meant no harm.

"Oh, I understand you just fine. Now how 'bout you understandin' me and get the fuck outta here?"

Harry nodded, nice and easy, and backed away, maybe two steps. Then he kicked out with his right foot and broke the black man's kneecap. The man screamed and fell like a deadweight. The friend came hurtling into the yard, but before he got too close, Harry had a gun in his hand and had it pointed.

"I hope you're not as rash as your friend," Harry Wagner said calmly. "But if you are, I'll give you to the count of three to decide which part of your body you feel you can best live without. One . . . two . . ."

The second black man stopped short, deciding it was best to pay some attention to this clearly crazy white man, and began backing off.

"Now." Harry turned back to the woman with Luther Heller's eyes. "I'd like you to take me to Momma One-Eye's house."

They drove deep into the woods. Luther's daughter sat in the front seat, next to Harry; the little girl sat in the back. The little girl stayed silent, barely moving.

"Your daughter is very well behaved," Harry said. "You must be a good mother."

"What you want, man?" the woman asked. "What's your business?"

"I tried to tell you my business," Harry said. "You chose not to respond. Now you've lost the right to ask any questions. Those are the rules."

"Rules?" The woman looked at him incredulously. "What rules you talkin' about?"

"My rules," Harry said. "The only ones that count."

It took them twenty-two minutes to get there. The woman known as Momma One-Eye lived in a small shack at the end of a rutted dirt road. Harry walked around to the other side of the car, opened the door for the woman in the front seat, and motioned for her to step out. She looked into the backseat, saying nothing, but Harry knew she was asking him to leave her daughter in the car. Harry smiled apologetically and shook his head. He opened the door to the backseat and waved his hand in a grand gesture, welcoming the little girl to their new destination.

Harry knocked on the door to the shack and got no answer. He hadn't expected one. The wood was so thin, it was not worth picking the lock. He just kicked out again and the door flew open. The little girl flinched at the noise and ran into her mother's arms. The older woman grabbed her daughter, lifted her up against her chest, and held her tightly. She whispered something to the girl, and Harry smiled sadly when he heard what she was saying.

It's going to be all right, baby.

It's going to be all right.

He had his detestable job to do, so he ushered the two of them into the one-room cabin. There was a fireplace, which he guessed was the only means of heat. The furniture was scarce, and what was there was simple: a single bed, two high-backed wooden chairs, a round kitchen table that could seat four, a small refrigerator and stove. He politely asked the woman to have a seat in a wooden rocking chair in the middle of the room. Never letting go of her daughter, she sat. The little girl soon settled on her lap. Harry Wagner then removed his suit coat, rolled up his shirtsleeves, and began to search the room.

The kitchen cabinets had several cans of beans and Jolly Green Giant vegetables. There was one closet and that was cleaned out of everything except four wire hangers. Under the bed there was only dust. He was thorough, as usual, but the search didn't take long and he found nothing of any interest. Nothing that would make his employer happy. And he knew he wasn't going to find Momma One-Eye, either. Not today. But he'd been told to make sure this was not a wasted trip. At the very least, he'd been ordered to leave a warning. One that served a purpose.

So he picked up a kitchen knife from Momma's counter and took a deep breath.

His job had just become twice as detestable. He was not going to kill one person. He was going to kill two.

Without saying a word, he took three steps toward the middle of the room and slit the throat of the woman sitting in the rocking chair. Death was instantaneous. The woman never made a sound. She didn't even look surprised. She merely toppled back into the chair as her blood spurted onto the front of his shirt and tie. He glanced down, revolted by the deepening stains, but he knew he couldn't let that distract him. The little girl was free now and screaming. She was running toward the front door and she was fast, but not as fast as he was. He had her by the arm and he swung her around, hard enough that he heard something pop, probably her shoulder. That was the end of her resistance. She wasn't screaming now; it was more of a whimper. She was too frightened to scream, even when he ripped her clothes off. Her head was down, tucked against her flat chest. She wouldn't look at him, as if, somehow, not seeing him would make him go away. He took her hair and pulled her head back, forcing her to look into his eyes. When he pulled the knife up, she shut her eyes tight, contorting her face into such an exaggerated expression, he almost laughed. But he didn't laugh. Instead, tears of grief began to roll down his cheeks. "I'm sorry," he whispered. "I'm so very sorry." Then, with one more slice, he slit the little girl's throat from ear to ear. She was so fragile, he nearly cut straight through the bone. As she slumped back to the floor, her head was tilted so far to the side, it looked like it was about to fall off.

It took Harry several minutes to compose himself. He did it by forcing himself to look at what he'd done, willing himself to study the carnage and confront the reality of his deeds. When he knew the scene was embedded in his memory, so deeply that he would never forget the most minute detail of this horror, Harry went outside to his rental car, opened the trunk, and took out a small, leather overnight bag. From that he removed a starched white shirt and a tie identical to the one he was wearing. He went back inside, took off his bloodstained shirt and tie, tossed them on the floor. There was an oil lamp on the mantel above the fireplace and he picked it up, holding it at chest level, then dropped it onto the wooden floor. He took out a cigar, a Dominican with Cuban leaves. It was one of the few unhealthy vices he allowed himself. Harry removed the wrapper, cut off the tip, and put the cigar in his mouth. He lit a match and held it to the end of the cigar until he was drawing in large, satisfying bursts of smoke. With a last look at the two bodies, one still rocking ever so slightly in the rocking chair, the other sprawled on the floor by the door, he dropped the lit match onto the spreading puddle of kerosene and walked out the door.

As Harry got into his car, he heard the noise, the lovely whoosh of flame as it starts to catch and spread. He felt the warmth and then stared at the magnificent flames, beginning to roar higher and higher, out of control now, crackling and spitting, as Momma One-Eye's cabin began to burn to the ground.

Heading out of town, Harry drove evenly and steadily, slowing down only once, as he passed a ragged football field. The letters on the scoreboard read "Go Owls." The w in the team name was crooked, tilted to the right. The field itself was in disrepair. The grass was brown, and there were clumps of cans and bottles on what should have been the fifty-yard line. One crossbar was missing, and the other was leaning at a 45-degree angle. Still, it was a school field, and Harry smiled as he passed by, remembering the feeling of pulling on a helmet and running out to play as cheerleaders screamed and parents roared their approval. Harry flashed back to those glorious days of stardom, losing himself momentarily in the past, then shook away the cobwebs of memory, put his foot on the gas pedal, and got the hell out of there.

Back on the highway, cruising at precisely the legal speed limit, H. Harrison Wagner realized he didn't have to be in New York until the next afternoon. A whole day off. And the kid he was supposed to see, the writer, he'd be easy. He didn't know what was going on. Didn't even have a clue. Harry now knew enough about killing to know he much preferred dealing with people who didn't have a clue. As with everything else, they made it much easier to do what had to be done.

Harry thought about the trap he'd allowed himself to be caught in. He didn't know whom he hated more: the person who'd caught him, or himself, for being caught. But, as always, his urges soon overcame any sense of self-reflection. So, as he drove, Harry Wagner decided he was going to spend the night in Nashville. And do his best to fall in love for another twenty-four hours.

Yes, he admitted to himself, underneath it all he was so, so weak.

But what the hell. If he was going to be weak, he might as well enjoy it.

chapter 3

arl rang the buzzer to Maggie Peterson's apartment and waited for over a minute before ringing again. When there was no answer after his third ring, he leaned against the elegant wrought-iron gate that shielded her front door from the street and began wondering if he'd imagined their entire conversation earlier that morning.

The rain had stopped, the sky was clear and bright, and the sidewalk outside Maggie's lavish East Side brownstone looked freshly washed. Nannies and young mothers were out on the street pushing baby carriages. A couple of teenage boys were kicking a soccer ball in and out among the parked cars. He'd been waiting, pacing in front of her stoop, for fifteen minutes when an errant kick from one of the teenagers sent the soccer ball Carl's way. He was in the process of making a nice little dropkick back to them when a black limousine pulled up directly in front of his pacing path. A chauffeur stepped out from behind the wheel and walked around the car to open the back door on the passenger side. As he did so, he glanced at Carl, a conspiratorial glance that seemed to wonder why the passenger couldn't open her own goddamn door. The answer was that Maggie was the passenger and Maggie clearly did nothing on her own that she could have someone else do for her. She did not apologize to Carl for keeping him waiting; she just strode silently past him, unlocked the glistening iron gate, then the door to her apartment, and whisked herself inside. Carl followed and found himself in a chrome and black-leather living room. He sensed a theme, since she was still dressed in black leather, although it was a different black leather outfit from the one she'd worn at the funeral. This one was a vest with, apparently, nothing underneath it, and a short, skintight skirt, along with ankle-high boots. She blended in perfectly with her furniture.

When she sat on the couch, leaned back, and crossed her legs, her white arms, legs, and face took on a free-floating, almost ghostly appearance.

"How do you like it?" she asked, and he wasn't sure if she meant the apartment or her outfit. He had to admit, he liked them both just fine. The living room opened into a gourmet kitchen. The six-burner Viking stove alone would have taken up most of the space in Carl's entire apartment. The rest of the apartment seemed just as opulent. As distracting as Maggie was, lolling on her couch, the view behind her was even more distracting. French doors led out to a brick patio and an elegant, English-style garden in full and brilliantly colorful bloom. Somewhere down the black and white tiled hallway, he assumed, was at least one bedroom. Probably two or three. He couldn't help but wonder if she'd be inviting him down that hallway to check out that view.

Carl finally responded to her question and, indicating the apartment, said that it was beautiful. He then took the plunge and began rattling off how pleased he was that she'd liked his novel, that it was very personal and important to him, the whole idea of a small-town basketball coach and what happens to him when he lands a once-in-a-generation player. He hoped she liked the title, *Getting Kiddo,* because he felt very strongly about it—well, not so strongly that he wouldn't think about changing it if she really hated it. He was just telling her how thrilled he was that she thought it could be a success, that he'd work incredibly hard, do whatever it took to help, when she held up an imperious hand, cutting him off, and said, bluntly, "Your novel won't sell for shit."

That stopped him cold. Which she didn't even notice. She was too busy pouring some Evian into a crystal glass filled with ice cubes. She didn't offer him any, just took a sip, sighed with pleasure, and put the glass down.

"It's too damned good to be successful in today's market," she explained. "But I *will* publish it. And I'll do the whole number—fancy advance galleys, a reading tour at the good independent stores, the three or four of them that are still left . . ."

Carl shook his head at her, confused. "Maybe I'm missing something here. Why do you want to take on a book that won't sell?"

"Because I want you to take on something for me that *will* sell. Something big. I'm talking number-one best-seller big. Are you listening?"

"I'm listening big," Carl said. He was also noticing that she had a wall of original Nan Goldin photographs. It was a disturbing display of junkies, transvestites, and asexual body parts.

"I've landed something that's so unbelievably hot we're doing it as an instant book. Written quickly, published even quicker. The kind of thing we usually save for terrorist attacks, wars, or dead royalty."

As she talked, her face lit up as though it were Christmas morning and she'd just been given the ultimate present. At that moment Carl saw right into the essence of Maggie Peterson, and that essence was pure, unadulterated greed.

"I've got an inside source in Washington," she went on. "A certain someone who has an amazing story to tell, every bit of it true. And when that story is published, it will change the course of history."

"That's quite a statement," Carl said, somewhat skeptically. Hype was, after all, what Maggie Peterson was best at.

"I mean every word of it. I am not exaggerating. This book will change the course of history."

"Who's the inside source?"

"Someone who, for personal reasons, wishes to be known only as Gideon."

"Gideon," Carl repeated. "Okay . . . but who *is* Gideon?"

Maggie drained her glass, uncrossed her legs, and leaned forward, narrowing her eyes at him. "The first and only thing you need to know about Gideon is that you'll get no answers whatsoever about him. None. You will never meet him, you will never speak to him, you will never have any contact with him. So don't even bother asking questions. Gideon is in an extremely sensitive position. And terrified of being outed. He will deal only with me. No one else. Understood?"

"No," he said slowly, frowning.

"Then keep quiet and listen." Her words poured out of her in machine-gun style, quickly, violently, and dispassionately. "I need a ghost. Someone who can write, because Gideon can't. At least, not well enough for a book. Furthermore, I need someone who can do this as fiction—a tight, well-crafted commercial novel. Because if Apex tries to publish this as nonfiction, we'll get sued for billions of dollars."

"By who?"

"I really don't like repeating myself," she answered testily. "You will get no answer from me about Gideon."

"Look, I'm not trying to be dense," Carl said. "But how do you expect me to agree to write a book when I don't have the slightest idea who or what it's about?"

"I'm talking about a rush, rush assignment," she snapped, as if that answered his question. "I'll feed you information, highly confidential information delivered directly to you. You will absorb it, then turn it into fiction, adding color, texture, and atmosphere but keeping as close to the facts as possible. You'll get it back to me, chapter by chapter, and I'll edit it as you go along. The timing is vital. It *must* be published in six weeks. *Now* do you understand?"

"No. I don't understand *anything*."

"What else do you need to know?" she asked.

"Let's start with why you picked me."

"Because I need somebody who's a nobody."

"Well, thanks for clearing that part up."

"I'm sorry if that sounds harsh," she said. "But I can't let a name journalist anywhere near this—he'll try to find out who Gideon is, and the whole project will go up in smoke. If I go get an established novelist, I'll have ego problems. They'll all want their name on the book."

"What if I want *mine* on it?"

"The only name on this book will be Gideon's. I need a true ghost, someone who will do this job totally without credit and keep quiet about it. Forever. No one can know you're working on this. You can't tell a soul—not even your girlfriend."

"First of all, I'm not working on this yet. And second of all, that's not a problem. I don't have a girlfriend."

"Of course you don't. You and Amanda have been history for what, a year now?"

He cocked his head and squinted at her curiously. "You *do* do your homework, don't you?"

Maggie's lips stretched somewhat tightly across her face. He wondered if that was her smile. "You have no brothers or sisters," she said, "your mother died four years ago, and you and your father barely speak."

"What else do you know about me?"

"I know *everything* about you, Carl."

He hesitated, stroking his chin with his thumb. "I can't believe I'm saying this, I mean, especially to you, but I think I'll pass." She looked at him in shock. He wondered if anyone had ever said no to her before. "I don't like to be rushed," he explained. "Especially when I'm completely in the dark. I have a tendency to bump into things and hurt myself."

Maggie let out a weary sigh, rolling her eyes at him as if he were a recalcitrant child. Then she reached over and picked up a soft leather briefcase that was sitting on the floor. She placed it on the sparkling coffee table, opened it, and removed a glossy-looking pamphlet. It was Apex's summer catalogue. Without saying a word, she opened it to the centerfold, a double-page spread that read:

GIDEON

COMING THIS AUGUST . . . THE MOST EXPLOSIVE TELL-ALL STORY OF ALL TIME! IT'S SO SECRET, SO CONTROVERSIAL, WE CAN'T EVEN TELL YOU WHAT IT IS—EXCEPT TO TELL YOU THERE HAS NEVER BEEN A BOOK LIKE IT!
FIRST PRINTING: 1,000,000 COPIES

"A million copies," he said quietly.

"That's John Grisham and Stephen King territory. Do you know how many novels you'd have to write to sell a million copies?" she asked.

"About half a million," Carl said miserably.

"At least."

Maggie returned the catalogue to the briefcase. Next she pulled out an envelope, which she held in front of her, and gestured for him to open it.

He did. Inside was a check for $50,000 made out to him. The payer was Quadrangle Publications. A new imprint of Apex, she explained, that specialized in topical books of particular news value. *Gideon* was going to launch the imprint. Even as fiction it would be news.

"When you deliver a satisfactory manuscript, you'll get another check for a hundred and fifty thousand. Since I'll also pay you an additional fifty grand for your novel, you'll make out quite nicely. The contracts are being drawn up as we speak. But lawyers take forever, and I don't have forever. I need you to start right away. I suppose we'll have to find you a new agent, too, won't we?"

Carl was speechless. This woman was handing him the keys to the magic kingdom. She was saying, *Come right on in—you belong.*

"So," she said. "Here's the question: Would you like to make a quarter of a million dollars, have a number-one best-seller, and have the best publisher in New York throwing her weight behind you?"

Carl didn't have to respond to that one. He knew what his answer was, and so did she.

Instead he stepped over to her wall of black glass bookshelves and removed an object he'd been eyeing since the moment he'd come into the apartment. He held it in his hand, stroking it, almost as if it were alive. It was a small golden statue. An Oscar.

"Is this real?" he asked.

"I don't have *anything* that's not real," she told him.

"You won this?"

"I bought it. At an auction at Christie's."

He took his eyes off of the magical statue and looked at her, baffled. "Why?" he wondered.

"Because I always wanted one. And, in case you haven't realized it by now, I always get what I want."

She now removed a final item from her briefcase: a business card, which she also handed him. "There's a number written on the bottom. It's my personal cell phone. If you need me, call me there. Don't ever go through the Apex switchboard. Don't ever leave your name on an answering machine. And don't even *think* about coming here again unless I invite you, and if I do, it won't be for professional purposes. Officially I don't know you. Officially you do not exist." She held out the card, and he took it. Her hand lingered in his a moment longer than it needed to. When she spoke next, her voice was a low, sexy growl. "But unofficially, Carl, I may still have to fuck you."

Carl Granville put the Oscar back in its proper place on the shelf, then took her card and stuck it in his shirt pocket.

"Please," he said. "Call me Granny."

Several years ago, when he first moved to New York to become a writer, Carl had fantasized about that special day when he would at long last sell his first novel, *Getting Kiddo*. This was no idle fantasy on his part; he'd worked long and hard on refining and perfecting every detail. There were, he'd decided after much thought, three things he would do.

First, he would phone his mother and tell her the news. After all, she was his biggest—and for years and years his only—believer. His father? His father felt Carl should have gone to a proper, responsible business school and gotten a proper, responsible job. Preferably one that called for wing-tip shoes.

Second, he would buy himself a leisurely, solitary lunch at Tony's, a cozy neighborhood Italian restaurant on West Seventy-ninth Street that was his absolute favorite haunt. He knew exactly what he was going to order, too—a green salad, ravioli with homemade sausages, cannoli for dessert, a bottle of Chianti.

Third, he would split a very expensive bottle of Moët & Chandon champagne with his special lady. They would toast to *Getting Kiddo*, then they'd make love until dawn.

It was, he reflected now, still a lovely fantasy. Which was too damned bad, because his mother was dead, Tony's was now a shoe store, and there was no lady in his life, special or otherwise. It was, he reflected, awfully damned strange how the world can change around you.

Briefly he thought about calling his father and telling *him* the good news. Then he thought better of it. He thought about calling Amanda and telling *her*. Thought better of that, too. What it boiled down to was that there was no one in the whole world to tell.

Awfully damned strange indeed.

Still, Carl headed for home with a bounce in his stride and fifty thousand dollars in his pocket. He stopped at Citibank and deposited the money into his savings account. Then he bought that bottle of Moët & Chandon at a liquor store on Broadway. He would just go ahead and drink it himself. That much he could do. Hell, yes.

Oddly enough, his feet kept climbing when he reached his apartment door. They took him one more flight up, to Toni's door. Well, why not? She was gorgeous. She was friendly. She was there. He was just about to knock when the door flew open and she came running out, fumbling for her keys. She was frantic and out of breath and in a big hurry and she stared at him in surprise, evidently wondering what the hell he was doing standing outside her door. Suddenly he was wondering the exact same thing.

"Something?" she asked finally.

"Kind of," he said. "I was looking for someone to celebrate with. See, I wrote this novel and—"

"That's fabulous. I'd love to hear all about it, but I have an audition for *All My Children* in fifteen minutes and I haven't even seen the pages yet and they're looking for a new vamp and it's a great part and . . . oh, God, how do I look?"

She had her hair up, and she wore a tight black minidress with high heels. The effect was absolutely spectacular.

"You look like if they don't hire you, they're crazy."

"You're a bunny. Thanks! Bye! And congratulations!" Then she went dashing down the stairs as fast as her teetering heels would take her.

Carl sighed and stood for just a moment in the silent hallway, feeling the tiniest bit foolish. Then he shrugged, wondered if being a bunny was a good thing or a bad thing, and went back down to his place, unlocked his door.

He felt it before he saw it. As he stepped inside, he whirled to his left.

There was a guy sitting on his bed. He was puffing on a long, slim cigar.

"You brought champagne, Carl. How thoughtful. Listen, I couldn't find an ashtray. Where do you hide them?"

Carl swallowed, frightened. The man was calm, smiling in a relaxed manner. But there was something about him that made the hair on the back of Carl's neck stand on end. "I don't smoke," he said. The man grunted, dissatisfied. Carl suddenly wished he had something in his possession a little more substantial than the miniature Swiss Army knife in his pocket, which he'd carried since high school. It had just a two-inch-long blade and a nail file. He gripped the neck of the champagne bottle, wondering what kind of weapon it would make. "What do you want?"

"I want you to close the door," the intruder said. He didn't move from the bed. Carl realized the apartment was dark and shadowy. Whoever this guy was, he'd drawn the curtains.

"Look, I don't have any money on me, and—"

"Close it, Carl." He didn't raise his voice, didn't even sound impatient. No need. He was in total control.

Carl closed the door and stood there.

"Good man. Now I want you to go over to the desk, turn on the light, and sit down facing me."

Carl did as he was told and sat in his swivel chair. The man now stood. He was bigger than Carl, 6'3" or 6'4", and powerfully built. His hands were monster-sized. His movements were precise and compact, elegant, like a dancer's. He was maybe thirty-five, with a flat-top crew cut, a neatly trimmed mustache, and heavy black-framed glasses. He was an elegant dresser, to the point of foppish. He wore a fawn-colored silk suit, houndstooth, a linen vest, a lavender broadcloth shirt, and a yellow polka-dot bow tie. He went over and locked the door, pausing to tap his cigar ash into the kitchen sink.

"How the hell did you get in here?" Carl demanded.

A faint smile crossed the man's lips. "It was something of a challenge, I'll admit. Took me almost six seconds. You ought to invest in a Medeco dead bolt, Carl. Those can sometimes take me up to a minute, depending on the construction of the door frame."

Carl's apartment had been a formal parlor ninety or so years ago, before the old town house had been broken up into apartments. There was a fireplace, nonworking, and built-in oak bookcases with glass doors. In place of a chandelier, Carl's sixty-pound red leather Everlast heavy bag hung in the middle of the room. He'd gotten it the day after Amanda moved to Washington. It wasn't until three months after that that he'd realized there might be some connection between the two. For furniture he had his bed, a huge old iron one that came from a lunatic asylum in upstate New York, and his desk, a battered rolltop that once belonged to a railroad stationmaster. Also a small dining table, which had no story behind it whatsoever other than the fact it was cheap. It was set up in front of the bay window.

The intruder went over to the window, opened the curtain an inch, and studied the street outside carefully. That's when Carl saw it. Underneath the expensive silk jacket, over the white vest.

"You have a gun," Carl said slowly.

"Mmm," the man said in agreement. "Don't you like guns?"

"No," Carl said.

The man nodded his head sympathetically. "Well, get used to them. That's my advice."

Carl said nothing. For the first time the man looked impatient. "We have work to do." When Carl didn't move, just peered at him curiously, the man said, "It's a rush job. I thought you understood that part."

Carl let out a slow breath. It felt like the first breath he'd taken in months. "You're Gideon."

"I'm Harry Wagner," the man said, puffing on his cigar. "Short for Harrison, not Harold. And no, I'm not Gideon. I'm what is known in underground circles as the go-between. Rather a quaint, Regency-era term, don't you think? Carries with it the whiff of tender romance. Intrigue of the trembly, virginal heart. Most inappropriate, don't you think?"

"I wouldn't know."

"Then trust me. There's no love going on here, Carl. None at all. There's only people fucking each other." As punctuation, Wagner hit the heavy bag with a thundering right hand.

"What people?"

"Nice try, Carl. And I appreciate the effort. But I was told you also understood that part of our little endeavor—no questions."

Carl glowered at him, not liking any of this. Who was this asshole? What the hell had he gotten himself into? He had the card that Maggie had given him, the one with her cell phone number on it. Abruptly he reached for the phone and dialed.

She answered on the first ring. "What is it, Carl?"

Carl froze. "How'd you know it was me?"

"I haven't given this number to anyone else," she said impatiently. "Now, what do you want?"

"There's a very large white man wearing a very ugly tie in my apartment . . ."

Suddenly Carl felt Harry's fingers wrap around his wrist. This was not a gentle laying on of hands. This was an iron grip. One that, with so little effort, was causing extraordinary pain. Somehow the man had sprung across the room. Carl hadn't heard him, hadn't seen him move. But there he was, crushing the bones in Carl's right wrist as easily as one might crumple a paper cup. Carl looked up into Harry's eyes and was very afraid.

"Say 'Hold on,' " Harry Wagner said. His voice was low, as if, out of politeness, he didn't want the person on the other end of the phone to know he was interrupting. When Carl didn't respond immediately, Harry squeezed harder. Tears came into Carl's eyes.

"Hold on," he managed to say into the mouthpiece.

"For Christ's sake, what's going on?" he heard Maggie squawk.

"Now put the phone down," Harry instructed.

This time Carl didn't hesitate. The phone was immediately down on the table.

"And now let me explain something to you," Harry continued. His words had no emotion behind them. He sounded like a high-school teacher giving instructions for a pop quiz to a group of not overly bright students. "I'm very sensitive about my clothes," he said. "I know you thought you were probably being a smartass, and usually I don't mind. I appreciate wit, in its proper place."

"That's good to know," Carl said, but when he felt Harry's hand squeeze even tighter, he decided it was probably better to keep quiet.

"I don't like people making fun of what I wear. I take great pride in my outfits. They're quite expensive, and many of them are made to order. I realize that you're an artistic type; that's why you've been hired. And I will give extra leeway for your artistic temperament. However, and I mean this with all due respect for your talent and abilities, if you ever again make fun of anything I'm wearing, I'll hurt you. And not like I'm hurting you now. I'll hurt you very badly. Permanently. Now pick up the phone and finish your conversation."

Harry released Carl from his grip. Carl felt no need to say anything in response. Harry Wagner had made his point most effectively.

Trying not to rub his red wrist, Carl picked up the phone.

"What are you two assholes doing over there?" Maggie Peterson asked.

"Nothing," Carl answered.

"Then what's the problem? I *said* you'd be receiving material."

"I've received it."

"Then everything is satisfactory."

"More than satisfactory," Carl said. "My compliments on your messenger service."

"Don't call me again unless it's important," she said. And then hung up on him.

"Thank you for the kind word. I appreciate it," Wagner said, swirling a puff of cigar smoke into the air.

"May I say something?"

"You may now and always say anything you'd like. Well, almost anything."

"We've established that you can hurt me. And you can probably shoot me if you want." Carl was suddenly very angry. And suddenly, no matter what this asshole could do to him, he didn't care if that anger showed. "But this is still my home and I don't like people smoking big fat smelly cigars in it. So put that goddamn thing out. *Now.*"

Wagner sighed, thought about the request, and nodded. "Fair enough," he said. He took a final, wistful puff, rolling the cigar around in his fingers. Then he put it out in the kitchen sink. Moving to Carl's closet, he opened the door and rooted around until he found a wooden hanger. "Wire hangers," he said, "are your wardrobe's worst enemy." He took off his jacket and carefully placed it on the wooden hanger, then hung the coat on the hat rack by the front door. Next, Harrison Wagner undid his belt, unzipped his trousers, and dropped them.

A nine-by-twelve manila envelope was wrapped around his bulging left thigh.

Surgical tape held it tightly in place. Wagner bent down and roughly yanked the tape off, wincing as the hairs on his leg came off with it. "I hate this part," he said. Then he zipped himself back up and opened the envelope.

Inside were what seemed to be photocopied pages of an old diary, along with copies of old newspaper clippings and more photocopies of stamped documents that looked like birth and marriage records. There were a half-dozen handwritten letters, also photocopied.

"Here's the drill, Carl. You are going to study this material until you have fully and completely absorbed every single detail. Names of people and towns have been blacked out. Don't even *try* to find out the real names. That will be far worse than insulting my tie. Don't think about who these people really are, don't think about where these events really took place."

"If I can't know the real people and places, how do I—"

"Be creative. Make them up. That's why you're being paid the medium-to-fairly-large bucks, isn't it? You'll have more than enough description to help you out. Believe me, you'll not be wanting for material."

"What's to stop me from showing this stuff to somebody else? Letting *them* try to find out the real story?"

"For one thing, Carl, I'm here to stop you. And I think you'll already agree I'm a fairly effective stopper. For another, I'm not allowed to leave any of this material here with you, and you're not allowed to make a copy."

Carl nodded. "Can I at least make notes?"

"You can," Wagner replied.

"That's good, because I flunked my Evelyn Wood course. Question: What are you going to be doing while I'm doing this?"

"Answer: I'm going to be watching you."

Carl glanced at the stack of papers, frowning. "This could take hours."

"I'm very patient. And I have nowhere else to go." Wagner sat back down on the bed, crossed his arms, and diligently began watching Carl. He did not blink. He did not loosen his tie. "When you're done," he continued, "I will take the material and leave."

"I'll miss you," Carl said.

"You will start writing immediately. I'll return to pick up what you've written and to bring you more material."

"When will that be?"

"You'll know when you find me here."

Carl thought about chucking the whole thing right then. But then he thought about his novel and the fifty thousand dollars he'd just deposited in the bank. He thought about Maggie Peterson saying this project was going to change the course of history.

"Harry, you seem to be a fairly intelligent guy."

"Why, thank you, Carl. That's kind of you."

"Are you aware of just how fucking weird this whole thing is?"

"It's a fucking weird world, Carl. And getting weirder as we speak." Again Wagner smiled at him faintly. "You'd better get to work."

Carl dug a blank notepad out of the bottom drawer of his desk and started in on the diary. It was not easy going. The handwriting was tortured and faint, the prose rambling and disjointed and semiliterate. He found the content hard to follow, let alone absorb. Especially with that very large man sitting not ten feet away, staring at him like an immaculately groomed bird of prey. It took some getting used to. It all took some getting used to.

But this was his job, he told himself. It was just like stroking a fifteen-foot jumper with three seconds left in a tie game. You get in the zone. You block out everything else. You do it.

Carl Granville read, he made notes, he concentrated. Soon he was barely conscious of Harrison Wagner sitting there. Wagner, for his part, remained as motionless as a tree. And as silent. Not once did he so much as clear his throat or make any other effort to remind Carl he was there. He knew that Carl knew.

After a couple of hours Carl needed to splash some cold water on his face. Wagner allowed it, as long as Carl left the door ajar. Standing at the sink, his head spinning, Carl wondered just exactly what the hell he was reading. Clearly it was a woman's diary. The handwriting and spelling showed that she was uneducated; the content indicated that she was dirt poor and of no apparent significance. But who was she? And who were all of the people that she was talking about? Had one of them become famous? Maggie had mentioned that her source, Gideon, was based in Washington—clearly, this diary in some way had political implications. But what were they? None of what he'd read seemed in any way controversial or damaging to anyone. It was about a time long ago and far away. Distant, obscure people in a distant, obscure place.

And just exactly who was Harry Wagner? A bodyguard? A detective? A spy?

Carl wondered. How could he not wonder?

Wagner was making a pot of coffee in the kitchen. Waiting for the water to boil— "Electric kettle, Carl, that's the secret," he said—he used the bathroom himself. He kept the door open the entire time and ordered Carl to remain in the kitchen, far from the top-secret material on the desk.

Suddenly hungry, Carl began fishing around in the refrigerator for something to eat. The likeliest candidate he could find was a half-eaten turkey hero from Mama Joy's on Broadway, somewhere between seven and ten days old.

"Want part of a sandwich?" he asked Wagner when the big man emerged from the bathroom.

Wagner examined the food distastefully. "I would rather chew off my own foot."

"Good. More for me."

Carl finished making the coffee and poured them some. They both took theirs black. Wagner returned to the bed and sat there, sipping his coffee, waiting for Carl to get back to work. Carl ate his sandwich, as slowly as possible, over the kitchen sink. He drank his coffee. Poured himself another cup.

Then he went back to the diary.

Finally he could absorb no more. His eyes were glazing over, and his head was like a pinball machine, with descriptions of people and places, snatches of dialogue, and an unknown woman's memories and observations, both naive and harsh, careening around in there full tilt. He set the diary aside, puffing out his cheeks in exhaustion. He had been at this for more than six hours.

"Had enough?" Wagner asked pleasantly.

Carl nodded dumbly.

Wagner promptly gathered everything up, returned it to the manila envelope, and taped it back around his bare leg with a roll of surgical tape he'd brought for just this purpose. He put on his jacket, went to the curtain, and looked outside, intently studying the street. Satisfied, he went to the door, opened it, and started to leave without so much as a goodbye.

"Will you do me a favor, Harry?"

"What's that, Carl?"

"Will you fucking knock next time?"

Wagner let out a short laugh. "I'll think about it."

And then Harry Wagner was gone.

Carl needed a serious blow. He stripped to a pair of shorts and cross-trainers, put on his leather gloves, and pummeled the heavy bag with both hands for thirty minutes, staying up on the balls of his feet, dancing around it, punishing it, grunting from the exertion, until he was exhausted and his bare chest was drenched with sweat. He took a shower, first hot, then cold. He filled a tall glass with ice and poured in what was left in the coffeepot, adding a scoop of Häagen-Dazs chocolate chip. He returned to his desk and read over his notes while he drank. Then he flicked on his computer. He created a folder called "Gideon" and broke it into a dozen chapter files. He opened up Chapter 1. He closed his eyes and breathed in and out a few times, getting in the zone.

And then Carl Granville started writing.

chapter 4

Rayette ran off with Billy Taylor because he was the first boy she'd ever met who made her laugh. She had met boys who made her tingle all over the way they kissed her, lying out by Grinder's Creek in the moonlight. She had met boys who made her want to punch them the way they lied to her, lying out by Grinder's Creek in the moonlight. But she had never met a boy who made her laugh like Billy Taylor did.

Of course, in her fourteen years of life in Julienne, Alabama, Rayette had never had much to laugh about.

Rayette was born a year to the day after the great stock market crash of 1929. Her father, Enos Boudreau, was a salesman, and as snakebit as a man could be without actually dying of bad luck. The Depression didn't really change Enos Boudreau's life. All it did was prove to him that he was indeed ahead of his time: It had just taken the rest of the country some years to catch up with his failure.

Enos talked a lot about the good times, which seemed to be back when all you had to do was knock on a door, open your sample case, then tuck the money that people threw at you right into your front pocket. Rayette had heard much about those times, but she didn't actually remember them. What she remembered was her father trying to sell encyclopedias to white folks who couldn't read, vacuums to niggers who had dirt floors, and insurance to anyone for anything anytime. People in Julienne weren't too interested in insurance. What was broke they could mostly fix, and when it came to dying, well, death didn't seem to worry them much. Life seemed much more troublesome.

Enos still went out every morning looking to make his commission. He still returned every evening with dust on his shoes and whiskey on his *breath but nothing in his pockets. Rayette didn't pay much attention to her father's daily routine. He had never been very affectionate. Nor, for that matter, was he particularly talkative. He would nod at her in the morning over breakfast, and he would nod at her when he came back home. Sometimes, after he would flop down on the big, comfortable chair in the living room, his shoes off, his toes poking through the holes of socks that had been darned too many times, he would say to her, "Get the jar." The jar was given an honored place in the kitchen—on the second shelf, to the right of the icebox, right next to all the homemade jams—and it was kept full of moonshine whiskey. Every evening, when Enos would sit in that chair, he would hold the jar up to his mouth and drink from it until he had no choice but to sit because he could not gather his legs up underneath him. Once, when Rayette was seven, Enos had passed out cold, sliding half out of the chair, his legs stretched out onto the floor, his head resting on the seat cushion. The jar had fallen with him, and Rayette had gone to see what all the fuss was about. She picked it up and took a drink, a deep, full gulp, and the force of the whiskey hit her as hard as if she'd run straight into a brick wall. She choked and gasped and made so much noise that Enos rose from his stupor. The first thing he saw when his eyes finally opened was his little daughter, holding his beloved jar, letting its even more beloved contents spill onto the floor. He reacted the way he reacted to most things when he'd been drinking—violently. Enos slapped Rayette across the face, hard enough to make her head snap back. Hard enough to leave the imprint of his hand visible on her cheek for most of the week. Hard enough so she never forgot the hurt of it. Never stopped being afraid of him. Hard enough so that she never stopped hating him.*

That was not the first time he had hit Rayette, and it most certainly wasn't the last. By the time Rayette was fourteen and was laughing with Billy Taylor every night up in the old tree house that Billy's daddy had built, laughing and naked and tingling between her legs when she let Billy stroke her and kiss her all over, she had been beaten many more times than she could count. Enos had twice broken her nose with the force of his fist. Once he'd broken her eye socket. When Doc Greeby had come to the house that time and wanted to know what happened, Enos said she'd been playing baseball with the boys, was catching for them because no one wanted to be catcher, and been hit in the face with a swinging bat. The bruise was so bad the doctor didn't even question it. Alone at night, she sometimes wondered how her father could hit her so hard that his hand could cause the same damage as a baseball bat. But she didn't wonder too often, because then she'd also have to ask herself how he could kick her down the basement stairs, which he did once, and how he could light a match and hold it to her bare back, which he did twice.

If Rayette started wondering, she'd have to wonder about her mother, too, and she didn't like to do that, either.

Sulene Boudreau, born Sulene Jackson, was a saint. At least that's what everybody in town said. When Rayette would go into Julienne's general store, run by Abigail Brock, that's what Abigail said every time. She would pat Rayette on the head and say, "You know, honey, you are almost as pretty as your momma was. And your momma was the prettiest girl I ever saw. 'Course, your momma was a saint, too. Never knew no one like your momma."

No one had ever known anyone like Sulene. Pretty. Gentle. Quiet and soft-spoken. And smart as a whip. Even as a child, Sulene had a kind word for everybody. She was a little girl who saw no bad in anyone and, even growing up in Alabama in the early part of the century, didn't know black from white. She was courteous to all, helpful to anyone who needed help, never had anything but a smile on her face.

Of course, Sulene Jackson was also crazy as a loon.

Nobody spoke about it, but everyone in town knew it. They all loved this child, but she also scared the devil out of them.

She'd been a wonderful little girl, already making money for the family by the time she was ten years old, helping her own momma take in laundry. She didn't talk much—sometimes she could go a week or two without saying one word—but no one paid too much mind about that. She was thoughtful, they said. It was too bad more children couldn't be like Sulene. Nice and thoughtful and quiet.

She stayed quiet even when the first incident happened. That's what was so scary about it. So creepy. She'd been helping with the laundry, doing the

*ironing for Miss Pritchard, the teacher. Miss Pritchard would give little Su-
lene private lessons in exchange for some housework. That evening Miss
Pritchard had been working with Sulene on her multiplication tables. It had
gone well, as usual; Sulene was good with numbers. After the lessons, Miss
Pritchard was reading over by the window when she thought she smelled
something strange. It was like something was on fire. She looked up to see
that Sulene Jackson was standing at the ironing board, the hot iron pressed
down on her hand. How long it had been there, the teacher didn't know.
Long enough to permanently turn the little girl's left hand into a misshapen,
scarred ball. Long enough to melt two of her fingers together.*

*Miss Pritchard had picked the girl up and carried her six long blocks to
the doctor's, running the whole way. There wasn't much the doc could do,
though. He could ease the pain—that was it.*

*Miss Pritchard never gave Sulene private lessons again. It was the si-
lence, she said. During the whole time the little girl had the iron on her
hand, the whole time she was being carried down the street, the whole time
she was at the doctor's, Sulene never said a word.*

*There were no more incidents until two years later. That's when Sulene
jumped off the roof of her house. It was a miracle she wasn't killed that
time. She had climbed up to the top of the three-story wooden structure,
stood there for several moments—long enough for her mother to look up
and see her and cry out—and then spread her arms and jumped. For a second she looked like nothing more than a lovely bird in flight. But when she
hit the ground, she broke her leg and her collarbone and gave herself a
concussion.*

After that, people pretty much left Sulene alone.

*A year later she jumped again. From a higher building, the Baptist
church right in town. This time she didn't even break any bones. She walked
away unhurt. And still silent.*

*Six months after that, she was swimming by herself and disappeared
under the water. Two other children, the Clarkson twins, were swimming
nearby and saw her go under. They swam over to the spot, dove repeatedly,
finally grabbed hold of the girl and pulled her to shore. They later swore
that Sulene had been below the surface for well over five minutes. But when*

they brought her up, she wasn't even gasping for breath. She just looked at them, gently nodded, and walked on home.

After that, there were no more incidents. But people still looked at her funny—half in fear, half in praise. This was a little girl who seemed to be indestructible. This was a little girl who just might be something special.

When she was seventeen, Enos Boudreau started coming to call. He was handsome, he did some selling, and he didn't mind about the deformed hand or the fact that she still didn't talk much. In fact, he liked her silence. He liked it even more when they got married, for he could hit her as hard and as often as he wanted and she never cried or whimpered or screamed. She only stared right into his eyes, which never really bothered him.

When Rayette was born, two years after the wedding, Sulene kept quiet during the birth. And as far as the rest of Julienne was concerned, she kept quiet, for the most part, after that, too.

But not when she was with Rayette.

She talked to Rayette. Softly. Gently. Lovingly. Holding her little baby girl in her scabbed and rough-skinned arms, she told her all about the different kinds of flowers, and how animals could know things that people never knew, and about God, who was looking down at them at all times, looking out for them, saving them up for some wonderful plan he had for all living things. She told her baby how death was not something to be feared. How death was not something to run from. There was only one thing to be feared, Sulene told her tiny daughter. And that was life.

Rayette was five years old when she found her mother's body in the bathroom, blood everywhere. Sulene had found something even she could not survive: a razor blade. With Enos passed out in the living room and Rayette playing with her favorite doll, Sulene had gone behind the closed door and calmly slashed her wrists. It took her about twenty minutes to die. And in those twenty minutes, Rayette heard only one sound coming from inside the room. It was the first time she'd ever heard this sound.

It was the sound of her mother laughing.

After that, something inside Rayette told her she'd better grow up quite different from her mother. And that's exactly what she did.

She did not believe that God had any great plan for everyone on earth. She did not much care about the beauty of flowers or the intelligence of animals. And she did not care to be quiet. She liked to talk and laugh and moan and cry.

That was one thing her mother's death taught her: It does not pay to keep your mouth shut.

By the time she was twelve years old, Rayette could drink a pint of whiskey and be none the worse for wear. She had the face of an angel to go with the body of a mature woman. Boys couldn't stay away from her. And the later she stayed out and the worse her reputation grew, the harder Enos would punch her. Rayette spent her nights in ecstasy and her days in pain, and she thought that was pretty much life's normal cycle.

Until she met Billy Taylor, who not only brought her ecstasy with his big, hard cock and his miraculously soft, gentle hands, he could make her laugh. Day and night.

She laughed right after the first time she kissed Billy; his scrunched-up face was just so funny. She laughed the first time he saw her naked; he was dumbfounded by her body and could barely speak or even look at her. She laughed after she first had sex with Billy; even though he was four years older than she was, he'd been a virgin, and he was so pleased, so proud. She laughed when he proposed to her and when they ran away to get married by a preacher whose only stipulation was that he get paid two dollars in advance to perform the ceremony. She laughed the night they first made love as husband and wife, and she laughed as hard as she could when they spent the first night in their very first apartment in Chesterville, Arkansas, which was where they'd run off to, telling no one, not Enos, not Billy's folks, not any of their friends from Julienne. She laughed hardest that night because she knew she'd never have to see anyone from her past ever again. She'd never have to wonder about Enos's fists or Sulene's blood or dirty little boys wanting to put their things in her mouth.

Rayette kept laughing for most of the first year of her marriage to Billy Taylor. She only really stopped eleven months after their wedding, the Saturday when Billy went out hunting and never came back. It was an accident, they told her that night. You know Billy, they said. He was always clowning around, always making jokes. Only this time while he was joking, he tripped and fell and his rifle went off and he blew a hole the size of a beer can right through his chest.

Two weeks after that, she was laughing again. But she was also crying and screaming. She had never had anything hurt this much, not even Enos's punches. And yet she had never had anything fill her with so much pleasure. So much pride. And so much fear.

It was a new year. 1945. A cold but sunny January day.

The day Rayette Taylor's son was born.

chapter 5

When Carl woke up, he was still sitting in his desk chair. He'd crashed there while the damned pages were printing out. Bleary-eyed, he glanced at his watch. It was nearly noon, five hours later than the last time he'd looked. He yawned. He knuckled his eyes. He stretched his stiff neck . . .

And he screamed.

Harry Wagner was standing there in his kitchen, calmly making breakfast.

"I thought you were going to knock, you fuck!" Carl cried.

"What I said was I'd think about it." Wagner expertly broke some eggs into a bowl. The coffee was already made. His jacket was off. Cream-colored linen trousers today. Pink shirt. Maroon bow tie. The man looked maddeningly fresh and alert. "You need a proper omelet pan."

"I'll rush right out and get one," Carl said sourly.

He got up out of the chair, groaning and muttering, and went into the bathroom to shave and take care of other matters. As an act of rebellion, he closed the door. When he reached for a towel, he discovered that Wagner had—using a wooden hanger, of course—hung his linen jacket on the hook that was screwed into the back of the bathroom door. Carl hesitated, then gently pulled the coat back to reveal the lining. The clothier's name, Marco Buonamico, was smartly stitched on the inside left breast pocket. It was a name Carl didn't know. With another glance at the door, he checked the pockets. Nothing.

Nothing to tell him who the hell was making breakfast in his kitchen.

When he came out of the bathroom, Wagner was sliding a fragrant, golden omelet onto a plate. There was sour cream in it, chopped scallions, shiitake mushrooms. While Carl ate, Wagner perched on the bed, reading Carl's output. Carl found himself watching the big man carefully for a reaction. He couldn't help it. And he couldn't believe he was craving feedback—criticism, praise, something, anything—from this big ape. But Wagner's expression revealed nothing. He merely set the pages aside when he was done reading and sat there, stone-faced, waiting for Carl to get to work. The manila envelope with the diary in it lay on the bed next to him. For Carl, this was sheer torture.

"Well, what do you think?" he finally demanded when he could stand Wagner's silence no longer.

"That's not really my department," Wagner replied.

"You've got to have some kind of opinion."

Wagner hesitated. "Are you asking me?"

"I'm asking you."

"It could use some tweaking."

"Who asked you?!" Fuming, Carl poured himself more coffee. "You know something, Harry? Last night, when I was hitting the heavy bag, it was your torso I was seeing. You were pissing blood by the time I was done with you."

"I thought we were getting along so well."

"You're really starting to get on my nerves. Although I have to admit, you make the best fucking omelet I've ever tasted."

"Got that all out of your system now, Carl?"

"Maybe," Carl replied, scowling.

"Good man. Let's get started. Time's a-wasting."

It became a routine. Everything became a routine, Carl realized, no matter how bizarre it might seem. No matter how grueling it might be.

By day Carl would study the diary and letters and clippings, making notes under Harry Wagner's unblinking, unwavering eye. By night Carl would convert the material into a novel, catching as much sleep as he could before Wagner returned the next morning to pick up his nightly output and bring him more material to study.

And to cook him breakfast. Breakfast became the highlight of Carl's day. Wagner was an amazing cook. One morning he showed up with day-old challah from a Jewish bakery, which he promptly turned into mouth-watering French toast. Another morning he baked buttermilk cheese biscuits with bits of bacon in them. The man was marvelously skilled. He was also tidy as a cat. He washed every dish the moment Carl was done eating. One day he brought Carl a new sponge. Another day he brought a scouring pad. The kitchen sparkled as it never had before.

Always Wagner would go to the window and check the street below before he left, to make sure the coast was clear.

Always he seemed satisfied that it was.

By day three, Wagner was bringing Carl's manuscript pages back to him, marked up by Maggie Peterson. She wanted a little less dialogue. She wanted a bit more feel of the weather and local geography. She liked the tone. The pacing was good. She was pleased with what he was doing, which gratified Carl immensely. That gratification and the brutal schedule kept his curiosity in check. He still didn't know whom he was writing about or what possible importance it all had. But he was caught up in the process now. The characters he was creating, the world he was describing, had started to come alive. And that was enough for him. For the moment.

By day four Carl Granville had lost all track of the outside world. He could no longer identify what day of the week it was. In fact, he had to think a minute to recall what month it was. By day seven he had no clear, fixed memory of what his life had been like before he started this project, even who he had been.

By day ten he was going totally stir-crazy and felt sure he was about to explode.

This feeling came over him at one o'clock in the morning. He was all written out for the night, spent, exhausted—but wired to a caffeine high. Sleep was out of the question. The walls were closing in. He needed to take a break. Not a half-hour break on the heavy bag, either. A real, honest-to-goodness break. Carl knew exactly what he needed.

He needed to go to Son House for that beer.

It was warm out. Once summer hits, it never cools off at night in the city. His street was still active, even at one A.M. Couples were coming home arm in arm, giddy with drink and laughter. A Con Ed crew was tearing up the pavement at the corner. Still, as Carl started down the block toward Broadway, where cabs cruised all night, a strange feeling came over him. A feeling of unease. A prickly feeling on the back of his neck. It was crazy, but he felt it.

Somebody was following him.

He shook it off. The work was getting to him, that was all it was. He was tense, he was spooked. But he was definitely not being followed.

He went to the cash machine at the Citibank on Eighty-sixth and Broadway. He'd done this several times since he'd been hired by Maggie Peterson. It was silly, he knew, immature. But he couldn't help it. After punching in his code, he followed the instructions, telling the machine that he wanted to use the English language, that he wanted to deal with "Your Money in the Bank," then that he specifically wanted to see his savings account. And there it was. Just as it had been since he deposited it. Fifty thousand dollars. He smiled and thought what he thought every time he came by this machine: *So it is real. It is happening.*

But now Carl did something he had never done before. He pressed the instructions for "Get Cash." And he took a thousand dollars out of his account.

He had actually never held that much money in cash before, and he shoved it all quickly into the right pocket of his jeans. Why the hell had he taken it out? What was he going to do with it? Spend it? Lose it? Give it all away? He didn't really care. He suddenly felt exhilarated and couldn't wipe the smile off his face.

And that's when he was *sure* someone was following him.

He spun around and looked in every direction. But he saw nobody. He ran to the corner, but he heard no other footsteps in pursuit. Jesus. He shook his head and gave a little half laugh. He really *was* acting crazy. Too much Harry Wagner. Too much time cooped up with Rayette and her baby and their dreary journey through the South.

Blow it out your ear, Maggie. Shove it where the sun don't shine, Harry. Get out of my life, Sulene and Rayette and Billy Taylor and all the rest of you. I'm in the mood for a good time, and I've got money to burn.

Smiling again, Carl Granville stuck out his hand and waved it in the air, instantly caught a cab, and headed downtown.

Son House was Chelsea's answer to a down-home, shit-kicking roadhouse. The walls were of aged barn siding and studded with dented hubcaps, chrome bumpers, and old Louisiana license plates. There was sawdust on

the floor and Stevie Ray Vaughan blasting from the jukebox. There was rau-
cous laughter, lots of people having fun. There was life.

There was Toni with an *i*.

He found a table and waved her down. She seemed a bit frazzled and
exhausted, but she did seem happy to see him. And she was as gorgeous as
he remembered. Maybe more so. The sight of her standing there in her Son
House T-shirt and tight black jeans made his palms start to sweat. And those
arresting blue eyes turned his mouth dry.

"Did you get the part?" he asked when she brought him his Corona—
on the house, ice cold, with a wedge of lime. When her eyes narrowed, not
understanding, he said, *"All My Children."*

"Oh," she said, and shrugged. "I've already lost three more parts since
then."

The place was busy, so he quickly drank his Corona and watched her
work. Toni was easy with the customers, lively and friendly and engaging.
He could tell by the way she moved that she knew he was watching her. She
brought him another Corona when he finished the first one. Also a pulled
pork sandwich. He grinned at her. His best Granny grin. She smiled back,
coloring slightly.

He devoured the sandwich. It tasted great. Freedom tasted great.

When the place quieted down, a little after two, Toni grabbed another
couple of cold ones and flopped down next to him.

"They sure make you hump for a buck here," she said, blowing a wisp
of blond hair from her eyes. "I have got to get me a good part."

"You will."

"I suppose. But it's damned hard to keep going sometimes. Because
you're nothing but a face and a bod to them. Acting is supposed to be about
what's inside of you, but they're not interested in who you are or what you
think or what you feel. All they do is stare at you like they're wondering
what you look like with your clothes off."

"Only because they are," said Carl, who after several days alone in a
room with Harry Wagner was wondering the exact same thing himself.

"You know what it's like?" she went on, growing more animated. "It's
like the whole business is being run by fourteen-year-old boys."

"Hey, the whole country is being run by fourteen-year-old boys."

She let out a laugh. "Are you always so cynical?"

He stopped to think about that a moment. "No. No, I'm not. At least, I didn't used to be. Something about this job, I guess."

"Your novel?"

"A ghostwriting gig."

She lit up. "Really? Anybody famous?"

He wanted to tell her. He needed to tell someone. And he hesitated. He closed his eyes, willing the words to come out. But he couldn't do it. He'd given his word. He could never tell anyone about Gideon. So he just shook his head and sipped his beer.

"I've always admired writers," she said. "I guess because I wanted to write myself."

"Why haven't you?"

"Don't have anything to say."

"You're doing fine so far."

"I mean . . ." Toni paused, looking down at her hands in her lap. "I figured I wasn't smart enough."

"That's never stopped me."

"Did you always want to write?"

"I did," he replied, turning serious. "And when I was growing up, it caused some serious friction between my father and me. Actually, it still does. If it hadn't been for my mother, I'd probably be a—" He broke off, swallowing. Maybe it was the lateness of the hour, maybe it was the Coronas. Maybe it was because he hadn't talked like this to anybody in a long time, not since Amanda. But suddenly he was feeling very emotional. He took a deep breath and ran a hand over his face. Maybe he was just tired.

"You lost her, didn't you?" Toni said, watching him.

"Four years ago." Carl gazed at her curiously.

"I could see it in your eyes." Her own big blue eyes began to shimmer. "I lost mine, too. Last year. I miss her every single day. And it still hurts every single day."

"Every single day," Carl echoed.

"There are things I want to tell her. My triumphs. My failures. Mostly my failures these days. Only she's not there anymore. . . ."

"And never will be," Carl said softly. "I know."

They were silent for a moment. Something had changed between them. There was a feeling of closeness. Of intimacy.

She was the one who broke the silence. "So the other day, how'd you celebrate? Your novel, I mean."

"Never got around to it."

"That doesn't seem fair."

"No," he said. "It doesn't."

Within minutes she had punched out and said her goodnights to her coworkers and they'd caught a cab uptown. They were in each other's arms by the time they crossed Forty-second Street, kissing each other with a passion that bordered on the feverish.

"Oh, God," she gasped, panting for a breath. "Here I go again."

"Meaning what?" he said, his chest heaving.

"I have really bad taste in men."

"Sure, now you tell me."

"No, it's just . . . they always end up hurting me."

He gazed deeply into her eyes. "Let's make a deal. I won't hurt you if you won't try to change me."

"Why would I want to?"

"It's been known to happen. Is it a deal?"

"You know it is, Carl," she said softly, melting into him.

"I think you should start calling me Granny."

"Okay . . . Granny."

They did no more talking after that.

When they arrived at their building, she went up to her apartment to shower and he stopped off at his place for the bottle of champagne that was still in his refrigerator and a couple of glasses. As he opened the door, he was suddenly terrified that he'd find Harry Wagner inside, rustling up some gourmet grub. But happily, there was no sign of the man, and he rushed out and up the flight of stairs. Toni had left her door open for him. Her bathroom door was closed, and he heard water running in there. The ugly green chair was exactly where they'd left it. Cartons were still piled everywhere. He went into her kitchen, popped the cork on the champagne, and poured. He raised his glass. In silence he toasted Maggie Peterson. Then he toasted himself and his genius and his luck.

"I decided to take a bath instead of a shower," Toni called out to him over the sound of the water. "I don't suppose I could have my champagne in here, could I?"

"I think that's allowed," he said. He carried her glass over to the door, pushed it open, and with great propriety said, "Madam's champagne."

She was in the tub, naked and pink and slippery as can be. She was not the least bit self-conscious about her nakedness. Not that she had any reason to be. Carl stood there a moment, his eyes feasting on her, the fragrance of an exotic bath oil filling his nostrils.

"Are you going to stand there gawking all night," she said, "or are you going to get in here with me?"

It was only a few moments before she was in his arms, splashing and wriggling and laughing. They were both laughing. He couldn't remember the last time he'd laughed so hard. And then the laughter gave way to long sighs and even longer moans. She straddled him right there in the tub, lowering herself slowly, achingly, down onto him until he was buried deep inside her. They stayed locked together that way, motionless, as long as they could, wanting it to last a long, long time. And it did. Until neither of them could wait a moment longer. The water was cold by then. They didn't notice. They didn't notice anything. Just each other.

It wasn't love. Carl knew that. Christ, how could it be? He barely knew this woman. But this wasn't some casual fuck, either.

It was something special.

Afterward they dried each other off and Carl carried her to her bed, and it began all over again as the dawn sky grew purple outside her window. The two of them were even hungrier for each other this time, if such a thing was possible. And they made it possible.

For one special night, Carl decided, all things were possible.

The diary seemed particularly unintelligible to Carl the next morning. Almost like a foreign language. He couldn't concentrate on it. Hell, he could barely focus on it. He just sat there at his desk gazing blindly at the scrawled handwriting, absorbing nothing. His head ached. His mouth tasted like fish glue. And his mind kept straying back to Toni. The feel of her, the smell of her, the taste of her . . .

His mind wasn't here in his apartment at all. It was still upstairs, locked in her fragrant embrace.

She had been gone when he woke up. Left him a note on her pillow. Also her spare key. The note read: *Granny—Off to a class. Didn't want to wake you. For some reason you seemed really worn out. Please lock up. —Toni.*

Grinning, he had climbed into his jeans and his shirt and staggered downstairs to find Harry Wagner whipping up thin, golden brown johnny-cakes topped with poached eggs and caviar. He had devoured them, then showered and shaved, and now he was staring dumbly at the diary, a bulging folder with Maggie's marked-up changes waiting next in line for his attention, courtesy of Wagner, who sat on the bed in a light gray silk herringbone suit, watching him as always.

"You're doing a good job, Carl. Making decent progress. They're quite happy."

"Whoever they are, I'm glad," Carl said, slumping back in his swivel chair.

"Tell you what," Wagner said, getting to his feet. "Why don't we give it a rest today? Just work on Maggie's changes."

"You're all heart, Harry," Carl said gratefully.

"Carl, I'm going to say the truest words I've ever said to you: I have almost no heart whatsoever. But for some reason I've grown strangely fond of you. You're a professional. I admire professionalism."

You're a professional, too, Carl thought. *But a professional* what— *that's the question.*

"But sometimes," Harry went on, "there's more to life than professionalism, don't you think?" Carl didn't answer. And Harry continued as if he hadn't expected him to. "Sometimes it's important to just be whatever it is you are."

"All right," Carl agreed. "So what *are* you, Harry?"

"I'm not talking about me. I know what I am, and it's too late to ever change that. I'm talking about you."

"No offense, but I don't think you have a clue as to who or what I am."

"I know you need looking after."

"I do okay for myself."

"You shouldn't be so dismissive. I happen to be very good at looking after people. And I'm offering you something that's very difficult for me to offer."

"What's that?" Carl asked.

"My friendship," Harry said.

Carl hesitated. The man standing before him had threatened him. Bullied him. Hurt him. The man before him scared him on a deep and visceral level. But for some unknown and probably foolish reason, Carl realized that he trusted this man. "I don't know if this is exactly how Damon and Pythias started," he said, putting his hand out, "but I accept."

They shook firmly. And as they released their grips, as if the physical contact had created a more powerful bond, Harry said quietly, "Do you have any idea what you're mixed up in?"

The big man's tone made Carl pay attention. It frightened him. "Some kind of best-seller," he responded. "It has to be done as fiction or there'll be a major lawsuit. It's controversial. It's big. Apex is printing a ton of copies."

Wagner spoke quietly again. "You have no idea at all, do you?"

Carl frowned at him. "So why don't you tell me, Harry? What am I mixed up in?"

Wagner didn't answer him, just gathered up the diary and Carl's latest output. He went to the window and studied the street. "You know what I wish, Carl? I wish you appreciated the wonders of a good cigar." He took one from his jacket pocket, unwrapped it, and carefully sliced off the tip with his sterling silver cigar cutter. He stuck the cigar in his mouth, unlit. "Tell you what." He removed another one from his pocket and laid it on the desk in front of Carl. "A victory cigar. For when we finish."

Carl shook his head. "I'll never smoke it. I hate cigars."

"Keep it. I insist." He tossed Carl a book of matches. "Maybe you'll change your mind."

"Now, why would I do that?"

"You never know about these things, Carl." Wagner went to the door and opened it. "You just never know."

"It's not that I'm not appreciative," Carl said before Harry could escape, "but why this sudden desire to be my friend?"

Harry looked thoughtful, giving the question serious consideration.

Then he nodded, satisfied that he had the proper answer. "Because I want someone to understand why I'm doing this. And because everything in life is reciprocal. Do you understand what I'm saying?"

"That you might need a friend yourself sometime."

Harry smiled, pleased. And then he was gone, leaving Carl to wonder just exactly what it was he had been trying to tell him.

chapter 6

The Closer sat there in the darkened room staring at a talk show on the television set. Something to do with Arnold Schwarzenegger and Maria Shriver. The Closer couldn't tell what, or care less. The sound was not on. Noises of any kind interfered with the Closer's ability to stay focused. So did lights.

The Closer sat there in the dark, focusing.

Until the phone rang.

"Now," said the voice on the other end of the line, "would be an excellent time."

The accent was veddy, veddy British. Upper-class on the surface, but salted with a street coarseness—if you knew how to listen. The Closer knew how to listen.

"So soon?"

"We've accomplished what we needed to accomplish. If we wait . . ."

"Yes, I know," the Closer said. This was not the first time the voice had expounded on the subject. "Procrastination too often means failure."

"There are many complications this time. It is best to remove them as quickly as possible."

"It usually is."

"Will that be possible?" the voice finished.

"Anything is possible."

The Closer hung up the phone and promptly got dressed. The navy blue linen suit. White silk shirt. Red bow tie. Black ankle boots polished to a high gloss. The Closer turned off the television set, locked the door, and left.

The street outside was still active at this late hour. People coming home from their evening out. Cabs were plentiful. The Closer hailed one and took it way downtown to where Greenwich ran into Duane Street. Here there was only darkness and quiet, the warehouses and offices and small factories deserted now.

"You sure this be where you want to get out?" asked the cabdriver, who had a thick Russian accent.

The Closer handed him a ten-dollar bill, got out, and walked down the block, stopping at an unmarked steel door. There was a buzzer. The Closer pushed it and was buzzed in.

Inside was a dingy stairway littered with broken pint bottles of peppermint schnapps, disposable syringes, used condoms. A steady, rhythmic thudding shook the building. At the top of the stairway was another unmarked steel door and another buzzer. The Closer climbed the stairs and pushed the buzzer.

The man who opened the door was as wide as the doorway and hugely muscled. He wore a tank top and sported numerous tattoos on his pumped-up biceps, which were nearly the same size as his shaved head. He grinned at the Closer and stepped to one side.

The Closer entered.

Now the thudding took on a melody. It was house party music. And ahead lay a winding maze of shadowy rooms where people danced and got high and talked to each other. An after-hours club, the kind with no name, no address, no license, and no limits. Models and dancers hung out here. Performance artists. Fashion photographers. Musicians. Athletes. Hangers-on. Black and white. Latino and Asian. Straight and gay. All of them young, their sinewy flesh shiny with sweat. For it was very warm, the air heavy with musk and marijuana smoke.

The Closer moved through them, searching for a particular someone. Finding a back room where there were sofas, chairs, a makeshift bar. Finding that someone—a blonde sitting alone at the bar, drinking a martini. She was a big, creamy blonde with a great body and even better legs. She wore a flimsy black silk minidress, and spike heels, and nothing else. No more than twenty-five years old. She was perfect. Ideal. The Closer eased over next to her and ordered a martini from the bartender, who wore a ring through her lower lip.

When the drink came, the Closer took a long sip, then turned to the blonde and said, "Mind if I join you? I always get hit on here if I sit alone."

The blonde raised an eyebrow, a smile forming on her lush, pillowy lips. "Does that line actually work?"

"Hasn't failed me yet. What have I seen you in, anyway?"

"Seen me in?"

"You're an actress, aren't you? You must be. God, you have to be."

She colored slightly. "Well, kind of. I mean, I'm trying. I just got my SAG card, and I *was* in a Smashing Pumpkins video."

"That must be it. How about another one?" Meaning a martini.

The blonde shrugged and said sure.

One more round after that and they were leaving together, the blonde giggling and falling all over the Closer. "I can't believe how drunk I am," she jabbered. "I didn't have anything to eat today. That must be it. I mean yesterday. Because today is tomorrow. Shit, I can't *belieeeve* this. . . ." Giggling again. Just enough to let the Closer know she *did* believe it.

She was still giggling when they fell into the cab.

And each other's arms.

They kissed, wildly, passionately, teeth clanking as the cab pulled away with a screech. One strap fell away from a milky white shoulder, half revealing a naked, perfect breast. The Closer yanked it the rest of the way off, tonguing her nipple, sucking. The blonde let out a soft moan, twisting sideways on the seat, her gorgeous, satiny, naked legs thrown wildly over the Closer's shoulders. The Closer's mouth burrowed deeper, deeper . . . *there* . . . where it was slick and wet and pulsing. The blonde let out a gasp, shuddering. She held on tight.

She was a very strong girl, and she hadn't had a thing to eat.

When they arrived at the apartment, they tumbled out of the car, panting, laughing, flying. There was no elevator. And very little furniture. There was a bed, and they fell onto it immediately. Her dress was off now, her flawless skin glowing like a pearl in the city lights that came through the window. Her nipples were erect and hard and long.

"I've kind of got a boyfriend," the blonde confessed.

"Me too."

She let out a giggle. "You're funny. Anyone ever tell you that?"

"Not recently, no."

"One of us," the blonde said coyly, "is still dressed."

"You're right," agreed the Closer. "You're so very, very right."

Off came the jacket, which the Closer hung in the closet, because linen wrinkled so easily. And off came the boots, because hidden in the right one was where the present was.

"I have a little surprise for you," the Closer said. "Something I've been saving."

"For me?"

"Yes," the Closer said. "Just for you."

The blonde squealed with delight. "What is it?"

"A special present. But you have to close your eyes." The girl feigned a pout, and the Closer wagged a finger. The Closer knew how to be strict. "Promise me you'll close your eyes, okay?"

She promised. She was an obedient girl, a good girl.

The Closer carried the present over to her, clutching it tightly in one hand, and positioned it directly between her eyebrows, which, in the taxi, had felt like two strips of velvet to the touch.

"Ooh, it's *cold*," she whispered. "What is it? Wait, don't tell me—a bottle of champagne, am I right?"

"Not exactly."

It was a Smith & Wesson .357 Magnum revolver, equipped with a silencer.

"Can I open my eyes now?"

"Honey, you can do anything you want," said the Closer, who smiled and pulled the trigger.

chapter 7

When Rayette's son was born, she made a vow that she would never hit him. Determined to spare him the pain of her own childhood, she bent over backward to smother him with love and affection. Although she had very little money, whatever she had was spent on Daniel Taylor. After Billy's death, Rayette also had very little love to dispense, and whatever she had in reserve was lavished on the boy.

Little Danny Taylor was a precocious young fellow. By the time he was two he was speaking in complete sentences. At the age of four he was reading the sports pages in the Arkansas newspapers. And at five years old he was bright enough to realize that his mother was very different from other mothers.

Danny didn't seem to make many friends at school. The other mothers weren't anxious for their children to play with him. They were especially reluctant to let them come to Danny's house, and Danny just didn't understand this. The house was nice enough. Not as big as some of the other ones nearby, maybe, but it was warm and friendly and he had plenty of games and toys. And his mom was always around. She worked at night a lot, sometimes in bars and restaurants, but during the day she was at home. And she had a lot of friends come over. Men friends. Sometimes his mom told him they were his uncles, but he didn't see any of them more than a few times. None of them stayed around long enough to play catch or take him fishing. His mom's friends would only come over for an hour or two. They would drink and laugh and then they would go into the bedroom to talk and laugh some more. They almost always came out happy. Once in a while his mom came out crying and Danny would get very upset. But Rayette would hold him and kiss him on the back of his neck and tickle him on the stomach and soon he wouldn't be upset anymore.

When Danny was five and a half, Rayette got married again. Danny had met his new dad only a few times and didn't really like him much. His name was Marcus and he hardly ever smiled, except for when he was coming out of the bedroom after talking to Rayette. He didn't talk to Danny very often; usually he just nodded at him nervously. His new dad was very nervous, Danny thought. His leg was always jiggling up and down a million miles a minute. Rayette said it was because his new dad was always waiting for something big to happen. Rayette said that something big was right around the corner. Something that would make them all very happy. So Danny didn't mind when Rayette and Marcus got married and they left Chesterville to move to Huntington, Mississippi. He was looking forward to something big happening so they could all be very happy.

Marcus was very nice to Danny after he married Rayette. When Rayette was off working—she'd gotten a waitress job at a cocktail lounge a few miles from Huntington—Marcus would always tell his new stepson to climb up on his knee. Then Marcus would tell him stories and tickle him and sometimes even kiss him. Sometimes he kissed Danny on the mouth. Danny would pull away when that happened, but Marcus would talk to him very softly and seriously, telling him that it was all right, that's what daddies did when they loved their little boys. Marcus smelled nice—Danny loved the odor of the greasy stuff that Marcus put in his hair—but Danny still didn't like him very much. He didn't like the way he tickled him, didn't like the way he kissed him. Didn't like the way he sometimes touched him.

One day about six months after she'd married Marcus, Rayette came home early from work. She had a headache, she said. But Marcus yelled at her, said she wasn't really sick, that she was checking up on him. "You're goddamn right, I'm checking up on you," Danny heard Rayette yell. "Sittin' naked with my boy on your knee. What the hell you been doin' with him?" Marcus said he hadn't been doin' nothin' with Danny. He came out and told Danny to tell his mother that he had never hurt him. But Danny just ran into his mother's arms, and soon they weren't living with Marcus anymore. They were back in Alabama. Not in Julienne, but in another town, in another county. And in this town, when Rayette was asked her name, she said it was Louisa. Danny asked his mother why she was calling herself by a different name and she said, "Because here I'm a different person, honey chile. I ain't no whore and I ain't married to no sick bastard."

They lasted nine months in this town and then they moved again. Rayette had been all excited because she thought she was getting married again, this time to a really nice guy, she told Danny. Only the really nice guy turned out to be married already. So they went to another town. And soon after that another, and then another.

One of those towns was Simms, Mississippi. It was a small town, not rich but surviving in a changing South. Those who didn't work in the stores along Main Street mostly worked shifts at the battery factory along the river. It was in Simms that Rayette—who was calling herself Leslie Marie now—got pregnant again.

She wasn't exactly sure who the father was, she told Danny, but she was sure he was a really nice guy. She only went with nice guys, she said. It was important for Danny to understand that. She would only go with nice guys.

Life was lonely for Danny in this latest town. He had long since given up trying to make friends. So he disappeared into a world where he needed no one. He read all day long, magazines about movie stars and car engines and black women in South America who carried around live poultry in baskets on their heads. He read any book he could find. Even those he didn't completely understand. Gone with the Wind, *he read. And* Around the World in Eighty Days. *There was a motel maybe five, six miles from the house, and sometimes he would walk out there and scrounge around their trash looking for books that people had thrown away. He found* The Time Machine *there, in the garbage. And a biography of Robert E. Lee. He went for walks by himself and learned to tell the difference between different types of flowers and plants. He carved things, too. Once he made a beautiful walking stick for Rayette, carved a rooster's head onto the top of it. Rayette had loved it, showered him with kisses when he gave it to her, told him how smart and clever he was. She took it everywhere she went. But two weeks after he gave it to her, she came home late one night without it. And he never saw it again.*

He had two favorite retreats. One was the small town square. It was just a patch of cobblestones, really. But growing up out of those stones was a magical oak tree. Magical because it was so big, its branches so strong and sturdy and so full with leaves. Someone—some little boy, Danny always thought, long before Danny was born—had put a swing there, had hung it from two of the strongest branches. It was just the right height for Danny, and he liked to sit on the small wooden plank held up by the thick rope, and he'd kick his legs off the ground and go higher and higher, higher still, and think about anything but where he was and what he was doing and what his life was turning out to be.

His other special place was the football field. It was about a mile from their house, near the high school. It had rickety bleachers on both sides of the field and chalk lines for yard markers, lines that were bright white and clean and never seemed to fade into the dirt and grass. Almost every afternoon when school was done, he'd walk all the way to that field, stand in one end zone, take a deep breath, and then start running. He'd run a hundred yards until he reached the other end zone, catch his breath, and then run all the way back, a hundred more yards. He would do this sometimes until it got dark, running back and forth, sweating, exhausted, sometimes even just walking because he couldn't run another step. When he was done, he'd hug one of the goalposts, using it for support, sucking in air, until he had the energy to begin his walk back home. On the goalpost at the north side of the field, someone, years ago, probably long before Danny was born, had carved a small heart. Inside the heart was carved JD + SE = LOVE. When Danny was running back and forth, faster and faster, he used to think about the carving on that post and wonder if he'd ever meet JD or SE. He'd also wonder if they were still in love.

The fatter Rayette got, the more moody she became. This was a hard pregnancy. She was sick almost every morning and often at night. The factory was nearby, down by the water, and the smell that floated into the air and seeped into the very ground drove her wild. She complained that it was attaching itself to her body, that it was leaking out of her pores, and sometimes the pain in her belly was so sharp she couldn't get out of bed. Once Danny didn't finish his dinner when she told him to and she yelled at him, really screamed, and then she raised her hand to slap him. He didn't flinch, just stood there waiting to take it, but Rayette didn't hit him; she slowly lowered her hand and began to cry. Then she took him in her arms and held him for a long, long time, calling him baby and honey and sweetie and telling him how much she loved him, how sorry she was for everything. He told her she didn't have to be sorry. She was his mother and she could do anything she wanted. She hugged him tighter and said the same thing back to him. "Whatever you do, I'll always love you. Whatever else happens, just know that."

Danny knew how much she loved him. And he loved her just as much. She was the only thing he loved, and he was determined that he would never let that love slip away. It was the one thing in his young life that he was absolutely sure of.

When Danny was nine years old, his baby brother was born.

Rayette had made a list of names that she and Danny had discussed long into many nights. But they couldn't pick a name until they'd seen the baby, she said. A name had to be exactly right, and the only way to get it right was to hold the child, to feel the person, to understand exactly what kind of human being was coming forth into the world.

They were too poor to go to a hospital, so Rayette had the baby at home. It was a long and painful labor, but Danny stayed by his mother's side the whole time. He stood next to the black midwife who had come to help and did whatever she told him to do. He got a cold towel when Rayette's brow needed to be mopped, and he boiled hot water when something needed to be sterilized. The midwife was wonderful—her hands were magic, moving this way and that, soothing Rayette when she screamed out in pain, gently turning Danny away when she felt there was something he shouldn't see. Danny liked the midwife very much. He liked her voice, which was soft and gravelly, and he liked how bony she was, so thin she looked as if she might break in two at any moment. He liked everything about her—especially the strange thing on her face.

He couldn't stop staring at her face.

She had a big circle around her left eye; it almost looked like it was painted on. It was perfectly round and very black, much darker than even her dark brown skin. It started at the top of her nose and went around the eye, onto her cheek, and then back up to the nose. It was so shiny it almost glowed. And it didn't touch the right side of her face. That side was smooth and unblemished. The mark was the most amazing thing he'd ever seen.

When he had run to fetch her, to tell her it was time to come, she noticed his stare and she smiled. "It's all right," she said, "it don't bother me none. It's just a birthmark. It's just His way of tellin' me I'm chosen for somethin' special." But Danny still couldn't stop staring. Even while his mother was screaming and moaning in pain, he was gazing at the black woman's face, at the eye that she said was a gift from God.

The baby was born at ten minutes past midnight.

Within seconds they knew that something was wrong.

When the midwife pulled the child out from between Rayette's legs, she didn't say anything, but Danny saw her shudder. The baby was crying, screaming its head off; it was all red and wrinkled. It looked the way a baby was supposed to look, Danny thought, but even he knew that all was not right. It was the look in the baby's eyes. And the way the baby was crying. Danny thought it sounded like a cry for help.

It was only a matter of days before it was clear that this was not a normal child. He never stopped crying. And he didn't seem to respond to any of them, not Danny, who tried to pick him up and talk to him, not the black midwife, who came by every day to feed him, and definitely not Rayette, who held the baby moments after he was born, put him down, and then refused to ever look at him again. When Danny asked what they were going to name him, Rayette said that the baby didn't deserve a name. He was not normal. He scared her. He could not have a name like any other little boy.

It was the devil, the midwife said. It was the devil that had done this to the child. No, Rayette said. It was the smell. The smell from the factory. It had gone from the smokestack into the air, then into her bones. And then into the baby's blood.

Whatever the reason, devil or man, the baby had caused her great pain. And Rayette knew the pain wasn't over.

By the time the baby was six months old, Danny hated him.

As soon as Rayette was up and around after the birth, she went back to work at a local bar. She stayed away from the house as much as possible so she wouldn't have to be near her second son. It became Danny's job to watch him, to feed him, to care for him. To listen to him cry.

When the child was a year old, Rayette still had not given him a name.

He did not seem to hear when anyone talked to him. He showed no signs of intelligence. He had no coordination. And he made no effort to talk or coo. All he did was eat and cry. Eat and cry.

As far as the outside world was concerned, the child didn't seem to exist. It was 1955, and in the deep South a severely retarded boy was something to be feared and shunned. Rayette was ashamed and humiliated that she had given birth to such a creature. She could not afford to give him proper care, nor could she afford any further social ostracization. So the baby stayed home. During the day, the black midwife would come and look out for him. When school was over, Danny would come home, still alone, and listen to the screams.

By the time the baby was eighteen months, Danny blamed him for the loss of his mother. Oh, she was still there, she still lived in the house. But she rarely came home anymore. She never hugged Danny or kissed him or told him how much she loved him. She drank more than she ever had. And she took more men friends than ever before, although she never brought any of them home.

Three days before Danny's eleventh birthday, a girl in class had a birthday of her own. As a present for her birthday and to welcome in the new year, her parents gave her tickets to see a new teenage idol who was performing twenty miles away at a local auditorium. The singer's name was Elvis Presley, and everyone in Danny's class talked about no one else. They imitated him, dressed like him, combed their hair like him. Danny had never seen or heard Elvis, had vaguely overheard some of his classmates talking about how cool he was. So when the girl announced that she had ten tickets to see the King, it was the biggest news ever to hit Danny's class. Everyone courted her favor, hoping to be one of the chosen nine. Over the course of the week she chose four boys and four girls. There was one more slot open. No one was more surprised than Danny when she tapped him on the shoulder after class and asked if he'd like to come see Elvis. He stuttered, "Y-y-y-yes, sh-sh-sure," and then she ran off, giggling.

He raced all the way home and banged through the front door to find Rayette sitting on the living room couch, a half-empty bottle of bourbon on the table next to her. Danny had never been so happy, and he yelled so wildly at her that she had to tell him to calm down and talk slowly. He excit-edly told her that he was going to see Elvis Presley that night and he waited for her to ask who Elvis was, hoping to show off his knowledge. She didn't ask him anything, however; she just looked sadly at him and told him he couldn't go anywhere. She had a date that night, a date with a very nice guy, and he had to stay home to watch the baby.

Rayette left the house at five o'clock for her date. The children going to the concert were supposed to meet at six in front of the school. At five-thirty the baby was crying, screaming its head off. Danny knew he was hungry, that Rayette wouldn't have bothered to feed him earlier, but he didn't care. He didn't want the baby to eat. He didn't want the baby to live.

At five-forty-five the baby was screaming louder than before, louder than Danny had ever heard him. He went into the mudroom, which was where Rayette kept him. The baby was all red, waving his hands and feet spastically, screaming and crying, making ugly rasping noises. Danny looked down at his brother, not yet two years old, and knew that he had to stop the crying. Had to stop the noise.

He went back to the living room, picked up a pillow from the couch. When he went back to the baby's room, he stood frozen for several seconds, then bent down. He put the pillow over the baby's face, over his whole body really, and began to press down. The crying was muffled but stayed just as fierce as before. Then, gradually, it slowed. It got quieter. Danny pressed harder, then harder still. And soon there was no more crying. Soon the house was quiet.

Danny did not stay in the mudroom long. He went back to the living room and put the pillow back on the couch. Then he ran out the front door, letting the screen door slam against the frame.

He sprinted all the way to the school, arriving just seconds before the other nine children were about to leave. To the sounds of taunting boys and girls yelling for him to hurry up, he hopped into the station wagon that was waiting to whisk them away.

At seven-thirty that night Danny was laughing and jumping up and down and cheering, just one of fifteen hundred fans lucky enough to be at one of the King's greatest concerts.

At long last Danny was happy.

And he knew that when she found out, his mother would be happy, too. And she would love him again.

She would love him forever and ever and ever.

It was three A.M. Almost one full hour since Carl had slid the power button on his computer to the left, had watched the glowing light on the screen fade and the machine go dark.

Wham!

He nodded, pleased. That was a solid left, straight, short, and hard into the meat of his heavy bag. It might not have stopped Holyfield, he told himself, but it would have backed him up. Well, it would have taken the smile off his face, anyway.

He'd been punching away since he'd stopped writing. He didn't wear gloves. He wanted the immediacy of flesh against leather, the strangely pleasurable pain that he knew would soon flow all the way up his arms and to his shoulders. A right hook followed by a left jab, a little dancing, a quick Ali shuffle, then *pop pop*, two quick jabs and a thundering right. His hands were hurting now; he could feel the skin scrape off his knuckles. His chest was starting to burn and his throat was dry. He was exhausted. The book he was writing was starting to drain the very strength right out of him. But he wouldn't quit the workout.

Sweat was dripping from every pore in his body and he could wring water out of his hair, but he needed to keep lashing out, to hammer at something. So it was *whap*, a solid body blow. And another. *Ssssttt.* A slicing jab to the top of the head. And yet another. And one more. This one sent a wave of pain up his right arm. He smiled and grunted. And struck at the bag as if it were possessed by demons, as if every wrong in the world could be righted if only he hit it hard enough and often enough.

Carl was breathing hard now, had been for a good twenty minutes. But he hadn't yet accomplished what he needed to. He hadn't gotten the night's work out of his system. He had not gotten his brain to stop working, which was what he wanted more than anything.

He wanted to stop thinking about Gideon. *Needed* to stop. And the only way he knew how to do that was to move and hit and sweat until his muscles ached and his body collapsed.

It wasn't just the pleasure or the exertion of writing so quickly. Sure, that was draining. But there was something wrong with this whole thing. Something that was starting to bother him, gnaw away at him. Gnaw, hell. He might as well admit it. Something was starting to eat him up inside.

The story he was writing had started out innocently enough, but it had quickly turned dark and deadly. According to the diaries, notes, and documents he had been fed, someone had, as a young boy, murdered a small child. Not only that, he had gotten away with it. But by the very nature of Maggie Peterson's endeavor, that someone was obviously vulnerable today because of it. The question was who. Who was the boy who had done it, and who was the man he had grown up to be?

And who the hell was Gideon?

Thwappp!

He winced as the jolt of that shot traveled all the way up to his elbow. He shook it off, moved his feet, bobbed and weaved. *Just keep moving,* he told himself, *and no one'll lay a hand on you.*

Maggie had said the source was in Washington. Did that mean the real-life Danny had grown up to be a politician? If so, an elected official or a member of the cabinet? How high up did this thing go?

Bam!

Or maybe it was a power broker. A member of the media. The owner of a newspaper or a television anchor. Or someone from the religious right who'd built up an influential following.

It was impossible to tell from what he'd seen so far. But what he *could* tell was that this book was not merely a commercial enterprise. It was not a thinly veiled kiss-and-tell, meant to titillate with gossip. *Gideon* was not meant to be just a potential best-seller; it was going to be used to destroy someone's career. Perhaps his very life.

Pop. Pop. Pop. Thwappp!

For the book, Carl had made up the names of those involved. The real names had been carefully covered over in every document he'd received, and Harry Wagner never gave him enough time to try to get to the truth. Without the truth, he had begun to think of these people by the names he'd ascribed to them. And slowly, as he added personalities and feelings and emotions to go with those names, they had begun to come alive for him.

They had become flesh and blood. Christ, they *were* flesh and blood. And the more he wrote, the more he needed to find out what had really happened to them, the more he needed to know how the lives he was creating on paper had turned out in real life.

He knew he was becoming obsessed. How could he *not* be obsessed? Especially after what he'd read and learned that day. He had stopped writing at two A.M., but he hadn't stopped thinking. There was more material, more information he'd gotten from Harry Wagner. And he'd read it all.

The woman he knew as Rayette had come home late the night of the murder. Thinking about her, Carl could visualize her handwriting. A sloppy, thin scrawl, somehow harsh yet strangely elegant and sad. Like the woman herself, he thought. He could see her, picture her stepping through the front door. Danny had already returned from his concert. He was sitting in the living room when she walked in, and from the silence in the house she immediately knew something was wrong. Mother and son had stared at each other. Then she went in to see the infant. Rayette was used to looking at the child in quick glances. She could not bear to stare at him for any length of time. But now she stared for long minutes. And when she was finished staring, she went back to the living room, back to her living son.

And she smiled.

They buried the baby that night under the cover of darkness. Danny dug a grave to the right of the ramshackle barn that stood behind the house. Rayette carried the baby out, wrapped in a blanket, then settled him into a small wooden box, a vegetable crate, and placed him in the ground. Danny shoveled the dirt back in and tamped it down as best he could. They said no goodbyes, spoke no prayers, held no ceremony. The whole thing took less than fifteen minutes. That was all the time needed to erase any trace that Rayette had ever had a second son and Danny had ever had a brother.

The next day they left town.

For the next several years, mother and son rarely stayed in one place for long. They moved all through the South, Rayette working as a waitress and an occasional whore. Danny became a good student. An excellent student, in fact—Carl had seen the report cards and the glowing comments from teachers.

Rayette married three more times, and she hit gold the last time. Well, if not exactly gold, a semiprecious stone. Her last husband was a decent man. He not only treated his new family well, but when he died, he left them some money. Not a fortune, but enough so Rayette could buy a better brand of bourbon and spend her days at the racetrack. Enough so Danny could go to a good college up north, could get out of the South and . . .

And what?

That was the question that was in Carl Granville's mind when he hit the bag for the last time. The punch lacked any power. And his legs were gone. He'd had it. Without even taking off his sweat-streaked T-shirt or his briefs, Carl sprawled out on his bed and was asleep within seconds after his head hit the pillow. It was a deep sleep, but one filled with dreams and disturbing images. Images of a poor dead child. Images of wicked people and wicked deeds in a past that only he was privy to.

And dreams of a troubling future.

A future unknown but certain to be feared.

chapter 8

The Closer waited patiently for the Target to arrive.

The Target was running late, and that was not a good thing. The schedule was very tight. There was no margin for error. None. But the Closer remained focused and prepared and patient, as always.

The walking helped. A steady, deliberate pace, up and down the block, always keeping the building within view. It was a warm evening. The air was heavy and still. It was one of those nights when the city holds on to the heat and won't let go. The Closer liked the heat, liked the feeling it brought that everything was closing in, liked the sense that it could, eventually, smother whatever it came in contact with. The Closer particularly enjoyed being in costume.

There was hardly anyone on the street. This was a neighborhood where people went to bed early, either because they worked hard or because they were old. The Closer could hear the hum of their bedroom window air conditioners. Feel the condensation as it sprinkled down onto the sidewalk below. There were doormen at one end of the block. They nodded and got a nod in return. The Closer smiled now, despite the lateness of the hour and the tight schedule, sauntering up and down the block, comfortable in the summerweight uniform, soundless in the rubber-soled black brogans. Smiling, sometimes even laughing quietly. Noticed by no one.

Except for one middle-aged couple in a Range Rover. They stopped to roll down their window and ask if the Closer happened to know where the nearest twenty-four-hour parking garage was. The Closer suggested they make a right turn, go three blocks, and try the high-rise apartment building that was on the far corner, right-hand side of the street.

The Closer was always very polite and helpful.

The black limousine finally eased up the block. It stopped in front of the Target's building and idled there. The Closer waited in the shadows across the street, three buildings down, watching. Two people were in the backseat. One was the client. The other was the Target. The two of them talked for a moment, the limousine continuing to idle. Then the driver got out and hustled around to the rear passenger-side door, opening it. The Target got out but still lingered. The Closer heard brays of laughter, the kind that comes when people are saying nasty things about other people they are supposed to be nice to. Then the Target stepped back and the limo driver shut the door. The driver got back into the long black car and the Closer watched it drive away.

The Target headed toward the building, keys jangling.

The time frame was still workable.

The Closer proceeded across the street.

"Excuse me, ma'am. I'm sorry to bother you at this late hour, but I tried you earlier and you weren't home."

The Target looked the Closer up and down. "What seems to be the problem, Officer?"

"There was a break-in upstairs earlier this evening, ma'am. The top-floor apartment."

"Again?" She cursed under her breath. "I hate this city. I really do."

"Yes, ma'am. I can't say I blame you."

"What did the fuckers take?"

"Small things. Jewelry. Silver. A laptop computer. They were very professional—in and out, no muss, no fuss. They even locked up behind themselves."

"So what do you want with me?"

"We just want to make sure that nothing in your place was disturbed. You do have the garden apartment?"

"I sure as hell do. And sometimes it scares the shit out of me."

"Yes, ma'am."

The Closer watched the Target shake her head and curse again. Then she said, "Come on in. Let's have a look."

The Target pulled out a key and headed toward her own entrance to the building, an iron gate that was at ground level directly underneath the raised front stoop. This would have been the servants' entrance back in the days when the town house belonged to a single family. Another key opened her front door. She paused in the doorway, smiling tightly. "By the way, I'm impressed. This is very thorough of you."

"We do what we can, ma'am."

The Target grunted in response, went inside, and started turning on lights.

The Closer followed her in and shut the door, simultaneously reaching for the standard-issue billy club that hung from the standard-issue belt.

"Doesn't look like anyone was here," the Target said. "It looks like I lucked out."

The Target was wrong. She had not lucked out. Because the Closer moved swiftly and surely now, striking the Target directly behind the right ear with a blow of tremendous force. The sound of polished hickory shattering her skull was like no other sound on earth. For the Closer, it was a most satisfying sound. The sound of completion. Still, the Closer left no room for doubt. As the Target lay on the floor in the entry hall, one shoe half off, blood oozing from the back of her head, the billy club was raised and lowered three more times. Each time the sound of wood striking bone was as loud as the crack of a baseball bat connecting with a ninety-five-mile-per-hour fastball. By the third strike, the Target's skull was crushed. Her face was a misshapen lump, resembling nothing so much as a smashed melon left on the ground to rot.

The Closer stood in the foyer and listened. No sounds now.

There were no witnesses.

And there was no more time.

The Closer left the apartment door open an inch and the front gate open wide. The sidewalk outside was clear.

The Closer stepped out into the night air.

There was still much to prepare.

There was still more work to be done.

chapter 9

The sound of the telephone sliced into Carl Granville's brain, and he sat up with a start. For a moment he didn't know where he was. His dreams had kept him in Rayette and Danny's world during the night, and when he forced his eyes open, he was surprised to find himself in his own bed. When the phone had begun ringing, Carl was dreaming that he had been buried in the dirt alongside Rayette's baby. He woke up gasping for air.

He let the phone ring several more times, focusing now. He groaned and squinted at the alarm clock on his nightstand. Nearly ten o'clock. He looked around at the apartment, surprised that Harry Wagner was not there. He was getting used to their routine. And the superb gourmet breakfasts.

Strange. It wasn't like Harry to be late. Especially with their deadline drawing ever nearer.

He answered the phone on the fifth ring. He cleared his throat and managed to squawk out a hoarse hello.

"Hi."

Well, well. The second surprise of the morning.

"Amanda," Carl said into the phone.

"I just wanted to make sure you're okay. Because the two of you . . . I mean, it looked as if the two of you were going to become . . . well, I don't know what. But I know how hard this must be for you."

Carl rubbed his tongue around his teeth and realized he was feeling a little annoyed that Harry wasn't there to give him a cup of steaming-hot coffee. "How hard *what* must be?"

Amanda was silent on the other end of the phone. "You haven't heard?"

"Heard what?"

"Maggie Peterson was murdered last night. It was on the wire when I got in. I'm sure it's all over the New York tabs."

His first thought was, *No, impossible, Maggie is indestructible.* But he heard the concern in Amanda's voice, and Amanda never got her facts wrong. Never. His next thoughts came in a jumbled rush: *Why? And who?* Then, briefly, selfishly, *How does this affect me?* A thought he shook away instantly, replacing it with, *This isn't about me. This isn't about a job or a book. This is about death. My God, this is about murder.* When he finally spoke, the words felt as if they were ripping his throat apart. "Where . . . how . . . ?"

"In her apartment. Someone found her this morning. Her head was beaten in."

"Oh, my God."

"*Savage* is the word the police are using," Amanda said. "I'm sorry. I thought for sure you'd know by now."

"Somebody just broke in and killed her?" Carl asked.

"There was no evidence of a break-in. They think it was someone she knew. An ex-boyfriend, maybe. Apparently there were plenty of those."

The words hung in the air, the silence Amanda's way of asking if Carl was one of those boyfriends. He said nothing. After a few moments she either decided his answer didn't matter or had gotten the response she had been looking for.

"Had she decided to buy your novel?" Amanda asked gently.

"She *did* buy it," Carl said. "Plus she hired me to ghost a—" He broke off suddenly.

"A *what*, Carl?"

"A . . . political memoir." The shock of Maggie's murder had momentarily overshadowed his vow of silence. But he realized he still couldn't talk about *Gideon*. He had made a promise to Maggie, and her death didn't necessarily release him from that promise.

"Politics? She wanted you to write something political? Whose memoir?"

"Nobody's. I'm sorry. I shouldn't have said anything. It's supposed to be a secret, but I'm a little shaken up. It's nothing important."

"Are you all right?"

"I'm fine."

"I . . . I still worry about you, you know. Can't seem to help myself."

"I know. And I'm glad."

They spoke for another minute, but there was really nothing else to say. Carl desperately wanted to tell her everything that had happened, everything he'd been working on, everything he'd learned. But he couldn't. And it wasn't just his promise to Maggie. It was all that had happened between them over the past year. So their conversation petered out until Amanda ended it with the words, "I've got to go back to work."

The moment he hung up the phone, Carl threw on a pair of shorts and a gym shirt and ran down to the bodega on the corner for the papers. It was pretty much as Amanda had told it. The *Daily News* had a photo of Maggie's building, the brownstone on East Sixty-third. Her neighbors had neither seen nor heard a thing. Apparently it happened late at night. According to the *Times*, she had been at a dinner party that evening with a bunch of other media heavy hitters to honor the prime minister of India. She had appeared in good spirits, although she had left early, saying she had a lot of work to do. The several hours between her exit from the party and her murder were unaccounted for. The Apex-owned *Herald* carried a statement from the publisher of Apex Books, Nathan Bartholomew, who said: "Maggie Peterson was the shrewdest editor in the business, with an unerring instinct not only for what was commercial but for what was quality. She was still a young woman. There's no telling what she would have accomplished. We will miss her. The entire publishing community will miss her. Not only because she was an invaluable asset but because she was our friend." Lord Lindsay Augmon, the man who owned and ran the Apex empire, was described by a spokesperson as "devastated."

That was a pretty good word to describe how Carl Granville felt, too.

There were other words that were applicable as well. *Confused. Anxious.* And finally *impatient.* It was impatience that won out. Which is why, after a twenty-minute shower under steaming-hot water and much soul-searching, he finally picked up the phone and began to dial.

The fifty-seven-story chrome and glass world headquarters of Apex Communications was located on Fifth Avenue at Forty-eighth Street. The building housed the offices of the *New York Herald*; several floors of high-fashion trendsetters who were running Apex's various women's magazines;

the television programming offices for TAN, The Apex Network; and the offices for the conglomerate's various book publishing divisions, hardcover,
paperback, and book club.

Nathan Bartholomew's office was on the thirty-fifth floor, the so-called
executive floor for Apex Books. The office was quite large and tastefully
furnished, befitting the publisher of the second-largest book company in the
English-speaking world. Almost everything in the room was white. A white
carpet. Off-white bookshelves covered with a most impressive display of
recent best-sellers. White sheers ran across the enormous span of windows,
which revealed a drop-dead view of St. Patrick's Cathedral. White curtains
partially covered the sheers. The desk, a dark, deep mahogany, was the only
thing in the room that wasn't white. But even that was covered with stacks
of white paper—memos, printouts, financial reports, sales figures.

Normally Nathan Bartholomew loved sitting in his office. It had taken
him twenty-two years to work his way up to this position, from salesman to
sales manager to publisher of the very profitable young-adult division, to
head of the whole shebang, a position he'd held on to for nine years now. The
spaciousness of this corner office, the sense of orderliness, infused him with
a feeling of power he truly relished, but today he couldn't wait to get out. He
had a twelve-thirty lunch at the Four Seasons with Elliott Allen, perhaps the
biggest agent in the business. Certainly the biggest asshole. It would be a
solid hour of listening to Elliott boast about the French impressionist art on
his office walls and the Italian marble countertops he'd had made specially in
Milan. He'd have to hear about the signed photographs from the various
politicians and movie stars Elliott represented. He'd even have to listen to
claims of the agent's sexual prowess, which Nathan had heard from a very
good source—Elliott's mistress, one of Apex's best-selling authors—was not
all that much to boast about. And, of course, he'd have to hear about the
Dalai Lama because, to the astonishment of almost everyone in the book
business, the Buddhist man of peace had decided to write his memoirs and
had picked none other than Elliott Allen to sell it. Bartholomew could hear it
already. *Can you believe it? Can you believe this Jew from the streets of
Brooklyn is representing the holiest fucking guy on the planet?* Of course he
could believe it. If Jesus Christ himself ever came back to earth, within five
minutes Elliott Allen would have sold his tell-all autobiography.

But he still couldn't wait to get out of his luxurious office and into the restaurant. He didn't care about any of Elliott's posturing or the phony kisses and waves coming from the other tables in the Grill Room, from editors looking for jobs and authors looking for bigger paychecks. Not today. Oh, no. *Especially* not today, when his life had turned to pure and absolute shit.

The book business was in the toilet, he reflected. The only books that anyone wanted to read were big best-sellers. Books by celebrities. By big-name writers. By war heroes and TV comedians and homosexuals coming out of the closet and Mafia hit men. By authors who wouldn't take anything less than a million dollars. A million? *Five* million. *Ten* million! If you paid ten million bucks for a book, you'd better sell a lot of copies. And how do you sell a lot of copies? Print a lot, which meant ship a lot—which meant, since booksellers had the right to return any unsold copies, you'd probably get most of them right back. Jesus. The business was impossible. No cash flow. Running on a 5 percent margin—in a good year. Pain-in-the-ass authors. Bigger-pain-in-the-ass agents.

Bartholomew shook his head. He was fifty-eight years old, with record high blood pressure, and what little hair he had left was absolutely silver. Was it any wonder? The worst part was that he didn't see an upside for his business. And unfortunately, upside was one of Lord Augmon's favorite things.

The only person who'd been making any money for the company was Maggie Peterson. A bitch on wheels, for sure, but she knew how to pick 'em. Very few people in or out of the company were aware of this, but Maggie was responsible for a third of the company's profit that year. She was humorless, arrogant, and, with her connection to Augmon, dangerous as hell and uncontrollable. But she was also a money machine. And impossible to replace.

It was typical of Maggie. She couldn't just resign. Or retire. No. The bitch had to go and get herself murdered.

Christ. Whoever had done it hadn't just killed the smartest, most ambitious, most foulmouthed woman Nathan Bartholomew had ever met. He'd murdered thirty-four percent of Bartholomew's profit! No wonder he had a headache.

The media had been all over him the entire day, from the moment he'd gotten to work. How many times could he say the same thing? *She was a treasure. She was a friend. Her potential was unlimited.* She should just be thankful he hadn't said a word about the time he'd found her giving a blow job to the Apex sales director in his office.

Maggie Peterson murdered. Jesus.

Well, God rest her fucking soul, but he had work to do. A *lot* of work to do.

He buzzed his secretary. He had plenty of dictation he needed to get through. And today she was wearing that pinstriped skirt and matching jacket with, as far as he could tell, no shirt underneath. There were worse things he could imagine than dictating to that. He buzzed again. Why didn't she answer?

What the hell was going on today? Maggie Peterson dead and his secretary ignoring him. Had the whole goddamned world gone mad?

"**M**r. Bartholomew's office."

"This is Carl Granville. I'd like to talk to Mr. Bartholomew, please."

"I'm afraid he's quite busy right now. People have been calling all day and—"

"I can imagine. But this is important. I've been ghosting a book for Maggie Peterson."

"Perhaps I can switch you to Maggie's assistant. Ellen is—"

"I need to talk to Mr. Bartholomew *personally.*"

"Well, I—"

"Please give him that message. He'll want to talk to me."

"I'm sure that Ellen can—"

"Just give him the message. Carl Granville. All right?"

"Yes. All right. I certainly will."

"Thank you."

Click.

"**H**ello?"

"Mr. Granville?"

"Yes . . ."

"I'm Ellen Ackerman. From Apex. I'm . . . I was Maggie Peterson's assistant. And I'm just calling to assure you that you'll be reassigned to another editor as soon as things calm down. Mr. Bartholomew is very committed to the idea of continuity and—"

"Ellen, I don't mean to be rude, but I don't think you can help me. I need to talk to Nathan Bartholomew."

"Okay, right, I know you do, but his assistant asked me to—"

"Yes, I'm sure she did. But I'm working on something very important and I can only discuss it with Mr. Bartholomew."

"Sure, okay, I'll tell him, but . . . um . . . what is it that you're working on?"

"I'll discuss it with Mr. Bartholomew when he calls."

"Right, uh-huh, but the thing is, I don't have a file on you, so when they asked me what you were writing, I had to tell them I didn't know. Which I don't. Which is probably why he didn't call back himself, so maybe you should tell me and—"

"Gideon."

"Excuse me?"

"Tell Bartholomew I'm the writer for *Gideon.*"

"Gideon?"

"He'll know. That's all you have to tell him."

"Okay. If you say so."

"I do. I really do."

Click.

Nathan Bartholomew looked at the young woman standing before him. She was nervous, not used to being in his office. And she looked out of breath, as if she'd sprinted all the way down the hallway after he'd summoned her. He wondered if he'd been this nervous around his superiors when he was her age, but he couldn't remember. It was too long ago.

"Ellen," Bartholomew said, taking a deep breath as if the subject were already too painful to discuss, "run this by me again, please. This, what's his name, Granbull?"

"Granville. Carl Granville."

"He says he's one of Maggie's authors?"

"Yes, but he's not. He said he's writing a book called *Gideon* and that you'd know all about it."

"Did he say why *I* would know all about it?"

"No, Mr. Bartholomew. But I checked the author files and there's no record of any contract with him. Or even a contract request. And there's no record of any book with that title, either."

"No record of *Gideon*?"

"No, sir. I called accounting and contracts, just to make sure. No contract's in the works, no check's gone out."

"Jesus." He shook his head and started to turn away. But the young assistant made no move to leave his office. "Something else?"

She nodded, kept nodding nervously, and for a moment Bartholomew was afraid she wouldn't be able to stop. Her head bobbed up and down like one of those Garfield dolls stuck on the back window of a car. "Well, I checked the correspondence files, and there *is* correspondence," she said. "With Granville. His agent submitted a novel several weeks ago and Maggie rejected it." She held up a manila folder she'd been cradling in her arms, removed several loose pieces of stationery, and waved those in front of her. Bartholomew took the papers and the folder and put them on his desk. He waited until her head stopped bobbing before speaking again.

"Thank you, Ellen. I appreciate it." The young assistant turned to leave, and Bartholomew began perusing the papers in the folder. As she reached the door, he muttered half to her, half under his breath, "There are some sick fucking people in this world." Then he punched the white button on his intercom and asked his secretary to come into the room.

"M r. Bartholomew's office."

"This is Carl Granville again."

"Mr. Granville, I've got to ask you to stop calling—"

"Look, I've got a serious situation on my hands."

"I'm afraid it's got nothing to do with us."

"I'm afraid it's got *everything* to do with you. I need to know who my contact is. I've got a problem and I need to—"

"Why don't you try another publisher?"

"Because *you're* my publisher! I know this is a very hard time for everyone, but—"

"I suggest you submit your manuscript somewhere else."

"*Goddamn it* . . . I'm sorry. Just let me talk to Bartholomew. All I need is two minutes with him and I'm sure everything will be fine."

"That won't be possible."

"Does he know I'm writing *Gideon*? Has anybody even *told* him that?"

"Goodbye, Mr. Granville."

Click.

.

The woman in the pinstriped skirt and jacket stood by the thirty-fifth-floor reception desk. She was explaining to the receptionist how busy she was, that her own assistant was out sick that day, that they were extraordinarily busy, that she needed a few favors. "First," she said, "call Elliott Allen's office—here's the number—and tell him that Mr. Bartholomew will meet him at twelve-thirty at the Four Seasons. Then," she continued, "if you could type up these letters so they can get out this afternoon. Mr. Bartholomew signs his letters 'best regards,' and he likes—"

"Excuse me."

She looked up at the young man standing before her. He didn't look like a messenger. Too nice-looking. Too well dressed. A little wild-eyed, maybe, but somehow that became him. Maybe he'd just started working at the company. That wouldn't be bad. Everyone was a little afraid of her, since she was the doorway to Mr. Big. Someone new wouldn't be so afraid of her. Someone new would—

"Excuse me. Do you work for Mr. Bartholomew?"

"I'm his executive assistant."

"I think we've talked on the phone. I'm—"

"Carl Granville."

As he nodded, she froze. Oh, God. It was him. The Nut. This was what she was most afraid of. That nuts like him would come up to the office and find her. Now he was pulling something out of his jacket pocket. He was holding it in front of her. *Oh, God, oh, God.*

"Look, I've written a letter to Bartholomew. I'd like you to give it to him, please."

"A letter?"

"Unless you have a better suggestion. This is the best I could come up with. Something very screwy is going on, and he's *got* to know about it. I was going to mail it, but this is fairly urgent. I want to make sure he gets this. Will you please give it to him personally?"

"He's not going to be able to see you."

"If you just give him the letter, I think he'll *want* to see me."

"You're not going to leave, are you?"

"I'm not trying to be difficult. Honestly. I just want to make sure he gets this letter."

"Marcy," she said, turning toward the receptionist, "would you please call security?"

"What?" he said. "Oh, come on. You don't have to call security. All I'm doing is dropping off a letter!"

"You'd better leave now."

"What is everybody so afraid of here? What's going on?"

"It won't do you any good to keep coming here. You're better off leaving."

"I just want to make sure Bartholomew gets—"

Carl heard the elevator door behind him slide open. He saw her shift her gaze, ever so slightly, to glance over his shoulder. When he turned, he was not surprised to see two uniformed guards walking toward him.

"What seems to be the problem?" one of the guards asked.

Carl thought briefly about lunging for the door that led back to Bartholomew's office. He thought about knocking one of the guards down in frustration. He thought about grabbing Bartholomew's secretary and shaking her until she let him in to see her boss. None of the thoughts made too much sense.

"I don't *know* what the problem is," Carl finally said, shaking his head. "That's the problem."

Nathan Bartholomew peered out of his office cautiously. As if he didn't have enough to worry about, now this nut was trying to force his way in to see him. One of Maggie's authors, indeed. As soon as something hit the papers, the wackos came right out of the woodwork. This letter took the cake. What a fruitcake. A secret, anonymous project. A $50,000 down payment. A fifty-year-old murder. Good God almighty. He thought he'd heard it all when, last year, Apex had published a best-selling biography of Janis Joplin. Within a week of the review in the *Times*, a woman showed up at their office threatening to sue. She claimed she *was* Janis Joplin, that she'd never died, had simply been in hiding all these years, and that all the info in the book was wrong. She could have tied them up in court for months, so they paid her $2,500 just to go the hell away.

Nice work if you can get it.

But this, using Maggie's death to con them—no wonder publishing was in the toilet.

"It's safe to come out, Mr. Bartholomew." His secretary smiled politely at him. He didn't bother to smile back.

"Where's the kook?"

"Security escorted him out of the building," she said.

"What a business," he said. "Who the hell needed security back in the old days? Did you put the little package together?"

"It's in your briefcase," she told him. "The new catalogue, the memo about the Clancy contract, and a copy of the Disney biography."

He walked to the elevator, nodding at the three or four people he passed in the hallway. He had no idea who any of them were, but he knew by the way they looked at him that they worked for him. Christ, this company had gotten enormous. When he'd started, he knew every single person who worked there.

Oh, well, he sighed to himself. *That's progress. You don't know who anybody is anymore, and you need security just so you can get some work done.*

The elevator was an express. It stopped once on the twenty-first floor, then went directly down to the lobby. Bartholomew strode out of the building, and saw his limousine double-parked right in front.

At least something's gone right today, he thought.

With midtown traffic in a snarl, it took fifteen minutes to go the six and a half blocks from Apex headquarters to the Four Seasons on Fifty-second between Lex and Park. The limo pulled up in front of the sleek, expensive-looking building, and Nathan Bartholomew didn't wait for the driver to open his door. He hopped out, briefcase in hand, and headed for what many considered to be the real hub of the book publishing industry—the front room of one of the world's most famous restaurants. He had done some serious eating there in his time, and some equally serious drinking. He'd had long talks with writers and agents there, had been told of his promotion to head of Apex there, and had made some of the biggest deals in publishing history there.

Nathan Bartholomew realized—and was surprised at the realization—that he didn't care much about writers anymore. Or books, or deals, or the respect of the publishing community, or about anything else except making his budget and holding on to his expense-account life. But he still cared about the Four Seasons. Coming there, being greeted by the maître d', having his regular table. That was what he'd worked for, he realized, all these years—so a little man in an ill-fitting tuxedo would grovel before him and lead him, three times a week, to the same small table at the far left of the room by the back.

"Your guest is here, Mr. Bartholomew." Martin, the maître d', led him toward the table for four. Even though there were only two people dining, Bartholomew liked a larger table. He liked the fact that they'd keep it free for him. He was partial to the larger table because he liked to sit facing the wall. There were fewer distractions that way.

But there was a distraction today. A big one.

Someone was sitting at his table.

And it wasn't Elliott Allen.

This was someone young, in his twenties probably, with blond hair that was disheveled and needed a trim. His face was unshaven and grubby. He was wearing jeans and a sport jacket and a tie, but the tie was poorly knotted and askew. He looked extremely excited. His back was to the wall, and when he saw Bartholomew he half stood. Bartholomew saw that whoever he was, his hands were clenched.

That's when Bartholomew knew. He didn't know how he knew. Or how this young man could have possibly tracked him down. But he was certain he knew the identity of the person who had just usurped his table and, it was beginning to appear, his life. It was the nut. The kook. The wacko who'd been trying to see him all day.

And the odds were that he was extremely dangerous.

Most lunatics were.

"I'm sorry to surprise you like this," Carl Granville said, as apologetically as he could manage, "but you're an extremely difficult man to get through to."

Carl realized he was breathing heavily. He didn't know why he was so nervous. There was no reason to be. He told himself to calm down. This was his publisher. This was someone who'd know what was going on.

"My guest . . . my *invited* guest . . . will be showing up any minute," Bartholomew said. His voice was surprisingly deep and cultured, although it had a falseness to it, as if it were really higher-pitched and lower-class but had been worked on for many years to give it the proper veneer.

"Not exactly," Carl answered. "I found out who you were having lunch with, and I called Elliott Allen's secretary to tell him you were canceling."

"Oh, shit," Bartholomew said.

"I told them it was an emergency, and she was very understanding. I mean, I didn't want them to think you were just blowing him off. And believe me, I know what you're thinking, but I had to see you," he concluded.

"Well, your timing is very bad. It's not only a busy day, it's an extremely traumatic one. Maggie Peterson was one of my closest associates, and this has not been easy."

"Yes, sir, I know. But, as I told your assistant, as I told her *many* times, I'm here because of Maggie. Did you read my letter?"

"I certainly did."

Carl breathed a sigh of relief. "So you understand what's happening."

"The only thing I understand is that you're playing a very disturbed game."

Carl stared at him for a moment, tense and confused. Then he suddenly relaxed, his shoulders sagging a bit, and he shook his head, in on the gag. "It's okay," he said quietly. "I know it's got to be a big secret. I probably shouldn't have put it in writing, but I didn't know how else to get through to you. I'm having some problems . . . with the book, I mean. I'm having some second thoughts. I was going to talk to Maggie about it, but, well . . . You're looking at me as if you don't know what I'm talking about."

Bartholomew stared at him without speaking.

"Mr. Bartholomew, it's okay to talk to me. Believe me, I know all about *Gideon*. Well, not *all* about it, but I know enough."

"And what is it that you know?"

"How important it is. And what a rush it is. I know enough to know that we're all going to need some serious help now that Maggie's dead."

The publisher looked away. Carl saw a glimmer of fear in his eyes.

"I'm not going to do anything rash. But I need to know who my contact is. And I have questions. I need to know certain things before I write any more." Carl hoped the urgency he felt was in his voice. "It's okay. You can *trust* me."

The waiter now came to take Carl's order. There was no need for him to ask about Bartholomew's lunch . . . he had exactly the same thing every time he came in—a baked potato, plain, a small salad with vinegar and lemon, no oil, and a glass of red wine.

"He's not eating," Bartholomew said quickly, and the waiter scurried away. The publisher then said, in a slower, more deliberate tone, "Mr. Granville . . . do you need money? Is that why you're here?"

Carl smiled, relieved. Jesus. For these few minutes he'd really believed that Bartholomew hadn't known about him, had never heard of *Gideon*.

"No, no. I mean, I wouldn't *mind* some more money, but I got the check for fifty thousand dollars. I'm supposed to get the rest when I deliver, which is going to be soon. And I'm supposed to be paid for a novel, too."

"We've hired you to ghostwrite a book *and* write a novel?" Bartholomew said.

Carl leaned across the table and grabbed hold of the publisher's arm. "Mr. Bartholomew, I *swear* I can be trusted. But I need to know what's going on. There's something wrong here, and I don't know exactly what it is."

"Mr. Granville," the publisher said slowly, "there's something *very* wrong here."

Carl nodded and released his grip on Bartholomew's arm.

"What's wrong," Bartholomew said, "is that in all the years I've been in publishing, I've never heard anything quite as preposterous as the story you tried to pass off in your letter. A check for fifty thousand dollars without a contract? Wouldn't happen. Impossible. *Couldn't* happen. My CFO wouldn't

let it. A two-book deal—and I've never heard of either book? Also impossible. There's no book that we buy that I don't sign off on. This is the sleaziest,
clumsiest move I've ever encountered. Maggie Peterson hasn't even been
buried yet, and here you are, sucking around, tracking me like some kind of
stalker—"

"No, you don't understand."

"I understand *very* well."

Carl leaned forward. He clenched his right fist, could feel the sweat
forming on his palm. "I'm writing *Gideon*. You *have* to know that. Why are
you doing this?"

"Young man, listen to me. There's no record of anything called
Gideon," Bartholomew said quietly. "No deal memo, no correspondence,
no folder—"

"There wouldn't be," Carl interrupted. "She wouldn't have kept anything in the office. You know that."

"There's no book called *Gideon* that's in the budget anywhere over the
next two years. There's no author by that name, either. There's no contract,
there's no mention of it in any of the editorial minutes. I checked with our
lawyers, with sales, subsidiary rights . . . it doesn't exist. Neither does any
kind of deal for one of your novels." The publisher was not speaking so quietly now. "And according to accounting, there has never been a check issued
to anyone named Granville, not for fifty thousand dollars, not for five dollars. Maybe you believe what you're saying; maybe your motives aren't as
crooked as I first suspected. I'll even give you that. But that doesn't change
the facts. You're living in a fantasy world, son, and I don't want any part of
this fantasy."

Carl stared at Bartholomew disbelievingly. He realized he was shaking
now, so he took a deep breath to calm himself down.

"Look," he said slowly, "I don't even know how to respond to you.
Everything in that letter is true. Maggie Peterson hired me to ghostwrite
a book called *Gideon*. She said it was your biggest book of the year. A
million-copy first printing." He snapped his fingers. "Okay, okay, how about
this? She told me it was going to launch a new imprint, it was the key book
for . . . for . . . Quadrangle! That's the imprint. Quadrangle. How would I
know about that if she didn't tell me?"

"It's a good question," Bartholomew said. "But I'm afraid even *I* don't know about it. We don't have an imprint called Quadrangle. And we don't have any plans to start one."

Carl was sweating now. Profusely. The back of his shirt was wet, and he could feel a swirl of hair starting to stick to his forehead. When he spoke, his voice was hoarse. Unsteady. He didn't know what the hell was happening to him. "It was in your catalogue," he said. "I saw it in your catalogue."

"Is that right?"

Bartholomew reached below the table and brought up his briefcase. He snapped it open, reached inside, and pulled out the Apex summer catalogue.

Carl lunged at the publisher, making a grab for the booklet, nearly causing Bartholomew to topple over backward in his chair.

"That's it," he said. "She showed this to me. In her apartment. You don't think *Gideon* exists? Then what the hell's it doing with a two-page spread right in the middle of your own goddamn catalogue?"

With that, Carl opened the booklet to the *Gideon* spread and held it up for Bartholomew to see. When there was only silence, he brought the catalogue down and turned it around. He stared at the spread in the middle. A spread announcing the publication of a new novel by a British thriller writer.

Carl gaped in disbelief, stunned and shaken.

"No *Gideon*," Bartholomew said.

"Goddamn it!" Carl exploded in a sudden rage. He stood up, knocking his chair over, oblivious to the stares of the other diners. "What the hell are you doing to me? Tell me the truth! Tell me the truth or I swear to God I'll . . . I'll . . ." He was too angry, confused, and frustrated to finish the sentence. He reached for Bartholomew's shoulders as if to shake the truth out of him, but the frightened publisher ducked away and Carl's fingernails scratched his throat. Bartholomew put his hand to his neck. A trickle of blood dripped onto his shirt collar.

Carl could hear his heart pounding in his chest.

"She bought my novel," he whispered. "She hired me to write *Gideon*."

"A book conveniently sold by a dead agent and just as conveniently bought by a dead editor. A *secret* book, which no one but you knows about." Bartholomew stared straight at him. "If you make any move whatsoever to pursue this insane claim of yours," he warned, now bristling with blatant hostility, "you'll find yourself on the receiving end of a fraud claim. Our lawyers don't settle nuisance suits. They fight back."

Carl closed his eyes. He felt as if the world were melting before him.

He glanced around the room. There was no sound throughout the restaurant. Carl faced Bartholomew, took a deep breath. Bartholomew relaxed as he saw the tension leave Carl's face. Then Carl bent down slightly, just enough to wrap his fingers under the edge of the table. With one quick flip, he turned the table on its side. Plates and silverware went flying and glasses spilled onto the carpeted floor. Everyone in the restaurant seemed frozen until the maître d' reached for the telephone by the front door. Carl heard the words, "Get me the police, please. Seventeenth precinct."

Carl stared down into Bartholomew's eyes. He was startled to realize that the look he saw there was one of pity. The publisher spoke softly to him now. "Betty Slater was your agent, wasn't she?" When Carl nodded numbly, Bartholomew continued. His tone had changed completely. It was as if they were in his office, having an after-work brandy and reminiscing. "Betty and I went back a long way. She told me about you, I remember that now. She used to get excited about real talent, even after all these years, and she said you were one of the ones with real talent. I don't like to see this happening to a talented young man; they're already too few and far between. Are you on drugs? Is that what it is? Because if it is, we can get you help. You can get back to your novel, back to the kind of work you should be doing. And if you do a good job, we can even talk about some kind of advance."

"I don't want money," Carl whispered. "I swear. I just want to know what to do."

"That I can tell you," Bartholomew said. He turned toward the grand staircase at the front of the room. The maître d' hung up the phone and nodded. "You can leave."

Two waiters were now moving toward him, a young one and an older one with a mustache, and Carl made his move. He lunged to the left, avoiding the sudden grab of the younger waiter. He knew he wasn't going to be able to outmuscle the one with the mustache, so he took two quick steps back, rocked forward, and jumped.

Carl thought the man would duck, would just get the hell out of the way, but no, he held his ground and braced for the impact. Hurtling through the air, Carl felt his knee crash hard into the mustached waiter's jaw, and his sense was that the man went down, out cold, but Carl never looked back. He raced down the marble steps that led to the ground floor and made a break for the door. The maître d', in no mood to tangle with a hard-charging maniac, made only a halfhearted attempt to trip him, but Carl easily shoved him out of the way. The coat check woman, his last remaining hurdle, was only too happy to let him pass, and he ran through the revolving door, out onto the sidewalk, and then straight into the street. A taxi slammed on its brakes and honked its horn. Carl vaguely heard someone swearing at him. And now a different voice was yelling at him. A cop.

Carl ran across Park Avenue, dodging the traffic. Sweat was pouring down his neck now. His shirt was sopping wet and stuck to his back. There was more yelling. And then he just turned and sprinted away.

Eventually the yelling stopped.

And, sometime soon after that, so did Carl.

Many blocks from the Four Seasons, on Fifty-fourth and Ninth Avenue, there was a small French-style bistro. Carl found an empty stool at the bar and ordered a calvados, a double, his voice sounding hollow in his ears. He sat there drinking and trying to make sense of what was happening to him. Trying to understand. Harry Wagner had asked him if he knew what he was mixed up in.

Clearly, he did not.

He didn't know a fucking thing.

Maggie had definitely hired him. She had paid him. So how could there be no trace of any of it? Who was the strange, semiliterate woman whose diary he'd spent these last weeks poring over? Who had been supplying him with all the other notes, documents, and background information? Who was the boy who'd coldly and brutally murdered his own unfortunate baby brother? Who was the inside source, Gideon? Why had Gideon leaked the material to Maggie? What was he hoping to gain? And who the hell was Harry Wagner? What was *he* hoping to gain?

It was in the middle of his third double calvados that it occurred to Carl for the first time: Was Maggie's murder connected to the book? Harry hadn't shown up that day. Had *he* murdered Maggie? Or were the two things totally unrelated? Was he starting to become paranoid? Was he as crazy as Bartholomew clearly thought he was?

Questions. He had tons of them. But what he didn't have were answers.

He paid for his drinks and wandered east and then north toward Central Park. At a pay phone he stopped to call Toni. He thought maybe she'd come and get drunk with him, then they could go home and spend the next three days in bed. Three days? Hell, three months. But his luck was consistent. Her phone machine told him she was out at an audition, that he could leave a message after the beep and she'd get back to him as soon as possible.

He left a message, saying he was sorry he missed her and he was even sorrier that his whole life was falling apart. He said that if she got home before he did, to wait for him so they could have dinner. Or just talk. Or . . . He hung up in the middle of his own message when he realized he was starting to sound like a lunatic.

Eventually he found himself back on the Upper East Side, in front of Maggie's apartment, where he had waited for her that day two weeks ago.

It had been one of the best days of his life.

It was a day he now wished had never occurred.

It was nearly five when Carl got home. He climbed the stairs to his floor and started to unlock the door to his apartment. Only there was no point in doing that. There was no point at all.

Carl stood in the doorway, frozen. The door was already open. The door frame had been splintered by a pry bar, the lock shattered.

Carl shoved the door open and charged into the room.

His apartment was in ruins. Everything he owned in the world had been ripped to shreds.

His clothing. His books. The contents of his desk drawers. His bed. Even his heavy bag. All of it was slashed and torn and heaped on the floor. It looked as though a hurricane had struck in the middle of an earthquake.

Slowly, numbly, he made his way through the devastation that had been his life. He had to reach his desk. He had to know.

His notepads were gone. His floppy disks were gone. His computer was no longer a computer. It was nothing more than a heap of spare parts. Whoever had been there had dismantled the damned thing, circuit plate by circuit plate. The hard drive was a shell. They had removed its memory.

And with it all trace of what he had been writing.

All record of *Gideon* was gone. Erased.

Carl stood there, unable to move, staring at the desk. That stupid cigar of Wagner's lay there, untouched in its wrapper. It was the only thing in the whole place that was intact. That and the book of matches he'd left him. Carl picked up both items and stuck them in the inside pocket of his blazer, a lame but instinctive attempt to salvage something from the rubble.

Do you know what you're mixed up in? Harry had said to him.

He did not.

All he knew was that they had succeeded in scaring the shit out of him, and it was now time to call the police.

He dialed 911. They put him in touch with the nearest precinct house. The desk sergeant was brusque and impersonal but switched him to another officer, Sergeant Judy O'Roarke, who was very patient and professional.

"How may I help you?" she asked.

"I'm not sure exactly," Carl said slowly. "I think I may know something about a murder."

"May I have your name, please?" the sergeant asked.

"Carl Granville," he said, and as he began to speak, the words came out faster and faster. He was almost helpless to stop them. "Something very weird is going on. I'm a writer. First my editor was murdered. Then my publisher didn't even know who the hell I was. Now my apartment's been broken into and ransacked. All my disks are gone. My computer is toast. My—"

"Slow down, Mr. Granville," O'Roarke said soothingly. "Please try to take it easy. Let's go one step at a time, okay?"

Carl took a deep breath. "Right," he said. "Okay."

"Now. You say your editor was murdered?"

"Last night. In her apartment. Her name was Maggie Peterson."

The sergeant was silent a moment. "Why, yes. Of course. And you say you know something about it?"

"No. Yes. I don't *know* what I know. I was working on a project for her. A book. And I just got home to find my apartment broken into. It's not an ordinary break-in, either. They didn't take my TV or my stereo or anything. What they took was anything that had to do with our project."

"Where do you live, Mr. Granville?"

Carl gave her his address.

"Okay, here's what I want you to do. I want you to lock your door—"

"I can't. The lock's no longer functioning."

"Then just stay put. Don't move. I'll be there in fifteen minutes, okay?"

"Okay. Fine. Thank you."

"No problem. Just wait right there."

Payton got there in five minutes, belching sourly from the corned beef on rye he'd been inhaling over at the Blarney Stone on Broadway and Ninety-fifth Street when the call came through. It had been a big mistake, no question. He should have ordered the tuna. Except Payton hated tuna. He was a man, not a house cat. So he'd ordered the corned beef. And now it lay there in his stomach like wet cement.

As he approached the brownstone on 103rd, Payton flicked his cigarette into the gutter and gobbled a couple of antacid tablets, the kind that were supposed to work instantly. They did shit instantly. He probably had an ulcer, but he hadn't gone to the doctor to find out. He didn't want to find out. He didn't want to know what his blood pressure was or if his cholesterol was high or if he was a prime candidate for a fucking heart attack in the middle of the night. He didn't have to be told that he was out of breath all the time, overweight, sluggish, out of shape. He also didn't have to be told that women got busy looking somewhere else when they saw him coming. Payton knew all those things. Not that he'd ever been one of those tall, trim glamour boys. He was a short, stockily built bull with thick, curly black hair and an oily, pitted complexion. His arthritic left knee ached most of the time, as did his lower back, and his flat feet throbbed *all* of the time.

Aw, what the fuck, he thought. *Overall, not bad for a sixty-year-old.*

Except in another two months and three days, he would turn forty.

He lit another cigarette, his twentieth of the day, crumpled the empty pack in his meaty fist, and tossed it onto the sidewalk. A pair of gang-bangers eased on by him in a shiny, chrome-emblazoned black Jeep Grand Cherokee, acting like they owned the whole damn block, their rap music blaring out of a pair of stereo speakers, each of which had to be the size of an Amana sixteen-cubic-foot no-frost. That drumbeat practically shook the buildings, thudding like some kind of primitive jungle rhythm. The two jigs glared at him as they drove by, their chins thrust defiantly into the air, their gold glinting in the sunlight. Payton glared right back at them, his jaw muscles tightening, his hands itching to take them down, to teach them some respect, to show them who really owned these streets.

It was his old rabbi, Big Sal Fodera, who had said it best, speaking for every foot soldier who was out there doing battle day after day, night after night: "Gentlemen, what we have here is a nigger problem."

The meatball who was backing Payton up was already there waiting for him outside the building. Payton muttered a noncommittal greeting and buzzed the apartment from the vestibule downstairs. When he got a response, he growled "Police department" into the intercom and was buzzed in immediately.

The meatball stayed put on the sidewalk.

Payton started climbing, weighted down by his flab and his bitterness. Another fourth-floor walk-up. Another shit detail. This wasn't supposed to happen. Not to him. There had been a time, and not so fucking long ago, when he got the high-profile cases. His name in the *Daily News*. Back then, he was wired to the top floor at Thirty Penn Plaza. On the swift track to Homicide and a lieutenancy, followed up by a nice, cushy security gig at a nice, cushy gated community down in Boca—just like Big Sal. Get himself a boat, maybe a nice little fitness instructor with a tight butt. There was a time, all right. There was a time . . .

Until it blew up. All because of one lousy, stinking piece of nineteen-year-old human filth named Yussef Gilliam, a stone-cold lying-ass baby killer who had to go and die on him while Payton was taking him in. A choke hold, they called it. Reasonable force, Payton called it. The kid was buggin' on him. He was high on crack and speaking no known language. He had just robbed a Korean produce stand at gunpoint and pistol-whipped the owner and his wife, who was seven months pregnant. She'd gone into labor right there on the dirty floor of the store, hemorrhaging blood like she was a goddamn fountain, losing the kid. What was he supposed to do when he saw something like that? Ignore it? Kiss the guy who did it? And how was Payton supposed to know that the piece of shit had a medical history of severe asthma episodes? More to the point, why was he supposed to care? This was a war. Us against Them. The mayor had declared it so when he ran and won on a law-and-order platform. Make the streets safe, he said. We want to feel safe, the public said. Well, what did they think that meant? And just exactly who did they think They were? The goddamn niggers, that's who. Anyone who didn't know was a fool. Or a goddamn hypocrite.

Or worse, a *New York Times* bleeding-heart liberal. That fucking paper. Police brutality, they called it. Institutionalized racism, they called it. A full-scale investigation, they demanded. And then along came the good reverends Al and Jesse, and before you could say the words *Rodney fucking King* Payton was going down for it—he and everyone else who had been in the precinct house that night, even if all they'd been doing was taking a leak down the hall.

And now here he was, a fat man in a cheap suit who had to jump when the Man said jump.

When he finally got to the fourth-floor landing, puffing, Payton found a tall, good-looking blond guy waiting there for him. He was young and sleekly built, a real big-man-on-campus type. The kind who end up becoming quarterbacks or politicians or news anchors. Payton detested him on sight.

"You Granville?" he asked, sizing him up, wondering if he would give him trouble or not.

"That's right," Carl Granville replied. "Thank you for coming."

He seemed spooked but in control of his emotions. Good. Payton knew it was harder to get anything done when people let their emotions take over.

"My name's Payton. How did they—" He looked over Carl's shoulder at the jimmied door. "Never mind. I guess I can figure out how they got in— your basic pry bar job. Want to show me around, pal?"

Payton could feel the guy's relief. It was the part of the job Payton always liked, always got off on. A guy like this, a hot-shit guy, smart, confident as hell. They were always glad to let a guy like Payton take over. They were always happy to let a pro come in and assume responsibility.

Carl led him inside the studio apartment. Payton stood there a moment, surveying the wreckage. The furniture had been slashed and overturned. Dishes were broken all over the kitchen floor. A computer was smashed to bits. Payton let out a low whistle, shaking his head. "Damn, these boys meant business, didn't they?"

"You think there was more than one of them?"

"Most likely," Payton replied, scratching his oily scalp. "We had us a pair working this neighborhood a few weeks ago. Passing themselves off as furniture movers. Had themselves a beat-up old van and everything. They been quiet lately, but I guess they ran through their dough and got back in business." He moseyed across the room, poking at the wreckage. "Weird that they didn't take your TV or your stereo. What'd they get, cash? Jewelry?"

"It's like I said on the phone, they were after anything that had to do with this book I've been working on. Sergeant O'Roarke didn't tell you?"

"Why don't you tell me?"

"Where's Sergeant O'Roarke, anyway?"

"Got another call. This may surprise you, but we get more than one robbery a day. He asked me to come instead since I was already in the . . ." Payton trailed off, cursing at himself. Shit, how could he make such a sloppy mistake? He never used to. He'd always been so careful. Alert. Then again, he reflected, maybe he'd get away with it. Maybe this guy was dumb.

Payton turned and shot a hopeful glance at him.

One look at the expression on Carl Granville's face told Payton he wasn't dumb.

Too bad.

He.

Payton had said *he* asked him to come.

Referring to O'Roarke.

He. Not she.

What took place next happened so fast, Carl never had time to think. The time for thinking was over.

Payton started to turn back to Carl. Only now his gun was drawn.

Carl stepped to the middle of the room, where his ruptured heavy bag still hung. For one brief instant it was between them, a moving sixty-pound shield. Carl had one chance and he took it.

He shoved the heavy bag at Payton with every ounce of his strength behind it, knocking his gun hand wide. Carl heard the shot, heard the bullet slam into the wall somewhere off to his right. Now he charged headfirst into the burly man with the oily air. The gun went clattering across the floor. Payton dove for it. They both dove for it, wrestling around on the floor among the torn clothing and bedding, grunting, gasping, straining. Payton was strong. But so was Carl. And he was fighting for his life.

Payton made a move, but he stepped on one of Carl's scattered socks, which slithered along the wooden floor. Payton lost his balance, leaving himself open, and Carl knew exactly what to do. He punched the man as hard as he could in the Adam's apple—a street fighter's move he'd learned from a Cornell teammate who'd grown up in the meanest end of Newark. It was a thundering right hand, and it instantly sent the man's windpipe into spasms, leaving him gasping for breath, his chest heaving, his face turning purple. As he doubled over, Carl kicked up with his right leg, and the hard toe of his shoe connected perfectly with the bottom of Payton's chin. Payton's head snapped back and he toppled forward. He lay on the floor, moaning, twitching. And Carl had no doubt what his next move was.

He ran like hell from the apartment, slamming the door shut behind him.

And he kept running, but not down the stairs. Payton would figure he'd run that way. And be right on his tail as soon as he recovered his breath. There'd probably be someone else waiting down there, too. So Carl ran *upstairs*. He still had Toni's key in his pocket. He could hide in her place, buy himself some time. Try to figure out what the fuck was going on.

Fumbling with the key, his hands shaking, he unlocked the door and dove inside. He shut it quickly behind him.

The apartment was silent and still and dark, the curtains drawn. She wasn't home. Good.

He threw the dead bolt behind him and stood there a moment, panting with relief, trying to catch his breath. Then he flicked the light on. And turned around.

Toni *was* home.

Unbelievable. She was in bed. Sleeping. He took a step toward her. How could she possibly sleep through all—

That's when Carl's hands flew up to his mouth, strangling the noise that was trying to escape. He couldn't let himself scream. He'd give himself away. He had to be quiet. *Had* to be. And when he had forced the scream back in his throat, he threw his head back, gasping for air, trying to hold himself together. He began to gag, and then Carl staggered into the corner, toward the Pullman kitchen, where he bent over and got violently sick.

When he was through vomiting, there was no more noise in the apartment. He stayed, facing the corner, as long as he could. Then he forced himself to turn around.

Forced himself to look.

Toni was on the bed, stark naked. With her head blown off.

Her face and her brains and her lovely blond hair were splattered all over the wall. All over the floor and the sheets.

It was the most horrible thing Carl Granville had ever seen in his whole life. He was unable to look. He was unable *not* to look.

So he stared at her there on the bed, devastated. He stared at this *thing* that had been Toni with an *i*, who had laughed at his jokes and held him tight and dug her nails into his back and cried out in his ear. Why her? Why had they killed *her*? She didn't know shit. She didn't even know what he'd been working on. How could they have gone after this woman just because he was having a thing with her? Who *were* they? What the fuck was happening?

A nightmare. This was a nightmare. That's what was happening.

He heard heavy footsteps on the stairs below. Payton. Going down. One flight. Then another. Then there was silence. Good. He was gone.

And then he wasn't.

Because now Carl heard more footsteps. Payton coming back up. Shit, he was climbing all the way up to the fifth floor. Carl hadn't fooled him. Not one bit. The fucker knew he was still in the building. Did he also know that Carl was alone in here with a dead woman? Had *he* killed her?

More questions. Still no answers. Only chaos. And death.

Carl saw the doorknob turn. He held his breath; he couldn't help himself. He knew it was locked, but somehow he thought Payton would still be able to magically open it. No. Nothing else was making any sense, but a locked door was still a locked door.

But for how long?

Carl went to the window and looked down to the street. An unmarked car was double-parked out front. Another uniformed cop stood there, gazing up at the building, his gun drawn.

He couldn't go down. He'd be a sitting duck. The only way was up. Just one flight up to the roof. That was all he needed. One little flight without getting shot.

He heard something crash against the apartment door. Payton, trying to kick it down. The frame around the door was beginning to splinter. Kicking it once . . . twice . . . three times . . .

He had no choice now.

Carl scrambled out the window and onto the fire escape. The cop down on the street spotted him instantly, and he raised his gun and fired as Carl started up the ladder toward the roof. The first shot pinged off of the iron railing next to Carl's head.

Don't look down. Don't stop. Just keep moving. Keep running.

The second shot thunked into the brick facing of the building. But by then Carl was on the last step, hurling himself onto the roof. He heard the crash of the door bursting open, heard one more bullet fly by his head. But he had made it.

He started running. He ran from one rooftop to the next, vaulting over skylights and sidestepping furnace chimneys. Toward the end of the block he found another fire escape. Scrambled all the way down it onto the pavement below. Dashed around the corner and kept right on running.

In moments he reached Broadway. It was the beginning of rush hour. Thousands of people marched down the street, heading for the subway, coming out of the subway, shopping, coming home from work. Thousands of people leading normal lives.

It was through these throngs that Carl ran. Ran down New York's most famous street. Ran away from the mayhem and violence and insanity he'd left behind and toward the anonymity he so suddenly and desperately craved.

Ran straight into the nightmare that had become his life.

book two

July 10—July 13

chapter 10

Marcel Rousseau did not like this country called French Guiana. He did not like this city. He especially did not like the crappy Auberge des Belles Îles, where they gave him hammock space in a room with twenty-five Amarinds and bush Negroes and several thousand mosquitoes, all for thirty French francs a day. Soon he could move in with his cousin Simon, but first Simon's loud and smelly mother-in-law had to go back home to her husband. She had caught him fucking some whore, and so she had come to stay with her daughter and Simon until her husband came to beg her forgiveness. But Marcel did not know how anyone could beg forgiveness of someone who smelled so bad.

Merde alors.

From the moment he'd stepped off the ferryboat at Cayenne—a very well named city, hot and peppery and coarse—he realized that by coming here, he had forsaken paradise for a total shithole.

The problem was, he couldn't make a living at home in Haiti anymore, not unless he wanted to bow and scrape before all the German tourists, working sixteen hours a day at the hotel for twenty-five gourdes an hour. Plus tips.

The way they said that—*plus tips*—as if it were such an honor. As if a tip from a soft, white *Allemand* was something fit for a king.

I spit on their "plus tips"!

It was Simon who'd talked him into coming: *You can work here, Marcel. There is much money to be made. There is much construction, Marcel. In Kourou. And they pay cash!*

So he had come one month ago, working his way over by boat, from Haiti to Suriname, then a ferry from St. Laurent du Maroni to Cayenne. The first thing Simon did was put him on another boat and take him the eighteen shark-infested miles to Île du Diable—Devil's Island. It had once been the most terrible prison in the world, Simon explained excitedly. Marcel was not nearly as excited as Simon was about seeing a prison. This earth was created to be a prison, he believed, and he did not need to see those made by man.

After that, Simon drove him to Kourou, where Marcel pitched his hammock amidst the thousands of mosquitoes and got a job in construction.

It was a good job, adding on to a building. Why they needed it bigger, Marcel didn't understand. It was already enormous. Right on the water. But he did what they wanted. And Simon was right: They paid cash. A lot of it. Which meant the work probably wasn't legal, not completely, but that was all right with Marcel. It was always so difficult for him to find a job, he didn't care if what he did was legal or not. He could not be very particular.

Marcel could not read.

Not a word. Not a letter. Not even his own name.

But he was big and strong and worked like the devil himself. He carried, he hammered, he walked on high spaces where no one else would walk.

That's what you did if you could not read your own name.

It was seven kilometers from Marcel's hammock to the construction site. Sometimes Simon drove him, sometimes he walked. Today he was walking, even though it had been five days since they had last needed him. Three weeks straight he'd worked, even Sundays, often into the night. Then they'd told him to stay away. Not forever. Just a few days. But Marcel was impatient. Five days was long enough without pay. If he went back today, maybe they would need someone to go on a high place where no one else would go.

The mosquitoes woke him before dawn. Even though work never started until eight o'clock, he decided he would start his walk. It would be cooler than walking under the morning sun. And he knew a nice, shady spot under the pipes and planks where he could take a nap in peace. He had done it before and no one had found him. Even the mosquitoes didn't know about this spot.

When he got to the construction site, all was quiet. Nothing seemed changed. The same tools were left outside, resting on the same bricks. The same wheelbarrows were on their sides. The same flies buzzed in the same circles.

But one thing was not the same.

There was something new, something Marcel had never seen before except in the movies. He had not known such things really existed outside of the movies. What he saw was beautiful, he thought. And Marcel was happy now. He liked working for men who could make such a beautiful thing. These men would use him again and pay him well, of that there was no doubt. Well enough to get back to his beloved Haiti. He might even stay at the hotel and tell a fucking German to bring him a mai tai.

Marcel was tired from his walk and lack of sleep. He went to his secret spot, where he rested and waited for the other workmen to come. When he fell asleep, he was still thinking of the Germans and how he'd give them a tip when they carried his delicious drink to him.

It was the noise that woke him.

At first he thought it was the roar of a terrible animal, but no animal was so terrible as that.

Then he thought: *An earthquake.* Then: *A volcano.* And then: *It is God. He is coming back to destroy this shithole and all the buzzing little mosquitoes who live in it.*

The noise was so loud he couldn't stand it. He screamed for someone to come save him from this wrathful God, but he could not hear his own voice.

He could hear nothing but the noise.

Then he saw it. And he knew what was happening. It was not God destroying the world.

It was man.

Marcel started to run. But as he ran he began to feel the heat, enveloping him, sucking him into it.

He stopped running.

Stopped screaming.

He just stood and stared, and the beauty of what he saw made him cry. The thing was rising up into the heavens, and maybe this *was* God, because he was crying the way he had always known he would cry when he came face-to-face with his maker.

This was the last thing Marcel Rousseau thought as the flames engulfed him, incinerating him almost instantly, melting his body as if it were nothing more than a thin strip of plastic tossed into the midst of an inferno.

Within seconds there was no skin, no bones, no hair. By the time the noise stopped, there was nothing left of the itinerant day worker but a tiny pile of charred ashes, already beginning to scatter in the face of the soft, fetid breeze coming in off the water.

chapter 11

From the *New York Mirror* on-line:

AUTHOR SOUGHT IN NOTED EDITOR'S SLAYING

New York City, July 10 (Apex News Service)—Police investigators today identified their prime suspect in the brutal slaying early Tuesday morning of prominent publishing figure Margaret Peterson. He is believed to be Carl Amos Granville, 28, a struggling author who they say recently had unsuccessful dealings with the victim over a novel he had recently completed.

Mr. Granville's whereabouts are presently unknown, and the NYPD is engaged in an all-out search for him.

Mr. Granville is also wanted for questioning in connection with another murder that occurred in his apartment building on West 103 Street yesterday. The body of Antoinette Cloninger, a 23-year-old aspiring actress from Harrisburg, Pennsylvania, was found by the building's superintendent last night. She had been shot twice in the face from extremely close range.

It is not presently known how or if the two murders are related. But, according to police sources, fingerprints were found in Ms. Cloninger's apartment that match fingerprints found throughout Mr. Granville's apartment. And those same fingerprints were found on an item of statuary in Margaret Peterson's apartment. Police have not yet confirmed that the prints belong to Mr. Granville, who has no previous police record.

According to police sources, Mr. Granville showed up unannounced at the Fifth Avenue editorial offices of Apex Books yesterday afternoon, demanding money for a book deal he claimed to have made with Ms. Peterson. Apex publisher Nathan Bartholomew, who declined to meet with him, says that no such deal ever existed.

"This was not our first contact with Mr. Granville," said Mr. Bartholomew. "Maggie Peterson rejected his novel in May. I have her rejection letter right here, taken from her file. She called the novel 'fragmented and disjointed' and said that the author 'did not have the voice or, I'm sorry to say, the insight to carry off an admirably ambitious attempt.' In other words, she said no. But he's one of those guys who just won't take no for an answer."

Shortly after receiving the rejection letter, said Mr. Bartholomew, Mr. Granville accosted the late Ms. Peterson at the funeral of his literary agent, Betty Slater, where he was abusive toward her and behaved in a threatening manner. "Maggie was very upset when she returned to the office that day. She described him to me as 'delusional' and 'greatly agitated,'" Mr. Bartholomew said. "And I can personally vouch for that, after what happened yesterday when I refused to see him."

What happened yesterday, recalled Mr. Bartholomew, was that Mr. Granville interrupted the publisher's lunch at the famed midtown restaurant the Four Seasons, insisting that Apex had entered into a contract for two books with him. When confronted with evidence to the contrary, Mr. Granville became violent, grabbing the publisher by the throat and threatening to get the truth out of him. The restaurant staff tried to subdue the irate would-be author, but Mr. Granville could not be quieted. The suspect bolted from the restaurant and down the street on foot before the police arrived. After the incident, Mr. Bartholomew was taken to the hospital for treatment of scratches on his neck and bruises on his arm.

Although Mr. Bartholomew has had no further contact with him, the veteran publisher is under police protection, and additional security has been added throughout the Apex office building.

"It was a scary experience," stated Bartholomew, clearly distraught. "He's strong and physically imposing and clearly thinks the whole world is suddenly out to get him. If I hadn't been so frightened, I would have thought it was sad. I really hope they find him soon, because he's dangerous. This is obviously a deeply, deeply disturbed young man."

Police are also questioning a witness, Mr. Seamus Dillon, of Douglaston, Queens, a limousine driver who works for the car service often used by Ms. Peterson. Mr. Dillon positively identified Mr. Granville as a man he saw loitering outside Ms. Peterson's building when he dropped her off there several weeks ago.

Ms. Cloninger, who was Mr. Granville's upstairs neighbor, was employed as a waitress at Son House, a blues bar in the Chelsea area. She was acquainted with Mr. Granville, a coworker has told police. Mr. Granville had visited her there when she was working recently. The two appeared to be "extremely friendly," according to the coworker, and they left together at the end of Ms. Cloninger's shift.

Mr. Granville is a 1992 graduate of Cornell, where he starred on the basketball team and edited the literary magazine. *New York Magazine* senior editor Rain Finkelstein, a Cornell classmate who has hired him to write occasional freelance articles in the past two years, described Mr. Granville as "a real all-American boy. The kind you'd take home to meet Mom. Clean-cut. Easygoing. I find all this real hard to believe."

She did, however, go on to characterize him as "a man on a mission. It was clear that what he really wanted more than anything in the world was to be a novelist. It was like a holy crusade with him. I guess when the crusade failed, he just went off the deep end."

Amanda Mays could not believe it. Not one word of it.

Carl Granville dangerous? Carl Granville a *murderer*? Her Carl? The man who used to brush her hair so gently, so sweetly, after a shower, then softly kiss her shoulders? Who would squeeze her fresh orange juice in the morning? The man who sat in his seat sobbing for ten minutes at the end of *Babe*? Okay, so he was a bit immature. Stubborn. Unrealistic. Infuriating. A great big blond mistake of a man for any self-respecting professional woman to fall in love with. A man whom she lay awake at night wishing she could flush clean out of her system—if only Drano would show some mercy and invent such a product. Carl was all of those things, to be sure. But a murderer? No way. Besides, she'd seen him talking to Maggie Peterson at Betty's funeral. She'd driven him home. He hadn't been agitated. Just his usual boyish, jovial, impossible self.

This wasn't possible. This *couldn't* be possible.

But there it was, jumping out at her from the screen of her office computer.

Amanda had first learned about it when she saw it on TV earlier that morning. She was up at five A.M., as always, wired and ready. She never slept past five. Too many stories working. Too much to do. She'd fired up the coffeemaker and flicked on the early morning roundup on Apex's All News Network. She'd stretched out on the living room carpet and begun her regular morning regimen of tummy tuckers, butt burners, and positive thoughts.

She loved her house. She was renting a converted brick carriage house that was out back of a colossal Georgian mansion on Klingle Street in Kalorama. The mansion belonged to the former U.S. ambassador to Brazil. She had two big bedrooms, a gourmet kitchen, skylights, her own patio, a garden. She adored her garden. Herbs. She could barely believe it, but she was growing herbs. She loved D.C. It had all of the energy and pulse and power of New York, but here she could live and breathe. She was one block from the National Zoological Park. Two from St. Stephen's Cathedral. The office was less than twenty minutes away. And that was another thing—she was crazy about her job, too. Yes, she was happy here. She was totally and completely happy here.

That's what Amanda was thinking as she lay there contorted on the floor, groaning and grunting, when suddenly a man's photograph flashed up on the TV screen. The man looked eerily familiar. It took her a second to realize why.

It was Carl's photograph up there on the screen. An old photo of him from his playing days at Cornell. And the announcer was saying that he was the primary suspect in the murder of Maggie Peterson. She watched, transfixed, as they showed a close-up of a letter Maggie had written, rejecting Carl's novel. They interviewed the publisher of Apex Books, who talked about Carl physically assaulting him in the Four Seasons. And they'd already begun digging into Carl's background—his solitary ways, his obsessive desire to become a successful writer. Jesus. They were making it sound like she'd once been in love with Lee Harvey Oswald.

Flabbergasted, she had logged onto her computer and surfed every news service she could find. Nothing more had come over any of the wires yet. No details. Trembling, her heart racing, she threw on a sweater and a pair of slacks, ran her hands through her unruly mass of red hair, wishing more than ever that she had the nerve to hack it all off. She jumped into her aging Subaru, yelled at it to please, please, start—it did, thank God—and floored it down Connecticut Avenue. At Dupont Circle she veered off onto Massachusetts Avenue and took the turn onto Fourteenth on two wheels. The *Journal*'s offices were across from Commerce. By the time she got to her desk, she'd found this latest story on the Apex news wire, confirming that it was so.

Carl Granville was wanted for murder. They were searching for him. He was missing. Missing and presumed guilty.

But how could this be? How?

Amanda took a sip from her fifth cup of coffee of the morning. She stared out through her glass partition at the newsroom, which was just beginning to awaken. It was still not eight o'clock. As deputy metro editor, Amanda was "against the wall," which officially meant she had a small glassed-in office next to the metro editor's large glassed-in office. Unofficially it meant she was on a fast track to the national desk, provided she didn't screw up or make any power enemies in management. For now, she had no window, half of a secretary, and her babies.

One of her babies was asleep on Amanda's couch, her long legs sprawled over the upholstered armrest. Shaneesa Perryman had one shoe on; the other was lying several feet away, as if she'd kicked the first off, exhausted, then didn't have the energy to bother with the second one. A cherry-red sweater was drawn up to her neck, substituting for a blanket. Shaneesa was Amanda's favorite. She'd come to the States from Jamaica thirteen years ago, when she was ten years old, and still had a touch of saucy island lilt to her voice. Her family didn't have a dime and she'd done her time in the projects, using her brain and her personality to help her escape. Shaneesa was fearless, funny, almost six feet tall, and could do things with a computer that Bill Gates hadn't even dreamed of. When she stirred, her unfocused eyes took in the room. For a moment she looked as though she didn't know where she was. Then her face softened when she spotted Amanda's concerned expression.

"Been here long?" Shaneesa murmured.

"That's supposed to be my question, isn't it?"

Amanda didn't have to ask why Shaneesa had spent the night in the office. There was a boyfriend who had the worst possible combination of personal traits: he was unemployed, he liked to yell, and he couldn't take a hint, even when the hint was as straightforward as "Get out of my life."

"Mmm. That coffee smells good."

"It is. So you might want to get yourself a cup—somewhere else."

Shaneesa *could* take a hint. Within seconds, both shoes were on, her sweater was tied around her neck, and she was heading toward the coffee machine at the far end of the newsroom. But before Amanda could return to the problem at hand, another one of her babies, Cindy, a tough little Asian woman from San Francisco, marched in and sat down. She wanted to talk. Amanda encouraged her reporters to come in and talk anytime they wanted to. Cindy was hot into a story about a local priest, the pastor of St. Stephen's Cathedral, who had disappeared. No body had been found yet, and there was no cause to suspect foul play. There *were* all sorts of rumors—possible accusations of sexual abuse, a secret wife stashed somewhere in Virginia, depression over a dead sister, even suicide—but Cindy felt there was something else going on. She'd cozied up to a few sources, had begun to get intrigued with this handsome and charismatic young priest. There was a lot of competition for this story—the man of the cloth was a rising star in Washington circles—but Amanda had fought for Cindy to stay on it and she had won. The story was theirs. Except there was one big problem—Cindy knew what she believed *hadn't* happened. But she didn't have one solid lead about what *had* happened.

If only Amanda could concentrate. But she couldn't. She hardly heard a word Cindy was saying.

Her secretary was buzzing her.

Amanda picked up her phone and said, "I can't talk to anyone right now. Please take a message."

"Okay."

Amanda hung up the phone and turned her divided attention back to her reporter. Or tried to. Her secretary was buzzing her again.

She answered impatiently. "Yes?"

"I'm sorry, Amanda, but he says it's urgent. There's some kind of emergency with your grandmother."

Her grandmother? Was this some kind of joke? She'd never even met one of her grandmothers, and the other one had died several years . . .

Amanda froze. She swallowed, composing herself.

"Did he say he's calling about my granny?"

"That's what he said. It sounded really important."

Amanda asked Cindy to please excuse her. She got up and closed the door after her, then sat back down. She picked up the receiver and slowly brought it up to her ear.

"Carl?" she whispered.

"So listen," he said with maddening calm. "I know we agreed to wait until next year, but something has kind of come up."

The moment she hung up the telephone, Amanda announced that she could be reached at home if anyone needed her and went flying out of the newsroom. She told her secretary that she was coming down with a virus, which was not totally untrue. It was fair to liken Carl Granville's effect on her physical and mental well-being to that of a virus—one of those nasty Hong Kong ones, the kind that every time you think you've gotten rid of it, it comes roaring back and flattens you all over again.

On the phone, she told him where her spare key was—under the flowerpot with the nasturtiums in it—and told him to let himself in. She also told him to stay put and that she'd be there immediately.

As she impatiently nudged her Subaru through the midday snarl of government office drones and tourists on Connecticut Avenue, what she was telling herself was something entirely different: *I am out of my fucking mind. I am jeopardizing everything I've worked for—my career, my reputation, possibly even my freedom. And for what?* As unreal as it all seemed, Carl was a fugitive from justice. By harboring him, she was aiding and abetting a man who was wanted for two savage murders. So why didn't she just turn him in? Why hadn't she just hung up on him? What on earth was she doing?

She knew exactly what she was doing. She was being a total fool. One of those hopeless, low-self-esteem doormats who end up on *Jenny Jones* when the topic for the day is "Good Women Who Love Bad Men."

Except he *wasn't* a bad man. He was Carl. Granny, for God's sake. The man she used to think she'd be spending the rest of her life with. And so she would hide him and help him and be there for him. At least until he answered a few questions.

Questions like: Did he actually kill those two women? If he didn't, then who did? And why was he being branded as the prime suspect? Why had he acted so crazy with that Apex publisher? Why was he running instead of facing this thing head-on? And, oh, by the way, just exactly who was this gorgeous upstairs neighbor, this blonde, this actress? Had he been seeing her? Sleeping with her? Was he in love with her?

Yes, Amanda had questions, all right. A million of them. And he'd better have some answers. Damned good ones, too.

She made one stop on the way, at the market. There was no food in the house. Not a crumb. Then she streaked home.

Klingle was a very quiet street during the day. She drove slowly past the mansion, looking for any sign that someone was watching it. But she saw nothing out of the ordinary. It did not appear that anyone was paying any attention to where she lived.

The shutters in the carriage house's living room were completely closed. She usually left the top half open. Otherwise, there was no sign of anyone being home. No hum came from the air conditioner in the living room window, even though it was a brutally hot day. Carl was being careful. This was good. She drove around the corner and pulled into the attached garage directly to the left of her little house. It was her greatest luxury—a private parking space. She got out of the car, closed the garage door behind her, and took a deep breath. Then she headed toward the back door, the one that led from the garage to her kitchen, unlocked it, and went barging inside with her groceries and her mixed feelings.

The television was on softly, tuned to ANN, the Augmon-owned news network. He was glued to it, staring at the screen as if it were his last link to the outside world.

She barely recognized him when he got up and came across the room toward her. The man who stood in her sweltering, airless living room was not the Carl Granville she knew. There was no easy smile, no calm and confident swagger. This man was hollow-eyed, ashen, and unshaven. His hair was uncombed and greasy. The white button-down shirt he wore was grimy and rumpled, and he smelled disturbingly like a public rest room. This Carl Granville was exhausted and shattered and desperate. He looked like a man who had been buried alive in a cave-in for a week.

It took every ounce of self-control she possessed not to run to him and take him in her arms and hold him. But she did not. She just stood there, gazing at him warily.

"Did you have any trouble getting in?" she finally asked him, her voice hoarse.

"Not really." His own voice sounded clear and firm. Even casual. How was that possible? "Just figuring out which one was the nasturtiums. I had to turn over every pot. Since when are you so—"

"Into growing things? Always." She went bustling into the kitchen with the groceries. For some reason she felt it was important that she stay busy. The floor plan in her carriage house was very open. An island separated the kitchen from the dining area and living room. She put the groceries down on the counter and flicked on the air conditioner. Right away the place started cooling off. "Are you hungry?"

"Starving. I haven't eaten since yesterday."

She had bought him some chunky peanut butter, grape jelly, and white bread. One of his favorite forms of sustenance. He immediately sat down at the kitchen table, made himself a sandwich, and tore into it like a ravenous stray animal. She had bought milk, too, so she poured him a glass.

He finished one sandwich, then made another and ate that, too. And then one more. Each sandwich was washed down by a tall glass of milk. Finally he sighed, leaned back in the chair, and looked at her, satisfied and grateful.

"Have you been away?" he said.

She shook her head. "Why do you ask?"

"There was no food in the house."

"If it's there, I eat it."

"You look skinny," he told her.

She saw the look of concern on his face, and she let a rueful smile cross her lips. "There's no such thing as too tall or too skinny." Before he could say anything, she said, "And besides, you've got a lot more important things to worry about than my diet."

That was when he noticed the groceries she'd laid out: a slab of corned beef, a head of cabbage, carrots, potatoes.

"It happens to be the only thing I know how to make, remember?"

"I remember."

That's when she saw it. The look. It was an expression in his eyes; he used to get it when he would watch her and he didn't think she was looking. It was a look of bemusement and familiarity and deep affection, along with a touch of confusion. She asked him about it once—she said she'd never seen anything quite like it—and he told her that what she was seeing was the fact that he was in love with her. Love combined with awe—he couldn't believe she was also in love with him.

She turned away. It was not the look she wanted to see right this minute. "Here," she said. "I also got you a few things I thought you might need." She began unloading them from the bag. "A package of underwear, socks. Also a toothbrush, a comb, disposable razors . . ."

He didn't respond other than to stare in dumbfounded amazement at all of the stuff on the counter. This look was quite different from the one that had been on his face just a few moments earlier.

"What?" she demanded. "What did I do?"

"Christ, Amanda, why didn't you just go ahead and advertise that you're harboring a male fugitive—with a size thirty-two waist?"

"All I did was—"

"All you did was put up a neon sign announcing that a man's staying in your apartment! Don't you understand? They're looking for me. Which means they're looking for anyone, anywhere, who might help me. Which means that sooner or later they're going to be looking for you. Watching you."

"Well, excuse me," she shot back defensively. "I don't have a lot of practice at this. And it's been a helluva long time since I've seen *Bonnie and Clyde*."

He took a deep breath to calm himself down. "You're right, you're right," he said hurriedly. "I've gotten totally paranoid. I'm sorry." And then very quietly he said, "I'm really sorry."

Amanda had never seen him look so vulnerable, and it rattled her.

"Believe me," he continued, "I understand the risk you're taking by letting me stay here. I had no right to barge in on you like this. I would've understood if you'd said no. I'll understand if you *still* say no."

"I'm not saying no," she said softly. Then she steeled herself. They did not have the luxury of sentiment. "Only it's time for you to explain what the hell is going on."

He ran his fingers through his hair and closed his eyes. For a moment she thought he was starting to drift away. Then his eyes opened. This time what she saw when she looked inside them was anger and bewilderment and a sense of utter helplessness. For the first time his own voice cracked with strain. "I don't fucking *know* what's going on!"

She poured fresh water into the Melitta coffeemaker and stood there watching it drip. She found it hard to look at him again. He looked way too much like a wild animal caught in a painful, even deadly trap. "Carl, if you didn't do these things—"

"If?" He stared at her. "*If*, Amanda?"

"Then why don't you just turn yourself in?"

At first he said nothing. Then the faintest smile crossed his lips. It lingered for the briefest of moments. Then he started to laugh. And then he stood up, started to pace, and began to talk. It all came spilling out too fast, and she had to periodically stop him, make him repeat himself, make him go slower and fill in more details so she could begin to understand.

He told her about his meeting in the apartment with Maggie Peterson and hearing about *Gideon* and the check he'd received. He told her about Harry Wagner and the diaries, all the information he'd been fed. He talked about how he began to worry that something wasn't right with the book he was writing. About her own phone call telling him that Maggie was dead. He told her about Bartholomew and the break-in at his apartment, the destruction, and Sergeant O'Roarke, and the cop, Payton, trying to shoot him.

He talked about finding Toni. Then running and hiding. It had been twenty-four hours since his world had turned upside down, but he already felt as if he'd spent his entire life running and hiding.

When he stopped, Amanda lit a cigarette. She waited, but he was so stressed out that he didn't even make a snide comment. "What happened then?" she asked softly. "Where did you go?"

"Uptown into Harlem. Figured they wouldn't think to look for me up there. What white man is going to hide in a black part of town, right? From there I took a cab out to the Amtrak station in Newark. A gypsy cab. No medallion and no questions asked. I hid in a stall in the men's room until the Night Owl came through on its way here from Penn Station."

Well, that explains the smell, Amanda thought.

"It stops in Newark at four-oh-nine A.M., in case you're interested," Carl went on. "I paid on board for my ticket. I was afraid to wait in line. Paid cash, since I couldn't use my credit card—they'd be able to track me that way. Same with my ATM card. At least I took some cash out, on a whim." He grinned sheepishly and shrugged. "So I'm not going to have to borrow any money from you." He took a deep breath now. He was almost up to date. "The train got into Union Station just after eight this morning. That's where I called you from."

"No one recognized you on the train?"

"I don't think so. The hat and shades helped." He indicated the gaudy New Jersey Nets cap and wraparound sunglasses that were lying on the dining room table, an old oak worktable that she'd picked up in the Shenandoah Valley on one of her solitary weekend jaunts. "I swiped them from a shop at the station. After I talked to you, I took the subway straight here and—"

"Metro," she broke in, ever the editor.

"Huh?"

"They call it the Metro here. Not the subway."

"Yeah, right. Whatever. I didn't want to risk taking a cab. I didn't want anyone to remember bringing me here."

The coffee was ready. She poured them both some. He sipped his, gripping the mug tightly with both hands. He seemed a bit steadier now. His color was returning. The food seemed to have helped. And the talking.

"The weirdest thing," he said, shaking his head slowly, "is how they've concocted this serial killer, turning me into some evil psycho version of myself. My shitty relationship with my father. An obsessive desire to become a novelist. It's crazy, it's all skewed and wrong, it's all a lie, but it's in the papers, it's on TV, it's all over the Net . . ."

"And so it's true."

He nodded miserably. "When I read it, when I hear it, sometimes even *I* feel like I don't know what the truth is. So how could anyone else?" He peered at her suddenly, jerking his head up. His whole body tensed. "Have they contacted you yet?"

"Has who contacted me yet?"

"The police. The FBI."

Dread immediately began to gnaw at her. "No. No, they haven't."

"They will. And soon. Lots of people know about you and me. I won't be able to hide here for long. I'll have to keep moving." He looked at her and shook his head as if he was angry about something. "I shouldn't have come here," he said. And then he slumped back down into a dining chair. "I just needed to . . ." He trailed off and ran a hand over his stubbly face, knuckling his puffy eyes. "I was just so *tired.*"

"You're safe here for now," she assured him. "You're safe with me."

There was so much more she needed to know. But now wasn't the time. He needed sleep. "Why don't you take a shower and get some rest? I'll make up the bed in the spare room, okay? There are fresh towels in the linen cupboard. And I *think* I can even find something clean for you to wear." Again she started bustling around. A frayed old pair of his gray athletic sweatpants had found their way into her rag drawer in the kitchen, buried deep. And one of his soft, comforting shirts, a blue and white cotton New York Giants practice jersey, was hanging in the bedroom closet.

He peered at the shirt suspiciously when she brought it to him. "I thought they lost that at the laundry. How'd *you* end up with it?"

"I stole it," she confessed. "It always looked better on me than it did on you." She did not, however, confess that she had worn it to bed every night for three weeks after they broke up.

They stared at each other for a moment. And *wham*—suddenly it was there. The uneasiness. The tension. The silence. The past.

He looked away, swallowing. "Look, about Toni . . ."

"I didn't ask about her," Amanda pointed out frostily.

"I know you didn't," he acknowledged. "You never would. You're way too classy. But I'm going to tell you anyway."

She was, she realized, not breathing. She forced air into her lungs, then exhaled slowly. "Okay."

"I was lonely. She was there. I barely knew her. No, that's not true. I did know her. Not well enough to be in love with her. But she made me laugh, she made me feel good, and I cared about her. And . . . and when I found her body, it was the worst thing I've ever seen in my life. I never want to see anything like that again. Not ever." He broke off with a shudder. He glanced around at her snug living room. The fireplace and bookcases and good, worn leather chairs. The butler's tray with the cut-glass decanters of single-malt scotch and Calvados. The walls that were lined with the framed originals of vintage political cartoons and caricatures that she collected. The massive walnut desk that had belonged to her father, who had been a small-town bank president in Port Chester, New York, until he was struck down by congestive heart failure at the age of fifty-six. "I like your place. It's very . . ."

"It's very what?"

"Grown-up."

"Well, guess what, Carl. I'm a grown-up." Or at least she had been until an hour ago. "Now please go take your shower." She gently shoved the clothes and the things she'd bought for him into his arms.

Meekly he stumbled into the bathroom, closing the door behind him. She immediately grabbed her cell phone, stepped out onto the patio, and called the paper. "Talk to me," she commanded her secretary when she got through.

"Cindy phoned in. They started dredging the Potomac for that missing priest. Somebody thinks they saw him walking along there, not far from the basin, a couple of nights ago. She said they're not ruling out suicide at this point."

"Anything else?"

"Yeah, some guy from the FBI called, said it was important. I told him you were home sick. I hope that's okay."

"Not a problem." She thanked her. She rang off and then jumped two feet in the air.

There was a man in a crisp tan suit standing right there before her on the patio. He was tall and sunburned, with a blond crew cut and white-blond eyebrows. No more than thirty. And clean enough to eat off.

"Miss Mays? I'm sorry if I startled you. They told me at your office that I'd find you here. I'm Special Agent Shanahoff, FBI." He showed her his badge. His manner was very calm, impassive. If his resting pulse rate was more than forty-seven, she would have been shocked. "I wonder if I could talk to you about Carl Granville."

She gulped, collecting herself. Her heart was pounding. "Yes," she said quietly. "I had a feeling I'd be hearing from someone."

He had very blank eyes. Humorless and cold. She did not like his eyes. They made her very afraid for Carl. "May I come in?" he asked.

His question froze her momentarily. She *had* to let him in. If she didn't, he'd know she was hiding something. Or, more precisely, someone. And if she did, well, Carl was in there taking a shower. She had never totally understood the expression "between a rock and a hard place" before. Well, she certainly did now. Because that was exactly where she was caught.

"Miss Mays," he persisted, a slight edge to his voice now.

"Yes. Yes, of course. I—I'm sorry . . . Agent Shanahoff? I'm not feeling very well. When I saw the news this morning, I just . . ."

"I gather that the two of you were close," he said, not unkindly.

"We *were* very close."

"Until?"

"Until, well . . . until we weren't anymore. That's when I moved to Washington."

"This was last year?"

"Last summer."

"August twenty-fourth."

She nodded. *Okay,* she thought. *Chalk one up for him. The FBI can be thorough when they need to be.* She exhaled slowly. "Please, come inside."

They stepped into the living room. She did her best to smile graciously. But all she was thinking was: *Please, Carl. Don't make a goddamn sound.*

"Whew, much cooler in here," he said gratefully, pausing in the doorway to take in as much of the apartment as he could. "I want the name of your realtor. These old places have so much character. You should see my place. It looks like the inside of a shoebox."

"Have a seat," she told him.

He stayed where he was, his eyes narrowed slightly. "Do I hear water running?"

She jumped up and rolled her eyes at her own foolishness. "Thanks for reminding me. I was just running a bath. I thought it would cheer me up." She crossed the living room and started down the narrow hallway to the bathroom. She stopped at the bathroom door to glance over her shoulder. The agent had not followed her. She reached for the doorknob. *Please, please don't make any noise. Don't splash, don't ask a question or say a word.* She turned the knob and ducked inside.

It was thoroughly steamed up in there. Carl's clothes and things were heaped all over the counter next to the sink, and towels were strewn everywhere. Nobody, in Amanda's experience, could mess up a bathroom like Carl Granville. She yanked open the clear vinyl shower curtain and reached around Carl's slippery, soapy body. She saw the surprise on his face, but before he could so much as breathe, she turned off the water and clamped a hand tightly over Carl's mouth.

"There is an FBI agent out there," she whispered urgently in his ear. He froze immediately. "Do not move. Do not make a sound. Understand?"

He nodded obediently, his eyes wide with fear.

She released him. They stared into each other's eyes a moment. An unspoken closeness passed between them, a bond. Something that had always been there—and was still there, whether she wanted to admit it to herself or not. She eased the bathroom door shut behind her and took a deep breath, trying to calm herself but failing. She returned to the living room.

Agent Shanahoff had not sat. Far from it. Rather, he had moseyed casually over toward the kitchen, the better to take stock of things. Such as the two coffee cups on the kitchen counter. Such as the remains of Carl's peanut butter and jelly feast.

Such as his cap and sunglasses on the dining table.

"I always eat peanut butter when I'm upset," she blurted out from the doorway. "Comfort food."

"Yeah, I know exactly what you mean." He smiled at her. Or at least his mouth did. It never caught up to his eyes. "I'm a meat-loaf-and-mashed-potatoes man myself."

"Can I get you some coffee, Agent Shanahoff? Or something cold?"

"Please, call me Bruce. And no, thank you," he replied politely. "I won't stay long." His eyes flicked back to the cap on the table. "I see you're a big New Jersey Nets fan."

She forced out a laugh. Not a very good idea. She wondered if he could hear the brittle edge of hysteria to it. "No, my nephew is. He sent it to me. Actually, I couldn't name a single member of the team if my whole life depended on it."

"I doubt anyone else in the New York area could, either," he said pleasantly. "I used to be assigned there. Just been in D.C. a few months myself. Hardly know a soul yet." He paused, thoughtfully scratching his solid, square chin with his thumb. "Maybe we're kind of in the same boat that way."

"Maybe we are." Unbelievable. He was hitting on her. Well, maybe this wasn't so bad. In fact, this was all right. She could deal with this. She sashayed by him into the kitchen, working her hips. She got started on the dirty dishes, the better to give him a nice view of her tush. "What would you like to know about Carl?" she asked him over her shoulder.

"Anything you can tell me, Ms. Mays."

"He was the boyfriend from hell," she said, and was surprised at the bitterness that crept into her voice.

"Abusive?"

"Oh, God, no."

"Did he cheat?"

She shook her head. "Never."

"Did he steal from you?"

"Carl Granville is probably the most honest person I know."

"That right?"

"He once found twenty-five hundred dollars in an envelope in a taxicab—somebody'd left it there. He was broke and he really needed the money, but you know what he did?"

"Used it to feed needy orphans?"

"He turned it in to the police. And there's no need to be snide."

"Sorry. But I'm a little confused. I was under the impression that Granny was someone you're not very fond of. But it doesn't sound that way."

For some reason it bothered her that he had referred to Carl by his nickname. Like it was some kind of psychological test.

"Look, Agent Shanahoff—"

"Bruce."

"I was in love with Carl. But he's not a man who is emotionally capable of maintaining an adult relationship. I had to get away from him, so I did. Consider it an act of self-preservation. Or personal survival. It wasn't easy, and I can't pretend I don't have feelings for him, but I did it. And now I'm getting on with the rest of my life."

"And when was the last time you saw him?"

"At Betty Slater's funeral in New York a few weeks ago. She was someone we were both close to. I hadn't seen him for several months prior to that. I gave him a lift home." Her mind leaped to him standing in her shower right that very second, covered in lather. She forced the image out of her thoughts. She didn't believe in ESP, but there was no sense in even tempting fate with this federal agent standing in her kitchen.

"Was it friendly?"

"As a matter of fact, we had a rather heated quarrel in the car."

"May I ask about what?"

"About nothing. About everything. I'm sure you know how it is, Bruce."

"Did he strike you? Threaten you with physical violence? Anything like that?"

Amanda turned to face him, tossing her mass of red hair. "It's inconceivable to me that Carl would be capable of violence."

"Maybe to you. But not to the people he's killed."

Amanda stood there, motionless. The words hit her hard. But they weren't true. They couldn't be true.

"Miss Mays—"

"I wish you'd call me Amanda . . . Bruce," she said huskily. She ran her fingers along the bare, creamy white skin of her throat and could feel herself perspiring. Playing a femme fatale was not her favorite role.

"All right." He flashed another smile at her. This one almost made it up to his eyes, but still not quite. She really did not like those eyes. "I'm going to ask you this straight up, Amanda—have you heard from Carl Granville since he took flight?"

"No, I haven't." *Dear Diary, today I lied straight up to a federal agent.*

"No phone call, no note?" he said, a bit doubtfully. "He hasn't tried to contact you in any way?"

"No, he hasn't."

He moved in closer, towering over her. On the surface his manner didn't change, yet somehow she could feel him turn stern and steely. Suddenly there was an air of quiet menace about him. "I hope you're not lying to me," he said. His voice was even but remarkably hard and unbending.

She tensed. *Steady, girl.* "You're not listening to me, Agent Shanahoff," she said in what she hoped was an equally even tone. "I just told you I haven't heard from him, and I don't expect to."

He backed off, satisfied. For now, anyway. The hard-to-read smile was back on his lips. "Well, I'm sorry to say that you *may* hear from him. An Amtrak conductor identified his photo this morning. We believe he's in D.C. I probably don't need to say this, but if he does contact you, be aware that he's no one to mess with. Despite what you think, we've got a lot of evidence that indicates he's murdered two people. We're talking about one dangerous puppy. Understood?"

She nodded.

"Do you have any idea where he would go? Any idea at all?"

She ran her tongue slowly along the edge of her lower lip. His eyes never strayed from the tongue. God, men were easy. "He used to talk a lot about his playing days at Cornell. Maybe he's running to one of his teammates, like O.J. did. All those old jocks stick together." She looked Shanahoff up and down his six-foot-plus frame. "I'll bet you used to play some basketball yourself."

"Captain of the golf team at Creighton," he said blandly.

She tried to think of something flirtatious to say about golf. What came out was, "Well, that's a fun game. And you get to wear those cute pants." *Fun game? Cute pants? Relax, girl! You're blowing it.*

"Know any of his ex-teammates?" Shanahoff asked. "Or if any of them lives here in the D.C. area?"

"Um . . ." *Oh, God.* Was that a noise she'd just heard coming from the bathroom? What the hell was he doing in there? She glanced at the FBI agent. He hadn't reacted. *Carl,* she thought, *you're giving me a heart attack.* "Um . . . no, I don't. They're scattered all over, I would imagine. But the Cornell Athletic Department ought to be able to help you out."

He nodded. "That's a good lead. Thanks."

"It's not for free. I expect something in return."

Agent Shanahoff raised an eyebrow at her curiously. "What's that?"

She reached for her purse on the counter, dug out one of her cards, and handed it to him. "The story. If you catch him, I mean."

"Oh, we'll catch him," he assured her, inspecting the card carefully. "Deputy metropolitan editor, huh?"

"I'm trying to make a name for myself," she said. "Same as you. I could use a break."

"And maybe a little personal revenge?"

"Maybe," she conceded. "I'm only human, after all. Deal?"

"I'll certainly think about it." He slid the card into the breast pocket of his shirt for safekeeping. He paused. Again he thumbed his chin thoughtfully. Somebody must have told him once that it made him look sensitive. "Maybe we could discuss it over dinner some night?"

"What, meat loaf and mashed potatoes?"

"I do eat other things."

She smiled at him, her biggest, brightest smile. "I'd like that, Bruce."

"Great. Thanks for your time, Amanda." He started toward the door. Amanda thanked God he was leaving. He was actually leaving. It was going to be okay. He'd bought it—the flirtatiousness, her sob story, her anger. He'd bought it all. She'd survived. *They'd* survived. He was almost to the door . . . he was reaching for the doorknob . . .

And then abruptly he stopped, turned back to her, and said, "Listen, I've been on the run all day. Would you mind if I used your bathroom?"

Amanda's heart stopped beating. It honestly did.

"My bathroom?" she said. "Um . . . it's kind of a mess." She heard the quaver in her voice. It was a wonder she could speak at all.

"I grew up with two sisters. I promise not to notice." He was already heading across the room to the hall, moving with the utter self-assurance of the white male master race.

What could she do, faint? That hadn't worked since Lillie Langtry bit the dust. Besides, she didn't know how to faint. All she knew was that this man, this FBI agent, was going to open the door to her bathroom and find Carl Granville and she was dead. No two ways about it. *Dear Auntie Sheila, I'm going to be out of town for the next five to seven years doing extensive firsthand research for a series of articles on life in a maximum-security women's prison. Please don't try to contact me.* "Well, okay," she said finally, puffing out her cheeks with weary resignation. "Only . . ."

Bruce Shanahoff pulled up, frowning at her. "Only what, Amanda?"

Oh, hell, she thought. He'd find out soon enough for himself. "Only you might have to move a few stockings."

He smiled. "I'll just be a second."

That's what you think, she said to herself. She thought about crying out, warning Carl. But what good would that do? There was no way for him to escape. The bathroom window was too tiny. She thought about running out the door and never coming back. But running away was not her style. So she just stood there, resignedly awaiting her fate. Waiting for that crisp, clean bastard to return with his prize catch of the day. Waiting, the seconds interminable, the silence deafening. Waiting. Hearing nothing.

Absolutely, totally nothing.

What was going on?

Then she heard the toilet flush, the bathroom door swing open on squeaky hinges, and confident footsteps in the hallway. *One* set of footsteps.

And there he was, bladder emptied, hair combed, hands washed, a thin smile on his lips, the same empty expression in his eyes. Most important, he was alone.

Where was Carl?

"I really am going to have to get the name of your realtor," he exclaimed admiringly. "This place would serve my needs perfectly."

Where was Carl?

"Th-Then I hope you get to spend some more time here," she stammered, baffled, amazed, incredulous.

Where was Carl?

"I hope so, too," he said. And then he was out the door. Gone.

She darted to the window. Through the shutters she watched him go down the stone path to the street. She waited all of three seconds. Then she sprinted for the bathroom.

It was immaculate. No towels strewn about. No dirty clothes. No clean clothes. No razor, no toothbrush, no comb. Above all, no Carl.

Where was Carl?

chapter 12

The instant Amanda left him alone in the bathroom, Carl began to move. He dried himself off and stuffed his dirty clothes, his towel, and all of the other shit she'd bought him into the clothes hamper. Swiftly and silently he removed every observable trace that he'd been there, his mind racing, searching desperately for a way out.

He knew he didn't have much time.

If *she* had come in there, the agent would make damned sure *he* came in there, too.

Carl knew this. It was not conjecture, it was fact. He had been on the run for over twenty-four hours now and his survival instinct was operating in overdrive. He reacted to danger like a hunted animal. He *was* a hunted animal. Heart pounding, mouth dry, he weighed his options.

They sucked. The window was out—too narrow. The door was out—the hinges squeaked. So did the floorboards out in the hall. The bastard would hear him. Maybe even see him the second he appeared. Hide right there in the tub? No chance. The shower curtain was, unfortunately, see-through. Why couldn't she have gotten something with a design, maybe a nice floral pattern? He knew why, unfortunately. That was his own damned fault. Because *he* was the one who had taken her to see *Psycho* at the Film Forum. No, the tub was out. Which left him . . . what? *Think, damn it. What are the other possibilities?* Well, there was down. Sure, sure. He could tunnel out through the floor tiles with a pair of Amanda's fingernail clippers. Should be out of there in what, six, seven months? Great plan. That left . . .

Up.

As he began to examine the ceiling, at first he thought he was hallucinating. But it was definitely there—a small wooden hatchway. An attic crawl space.

By climbing up onto the sink, he was able to reach it. He pushed up, testing, and the hatchway shifted with a slight grating noise. He froze, expecting his very own junior G-man to come bursting through the door, gun in hand. But no. Nothing. He lifted the hatch as silently as possible and moved it over to the right. Ordinarily one would use a stepladder to get up there. Carl had no ladder, only his arms and his legs and his feverish desperation. Grunting, straining, he hoisted himself up, up, up, his feet kicking feebly in midair, then scrabbling along the wall, the ceiling . . .

With his last gasp of energy, he managed to pull himself over and in. He lay there a brief moment, panting. Then he glanced around.

It was a narrow crawl space, no more than two feet high. The roof slanted directly overhead, the nails from the roofing shingles poking through from outside, shiny and deadly sharp. There was ductwork, a network of rusty pipes, dustballs, filth, cobwebs. The ceiling joists were about sixteen inches apart with rolls of pink fiberglass insulation laid out in between them. Sprawled there directly under the roof, Carl gently slid the hatchway back into place, immediately plunging himself into pitch blackness.

He stretched out on his side in between two of the joints as best he could. The glass fibers of the insulation prickled his skin, making him itch all over. Lying there, he could hear himself breathing. He could hear something else, too—their voices from the kitchen. The sound carried. He heard the guy call him a dangerous puppy. A murderer. Heard her swear up and down she hadn't seen him, her voice insistent but admirably calm.

He heard the guy ask if he could use the bathroom.

Carl lay there, unmoving, soundless and sightless, as the heavy footsteps came closer and the door swung open directly below him. Then it swung shut. The guy was whistling under his breath. One of those insipid Spice Girls songs. Suddenly he realized that this would be the perfect ending: hiding in the bathroom, captured by some cretin whistling a Spice Girls abomination. As he lay there, the insulation tickling his bare side, he made a vow to the heavens: If he ever got away with this, if somehow, some way, he could ever resume a safe, sane, normal life . . .

But he couldn't. This wasn't a rehearsal, this was real life. *His* life. He couldn't just stop the tape, play it back, and redo the past twenty-four hours.

God, he felt lost. He couldn't remember ever feeling this lost. Not when Amanda had told him she was leaving to go to Washington. Not even when his mother died. He also couldn't remember ever feeling as relieved as he had when Amanda walked in that door with all of those groceries. It had taken every ounce of self-control he had not to hug her and kiss her and hold her tight. But he could not. Because that was not who they were anymore. That was over. Although he could have sworn that a brief flicker had passed between them a few minutes before, when she came in to warn him. For a second he had thought the old magic was still there. But then *poof*— the flicker was gone. Most likely it had just been fear.

The guy was taking a leak now. The longest, slowest leak in recorded history. What did the man do, store it up? Urinate once a week? God, that insulation tickled. Carl was desperate to scratch himself, only he didn't dare move. And then, to his utter and complete horror, Carl discovered that it wasn't the insulation that was tickling him.

It was a mouse.

No. *Jesus.* It was two mice.

No, three!

He'd disturbed an entire nest of the little fuckers.

He hated rodents. Mice, rats, hamsters, they were all the same to him. Even cute, friendly squirrels in the park. They made his skin crawl. Always had.

And now one was scurrying up his bare leg.

Carl wanted to yell. He wanted to jump up, scream at the top of his lungs. But he could not. He could not move. He could not make a sound. Not with that FBI agent right below. He just had to lie there in the blackness, shuddering, while the repulsive creatures scampered onto his neck, his chin, his face. One perched on his lips. One ran down his chest—he could feel its little legs working their way under his armpit. He could feel another one nibbling on his ear. He lay there, his stomach turning, a cold sweat flooding from his pores. But he didn't move. He didn't scream. He closed his eyes and prayed that this would be over soon.

Down below, the guy was flushing now. Washing his hands. Drying his hands. No doubt glancing about. Had Carl remembered to hide everything? Had moving the hatchway left any sawdust on the floor?

Was there any telltale sign of his presence? Anything to arouse the shit-head's curiosity?

Finally Carl heard the door swing open and the footsteps recede. He wanted to move instantly, to stop the furry creatures from crawling and bit-ing, but he waited, forcing himself to stay still, making absolutely sure the agent was gone and wasn't coming back. He heard voices in the living room. Heard the front door open and close. Then silence. It was safe. It *had* to be safe. He rolled over frantically, scratching and clawing at the tickling on his body. He pounded at his back and saw a mouse scurry by on the floor and disappear under a floorboard. He struck out with his fist, smashing it against the wood. For a moment he thought he might vomit; then the wave of nausea passed.

Amanda was down below now, calling out his name. He fumbled in the darkness for the trapdoor, shoved it aside, and tumbled back down to the bathroom floor below, practically landing right on top of her.

He lay there naked, sprawled on the tile, hoping he hadn't broken any-thing. She stared down at him, astonished. It was the first time in his life he'd ever seen her speechless.

"Do you know," he said to her as soon as he caught his breath, "that you have goddamn *mice* up there?"

"I didn't even know I *had* an up there," she replied. She still stared at him, dumbfounded. "Are you all right?" And before he could even answer, "How'd you know he'd come in here?"

"If he was a real agent, he was coming in."

"He had a real badge. And he was a real jerk."

"He couldn't search for me, not without a warrant. Not unless there was probable cause. Since he didn't turn the place upside down, I guess that means he was the genuine article."

"Do you think he believed me?"

"You were pretty convincing. *I* would have believed you."

"That's a no, isn't it?"

"I'm afraid it probably is."

"They'll be watching this place from now on, won't they?"

He nodded grimly. "Probably tapping your phone, too." He reached his hand out to her, and she helped him stand. "Amanda," he said, "I really am sorry I got you into this."

She started to tell him that it was okay, not to worry. But she stopped herself. Because it wasn't okay. And because there was every reason to worry. Her life had been crazy enough before he'd come back into it, and now not only was she harboring a wanted criminal, she wanted to run into his arms and make love to him. She wanted to return to what they'd had; she wanted to go forward into the future she'd always envisioned. The one with him by her side, in her bed, inside her every thought.

Damn, damn, damn. He had broken her heart once already. She was prepared to let him disrupt her life. She was willing to fight for him, ready to help him prove his innocence. But she wasn't going to risk falling in love with him a second time. No, thank you. On that, she'd take a pass.

He was watching her, she was sure he knew what she was thinking. Standing together in the small bathroom, they both became acutely aware of his nakedness. And so she muttered something vague under her breath, turned away, and slipped out the door, leaving him to put on his clothes.

Alone in the bathroom, Carl slowly got into his old Giants shirt and sweats. Then he looked dead-on into the rectangular mirror over the sink. The man gazing back at him looked much older than Carl remembered. Sadder. A little desperate.

Carl didn't like what he saw in the mirror. It scared him. That's why he slowly raised his right hand, curled it into a fist, and then jabbed it violently into the glass, causing the image to shatter into a hundred pieces.

The knuckles on his hand turned pink and raw, and a thin trickle of blood ran between the index finger and forefinger. He put the hand under the tap, let a spray of cold water wash over it.

Staring into the mirror, his face distorted by the cracks and the breaks, he stayed in the bathroom until the bleeding had stopped. Then he opened the door and went to join Amanda. Went to figure out what the hell they were going to do to try to stay alive.

chapter 13

The Closer took a taxi from a midtown Manhattan hotel out to La Guardia Airport. The driver wore a turban and had suffocatingly bad body odor. He smelled of curry and turmeric, and the combination was faintly nauseating. The traffic was slow, the drivers testy. Many rode their horns incessantly. If vehicles had come equipped with turret-mounted machine guns, the Closer had no doubt their drivers would have used them to annihilate their fellow drivers. The summer heat—combined with their miserable jobs and even more miserable marriages—did that to ordinary citizens.

Having no spouse, as well as employment that offered an infinite amount of variety and challenge, the Closer was able to remain calm and focused.

Leaving from La Guardia, the two P.M. shuttle to D.C.'s National Airport was three-quarters full. The man who was seated next to the Closer was clutching a three-ring plastic binder. The words *Environmental Protection Agency* were stamped on its face. He appeared to be very tense. Possibly he did not like to fly. He did not attempt to speak to the Closer, who had no interest in speaking to him, anyway.

The car, a year-old midnight blue eight-passenger Chevy Suburban with Vermont plates, was waiting in the long-term parking lot. The Suburban was registered to a child day care center in Putney, Vermont. The slogan *Putney Day Care—We're There* was emblazoned on the driver's and front passenger doors, underneath a playful cartoon drawing of smiling, happy young faces, balloons, and lollipops. The Suburban came equipped with a fifty-gallon fuel tank for long-distance cruising. The tank was full. The keys were in the Closer's pocket. In the glove compartment was a pair of high-powered binoculars, along with a German-made SIG-Sauer 9mm semiautomatic pistol. Tucked under the driver's seat was a .357 Magnum. There was ample ammunition for each. More than ample—the Closer rarely needed to reload a weapon.

Under the fold-down rear seat were two gallon-size Ziploc freezer bags. Each bag contained six eight-inch-long, three-quarter-inch-thick cylindrical sticks of dynamite. In the rear of the car, taped to the casing that held the spare tire, wrapped tightly in extra-thick aluminum foil and folded into a three-inch-by-three-inch square, were six blasting caps.

The Closer was pleased. All instructions had been followed to the letter. Even the musical request.

In the CD player could be found a collection of Dick Dale surf guitar instrumentals from the mid-sixties.

The Closer got in and eased the big, heavy vehicle to the exit kiosk, paid the bill, which came to $42.50, then steered out of the airport and onto the George Washington Memorial Parkway. Observing the speed limit. Admiring the lush green growth of the trees and lawns that grew along the Potomac. Wondering, as always, how Washington could remain such a beautiful and serene place when there were so many ugly and dangerous people in it.

The Closer took the Francis Scott Key Memorial Bridge over the river and picked up Wisconsin Avenue. Klingle Street was a twenty-minute drive from there. Upon reaching the destination, the Closer parked in a shady spot four doors down the street and shut off the Suburban's engine.

"Observe and report," the veddy, veddy British voice on the phone had said. The instructions were very clear. "I need information."

Hanging up the phone, the Closer had smiled. They lived in different worlds. One in which information was a valuable commodity, a form of money and power and strength. And one in which the only information of any value was that which led you to your prey. Or kept you alive.

After thirty minutes of listening to Dick Dale, an unmarked gray Ford Taurus sedan pulled up in front of the destination and stopped. A tall, blond, official-looking man got out and strode briskly up the bluestone path to the brick carriage house that was around back.

The man was inside for forty-five minutes. When he left, the Closer watched him turn and look back at the woman's house. The expression on his face showed confusion, indecision. Something was bothering him. As if he'd left something behind. Then he turned, walked back to the Taurus, and drove away. The Closer waited. And sure enough, within minutes, the Taurus returned. Parked in a different location on the other side of the street. The blond man turned the ignition off but sat in the car, waiting, watching the house from which he had emerged.

The Closer looked at the clock on the dashboard of the Suburban, then picked up the cell phone and dialed. It was time to follow those very clear instructions. The Englishman answered on the third ring and listened to the Closer's report but made no comment until all the information had been dispensed.

"Something new has come up. I have another job for you."

"What about *this* job?" the Closer asked.

"A minor change of plans there as well," the English voice said through the slight distortion of the cell phone. "Or should I say, of ratings."

"Meaning what?"

"Meaning it would be to my financial benefit to make this more newsworthy."

"How?"

"However you choose," he replied. "Knowing the details would only spoil my fun. I work hard for my money. I deserve to have some fun."

"We all deserve to have some fun." The Closer's palms were beginning to itch at the prospect of it. "But only a few of us are lucky enough to ever get the chance."

Lindsay Augmon hung up the phone on his most dangerous employee. He was not thinking of the Closer's vivid imagination or special abilities. Nor was he thinking about the consequences of those skills.

He was thinking about money.

Lord Lindsay Edward Augmon had made his first million dollars when he was twenty-two years old.

His father, Sir James Lindsay Augmon, was an Oxford don, distinguished, stuffy, quite righteous, and respected by all who met him. He revered the queen, supported Labor, and felt there was no higher calling than teaching poetry to young people thirsting for knowledge and beauty. Every seven years or so, Faber would publish James's own thin volume of poems, which ritualistically received glowing reviews, and every four or five years they would publish a volume of his criticism, most of which made it clear that no other modern poet had a clue.

Young Lindsay attended Oxford as well, as duly expected, but lasted just one month into his second year, when he was expelled for impregnating the sixteen-year-old daughter of the head of his college. Lindsay did not mind leaving England's greatest university behind him. He did not care much for his father—for his obsession with discipline, his stiff-upper-lip British reserve, or his phony liberalism, which in young Lindsay's mind had more to do with making the right social connections than anything else and allowed his father to love the masses from afar and treat his own son, who was quite close up, like a pile of rubbish. He also detested his father's retreat from reality into academia and had no intention of following in the elder man's hallowed footsteps. Lindsay had every intention of becoming a newspaperman. And a man of the streets. He loved the roughness of lower-class England: the smells, the language, the excitement. It was where he felt he belonged.

Within days of his arrival in London, in 1953, Lindsay Augmon had a job on Fleet Street. His reporting instincts were so unerring and his demeanor so fearless that within six months he was asked to move south to the coastal town of Falmouth to run a local resort paper, the *Sandpiper*. The paper was seasonal, the ad rates high but good for three months only, four months tops. However, Lindsay quickly changed the tenor of its news coverage. Instead of covering local yacht races and having full-page weather reports, the *Sandpiper* became political. Not surprisingly to anyone who knew the young Augmon, the paper's targets were the Labor Party and the queen herself. Both were attacked viciously and relentlessly, and Lindsay's specialty became the lurid tabloid headline. After another Labor victory in the national elections, Augmon's paper blared, "Entire Country Having Labor Pains," and, after a sex scandal within Parliament involving a minister named William Conklin, it ran "Willie's Willie—Will He?" The one that caused the most consternation and caused the greatest one-day sale of papers in the *Sandpiper*'s history was "Queen Eats a Rat." This particular headline was to become the symbol of Augmon and all his papers, as well as the modus operandi. The queen had not, in fact, eaten a rat. The story was about a London restaurant that was discovered to be serving rat meat in their stew and passing it off as chicken. When the owner of the Soho eatery was asked for a quote, he insisted that rodent made a perfectly fine meal. His quote was, "If the queen herself came in to eat, I'd serve her the little buggers." The fact that the queen *hadn't* come in to eat didn't stop Augmon. His headline was close enough to the truth for him—and apparently for his readers as well. Within a year, the paper's circulation had quadrupled and advertising rates were soaring year-round.

One year after going to work for the *Sandpiper*, he put together a syndicate to buy the paper. It turned out he had a flair for ownership. For *sole* ownership. One by one, his partners disappeared—quitting in frustration in the face of his ruthless business tactics or driven out by Augmon's economic pressuring. By the late 1950s Augmon owned seven newspapers in England and had expanded to Australia, where he owned four more papers. Each was small, tabloid in nature, and becoming more and more fanatically right-wing—all in the name of giving the working people what they wanted. In the early sixties he moved into TV, magazines, and books. By the late sixties he realized that England was a dead end, never again to be a world power, so he took his voracious appetite and his penchant for making up stories to America. During the seventies he took dual citizenship, becoming an American citizen so he could circumvent the law restricting foreign ownership, and began buying up American television stations as well as any magazine or newspaper that came up for grabs. He followed the same formula for each of his possessions: streamline the operation by any means necessary, hire hungry young people who had as few scruples as possible and who were eager to climb the corporate ladder, go for the blue-collar audience, and never worry about the truth if a lie will sell better. Reagan's America and Thatcher's England made the perfect foil for his schemes and vision.

By the time he celebrated his fiftieth birthday, he had been married three times. His second wife bore him a son, Walker. The relationship between father and son was not a good one. When Walker was sixteen years old, he was killed in a freakish accident. He was vacationing in the Middle East and was hiking in Jordan, in the spectacular ruins of Petra. While he was walking through the narrow ravine leading out of the ruins, there was a flash flood. Most of the tourists were able to cling to a high space. Walker, along with three others, was drowned. His body was flown back to New York, where his mother and father lived, but Lindsay Augmon did not attend the funeral. On that day he was buying a film studio and the funeral did not fit into his very busy schedule.

He was knighted in 1984 when he bailed out Britain's largest airline and kept it from going out of business. Throughout that decade, his formula never varied. The only thing that changed was his bottom line, which became more and more profitable as he moved into the business of satellite television, wireless communications, and blockbuster films. In 1988, the same year he became a naturalized American citizen, *Forbes* magazine listed him as the seventh richest man in the world, with a net worth of $6.8 billion.

In 1990 Lord Augmon had perhaps his most important revelation: It wasn't only Britain that would never again be a world power. *No* country would ever truly dominate again. Modern tools of communication had stripped governments of their real means of power—the control of information. If one wanted to be a ruler, one had to rule not with weapons, not with law, but with technology.

It was that simple. One night Lindsay Augmon went to bed with a new realization about the way of the future. The next morning he woke up determined to become the most powerful man in the world.

chapter 14

"**Y**ou've got to think," she said.

"If I think any harder," he told her, "I'm going to suffer a full cranial meltdown."

Amanda nodded, backing off. "All right, then let's take a break." She went to the refrigerator and took out a Bud Light. "I bought you some beer," she said.

"That's not beer, Amanda. That's more like monkey piss."

"Oh, I'm so sorry," Amanda snapped. "Next time I'm stocking a hideout for you I'll make sure to provide a full selection of handcrafted micro-beers."

They were eating the corned beef and cabbage that Amanda had made, and going through as many details as Carl could remember. Anything at all about the book he'd been writing, about the information he'd been given, the material he'd read. Dates. Any recognizable locations. Anything distinctive about the conversations he'd had with Maggie, with Harry Wagner. Anything at all he might have picked up about the identity of the unknown Gideon. He was clean-shaven now, hair slicked back, wearing the Giants jersey and sweatpants. It was good to be clean again. And it was even better to be sitting there listening as Amanda began to sink her teeth into the puzzle they had to solve. He almost felt like his old self. Except, of course, that he wasn't. And never would be again. That Carl Granville was gone. That Carl Granville was history.

In between bites of food, Amanda was taking notes, sorting through any information that seemed relevant, making lists, and trying to organize the whole thing according to time line, geography, and character involvement. She didn't have a lot to go on.

He had no real names. Just the boy he'd taken to calling Danny and the boy's mother, whom he'd tagged Rayette. And no real places. He had read real descriptions of the southern towns he'd been writing about, he'd gotten to know them so well he felt he'd lived in them himself, but all names had been excised from the diaries and letters he'd been given. They could have been anywhere. Louisiana. Tennessee. Arkansas. Alabama. Who the hell knew. So many of the details had blurred in his mind—he had absorbed so much in such a short time—but Amanda was a terrific reporter. She had gone through the story with him three times already, asking questions, taking him further and further into the recesses of his mind. Each time something new came back to him. Each time he felt they were making some slight step forward. The question was: What were they stepping forward to?

"All right," she said. "Tell me about Rayette."

"Poor, uneducated. Borderline hooker. Big drinker. Married several times—"

"How many?"

"I don't know. Three, four . . . three. There were three. No, four."

"Who were they?"

He listed the men he remembered. And described some of the small, shithole southern towns in which Rayette had lived. He remembered that Danny had been born in 1945. They had started moving around soon after his birth. His sense was that they'd moved from state to state rather than within one state. The baby brother—Carl had never even thought of a name to call the child—was born in '54. In 1955 Danny committed the murder, killing the year-and-a-half-old boy. Whatever town it had happened in had smelled really bad. There was something—a factory? a chemical plant? a slaughterhouse?—that fouled the air. It was a factory. Definitely a factory. And he had remembered that there was a midwife. With a birthmark covering half her face.

"What *kind* of factory?"

"I don't know."

"Think."

"It didn't ever say. I made something up. I said it was a battery factory, I think. Yeah, that's right. I did a little research on my own, and that seemed like a decent choice. They used to dump all kinds of toxic shit in the water back then. Cobalt, cadmium . . ."

"Those were the good old days for American industry, when they could dump anything they wanted to dump. I wouldn't be surprised if that's why Rayette's baby was born retarded."

"You think there's an ecological angle to all this? I mean, from Gideon's point of view?"

"I don't know. It's certainly possible." Amanda pressed on. "But we don't have enough to go on. You have to remember more."

"I can't even remember my own name," he said.

"Come on, Carl, there has to be something else."

"I'm blank."

"A school," she urged. "Or a church. Some kind of landmark. A store . . ."

"Elvis," he said.

"What?"

"Elvis!" His eyes were on fire now. "Elvis Presley performed in the town. At a small arena, maybe a high-school auditorium or something like that, for fifteen hundred people."

"When?" she asked.

"The day of the murder. 1955."

"Good!" Amanda sounded elated. "Very good."

Carl allowed himself a brief and triumphant smile. Then he shook his head and sagged back into his chair. "It's not much," he said, "is it?"

"No, it's not much," she agreed. "But it sure as hell is something."

Two and a half hours later they had very little else. Carl was struggling to stay awake, and Amanda was stuck for a new direction to take. They had gone through the story three more times and no new details had emerged. They were back at the starting point: Whoever Danny was in reality, he had grown up to be somebody very, very important. And someone else, Gideon, was trying to use Carl and the book he'd been writing to bring him down. Somehow Danny must have gotten wind of this plot. As a result, two women were dead and Carl was on the run. And here they were in Amanda's cozy house picking through the remains of lukewarm corned beef and cabbage, trying to make sense of the whole thing.

"We've got a few specifics now," Amanda said. "We've just got to figure out how to use them to find out who Danny really is."

"And Gideon."

"And why Gideon is trying to ruin Danny."

"Danny's obviously someone who has a whole lot to lose," Carl murmured.

"And not just money," Amanda added, "or we'd be talking about a simple case of blackmail. Danny's got to be someone with real power. Or position. Fame . . ."

"What about the new guy who just took over as head of that Christian right group?"

"The United in Christ Coalition?"

"There's been a real power grab over there, hasn't there?"

"He doesn't murder little boys," Amanda pointed out sharply. "He just diddles them."

Carl cocked his head at her. "Really?"

She nodded. "Common knowledge around town. If someone truly wanted him out, it would be a snap. They wouldn't have to bother rat-fucking him with a book. Do you have any other possibilities?"

He drained his beer and sat back in the chair, gazing up at the ceiling. "The hotshot governor of Alabama, the one who went to Princeton."

"Al Brady."

"He's very progressive. Putting a lot of money into public schools and job training. The *Times* keeps mentioning him as someone who has a national—"

"Why bother?" She dismissed this one with a wave of her hand. "He's been hospitalized twice for depression. His first wife divorced him because he's a bed wetter. And when he was in law school he lived with a drug dealer."

He stared at her for a long moment. "Nice crowd you're moving in."

"Look who's talking. Besides, people want to know what they're buy-ing. It's up to the press to look under the hood. Who else?"

He named the beloved anchor of the number-one-rated network news-cast. "He's the right age. And he grew up in Arkansas. But—"

"Right," she said, finishing the thought for him. "But so what? He'd lose his job. He'd write a soul-baring memoir that would go straight to number one on the best-seller list. He'd go on *60 Minutes* and cry. And probably just get an-other job on another network. Getting rid of him wouldn't change the course of history. It probably wouldn't even make anyone change the channel."

"So where the hell are we, then?" he asked. And when she didn't answer, he answered for her. "We're nowhere. That's where we are."

He was fading again. The mental strain and the physical pace he'd kept
up over the past several days had finally worn him out. Carl didn't even
make it to the spare bed, just lay down on the couch in the living room and
conked out. While he slept, Amanda stayed in the kitchen, smoking, drinking a diet Coke, and trying desperately to sort things out. After an hour, the
tobacco tasted stale, the soda seemed watery, and her brain was even more
muddled than before. She stubbed out her butt, went and stood over him,
watching him. Even asleep, he did not show signs of peace. He was tossing
and turning, breathing hard; from the kitchen she thought she'd even heard
him moaning and muttering. The terror he was living through had clearly
penetrated deep into his dreams. She stroked his hair and he stirred. For a
moment the tension left his face, and she grinned. There he was, the old
Granny. Then his eyes opened. He stared at her for a moment, uncompre-
hending, as if he didn't know where he was. When the fog cleared, he forced
himself to sit up. Took a deep breath and rubbed his eyes. Then it was time
to go back to work.

She told him that after a brief sleep, the brain sometimes did wonders.
New thoughts could penetrate, new memories could reveal themselves. So
they went through the story two more times. The first time she made him
tell everything he could remember about Harry Wagner. When he'd show
up, exactly what he'd said, what he cooked. The second time they concentrated on Maggie Peterson as their focus. Detail after detail came forth. He
recounted exactly what she'd said to him in her apartment. He told her
about Quadrangle, the name of the Apex imprint she said would be publishing the book.

"Who signed the check?" she wanted to know. "The check that Maggie
gave you."

"I don't have a clue," he told her.

"Was it a company check?"

"Of course."

"Well, what company?"

"I assume it was Apex."

"Bartholomew said no, didn't he?"

"That's what he said."

"Was it Quadrangle?" she pressed.

"Maybe." He shrugged.

"Your bank will have a record of it."

"Unfortunately," he pointed out, "if I try to find out, they'll also have me arrested."

"All right, we can work on that. What else?"

"Nothing else," he said. "Really. She told me why she wanted me to do the book, she liked the fact that I could keep a secret, she knew I could write fast—"

"That was important?"

"Very. I had about three weeks to write the whole thing. She said she wanted it to be published in six."

"That quickly?"

"That's what she said."

"Is that normal?"

"Not at all. Three *months'* delivery to publication would be an incredibly fast turnaround time for a regular book."

"When did you start?" Amanda asked.

"You know when. The day after Betty's funeral."

Amanda went and grabbed her calendar. "June eighteenth," she said. "That was the funeral."

"So I started that night."

"And three weeks from then is . . . that's now. Early July."

"Okay," he said. "What does that prove?"

"I don't know. But if she wanted it published three weeks after you turned it in, that'd put the pub date at the end of the month. Why?"

"Could be anything. Could be somebody's birthday."

"Or it could be something happening in July," she said. "An event. An opening of something, I don't know. What happens in July?"

"The fourth," he said. "That's an event."

"Very patriotic but pretty vague. What else?"

"The All-Star game. But somehow I doubt that's related."

She didn't dignify that with a response. They both sat in silence for a few moments. Then her mouth opened slightly and she turned her head toward him. Their eyes met and he nodded.

"I think I might be thinking the same thing," he told her. "But what does it have to do with Gideon?"

"The presidential convention," Amanda breathed.

"It's in New Orleans. In about three weeks."

"That's a hell of an event."

"A nonevent," Carl said, shaking his head slowly. "Adamson's the most popular president since Reagan. Even *you* like him, and you don't like *any* politicians."

"I do like him," she agreed. "He can remember his own name in a meeting without looking at a cue card, he can speak in complete English sentences without using a speechwriter, and he's managed to be president almost four whole years without getting sued by a member of the Bimbo of the Month Club. That gives him a major leg up on his predecessors. The fact that he's managed to keep the country from falling apart is pure gravy."

"Plus he's married to St. Lizzie."

"I hate that nickname. It's so sexist. Just because she's smart and strong on her own, she gets slammed."

"I'd hardly say she gets slammed. The press treats her like royalty."

"Well, she deserves a lot of it. She does a lot of good things. She's building a whole infrastructure of inner-city health clinics. She's doing more for education than anyone since God knows when. And the same for the rights of pregnant women."

"I'm not arguing. I voted for the guy and I love his wife. Why are we even talking about them?"

Amanda shrugged. "Just examining every angle. What else would tie in to a book pub in July?"

"You know," Carl said slowly, "as long as we're being thorough . . . Adamson *does* qualify in one regard. He's certainly got a lot to lose. He's a shoo-in for reelection in November, no matter who runs against him."

"Especially if it's Walter Chalmers. The senior senator from the great state of Wyoming presently trails the president by twenty points in every poll."

"Because Chalmers is a right-wing racist gun nut who's living in the nineteenth century and terrifies anybody who actually hears him speak. He's crazy." The words hung there between them. "I guess," Carl said slowly, "the question we have to ask ourselves is . . . just how crazy is he?"

"Are you asking if he was crazy enough to murder a little child?"

Carl exhaled a great swoosh of breath. "Yeah," he said. "I guess that's what I'm asking."

"Even if it were true, why would Adamson bother? It's going to be the biggest landslide election since . . ." She stopped short.

"Since Nixon and McGovern?" he finished. "When Nixon was ahead by twenty points in the polls and still went ahead with the Watergate break-in?"

"I agree he's a nightmare, but Senator Chalmers as Danny? And President Adamson as Gideon? It just seems too crazy."

"Maybe Adamson doesn't even know about it. Maybe it's one of his aides. Or maybe it's the other way around. Maybe it's Chalmers as Gideon."

"And the president as Danny?" She stared at him as if he'd lost his mind.

"Hey," he said, "we're just examining all the angles, remember? And some of them come into play. Adamson's from the South, he's about the right age . . ."

"Do you remember the campaign?" she said with an incredulous laugh. "You're talking about the most scrutinized president in U.S. history. How many biographies have been written? There isn't a detail of Tom Adamson's life that hasn't been pored over, investigated, and reinvestigated. If that man ever had a brother—a half-brother, a stepbrother, legitimate, illegitimate, black, brown, yellow, simian, alien—don't you think we would have found out by now?"

"What about Bickford?"

"What about him?"

"He's vice president. A heartbeat away. Maybe he wants to be the Man."

"First of all, if Jerry Bickford had wanted to be president, he would have run for president. He's a kingmaker, he's not a king. He's also the most honest politician we've had since . . . probably since George Washington."

He stuck his lower lip out, considering this. "I guess."

"There's also a rumor going around about him. That he's sick. A small stroke or something. He's kind of dropped out of sight the last few days, and no one's quite sure what's going on. But I guarantee you, Jerry Bickford's not involved in any of this. That's just crazy, Carl. It's really, really crazy."

"You're right," he said slowly. "It's crazy."

Without any warning, he stepped over to her and planted a soft kiss on top of her head. Then he headed toward the front door, his stride steady and purposeful.

"Wait a second," she said. "Where are you going?"

"I'm going to do what I should have done at the beginning—turn myself in. Before things get even crazier. And something even worse happens."

She almost smiled. "What could be worse?"

Without even a trace of a smile, he said softly, "They could come looking for you. That's the worst thing I could possibly imagine."

She walked over to him, gently rubbed the side of his cheek with her hand. Their bodies were close, touching when they swayed. "We're in this together," she told him, her voice low and urgent. "And I want you to stay."

His hand went up to touch hers. Their fingers entwined. "Amanda . . ."

Gently but firmly she untwined the fingers. "Don't start getting sentimental," she said. "This has nothing to do with you and me." She slipped her hand out of his grasp, but her body still leaned up against his. "This is strictly professional."

He frowned at her, not quite believing what he heard. "Professional?"

"Absolutely. You don't think I can pass up a story like this, do you?" And before he could answer, she said, "I'm a journalist. I'm supposed to be able to find people." She took a step back, gave him a determined nod. "So let's cut the shit and go find Harry Wagner."

chapter 15

Punching in the numbers on his cellular phone, placing the call that would irrevocably change his life, H. Harrison Wagner was afraid.

When he identified himself to the English voice on the other end of the phone and there was a distinct pause, Harry knew that he had the element of surprise on his side. With surprise came control. And, usually, with control came victory. Even over a man like Lindsay Augmon. But waiting for Augmon to respond, Harry did not feel victorious. His blood ran cold, a chill swept through his entire body, and he thought: *Hang up. Hang up and forget all your well-thought-out plans. Just run. As far and as fast as you can.* But then the man on the other end recovered his composure. He no longer sounded surprised when he calmly said, "How did you get this number?"

"Have you forgotten who I work for?" Harry said.

"No." Augmon sighed. "I haven't forgotten."

"Then don't ask stupid questions." Harry was pleased. His voice showed no sign of stress, no hint of nerves. "You've gotten my communications?"

Augmon hesitated. Then said, "Yes, of course I have." There was a resignation to his tone, as if this conversation had been inevitable. As if everything that Harry had asked for, everything Harry had done, had been preordained. The Englishman sounded weary and slightly impatient.

"I know everything," Harry said.

"You know a lot," the voice on the other end admitted. "But not everything."

"I know enough to fuck you up, pal," Harry said. "And fuck you up big time."

"Your threats have already been made and taken into consideration," Augmon said. "There's no need for you to embellish them. I have had greater experts than yourself try to intimidate me and, believe me, it's a waste of your energy and my time."

"Fine. No more embellishment. Let's just get down to business. Write down this number." Harry, clearly and distinctly, barked out a nine-digit number.

"Your bank account?"

"Good," Harry said. "I'm impressed."

"Cayman Islands?"

"*Very* good."

"And how much would you like wired into it?" the man wanted to know.

"For you, spare change. For me, my retirement fund. Five million dollars."

"May I ask how you arrived at that figure?"

"I'm not greedy," Harry told him. "I figure it's enough to keep me happy, not enough for you to bother coming after me."

"I'm sorry you decided to switch sides," the man on the phone said. "You could have been quite helpful."

"I'm not switching sides," Harry responded. "There's only one side. Always has been. Mine. I need the money by tomorrow."

"You can have it in thirty minutes. One hour, to be on the safe side. If you give me a number, I'll call you as soon as it's arranged."

"I'll call you," Harry said. "One hour." And without another word, he disconnected the phone.

Harry expected the fear to disappear when he hung up. But it didn't. It was inside him, clutching at his stomach and his kidneys and his throat. It would not let go, and that surprised him. Fear was not something he generally lived with. The fact was, he could only remember three times in his life that he'd been scared.

The first was when he was nine years old. He was living in Buffalo, New York, and his best friend, Timmy McGirk, was moving to Hawaii. Timmy's father was a career army officer and he'd been transferred there. Everyone in school was incredibly jealous. But not Harry. Harry was distraught. He cried when Timmy broke the news, and Timmy had to comfort him. Timmy told Harry he could visit anytime he wanted and they would learn how to surf.

Hey, maybe you can learn the hula, Timmy had said, poking him in the chest and laughing.

The young Harry Wagner never made it to Hawaii. Neither did Timothy McGirk. The plane carrying Tim, his younger sister, and both their parents crashed into the Pacific Ocean approximately thirty minutes before reaching Honolulu. There was some kind of electrical fire in the rear of the plane and the whole thing turned into a flying inferno. According to the newspaper accounts, it was highly unlikely that any passengers were still alive by the time the flaming hulk hit the water. They had long since been asphyxiated and burned to a crisp.

After that, Harry had been afraid to fly. Afraid of falling. The fear took over almost every waking minute. Looking out the window from the high floor of a building, he would break into a cold sweat and his knees would get weak. When his family was driving over a bridge, he would have to close his eyes and crouch on the floor of the car. Sometimes in school he couldn't even hear the teacher because all his brain was picturing was a huge jet, falling, falling, faster and faster and then . . .

And then nothing.

Over time the fear became manageable, but it was still present. Then, when Harry turned eighteen, he forced himself to take flying lessons. He was in college by then, the state university at Binghamton. He took a job at an all-night diner, throwing frozen potatoes into vats of boiling-hot grease, to pay for the lessons. Although his airborne performance was beyond reproach technically, every time he got behind the controls of that twin-engine Cessna he was frozen with terror. The instructor, whose name was Rigney, was extraordinarily handsome, in his mid-thirties. His skin was always a perfect bronze color, even in the dead of winter; his teeth were sparkling white; and his smile was as cocky as it was dazzling. Harry was in awe of Rigney, who, while in the air, would constantly regale the younger man with stories about his winter job. Every December Rigney would pack up, fly down to the Caribbean, and operate his own charter, carrying whoever and whatever needed carrying from island to island. It was four months, he said, of flying, sun, and pussy, the three greatest things in life. Harry would listen to the wild tales with his sweating hands wrapped around the controls, desperately wanting Rigney to notice him and tell him

he was doing a good job, desperately wanting Rigney to like him, but wanting even more to make it back down to safety, to get the hell out of the
clouds and feel his wobbly legs on firm ground. Rigney picked up on his
pupil's fear and didn't want to let him solo, even after he'd done the required
hours. But Harry had insisted and the instructor had no real reason, other
than instinct, to hold him back.

Harry believed that Rigney had picked up on more than just his fear. He
believed that Rigney, underneath his cocky smile and cynical eyes, knew
everything about him. He thought that Rigney had the ability to look inside
him and see the real him. See what Harry Wagner really wanted. See what
Harry Wagner really *was*.

On his off days Harry began to follow Rigney around. Secretly. Just
watching him from afar. He was certain that Rigney never knew, and Harry
got better and better at trailing him down the street. He could keep up with
him for blocks and blocks, ducking into doorways and dodging behind
passersby when need be. He even found out where Rigney lived, and sometimes he would go to his house late at night. He would hide in the bushes
and peer into the lit windows. Sometimes he would climb a big maple tree
in Rigney's front yard and crouch in the branches, just watching. There
were always women inside, young, attractive women who laughed at everything Rigney said and moaned loudly every time Rigney kissed them.
Sometimes Rigney would come to the window, one of his women begging
him to come to bed. But Rigney would stare out at the yard and Harry
would freeze, terrified that Rigney might see him. Once Rigney stood like
that, naked, his body framed in the light from the bedroom lamp. He stood
for fifteen minutes, maybe longer, just staring. Harry crouched down in the
branches of the tree, sweating, willing himself to disappear behind the
camouflage of the leaves. Then Rigney turned away, laughing, and jumped
into bed with his pouting partner.

The day before Harry's first solo flight, Rigney insisted on taking him
up one last time. Harry hadn't slept in a week, hadn't eaten in almost as
long. For over a month, minutes before every lesson began, he'd gone into
the men's room at the tiny upstate airport and gotten the dry heaves so bad,
he'd cough up blood into the rusty sink.

When they went up for their final session before the solo, Rigney was uncharacteristically quiet. No leering talk of flying babes in bikinis, no cheery chatter about three-martini flights and blow jobs in the pilot's seat. He told Harry he wanted to simulate the next day's solo flight, wanted Harry to feel as if he were totally alone. It didn't take long before they were soaring, encased in silence save for the steady hum of the plane's engine. As always, Harry's mind forced its way back in time, let the picture of the burning jet return in all its paralyzing glory. Soaring above the cottony clouds, looking down at the roads and bridges and buildings below, all reduced to an unreal miniature landscape, Harry kept his hands clenched on the controls and waited until the ordeal could be over and he could once again get his feet back on the ground.

Except this time it was not so simple.

At ten thousand feet, half an hour into the two-hour session, Rigney reached over and began to reduce the power in the right engine.

"What are you doing?" Harry asked through clenched teeth.

"I want you to demonstrate emergency single-engine procedures."

"We've done this," Harry said.

"That's right," Rigney told him. "And we're gonna do it again."

The plane dipped suddenly, dropping maybe a hundred feet, and Harry thought his heart would literally burst from his chest. Mouth open, sweat pouring down his face, he turned to Rigney, incredulous. But the instructor only looked at him and said calmly, "Gotta see how you do when things go wrong."

Harry fought the urge to panic. He tasted his own bile rising up in his throat but choked it back and forced his mind to focus. It was only a test, he told himself. Rigney was just reducing power, not destroying it. *Right the plane, get it level, show him you know what you're doing, and he'll bring the power back up.*

He looked to his right. Rigney was making no move to restore power.

"You're going too far," Harry said.

"Maybe so," Rigney said. "Shit happens sometimes."

Harry heard the throat of the carburetor constrict. *Christ, the engine's off!*

"Restore power," Harry said. "Restore the goddamn power!"

"I'd like to, son," Rigney said, his calm and even tone infuriating Harry. "But if you remember any of the shit I been crammin' into your brain, you'll remember that the carburetor heat comes from the manifold. And once the engine stops, what happens?"

"No manifold," Harry breathed. "You son of a bitch. You froze the carburetor. You stupid, stupid son of a bitch."

"You can swear at me all you want," Rigney said, "but that ain't gonna get us home."

"You piece of shit!" Harry screamed. "We're going to die!"

"Not if you do what you know how to do."

Think, Harry told himself. *This lunatic's ready to die with you, so think, think, think.* But he couldn't think. He couldn't move. He couldn't do anything except see himself falling, falling all the way to earth, a great big ball of fire plummeting toward his death . . .

"We're losing speed," Harry said. "If we go below sixty-five knots, we'll stall. We'll lose the other engine."

Rigney said nothing.

"Help me," Harry pleaded. "Please help me."

Rigney folded his arms serenely. "I ain't even here," he said.

Harry Wagner was frozen. Paralyzed. And in the few moments he was ruled by indecision, the plane began spinning wildly out of control.

That was when Harry shit himself.

The noise and the smell filled the small plane, and Harry was certain he saw Rigney sneer. He was humiliated. And livid. It was the humiliation that finally overpowered his terror, because it was at that moment he began to focus. And to act.

Okay, some inner voice seemed to say. *Single-engine procedure. Lower the nose to build up airspeed. You can't dip below sixty-five.*

They were down to eighty knots. Seventy-five . . .

Harry gripped the controls and lowered the nose of the airplane. They must have fallen five thousand feet, maybe six. They were down to seventy-two knots per hour.

Check the oil pressure so you can feather the prop.

The oil pressure held steady. He twisted the angle of the remaining working propeller so that the leading edge was facing forward and aft, into the wind. The drag on the plane immediately eased. The speed had dipped to seventy. Now it began to climb, back up to seventy-five, then eighty . . .

They pulled out of their spin. And they stopped falling. They were going to make it.

They were going to make it!

Harry threw his head back and laughed. He looked at Rigney, whose
expression had never changed. His arms were still folded across his chest.
He hadn't even worked up a sweat. He was just staring over at Harry, looking at him curiously.

Harry was suddenly aware that the front of his pants was stained and
wet. He hadn't just shit in his pants, he'd pissed all over himself, too. His
hands were sweating, his stomach was cramping now. But the plane was
steady and was turned around, heading back toward the airport. They had
goddamn made it!

When he'd landed expertly on the runway and the plane screeched
to a halt, Rigney turned to Harry. He still said nothing. Just gazed into
Harry's eyes.

Harry knew that once again the pilot was looking into his very being,
and he wanted to scream. It took him a long time to return the pilot's gaze.
When he did, all he could say was, "Please stop looking at me."

"You did better than I thought you would," Rigney said. "You acted like
a man. You'll pass your test."

"Thank you," Harry mumbled.

"Don't thank me," Rigney said. "Just don't ever come back here again.
I don't want to see you ever again. Don't take any more lessons, don't hang
around the airport, don't follow me down the street."

"I—" But Harry didn't get another word out because Rigney slapped
him, hard, across the mouth. Harry's cheek turned red and he felt a trickle
of blood seep between two of his top front teeth.

"I've seen you following me. I know when you're there. And I know
you're outside my house."

"Please," Harry started to say, "I can explain. . . ." But Rigney's hand
flew forward again, and this slap was even harder. It rocked Harry's head
back, and for a moment he saw only darkness.

"Do your solo," Rigney told him. "Do what I taught you. Make me
proud. But know that if I ever see you in the bushes, if I ever catch you
watching me again, I'll kill you."

Harry didn't bother to answer back. He unbuckled his seat belt, stepped unsteadily out of the plane, and walked away, never looking back at Rigney. The next day he showed up for his first solo flight. Nothing went wrong; the solo was as smooth as it could be.

Harry Wagner knew he would never be afraid of flying again.

The next time Harry felt fear was two years later. It was his first sexual experience.

The woman was twenty-seven, several years older than he was. She was divorced, with a four-year-old son. Her name was Helen and she had exquisite legs, long and muscular, and tiny breasts, almost nonexistent. Her hair was brown and thick, her skin was a little rough and slightly too pale, and he could smell her sweet shampoo when she stood next to him. They met at a party. Harry wasn't invited to many parties—even then he was a loner, separate from most of the other students—but he'd gone to this one. He wasn't sure why; maybe he'd been lonely, maybe he'd been looking for someone like Helen. And there she was. She said she'd come with a date but that he'd gotten drunk with his buddies and had disappeared. Harry thought she was lying, using that as an excuse to get rid of him, but he said that he wasn't trying to steal her from her date. He just thought they could talk. She smiled and nodded and looked pleased that she'd met someone with manners, so they talked quietly in a corner. And they drank. And soon Harry began to realize that she was staring hungrily at his muscular arms, at the lean V-shape of his body from shoulders to waist. He felt a gnawing in the pit of his stomach. He felt panic. He decided that this woman wanted him. He wanted her, too, and was surprised at how much he wanted her, but he didn't know if he could perform. He never had before. Harry felt himself begin to tremble, felt his throat constrict. He got drunk for the first time in his life that night, until he worked up the nerve to ask if he could go home with her. He had pictured in his mind exactly how it would be. She would nod and take his hand and lead him home to her apartment. But that wasn't how it was. When he asked if he could take her home, when he managed to get the words out, she looked at him curiously and said no. He was mortified, desperately embarrassed, and he apologized profusely. She laughed and said that she wasn't offended, she was flattered, but that he still couldn't come home with her. She had a son, she said, and she didn't bring men home to her apartment. Besides, they had just met. She said that perhaps they could go to dinner sometime, really get to know each other, but Harry knew that she was only feeling sorry for him. He knew that she didn't want to really get to know him better. She wanted him to leave.

So he left.

An hour later Helen left the party, too. Her apartment was not far; she walked the distance quickly, if a bit unsteadily after having had so much to drink. When she got home, she tried to unlock her front door, missed the lock with her key on the first attempt, chuckled aloud to herself, then used both hands to get the key into the slot. It took about five minutes for the baby-sitter to leave, cash still clutched in her hand. Helen was only inside the apartment alone for a few seconds before the doorbell rang. When she opened the door, Harry was certain she was quite surprised to see him standing there.

His closed hand went up so quickly she didn't have time to dodge the hard punch to the side of her cheek. She was knocked back so hard that she didn't utter a sound. He forced her to the ground and banged her head quickly against the wood floor. Not *too* hard, just hard enough. He wanted her conscious. He wanted her to be able to enjoy this experience.

He ripped off her skirt, tore her blouse in half. Grabbed her panties in his fist and yanked them free. She started to speak, but when she saw the look in his eyes, she stopped. She just closed her mouth and nodded. He climbed on top of her, placed his lips against hers, kissed her long and hard, forcing his tongue inside her mouth, bit her on the neck, then on the shoulder. When it was time, he didn't have to say anything; she took his penis in her hands and guided it inside her.

Harry performed. Quite well, in fact. He could tell by her passionate moans during the act, by her thrashing legs, by the way she lay so still afterward, never even bothering to cover her bare breasts.

He lay on the floor there with her for several hours. When it was near dawn and time to go, when he saw her glance toward a back bedroom, knowing that her young son might emerge sometime soon, Harry Wagner leaned down to her and whispered in her ear. When she didn't respond, he grabbed the back of her hair and pulled, hard. He leaned forward and whispered to her again. He could see the confusion in her eyes as well as the fear. He yanked harder on her. "I just told you something," he said. "Now don't you have something to say to me in return?"

She nodded. A quick, terse motion. She understood. He felt relieved. And happy.

"Well, say it, then," he prompted.

"I love you, too," she whispered.

After that night with Helen, Harry Wagner knew something about himself as a man. His knowledge was irrevocable and strangely satisfying. And he was no longer afraid.

In the years since, Harry Wagner had risen to the top of his profession. He had endured great pain, physical and mental, and even risked death on a regular basis. He had suffered loneliness and abandonment and even humiliation. But deep down, there had been no more fear in his life. Not even a twinge. Until now, standing in the living room of his small, comfortable, ranch-style suburban house. And this fear was the most overwhelming of his life.

Harry, above all, feared the loss of control. His ex-wife, Allison, had screamed at him, that messy day she'd gone away. "Jesus, Harry," she'd cried. "You want to control what I do, what I think, when I fucking breathe!" He had slapped her, hard, knowing what was coming. He didn't want to hear it, but she spit it at him anyway. "You're a fucking animal! You can't even control yourself! You can't even control your—"

That's when he hit her again. Harder, knocking her down. It was surprising how much pleasure it gave him. He had never really derived pleasure from hitting women. Then she left, gone for good, so he could never hit her again.

It had been several days since he'd realized that she was right, he had indeed lost control of his own life. They had taken it away, used his weakness to exploit and manipulate him, to blackmail him. It seemed impossible that he could be blackmailed. The word itself brought about a feeling of revulsion and contempt. But there it was: He was being blackmailed. He had thought this through, examined every angle, sifted through every bit of minutiae trying to find a solution. It was what he was good at. It was what he *did*—find solutions. But he had never been in a situation like this before. He had never come up against this kind of strength.

The first thing he had to do was to face the reality of this particular predicament. Pretense, false comfort, was of no value to him now. He needed logic, facts, if he was to have any hope of surviving. They had what they needed to destroy the life he'd so carefully built, and he knew they'd have no qualms about such destruction. The reality was that they had him by the balls and not only were they squeezing, they were letting him know that they could squeeze a hell of a lot harder whenever they wanted.

They had left him with only two options.

He could go on as he had been, doing what they wanted, when they wanted. He could do the dirty work and be a glorified messenger boy. In his head, he played that option out as dispassionately as possible. It did not come to a happy conclusion.

Harry understood that once the decision had been made to use Gideon, the stakes had gotten extraordinarily high. The game had risen to a new and extreme level. The bottom line was that the winner could not afford to leave the other players around once the game was over. They could not risk someone talking. Or thinking. Harry knew that he might last a little while longer, as long as he was useful. But ultimately his usefulness would come to an end. And when that happened, well . . . he didn't think they'd put a lot of stock in his loyalty. The editor, Maggie Peterson, had been loyal, as loyal as he'd been. Her loyalty had gotten her skull crushed. Ignorance was no help, either. The two women he'd killed down South had been innocent bystanders, murdered only to make a statement. The girl found in the apartment upstairs from Carl, also innocent. A nobody who hadn't even known she'd become a player in the game. Harry could hardly claim ignorance, in any case. He'd known what was happening, all right. Okay, not every detail perhaps, but he could connect the dots. He understood the level of power at which this game was being played. He understood that at this level, human life was unimportant. Even his.

He didn't know how many others had been killed along the way. He assumed there were several. He did know that Carl Granville had somehow managed to survive. At least until now. But he didn't have a prayer. The kid was dead meat. It was a miracle he'd lasted this long.

Well, it was too bad. He'd gotten to like Carl. But he'd done what he could for him. Harry didn't have time to worry about such things. He'd made his move. He had shown them that they were dealing with a player. Someone who knew the rules. And knew how to get around them.

In twenty-four hours Harry was going to disappear.

That was option number two, and it was the only one that made sense. If he stayed, they'd kill him. In the long run, that was a certainty. In the meantime, in the immediate here and now, his prospects weren't very pleasant either: servitude, obeisance. No, thank you. Been there, done that.

He had one key advantage, of course. He had been invisible to them for so long, they tended to underestimate him. He had stood nearby, as unimportant to them as a guard dog. But he had listened. He had learned. He understood the way they thought, the devious way they plotted. *One is not superior merely because one sees the world as odious.* Chateaubriand had said that. Harry smiled, knowing he had improved on it. He was not superior because he saw the world as odious. He was superior because he saw the odiousness before anyone else. And so he was prepared.

That's what he'd been doing for some weeks now. Preparing.

It surprised and depressed him a little just how easy it was to erase his life.

The furniture in the house had been sold in bulk to a company that rented out furniture for offices, parties, and unfurnished apartments. Taking cash in exchange for a greater discount, he'd managed to clear a little under ten thousand dollars for everything in the house. It had been arranged that all services for the house—phone, gas, electric, garbage pickup, newspapers— would be severed starting tomorrow, and everything had been paid in full. The house itself, he was just leaving. It was a rental, gotten through a company that specialized in relocating government workers, and it wasn't worth the risk to try to get back the three months' advance rent he'd had to put down for security. Better to eat the loss. Besides, it was peanuts. At least now it was. Comparatively.

He did own a small two-bedroom condominium nearby, just a couple of hundred yards from the water. He'd bought it long ago and had paid off the mortgage. Since he owned it free and clear, he was able to price it low, and it sold almost as soon as it came on the market. He cleared a hundred and fifteen thousand dollars—an all-cash transaction. He had thought about rolling over his income savings plan into another tax-protected account. But he decided, after several days of agonizing, that he couldn't risk tipping them off that he might be leaving his job. He hated to leave the money behind, but he couldn't afford to be greedy. Too often greed was the downfall of men looking to move from one life to another. Along with the sale of his stocks, bonds, and all other assets, he'd wire-transferred $147,000 to the Waverly Bank in the Cayman Islands. All local bank accounts under his own name were now closed. All charge accounts, closed. Because only birth certificates were checked, not death certificates, he'd gone to a nearby graveyard and appropriated the name of a dead baby found on a headstone—and as a result he had a new Social Security number and passport. He also had brand-new American Express, Visa, and MasterCard accounts, each listed under a separate and different name. In each of those names, he now had checking accounts set up through the bank in the Cayman Islands and accessible through a check-writing and financial-planning program installed in his computer. The final item on his economic checklist: Alimony checks were stopped. If he was disappearing, he might as well get in a final "fuck you" to Allison.

He had a roving 800 fax number built into his computer and a non-area-specific cell phone number as well. When he needed to give out such information, there would be no way to trace his actual location. His means of communication traveled with him.

Everything was set. Everything except the final phone call. And when that was completed, he'd have enough money to live on comfortably for quite a few years, depending on how thrifty he wanted to be. Four years should be long enough to see how it all played out. He'd know if it was safe to surface. If not, if he lasted that long, he'd certainly have figured out a way to make a living by then. If he needed to.

Harry picked up his cell phone and dialed the number he'd committed to memory. It was exactly sixty minutes since he'd hung up after his last call.

"You're very precise," the man on the other end of the phone said.

"You can skip the flattery. Was the transfer made?"

"All done," the voice said. "You can check to confirm."

"I intend to," Harry said.

There was a pause. "Well, then," the voice said. "I suppose I wish you luck."

"I don't need luck," Harry said. "All I need is twenty-four hours."

He hung up the phone. Immediately he went to his notebook computer, called up his financial service, and honed in on the proper bank account. Yes, there it was. Five million dollars. It was done. Tomorrow morning he'd be leaving. He would step into his little Cessna at eight A.M. It would take him four days of glorious, solitary flying, stopping in little airports across the country, to get to La Jolla, California. There he'd sell the plane to a less-than-reputable dealer he'd hooked up with on the Net. The price was half of what it was worth, but it was an all-cash deal and the recently counterfeited registration would not be looked at too closely, if at all. Then one night in San Diego. Then a four-hour commercial flight.

And then he'd be in Honolulu.

At long last he'd get to surf. *Hey,* he thought, *maybe I finally* will *learn to hula.*

And with that thought lingering, Harry Wagner decided he'd treat himself to one final celebration. Why not? He'd thought of everything. He'd done all that he could. He was as good as gone.

And suddenly Harry realized something. Something that, just fifteen minutes ago, he would not have thought possible.

He was no longer afraid.

chapter 16

They were still there.

The matches Harry had left behind on Carl's desk that day a million years ago. Carl had pocketed them while he stood, dazed and confused, in the ruins of what had once been his apartment. Now he dug them out of his rumpled, filthy blazer, along with Harry's celebratory cigar, which had miraculously remained whole inside its cellophane wrapper. He brought these to Amanda's dining table and laid them out there for the two of them to examine.

The matchbook was shiny and black. The striking surface was unused. There were three initials stamped across the face in raised gold lettering: *P.O.E.* Underneath, also in gold, was written the words *Port of Entry*. Nothing else was written on the front. The back was blank.

"Mean anything to you?" he asked Amanda as the two of them stood there studying it.

"Not a thing, other than the obvious nautical reference. You?"

"Could be where he buys his cigars," Carl suggested. "A store. A direct distributor. Maybe even some kind of wholesale outlet."

"Good answer. I like it. Based where, in New York?"

"Maybe. I've never heard of it, but then I'm not exactly a cigar maven."

Amanda considered this a moment. "Hmm . . ."

He peered at her curiously, knowing this particular doubtful sound only too well. "Yes?"

"Nothing. I was just thinking—wouldn't they have put their phone number on there? Or their address? If it were a business, I mean."

"You'd think so," he allowed, dropping the matchbook back into his pocket.

They turned their attention to the cigar. It was long. It was slim. It was Dominican. And it was no help.

"There must be *something* else," Amanda encouraged. "Something distinctive about him."

"What I mostly remember about Harry is he's really large and he makes a great omelet."

"Does he have any kind of an accent? Any inflection in his voice that might indicate what his background is?"

"None and no."

"*Concentrate,* Carl," she commanded, turning sterner. "Focus. Come on. Something the man said. Something the man did . . ."

Carl shook his head at her slowly. Until, abruptly, he snapped his fingers and said, "Would you settle for something he *wore*?"

She cocked her head at him, intrigued. "Explain."

"The name of his clothier. I saw it stitched on the inside pocket of his jacket once. It was Italian . . . it was . . ." Carl closed his eyes tight, trying to picture that expensive linen blazer hanging on the back of his bathroom door. Damn it, what was the name? What was the name? What was . . . "Marco," he exclaimed, his voice rising with triumph. "Marco Buonamico."

Her face broke into a smile. "That's good, Carl. That's really good."

"You know the name?"

"No, but I know someone who will—the fashion editor at the paper." Amanda started to reach for the phone on the kitchen counter, but Carl beat her to it.

"Wait!" he cautioned, and she froze in her tracks. His hand grabbed hers and guided it away from the receiver. "There's a good chance they're tapping your phone now."

"You really think so?"

"I do."

Amanda considered this a moment, her eyes narrowing. Then she shook her head. "They haven't had time to get a court order yet. And furthermore, I'm not even sure a judge would—"

"Time out. You're talking about the feebies."

"Well, yeah. Aren't you?"

"No," he said with quiet intensity. "I'm not."

She leveled a worried gaze at him, swallowing. "I see," she said. "You're talking about *they*."

"Whoever *they* are, that's who I'm talking about."

She reached for her cigarettes on the counter and lit one, dragging deeply on it. "There's always my cell phone . . . no, scratch that. Those are even easier to listen in on." Now she glanced at her watch. "I can go on-line," she said. "She should still be at the office."

"They can intercept e-mail, too," he said.

"No prob. I'll make it sound so totally innocuous that even if someone is intercepting my e-mail, they won't suspect a thing. It won't have anything to do with you. It'll just sound like I'm working on a story at home. Okay?"

He nodded. "Okay," he said. "Go for it."

She sat at her desk, fired up her computer, and logged on. Carl began pacing around the room, which was silent now except for the sound of her fingers racing madly over the keyboard. Amanda had worked her way through college typing term papers and dissertations. She was the fastest typist Carl had ever seen. Outside the window, it was dark. Inside, the air-conditioned little house seemed totally cut off from clock, from calendar, from reality. Briefly it reminded Carl of his own stint in college as a night-owl DJ on a radio station in Ithaca. Perched at the console in that sound-proofed booth, there was no sense of time. No sense of yesterday or tomorrow. Only right now.

Amanda fell silent at the keyboard, her eyes never leaving the screen. After a moment's pause, she said, "Come look." There was an edge of an-ticipation in her voice.

He hurried over to her. Standing over her shoulder, he read the reply.

```
Marco Buonamico is a très chic menswear boutique based in
Miami. Customers include Pat Riley, Sly Stallone, and their
reptilian ilk. Import their own line from Milan. Do a de-
cent catalog business. May expand to Beverly Hills soon.
What's your interest? Inquiring minds want to know.
```

"Well, shit," Carl fumed. "How am I going to get to Miami? It may as well be Mars. That's no help."

"Oh, yes, it is," Amanda said excitedly. "We are rolling now. Prepare to kick tush. Badda-boom!" She was now totally up—animated, enthusiastic, alive, cheeks flushed with color, nostrils flaring, eyes bright. The woman positively crackled with energy. She always got this way when she was hot after a story. It was one of the things that had first drawn Carl to her. Again her fingers started to fly over the keyboard. "I just have to find me Shaneesa."

"And who exactly is Shaneesa?"

"One of my babies. Straight out of the projects. She's six foot three with legs up to her neck, and the mayor gets silly every time she walks into the room. Her series on the D.C. government mess is going to earn her a Pulitzer nomination if I have anything to say about it."

"Okay, but what—"

"Do you remember that story last year about the sixteen-year-old boy from the projects who was arrested for rat-fucking the CIA's central computer?"

"Sure."

"Her baby brother. And guess what—it's a family gift."

"She's a hacker?"

Amanda nodded. "These days there isn't a major metropolitan daily in America that doesn't have one. We can't keep up with the tabloids without a hacker. They should teach a course on it at Columbia Journalism School. But in the meantime, it's a dirty little secret. Shaneesa is ours. Make that mine. I'm the one who found her. Aha! Got her . . ."

Carl read over Amanda's shoulder as they conversed on-line.

```
[What up, girlfriend?]
[What it is, back at ya.]
[Can you download catalog mailing list for male thread
emporium called Marco Buonamico and kick it my way?]
[Hmmm . . . may take a while, sweetness.]
[Define a while.]
[Three minutes?]
[God, you're good!]
[And God knows it, too. Now if only he'd pass the word
on to Mr. Grant Hill for me. Later.]
```

Amanda got up from her desk chair, arching her back, and went into the kitchen to put on more coffee. Carl paced the room like a caged animal, his eyes never leaving that computer screen.

Shaneesa was off a little bit in her prediction. It didn't take her three minutes to hack her way into the clothier's mailing list. It took her two.

"Success," reported Carl, who jumped into the pilot's seat and started scanning. "Here are the *U's* . . . *V's* . . . Check this out—Jim Varney buys his clothes there. . . . Wachtel . . . Waggoner . . . *Wagner,* H. Harrison. Amanda, you are not going to believe this."

She came out of the kitchen toward him. "He's a size forty-four long?"

"He lives in Bethesda."

"Maryland? That's less than ten miles from here."

Carl contemplated the implications of this, his exhausted mind racing. Was Harry associated with the government? If so, in what capacity? Who was he? What was he?

"Do you have a phone book?"

She bent down to the bottom drawer of the big desk and pulled out a stack of D.C. area phone books—Arlington, Alexandria, Annapolis, Silver Spring, and Bethesda. The only problem was that Harry had an unlisted number. He wasn't in the book.

"Looks like I'm going to pay the man a visit."

"*You're* going to pay him a visit?"

"That's right."

"Without me?"

"That's definitely right."

She already had her car keys out and her purse thrown over her shoulder. "I don't think so."

"Amanda—" was all he managed to get out.

"I'm going, Carl. That's all there is to it."

"Give me the car keys, will you?"

"No."

"This is a bad idea. A really bad idea. Trust me on this. You do not want to—"

"Whatever you think it is I don't want to do, believe me, I'm already doing it. And what do you think *you're* going to do? Just drive through the center of town, nice and slow, stopping at every stop sign so you can let everybody in town take a good look at a face that's been on the front page of every paper in the country and staring out at them from their television sets for the last twenty-four hours? Good thinking." She spun on her heel and started for the door to the garage. "Besides, it's my car and I'm driving it. Now, let's go."

"God, you're stubborn," he muttered.

She stopped, turned back to him, and smiled. "You missed me, didn't you?"

"Let's go!" he barked.

Carl got in the car first. Amanda waited for him to fold his large blond self—or try to fold his large blond self—into the leg space down under the Subaru's glove compartment before she hit the button that opened the garage door. If anyone were staking the place out, it would appear as if she were leaving the house alone.

"Are you going to be okay?" she asked, concerned at the awkward way in which he was squashed in.

"Fine," he groaned.

"I didn't know the human neck could bend that way."

"It can't. Just go, will you?"

The engine wouldn't kick over on the first try. Or the second.

"Glad to see you've had it serviced since I saw you last."

Ignoring him, she concentrated on turning the key in the ignition. On the fourth try the heap kicked over and she backed it out into the alley, her headlights off, her engine knocking. She aimed her remote control, clicked it, and the garage door slid closed. There was a crazy honeycomb of alleys behind her house. Here was where the service alleys built not only for the big Klingle houses but for the ones on Cleveland Avenue, Cathedral Avenue, and Thirty-second Street all butted into each other, converged, merged, and then broke off again in a million different directions. They existed on no map, but Amanda had gotten to know them well, even in the dark. Carl could feel every bump as she steered the little wagon at breakneck speed in between trash cans, around parked cars, and alongside garden fences. She veered onto the alley behind Cleveland on two wheels, brakes screeching, then floored it, braked again, and came out on Cathedral, where they joined the flow of conventional, law-abiding evening traffic.

No one was on their tail.

"I think I missed my calling," she burbled excitedly, flicking on the headlights. "I should have been a cabdriver."

Carl sat up in his seat like a person and tried to stretch the kinks out of nearly every part of his body. They drove in silence for several minutes. They were now out in the real world. No more strategizing, no more planning, no more Clint Eastwood–like fast rides through back alleys. They were stepping into a hole, and they didn't know how big or how deep or how dangerous it really was. He glanced at Amanda, who was a picture of intense concentration as she piloted the car through the city streets, her small, delicate hands tightly gripping the wheel.

"Carl," she said, driving along, "this Harry Wagner person. If he's one of *they* . . ."

"He is, Amanda."

"Then why do you think you can trust him?"

"I don't know if I can. I have a gut feeling, is all. I spent a lot of time alone with him in my apartment. I just feel that Harry's someone I don't have to be afraid of."

"The situation may be different now," she pointed out. "He might even be the one who's been doing all the killing."

"True," he acknowledged.

"So how do you know he won't try to kill you the second you walk in the door?"

"I don't," he told her. And when she turned her head ever so slightly to look at him, her eyes round and wide, he shrugged and said, "Hey, welcome to my world."

chapter 17

Harry Wagner had been sitting at the long teakwood bar for an hour and fifteen minutes and had been hit on by three people so far. Although he would have liked a little time to sit and drink alone, he didn't resent the intrusions. On the contrary, it made him happy. He was desirable, he knew. He had come to Port of Entry to be hit on. To feel desirable. That was the point. That was why he always went there.

The brunette had been an easy turndown, sweaty and nervous. And too skinny—*scrawny* was the word Harry would use. Besides, the pickup was a halfhearted one.

"You look lonely," the brunette had said, and smiled hopefully.

Harry hadn't even bothered to respond, just shook his head as if he didn't want to be bothered, and the brunette went away as if expecting the rejection.

The one with the streaked gray hair was borderline. A good body, perhaps a tad too chunky. But confident-looking. Calm. Not desperate at all. The conversation was boring, though. No spark. No real sign of intelligence.

"Me, I don't like politics," the gray-haired one said. "I'm into interpersonal relationships, you know what I mean?"

Harry knew. He passed.

The redhead was very close. Tall, muscular, reasonably interesting.

"What do you do?" Harry asked.

"I'm a jewelry designer. See this earring? I made it. Twisted the little rings myself. That's why I have such strong hands."

"Strong arms, too, from the looks of it," Harry said.

"And even stronger legs." The redhead's eyes blinked playfully. "Tennis is one of my favorite sports."

"You must be fast."

"On *and* off the court."

The redhead even liked football. A Redskins fan. Yes, the redhead was very close, and Harry might have gone along for the ride on a normal evening. But this was anything but a normal evening. This was a most special occasion. This was his farewell appearance. So Harry decided to sip his second Maker's Mark on the rocks and hold out for perfection.

And then perfection walked in the door.

Almost everyone in the bar turned as the man in the black jeans walked in—no, didn't walk, slithered. And it wasn't really a man. It was a boy. A glorious, lovely boy who couldn't have been more than nineteen. The most beautiful boy Harry had ever seen.

Harry Wagner could feel his heart pound and his cock stiffen, and he knew that for his special night, he had to have this very special creature.

It had been a long time since Harry had realized he was a homosexual. He suspected it when he used to lie awake in bed and think about his school friend, Timmy McGirk. It began to gnaw away at him when he would get knots of jealousy in his stomach watching the pilot, Rigney, make love to his steady stream of women. And he'd known for certain since the night he had made love, with Helen, for the very first time. He had not accepted this sexual identity at first. He'd tried to ignore it, then fight it. But it was what he was, and gradually he realized he could not change that side of him. It had cost him his wife and it was costing him his job, and ultimately it would cost him his very identity, but looking at this man-child, Harry didn't care. He would not have changed a thing. He was practically bursting from within, barely able to contain his excitement. This was magnificent. And it must be his.

The boy was close to six feet and slender, wiry and muscular with very white skin. He had the lithe movements of a dancer. His jeans were skintight, and he wore a loose, flowing white shirt under a black suede sport jacket. His eyes were large and piercingly blue. For Harry it was like peering into the blue of the ocean on a hot summer day, with the sun reflecting off calm water. The boy's white fedora was worn at a jaunty angle, but when he took it off, Harry saw that his hair was very black and straight, cropped short on the sides and just long enough on top for a few strands to tumble over onto his smooth forehead. When he sat at a table, he was immediately enveloped by a wave of middle-aged men offering drinks, food, and probably their very souls. He smiled politely—Harry was sure he was used to this kind of attention—and declined several of the drink offers while accepting several of the others. He spent the next hour fending off advances in a very gentlemanly but firm manner. Harry, watching him, knew that this boy was also looking for something special. This boy was used to something special.

In another hour the bar began to quiet down a bit. Harry was able to make eye contact with the boy. Nothing flashy, just a nod, a quick smile, something to acknowledge the gorgeous creature's presence. Their eyes held slightly longer than necessary. The boy nodded and his lips curled up ever so slightly in a silent communication of disdain for the crowd around him. At that point Harry knew that he had him.

Half an hour later Harry walked over and sat down at the boy's table. Without so much as a greeting or word of introduction, he signaled the waiter over and ordered a Maker's Mark and a dark rum and tonic, which was what he'd noticed the boy was drinking. He then pulled a Dominican cigar out of his jacket pocket and handed it across the table. They smoked the same brand and this pleased the boy, warmed his eyes.

Harry was tongue-tied, so taken was he with the beauty across the table. He started talking about the D.C. heat, the stifling humidity.

"I don't really want to talk about the weather, do you?" the boy asked.

"No," Harry said.

"Well, what *do* you want to talk about?" the boy said.

"You," Harry told him, and the boy laughed, pleased.

"That's a fascinating subject," he said, still smiling.

"It is to me," Harry told him. "It is to me."

So the boy told him a little bit about himself, in a throaty, smoky voice. He had an aura that seemed to belong to someone of a different era. Montgomery Clift, perhaps. His name was Chris and he was not as young as Harry had thought, but still young—twenty-two. He was from upstate New York, not too far from where Harry had grown up. He'd gone to school in Boston. Boston College, not Harvard. "No," he said with a husky laugh, "I'm not smart enough for Harvard." But he was smart enough to have a degree in finance, although he was in no rush for a job. He'd made a little bit of money playing the market and he wanted to travel a bit. That's what he was doing there now, traveling with some friends from Vermont. Having some fun. Before he became a grown-up, he said, he wanted to play.

"I like to play," he told Harry. "As long as I know the rules."

Harry was not interested in rules this night. He wanted fucking. He wanted passion, maybe even something a little rough. Something he'd remember.

It didn't take long before Chris was leaning over and touching Harry's arm, running his fingers up and down, and smiling. Everyone in the bar was watching. Harry loved being the center of attention. *Look at all these envious old queens,* he thought. *Let them get their own trophy. Keep away from mine.*

It was Harry who suggested getting out of there. The boy seemed reticent—not fearful, more like he was worried he'd been playing at a game that had just gone too far. But Harry soothed him, put no pressure on, made him laugh. And soon the boy nodded, looking Harry up and down, and said, "Why don't we go back to your place?"

Harry explained to him that he was in the process of moving. "I don't have any furniture," Harry said.

Chris just looked at him and smiled. "There's always the floor."

It was normally a twenty-minute drive from Georgetown and Port of Entry to Harry's house, but tonight Harry made the trip very slowly. The boy was following in his own car—a blue Chevy Suburban that he told Harry belonged to his friend from Vermont.

"It's fun to drive," Chris said. "It's so butch."

When Harry asked him about the cartoon and the logo stenciled onto the side of the Suburban, Chris shook his head mockingly and said, "Andy runs a day care center in Putney." Then he rolled his eyes and said, "Don't ask, don't tell—that's my motto."

When they got to the house, Harry mixed them each another drink. The boy sat on a window seat, sometimes gazing out the window, sometimes turning back to stare at his host. Harry was barely able to contain himself. It had been a long time since he had wanted to please someone as much as he wanted to please this lithe and lean dark-haired youngster.

When the boy beckoned Harry over with his finger, Harry knew that his real night of ecstasy was now about to begin. The boy never moved. He assumed that Harry would bend to meet him. And he did. Their lips met and they began to kiss. It was slow and elegant, tantalizingly erotic. Harry was getting aroused. This boy was extraordinary. Extraordinary!

They were standing now, near the middle of the living room, locked in an embrace. Harry's shirt was off. The boy's clothing was untouched. He was making it difficult for Harry. That was all right. Harry was prepared to beg if necessary.

When it felt right, Harry reached down and unzipped the boy's jeans. He reached in to grab the boy's cock. He could barely wait for the pleasure. Could hardly contain himself.

His hands moved. Both hands went inside the jeans. Harry knew it would take both hands to do this one justice. Feeling, groping, he was close. Oh, God, yes, he was so close. . . .

It was almost too easy for the Closer.

The bar had been filled with yuppie faggots. A lot of horny men with not enough taste and too much money. The Target had been easy to find and easier to seduce. The hunger in his eyes made him accessible and vulnerable and weak. That's what hunger did to men, the Closer knew.

The Closer had been briefed well, so the conversation went smoothly. All the right questions were asked, all the right answers were spoken.

In the bar, the Closer felt the Target's lust as strongly as if it were a third person sitting at the table with them.

In the Target's home, the Closer had been expecting the emptiness but not the sense of sadness. Of ordinariness. The Target had once been an exceptional man. Anything but ordinary. The bare house seemed to have reduced him, though, to its own shell-like level. The Target was like a structure with nothing inside. Nothing except his overwhelming lust and passion. And those were not enough to keep a man alive.

When the Target's hands unzipped the jeans, the Closer knew it was time. The game had gone on long enough.

The Closer's hands slowly reached toward the Target. The Closer's eyes beckoned. The Closer's lips drew nearer and nearer. . . .

Harry Wagner heard the click. Didn't realize for a split second what it was, but a chill ran all the way down his spine. He had been a player long enough to understand the smell of danger, and he knew instantly that he was caught.

They had taken the only thing that was left of him and used it to destroy him. He had been played for the fool, and now he knew he must suffer the consequences.

He looked at the lovely creature he'd brought into his own home.

Bastards, Harry thought. *Too strong.*

The kid, Carl, flashed before him. And then Allison, telling him he couldn't even control his cock.

The bastards, Harry thought again. And then, *I was so close.*

And then he was still.

chapter 18

The tree-lined street that Harry Wagner lived on was extremely quiet at one o'clock in the morning. It was a weeknight, and this was a neighborhood of midlevel government workers. Most were tucked safely into bed for the night, lights out, dreaming their dreams of early, taxpayer-funded retirement to Hilton Head or Fort Lauderdale. The only car they passed as Amanda's Subaru wended its way through this mid-Atlantic suburb was a dark blue Suburban, going slowly and carefully in the opposite direction.

The houses were small and squat, starter homes from the postwar boom, most of them faced with red brick. Harry's was no different from any of the others. With one exception, Carl was pleased to discover as they pulled over to the curb out front.

The lights were on. Several lights. And a Jeep Wrangler was parked in the driveway. The man was home.

Amanda shut off the Subaru's engine. A dog barked from somewhere down the block.

"I'm sure you'll argue this point," Carl said, his voice steady despite the loud pounding of his heart, "but I'm going in alone. There's no telling how he'll react, and if he gets violent, well, it's better for one of us to be outside."

She did not argue with him this time but just nodded, her eyes wide with fear. "You think he'll react violently?"

"Nah," Carl said, "not at all. But listen," he added. "If I'm not out in a while . . ." He ran a hand through his hair, letting his voice trail off.

"If you're not out in a while, *what,* Carl?"

"Nothing," he said softly. "I'll be out."

"Good answer."

They stared at each other in the darkened car. Again that bond passed between them. That closeness. For a brief moment Carl was overcome by regret over what had happened to them. He felt a powerful urge to take her into his arms and kiss her. But he did not. He smiled at her tightly and reached for the door handle.

"Carl?" she said, stopping him. "Don't do anything stupid, okay?"

"Don't worry. That's not part of my plan."

"You have a plan?"

"Well, no. But I've got all the way between here and the front door to work on one."

He got out and walked up the fieldstone path toward Harry Wagner's front door, lost in thought. Not a plan but a sorry reflection: *I am not supposed to be here. I am supposed to be comfortably ensconced in a cozy cabin in the woods writing the great American novel, a fire roaring in the fireplace, a loyal mastiff dozing at my feet. This is not me.*

But it is *me,* he realized. *So I'd better deal with it. More important, I'd better survive it.*

He rang the doorbell. No one answered.

He rang it again. Again no answer. He reached for the doorknob and turned the handle to the right. No luck. The front door was locked. He turned to face Amanda. The car was lit by the moon and the faint glow of a street lamp, but her eyes were hidden in the shadows cast by the trees. He turned back to the house. The blinds were drawn and Carl couldn't get a good glimpse of the front room. There didn't seem to be any movement. And he couldn't hear any noise. And yet . . . it was hard to pinpoint, but the place didn't *feel* empty. Maybe Harry was out back. Sitting in a lawn chair, having a brandy. He wouldn't necessarily hear the doorbell.

There was a path to the left of the house, bordered by an unruly row of hydrangea bushes on one side and by a hedge on the other, helping to hide the view of the neighbor's yard. Carl walked carefully until he reached the backyard. There was a small brick patio but no lawn chair, no brandy. No Harry. There was a back door, though, and Carl moved to stand before it. He tried to talk himself out of what he was about to do. But it didn't work.

He grabbed the doorknob, turned it slowly. The door was unlocked.

Carl took a deep breath, closed his eyes for a second.

That's when he felt the hand on his shoulder. He jumped two feet in the air and spun around, hands balled into fists. He started to swing blindly—

It was Amanda.

He hadn't heard her get out of the car.

"Shit," he hissed at her. "What are you trying to do, give me a heart attack?"

"What are you doing, Carl?" she asked.

"I'm going in," he said. "Who knows what he's got lying around? I might be able to find something important."

"It's breaking and entering."

"Believe me, Amanda, if I'm caught, my lawyers will be *happy* to plea-bargain down to breaking and entering."

"What if there's an alarm?"

"Then I'll leave a polite note and get the hell out of here."

"Carl . . ."

"I'm going in."

"All right," she sighed. "But I decided I don't like this waiting-out-here business. I'm going in with you."

It was his turn not to bother to argue. He just nodded and turned the knob to the right. Carl pushed the door open and ushered Amanda into Harry Wagner's house.

They prowled from room to room. There were two bedrooms. A bathroom. A powder room. A kitchen. A half dining room and a small den. Many closets. A full basement. And there was not a thing in any of them. Not one scrap of paper. Or a picture on a wall. Not one stick of furniture. Not one cleaning rag. There were no phone numbers scrawled in pencil on the wall over the phone. There was no phone. No slivers of soap on the edge of the sink. It was as if the whole house had been wiped clean, then boiled and sterilized.

Neither Harry nor Amanda spoke until they'd worked their way to the kitchen, the last room to be inspected. As they had in the other rooms, they made a thorough inspection. The cupboard under the sink: no garbage pail, no rags, no Ajax, not a speck of dust. The cupboards over the sink and counters: no dishes, no pots or pans, no coffee mugs. The silverware drawers: no silverware, not one utensil. The pantry: not a morsel of food. The only trace that anyone had ever lived in this house was a three-quarters-empty bottle of Maker's Mark on the kitchen table and two clean glasses sitting upside down in the dish tray by the sink. Amanda even opened the shiny stainless-steel professional oven and peered inside. She found exactly what she was expecting to find: nothing. She turned to Carl and shrugged forlornly. The refrigerator was also stainless steel, a large Sub-Zero monolith, and he slumped against it, dejected. He shook his head in frustration. Then, with his left hand, he pushed himself off the fridge and headed out of the kitchen.

"Well, I'm no expert," he said, without looking back, "but I'd say my good friend Harry has flown the coop."

Amanda followed. As she passed the refrigerator, she couldn't help herself. Never one to leave a stone unturned, she tugged at the handle of the freezer, pulled the heavy door open, and looked in. It was bare—except for four additional shelves neatly stacked on the freezer's top shelf. She moved her hand to the right now, to the refrigerator handle, and yanked. That door opened, just a crack and, when the light went on, Amanda glanced inside. She was silent a long moment, her hand resting on the open door, before she said very softly, "No, he hasn't, Carl."

She said it with admirable calm. But there was something odd about her voice. Odd enough for the hair on the back of Carl's neck to stand up.

He turned back and moved to stand behind her. Putting his hand on top of hers, he swung the refrigerator door wide open.

"Harry?" she asked. The question barely managed to escape from her lips.

"Harry," Carl answered, staring into the icy glare of the refrigerator.

H. Harrison Wagner, Carl's last and best hope, was wedged inside, fully clothed, looking surprisingly peaceful and normal except for the switchblade knife sticking out of his left eye.

Amanda backed slowly away, her legs buckling. All of the color had drained from her face. Her hands trembled, and she was blinking rapidly.

Carl reached for her and gripped her tightly by the shoulders. She shook her head almost imperceptibly, and he knew what that meant. It was her way of saying that she couldn't deal with this. But he only nodded, just as faintly. It was his way of saying, *Yes, you can. Even if* you *don't know how strong you are,* I *do.* She bit her lip to stop from crying. And then she

grabbed him, throwing her arms around his chest, falling into him and hugging him to her as if they were the only two people left in the world. As they
stood there, his eyes were on Harry. On the dead eye that stared back at him
from inside the refrigerator. On the blood that still oozed down his face
from the knife wound in his other eye.

On the man whose voice Carl had hoped would lead him out of the
wilderness. The man whose voice would never again be heard.

Special Agent Bruce Shanahoff of the Washington office of the Federal
Bureau of Investigation knew that something was wrong. He just didn't
know what. And it had him on edge.

He'd been told to lay off Amanda Mays—the bureau did not do well
when it came to screwing around with reporters. It was always a big mistake
to mess with the *Washington Post*, had been for years, but the *Journal*
wasn't too far behind. In fact, with the current political climate, they'd
pretty much pulled up to equal. They were splashier, sure, maybe a bit more
reckless with the facts, but the movers and shakers at the *Journal* had a lot
of clout, politically and socially. And while Mays was neither a mover nor a
shaker, she was an up-and-comer. In the short time she'd been in town, she'd
made a big impression, inside the paper and out. So better to leave her
alone.

Except . . .

Except leaving people alone was not one of Agent Shanahoff's best
things. Especially when he thought they were guilty as hell.

A car passed by, close to Agent Shanahoff's Taurus. Obviously lost. For
a moment Shanahoff thought the driver was going to stop and ask directions. That put him even more on edge. Agent Shanahoff was one of those
people who always seemed as though he knew what he was doing. He was
confident and smart, and he had the right look. He liked that about himself.
He liked the Look. And usually he *did* know what he was doing. Put him in
the middle of an emergency, he'd be the one acting calm and in control. Ask
him a question about how to get something done, he'd tell you how to do it.
But not when it came to directions. Much to his embarrassment, Shanahoff
could get lost going around the block. When he first came to D.C., it took

him three full weeks before he could get from his apartment to Bureau headquarters without making a wrong turn somewhere along the route. It frustrated the hell out of him when people asked him directions, because he hated not knowing the answer to a question. And when it came to directions, he not only never knew the answer, he never even had a fucking clue.

So he was relieved when the driver passed him by. He could concentrate on the problem at hand. Which was Amanda Mays.

Not that he thought she was a major criminal. But he was positive she'd been in touch with Carl Granville. Was pretty sure Carl had stopped off at Amanda's house. Shanahoff had no illusions about his appeal to women, especially women like Amanda Mays. She was out of his league. But she'd come on big-time flirtatious. Incredibly eager to please. Ready to open up. It wasn't natural. It wasn't her.

Which meant it had to be him. It had to be Granville.

There it was again. Shit. The car was circling back around the block. A Suburban. He liked them. Good and sturdy. He'd almost bought one when he moved to D.C. This one was definitely lost. Definitely coming back over to him to find out how to get someplace that he'd never even heard of. Shanahoff groaned out loud as the car's headlights shone through his windshield. He geared himself up . . . but the car kept going. Shanahoff shook his head, chagrined at his own discomfort. *What's the big deal?* he thought. *What's the big fucking deal?*

Carl Granville . . . now *he* was a big deal. The way the media were playing him up, maybe the biggest deal since Cunanan. It wouldn't hurt to be in on his capture. Which was why he was staked out in front of Amanda Mays's house, against orders. She was the best lead they had. She was gone now, but she'd be back. Couldn't hurt to just stick around. Do a little checking. Maybe nothing would come of it, but it sure couldn't hurt. All he needed was a little patience. And time. Hell, he had plenty of both. And—

And there it was again. The same car, moving at the same snail's pace. Agent Shanahoff frowned. Either whoever was behind the wheel had a sense of direction even worse than his own—which was highly unlikely— or something strange was going on. Shanahoff forced the relaxed-looking smile back onto his face. But he moved his hand inside his coat and onto the butt of his gun, which sat firmly in its shoulder holster.

This time the car pulled to a stop alongside the Taurus. The windows rolled down and the driver leaned out toward Shanahoff.

"I wonder if you could help me," the driver said, looking exasperated and hopelessly lost.

"I doubt it, but I'll try." Agent Shanahoff took his hand off his gun. *Jerk,* he said to himself. *There* are *some normal people in the world.* Then he smiled, his very best smile, giving the driver the Look. "What can I do for you?"

In response, the driver's hand came up. In it was a Smith & Wesson .357 Magnum.

The silencer attached to the revolver muffled the two quick pops. Special Agent Shanahoff didn't make a sound either as the back of his head exploded, all life went out of his eyes, and his body slumped down across the front seat of his car.

They went out the back door of Harry's house, Carl still holding on to Amanda, keeping her close. He helped her into the car. The street was as quiet as before, with no lights on anywhere. He told her he'd drive, but she was not even able to hand him the key. When she fished it out of her purse, her hands shook so badly she dropped it on the ground.

She still hadn't said a word, and Carl didn't blame her. What could she say? *I've seen the ugliest thing I've ever witnessed. I will never again be the same. I hate you for what you've done to my life.* Those seemed like the most likely choices to him, which is why he didn't speak, either. He couldn't disagree with her.

He started up the car engine, and as he turned the key he was thinking of Harry.

Why would Harry be killed? Because he *knew* things. When it came to dealing with Gideon, a little knowledge was clearly proving to be a dangerous thing, and Harry had more than just a little knowledge. He had read all the original material as well as what Carl was creating. He knew the truth; that's why he was killed.

Which brought them back to step one: What did Harry know and how

did he know it? That's what Carl had to find out. And then manage to stay
alive so that he could do something about it.

The chances of actually being able to do that did not strike Carl as being particularly favorable. Trying to be objective about it, he placed the
odds at about a million to one. If they could get to Harry, they could get to
anyone. How had anyone gotten close enough to him to kill him? It seemed
impossible that Harry would have let his guard down long enough for that.
There were many words to describe Harry Wagner—*dangerous, powerful,
paranoid*—but *careless* was not one of them. The guy wouldn't move without checking the street from behind the window curtains and making sure
the door was locked. He hadn't even carried a briefcase. He'd made sure he
hid his papers in his—

They were two blocks away from Harry's house when Carl slammed
on the car brakes. He glanced behind him, swung the Subaru around in a
U-turn and gripped the steering wheel tightly as his foot pressed down hard
on the accelerator.

"What are you doing?" They were the first words Amanda had spoken
since she'd found Harry's body.

"We forgot something."

"Carl, we went over every single inch of that house. What could we
possibly have forgotten?"

Carl tried to keep his voice even, trying not to sound as excited as he
felt. "We forgot to undress him."

The night was calm and undisturbed as the Closer pulled the Suburban up
to the small carriage house, stepped out from the driver's seat, and carefully lifted a three-gallon can of gasoline out of the backseat.

It did not take long to break into the house, perhaps four minutes to
pick the lock, and not much longer than that to do what needed to be done
inside.

The top twisted easily off the metal can. Then slowly, as if leaving a trail
for someone to follow, the Closer walked methodically through the apartment, pouring a constant stream of gasoline. On the kitchen floor and over
the kitchen counters. Into the living room, leaving a wet stream on the carpet, on top of the coffee table, over and around the couch. In the bathroom,

the puddle of gasoline spread into the cracks in the tile, and in the bedroom, the bed was thoroughly doused, as were the curtains. Still pouring, the Closer tracked back to the living room, stood over the desk and the expensive computer equipment. Lifting the can to chest level, the Closer drenched the keyboard and the screen, turned the can completely upside down and let its final contents splash over the modem.

From the time of the shooting through the moment the Closer lit the match, dropped it dead center on the casing for the computer's hard drive, went back out the front door, got into the Suburban, and drove away, exactly twelve minutes had elapsed.

For some reason Carl had expected the second viewing to be easier. But it wasn't. If anything, Harry's body, wedged inside the stainless-steel cubicle in the same twisted and folded position, was even more grotesque. They both stood before the open refrigerator door, a small blast of cold air enveloping them, neither one wanting to make the first move to do what needed to be done.

Finally Carl took a deep breath, reached inside, and took one of Harry's hands in his. He had never touched a corpse before, and despite his resolve, he flinched at the contact with the cold, dead flesh. Steeling himself, he grabbed Harry's wrist firmly, then bent down and put his right hand around Harry's ankle. He looked over at Amanda and, with his eyes, indicated that she should do the same. He saw her swallow nervously.

"Come on. As soon as you grab him, we'll ease him out. It's not so bad."

He could see her lips move almost imperceptibly as she counted to herself, getting ready: one . . . two . . . three. Then she grabbed Harry's hand and his ankle.

He heard her exhale, one long breath, then two quick ones, almost hyperventilating, then another long, slow inhale and exhale. She looked over at him and nodded. She was okay.

Harry Wagner was a big man. In life he had moved lightly on his feet, with the grace and quickness of a dancer. In death they could only move him slowly and awkwardly. There was nothing light or graceful about him now.

They got the top half of his body out without too much of a struggle.

He was leaning forward at a forty-five-degree angle, his butt pushing against the back wall of the fridge. Carl did a little maneuvering, and Harry's right leg toppled out and dangled, his shoe scraping along the kitchen floor. Carl had the sudden image of a 250-pound marionette. Another tug and Harry's left leg was free. There he was, propped up against the edge of the refrigerator in a sitting position, his head drooping to the left.

"Okay," Carl said. "I'm going to grab him under the arms and stand him up. Once he's up, you just keep him propped up, and I'll get his pants off."

She nodded grimly and he lifted. Christ, he was heavy. But so far so good. Carl spread his legs a little wider, as if preparing to do a squat. He pushed off, and Harry was upright.

"He's going to tilt toward you," Carl said. "All you've got to do is support him. All right?"

"All right." It wasn't the most enthusiastic of responses, but it would have to do. He let go slowly and felt Harry ease forward onto Amanda. She grunted as she felt the full force of his weight and he saw her right leg slip back a few inches. But she held him steady.

Carl reached down and undid Harry's belt, then gingerly unbuttoned his pants and unzipped the fly. He felt the body wobble a bit, and Amanda took another step backward, staggering. Carl bent down, grabbed hold of Harry's pants at the waist, and tugged hard.

Harry's pants came down to midthigh, but his upper body jerked forward, and Amanda buckled under the weight. Carl still had hold of the pants, and as Amanda slipped, Harry's legs flew up in the air, knocking Carl off balance.

The body twisted over in Amanda's direction, she started to go down, her arms wrapped around Harry's torso. Carl saw her eyes go wide, he lost his grip on the pants, tried frantically to grab hold of Harry's coat, his arm, anything, but missed and went flying backward. His hip banged into the kitchen counter, and as he spun around, swearing, he heard Amanda's voice, quiet and hollow, say, "Get him off me."

Then, louder, "Get him off me."

Then, louder still, and faster, "Get him off. *Get him off, get him off, get him off!*"

Carl ran across the kitchen, where Harry's lifeless body sprawled on top of Amanda's, pinning her to the floor. He tipped Harry over and pushed as Amanda scrambled out from under him and rushed to the sink, gasping, gagging, then breathing deeply until she once again gained control. Carl went to touch her, to hug her reassuringly, but she leaped back, shivering, not yet ready to be touched by anyone, dead *or* alive.

Carl thought she was finished as far as this scheme was concerned, but the trauma seemed only to toughen her resolve. He watched, amazed, as she was already turning back to the body on the floor. "All right," she said, half to Carl, half to herself, "let's do it."

They decided to leave him on the floor this time. They each untied one shoe, and there was something eerie about the act of placing them neatly together by the kitchen table. As Carl started twisting one of Harry's socks off, he pulled gingerly so as not to hurt or tickle, then realized the absurdity and ripped it off as quickly as possible. The pants were already halfway down. Carl stood over Harry, the body between his legs, and lifted up from the small of the dead man's back. Amanda braced herself by Harry's feet and pulled at the pants legs. They slipped off steadily until they rested down at his ankles. Amanda searched the pockets to make sure there was nothing of interest. There wasn't.

Harry's shirt was a struggle; the skin on his torso was icy and hard. But Carl got it off, and then the only thing left was Harry's underwear. Bikini briefs. Carl nodded grimly, got set, and pulled them down to Harry's knees.

Harry Wagner lay on the cold kitchen floor, naked.

There were no packets. No diaries. No papers. No clues. There was nothing.

"Can we get out of here now?" Amanda said quietly. When he didn't respond, just kept staring at the body, she said, "Come on, Carl, it's over. Let's go."

"I can't just leave him here like this."

"Carl, we have to—"

"Amanda, I *knew* the guy. Let's just get him dressed and put him back where we found him. Please."

The underwear and pants went back on first, then the shirt, socks, and shoes. Carl even tied the shoelaces back into a neat bow. Then they dragged the body to the refrigerator, opened the door, and awkwardly managed to shove him back in.

Carl stood before the body. For a moment he felt as if he should say a few words—pay his respects, apologize, something—but then he just closed the refrigerator door, turned his back, and walked out of the house.

Outside, standing in the driveway, they both sucked in the night air as if, while inside the house, they'd been holding their breath, afraid of inhaling the stench of death that had begun to permeate their lives.

"I'm sorry I didn't handle it better," she said.

"You were fine. Hell, you were more than fine. I'm the one who screwed up. I was positive we'd find something. It seemed so right. So logical."

"We *will* find something. I promise."

He managed a quick, grateful smile. Then they got back into her car. He put the key in the ignition, but his nerves weren't as steady as he'd thought. He realized he wasn't quite ready to drive—he needed a moment to collect himself—so he put his hands on the steering wheel and they sat in the dark driveway.

"You know what was the creepiest thing?" she said. "How, after a few minutes, it didn't seem so creepy. The fact that he was dead, I mean. I almost felt like a doctor must feel, objective and analytical. I stopped thinking about him as a human being and I could go, 'Oh, he wore Armani pants, that's interesting,' and I could look at the wound and not get grossed out, and focus on *bienvenue* and wonder what that meant—"

"What?" Carl asked. "What do you mean, *bienvenue?*"

"His tattoo."

"Harry had a tattoo?"

"On his forearm. His right forearm. Wait, it was to my right, so it was his left." She tapped a spot several inches above her wrist. "It was right here."

Carl took his hands off the steering wheel.

"Oh, no," she groaned. "Don't tell me. Carl—"

But he didn't hear the rest of her sentence. He was already out of the car and moving quickly toward the house.

This time their stay inside was brief.

Carl pulled the body partway out of its storage place. This time there was no skittishness as he touched the corpse's skin. This was all business.

Amanda rolled up Harry's shirtsleeve just far enough to reveal the small tattoo on the inside of his left forearm. It was the word *bienvenue* written in small, neat script letters.

Staring down at it, Carl said, "He always had his cuffs rolled up. When he was cleaning up after himself, washing the dishes, or just if my place got too hot. I'm telling you, he did not have this tattoo a week ago."

"So maybe he got one since you saw him."

"Clearly. The question is why."

"Bienvenue," Amanda said, mulling it over. "What does it mean?"

"It's French," Carl said. "It means 'welcome.' "

"So what does *that* mean?"

"I don't know." Carl gave a quick salute to the upside-down corpse, half in and half out of the refrigerator. "But Harry," he finished, "I'm sorry I doubted you."

The flames slithered across the bedroom floor, skating from doorway to bedpost, engulfing the blue and white summer quilt, then leaping to the French lace curtains protecting the windows. The powerful red and blue flames devoured the white lace, spit their way into the walls and beams of the ceiling, then roared through the entire room, peeling back paint, splintering wood, shattering glass, and turning plastic into a path of molten lava.

The bathroom was a sauna of black smoke and poisonous fumes. It did not take long for the enamel tub to char and become disfigured. As the pipes ruptured, they spewed forth water. The torrents of liquid met the crackling flames, and the hissing and steaming sounds began to scream throughout the neighborhood. It was a mundane inferno, claiming not souls but shower rods and toothbrush holders and cracked tiles.

In the living room, the couch was swallowed in one great whoosh of motion. Antique tables and desks that had survived and functioned for two hundred years were shattered like the cheapest plywood. The computer lasted mere seconds in the furious heart of the blaze. Keys melted. The screen blackened. Its insides were destroyed, bursting apart like ruptured organs.

Working its way through the kitchen now, the flames kicked out into the back alleys. Sparks flew into the night. Great spurts of color rose up toward the sky. Crackling laughter called out to anyone within hearing distance.

It was leaving the confines of its origin now. Spreading into the real world. Terrifying in its beauty. Magnificent in its pure destruction.

Spreading now. Out of control. Burning. Grabbing. Reaching out . . .

They didn't speak during the ride back to Amanda's. Both of them were racking their brains, trying to figure out the meaning of *bienvenue*. If indeed it had a meaning. But Carl was certain that it did. Harry was not the type to cavalierly go off and brand himself. Not unless there was some purpose. The French meant nothing, as far as he could tell. Welcome? What the hell was that? He didn't have a clue. But what else could it be? The name of someone? A girlfriend? A wife? A pet name? A last name? A boat? An acronym? The possibilities were endless.

When they were three blocks from her home, Amanda suddenly sat up straighter in her seat.

"What's that smell?" she asked.

"Something's burning," he said. And then: "Listen."

They heard sirens. And fire engine horns. They seemed distant, but within seconds the noises were right on top of them.

"Oh, my God," Amanda said slowly. And then in a long, mournful keen, "Oh . . . my . . . God . . ."

He followed her gaze and he could see it. Flames rising high above the houses.

Amanda flung the car door open and jumped out of the car. She began sprinting wildly down the street, her screams barely audible under the overwhelming sounds of the trucks and sirens and ambulances.

Carl ran after her, calling her name. She was really moving, and he didn't catch up to her until they were half a block away from the fire.

"It's my house," she screamed. "It's my house!" She tried to break away from him, wrenching herself free to run closer, but he grabbed her, yanked her backward. Held her tight and wouldn't let her go.

"Amanda, no!" he said.

"It's my house," she said, and now she wasn't screaming. It was more like some kind of plea. She slumped forward, rocking on the balls of her feet, and he thought he'd never seen such a sad expression on anyone's face.

Even from this distance, the heat was overpowering. Police officers and firefighters were converging on the area. Hoses were being unleashed. Questions were being asked of the gathering onlookers.

Carl was suddenly exhausted. The idea of running again was almost incomprehensible. Maybe it was time to just give up. What could they do to him? The idea of surrender seemed blessedly peaceful. This would all be over. No more hiding. No more terror. No more death . . .

He saw the short, thick body wending its way through the crowd. He couldn't see the face, just the profile in a quick glance, but Carl knew who it was. Shivers ran down his spine, and he instinctively stepped back. Then the body turned and he got a glimpse of the pockmarked face, the thick-lipped sneer, the dull, malevolent eyes.

Payton.

It was definitely Payton. The cop who'd tried to kill him in his own apartment.

Just when you thought the insanity had reached its peak. Maybe there is no peak. Maybe the lunatics have stormed the asylum doors and are now running the world.

Payton was searching. Sniffing him out. Those eyes were darting through the crowd. He sensed something . . .

"We've got to go," he whispered urgently to Amanda. *"Now."*

Two more police cars pulled up in front of the fire, sirens blaring and lights flashing. And now Payton's instincts took over; Carl could see him react, like a bloodhound moving in for the kill.

Payton's neck swiveled. His eyes locked onto Carl. The thick lips quivered. A smile. And then he began to run, his arms pumping, his round, fleshy legs moving quickly, surprisingly light on his feet, dodging through the gathered crowd.

"Amanda, *please.* We can't stay here."

She let him pull her back toward the car. He opened the door and gently shoved her back into the rusty Subaru. Then he went to the driver's side, glanced backward. Payton was still sprinting—he was close now, too close.

Red in the face and panting, but he hadn't slowed down. The veins in his neck were popping. He was so damn close.

Carl jumped behind the wheel, turned the car around, and tore away, tires screeching. In the rearview mirror he saw Payton still running, saliva flying from his open mouth. For a moment Carl thought the impossible was happening. He thought Payton was still gaining on them. But his image slowly began to recede in the mirror. He slowed down, then stopped, then bent over, hands on his knees, gasping for air, barely able to look up at their disappearing taillights.

As he rounded the corner, he saw Amanda turn to look behind her. She was not looking at Payton. She didn't care about an obsessed cop who wanted to kill them. She didn't care about a tattoo or the meaning of *bienvenue*, either. None of that mattered to her. She stared instead at the crowd, at the spinning lights, at the shooting sprays of water, at the horrible flames, caring about everything she ever owned or ever was, which had just disappeared from the face of the earth.

chapter 19

Partial transcript of the July 11 edition of *Sunrise News*, the one-hour ANN morning news program, airing at 5 A.M. Eastern time:

Dan Eller, anchor: *Good morning. We have a tragic update on the hunt for Carl Granville, the young writer already wanted for questioning in the death of two women, one of whom was flamboyant publishing executive Margaret Peterson, here in New York City. As of yesterday morning, FBI agents tracked Granville's flight to the Washington, D.C., area, where Amanda Mays, deputy metropolitan editor of the* Washington Journal *and an ex-girlfriend of Granville's, lives. In what appears to be a clear case of arson, Ms. Mays's house has been burned and nearly one hundred percent destroyed. Firemen appeared on the scene at approximately one-thirty this morning and are still doing their best to salvage what remains. Ms. Mays is missing, although there is no proof yet that she was in the house when the fire began. When police and firefighters arrived at the blaze, they found FBI Special Agent Bruce Shanahoff in his car, which was parked in front of Ms. Mays's house. Agent Shanahoff was dead when discovered, shot once in the head.*

We have no more details at this time. Neither police nor FBI officials are commenting on any possible link between the D.C. fire, Agent Shanahoff's death, and the two murders in New York. We hope to be able to provide more information when Wake Up America *airs, following this program, in one hour.*

On a lighter note, the Bronx Zoo announced last night that Brownie, a fourteen-year-old camel, gave birth to twins. The baby girl is named Humpty and the handsome young boy is Dumpty. . . .

From the July 11 FBI Website, http://www.fbimostwanted.com:

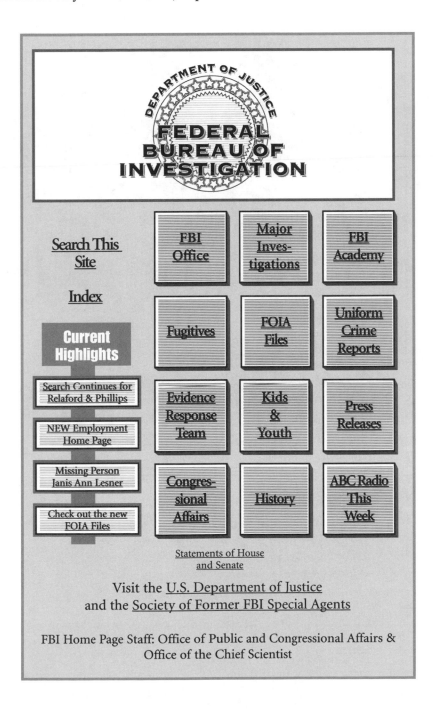

Enos Lewis Perkins   Carlos Gonzales   Carl Amos Granville   Raymond Allen Jr.

The **FBI's**

TEN MOST

WANTED FUGITIVES

Rasheed Duke   Manuel Velasquez

Henry Johnson Brown   Fawaz Ahman   Randall P. Ellington   Abdullah Al Magreb

The FBI is offering rewards for information leading to the apprehension of Ten Most Wanted Fugitives.
Check each fugitive page for the specific amount.

Ten Most Wanted Facts • **FBI Field Officers**
Home Page • **Fugitives**

WANTED BY THE FBI

Carl Amos Granville
ALIASES: Carl Granville, Granny

AGGRAVATED ASSAULT—ARSON—MURDER

**PRESUMED ARMED AND
EXTREMELY DANGEROUS**

DOB: April 23, 1971
Sex: Male
Height: 6' 1"
Weight: 185 pounds
Hair: Blond
Eyes: Blue
Race: Caucasian

THE CRIME:

    <u>Carl Amos Granville</u> **is wanted for the July 8 murder of Margaret Alexis Peterson, the July 8 murder of Antoinette Louise Cloninger, and the July 11 murder of FBI Special Agent Bruce Leonard Shanahoff. In all three cases, Granville fled before he could be charged and indicted. He is last known to be in the Washington, D.C., area where he is also wanted by local authorities as a suspect in a July 11 alleged act of arson, the burning of a house lived in by Amanda Dorothy Mays. Amanda Dorothy Mays is missing and feared dead in said fire. Granville is also wanted in connection with her disappearance. FBI Special Agent Bruce Leonard Shanahoff was found shot near the scene of the alleged arson.**

    Ballistic reports confirm that the same gun was used in the murder of Antoinette Louise Cloninger and FBI Special Agent Bruce Leonard Shanahoff.

    This information is valid as of 7 A.M., Thursday, July 11

<u>FBI home page</u> • <u>More info</u> • <u>More photos</u> • <u>Fugitive list</u>
<u>Next fugitive</u> • <u>FBI field offices</u>

Partial transcript from the July 11 edition of *Need to Know*, one-hour tabloid journalism show broadcast daily, 9 to 10 A.M. Eastern time, on ANN:

GINNY STONE: Unfortunately for his two newest alleged victims, it seems that Carl Granville, the man already being dubbed the "Literary Killer," is intent on proving that the sword—and almost any other weapon at his disposal—is mightier than the pen.

As you can see from the charred ruins behind me, it appears as if Granville has struck again. You're looking at what used to be One thirty-two Klingle Street, in the sedate Washington, D.C., area called Kalorama, where the frustrated and out-of-work novelist's ex-girlfriend lived. Amanda Mays ended her relationship with Carl Granville a little over a year ago. Now it appears that Granville, in a clear case of arson, has ended her life as well as the life of thirty-one-year-old FBI agent Bruce Shanahoff.

The dots are slowly being connected, and they're forming a horrific and deadly picture. At approximately two o'clock yesterday afternoon, Agent Shanahoff came to this once lovely two-story house to interview Ms. Mays. At that interview, he warned her that Carl Granville might be armed and dangerous but, according to FBI sources, Agent Shanahoff received no cooperation. He allegedly reported to his superiors that he suspected Granville had already paid Ms. Mays a visit. It seems he also suspected that Granville would return—for Agent Shanahoff, apparently acting on his own, staked out the house on Klingle. It was to be his final act of heroism.

I have with me here Dr. Ruth Matthiesson, a psychologist who specializes in obsessive sexual relationships and is the best-selling author of From Bundy to Cunanan: Love, Hate, and Murder. *Dr. Matthiesson, what patterns, if any, can you recognize in the tragedy that's unfolding before us?*

DR. RUTH MATTHIESSON: Of course, Ginny, you have to understand that I haven't yet spoken to or worked with Carl Granville, although I certainly hope to at some point. But the pattern is exactly the same as I laid out in From Bundy to Cunanan. *What we clearly have is someone who grew up in a troubled home and who is desperately seeking love and acceptance, both on a personal level and on a professional one. In this instance, the killer is some-one who would have come to this house with the intent of destroy-ing it. In a sense, he turned the house into a person. It became more than a symbol; it merged, as an image, with the woman who inhab-ited it. The killer is someone unable to create a domestic home life for himself and, out of jealousy, would refuse to allow anyone, par-ticularly an ex-lover, to enjoy one without him.*

GINNY STONE: And how would the death of Agent Shanahoff fit into such behavior?

RUTH MATTHIESSON: Well, anyone who would get in his way, who would try to interfere with his mission, if you will, would be fair game.

GINNY STONE: Thank you, Dr. Matthiesson. As this sedate com-munity is thrown into an uproar and as police search through the rubble for the body of a woman close friends describe as "intelligent, caring, and unwilling to give up on a troubled and unstable lover," questions still remain. How was the killer able to get close enough to shoot, at point-blank range, an experienced FBI agent? Where is Carl Granville now? If he is innocent, which seems more and more unlikely, why is he hiding? And, most disturbing of all, if he is guilty, where will his murderous spree take him next? Right now all we know for certain is that there is a growing myth of invincibility that is beginning to surround Carl Granville. Let us hope that that myth is shattered and sanity can be restored before it's too late.

From the July 11 *Washington Journal*:

EDITOR'S LIFE TOUCHED MANY OTHERS

by Shaneesa Perryman

Journal staff writer

The lurid details on page one tell it only too well: An FBI agent shot to death in his parked car. A Kalorama carriage house burned to the ground, its tenant, thirty-one-year-old journalist Amanda Mays, missing and presumed dead. Her ex-lover, Carl Granville, missing and presumed guilty, and now the object of one of the largest manhunts in modern criminal history.

But the story on page one doesn't tell it all. Not really. Because for those of us who knew and worked with and loved Amanda Mays, she was not just another name in the newspaper, another victim, another statistic. She was our big sister, our coach, our nursemaid, our friend. She was a shoulder to cry on, a sofa to crash on. She was Amanda.

It was Amanda Mays who took a chance on this reporter that cold, gray morning last winter when I showed up here at the Journal looking for a job—a gangly, knock-kneed young black woman with no experience and no clue, unsure whether I had what it took. Amanda told me that I did. Amanda believed in me.

And now she is gone.

Amanda smoked too much and drank too much coffee and was way too honest with her superiors to ever be considered a team player. She was always fretting about her weight, although plump was not a word that ever applied to this particular woman. She liked to dress in the color purple even though she looked much better in softer colors. She had the most beautiful red hair I've ever seen. If she was reading something that she didn't care for, she would wrinkle her nose, as if smelling something unpleasant. When she was excited about a story, which was often, she seemed more alive than anyone I've ever known.

And now she is gone.

Amanda was born and raised in Port Chester, New York, where her father was a local banker. She was an only child. In high school she was head cheerleader and went steady with the captain of the football team. "A full-time practicing bimbo, complete with pink nail polish," was how she described herself in those days. Her father died when she was a freshman at Syracuse University. Her *mother, whom Amanda called "the last truly authentic housewife in America," died less than a year later. "She lost her will to live after her man was gone," Amanda told me late one night over beers. "I will never, ever let that happen to me."*

And now she is gone.

It was at Syracuse that Amanda discovered her love of journalism. Because she was so lovely, her professors tried to steer her toward a broadcasting career. She resisted, preferring the meatier, less glamorous world of newsprint. After two years at the Albany Knickerbocker *she was hooked on politics. After two more years at* Newsday *she was hooked on New York City. Living in Manhattan now, she began writing pieces on city government for the* Village Voice *and* New York Magazine.

It was at a publication party for a friend's book that she met a promising young writer named Carl Granville. "He was," she later told me, "exactly the man I had dreamed about when I was a little girl lying in bed at night, hugging my pillow. He was my Prince Charming, my white knight, my everything."

And now she is gone.

They shared a love of good books, foreign films, Chinese food, and each other. "They were so good together," says an old friend who knew them both. "Everyone thought it was a real shame that they couldn't make it work." According to Amanda, she was ready for a greater commitment and Carl was not. Never one to stand idly by, Amanda promptly moved to D.C., where she became the Journal's *deputy metro editor and a den mother to us young cubs. Her babies, she used to call us. She changed our diapers, encouraged us, guided us, touched us. And she still had time and heart enough to be proud of her ex-lover. "He's really doing well. He's writing a secret political memoir," she told us. "For one of the top editors in New York."*

And then that top editor was found murdered.

And then Carl Granville followed Amanda here.

The rest of the story is found on page one.

As I sit here writing these words, I can't imagine how I will get along without Amanda Mays. But I will have to try. We will all have to try.

Goodbye, Amanda. I don't know how to thank you, but this is me trying, girl.

Love, Shaneesa.

chapter 20

Amanda had to fight back the tears as she stood in line at the Gourmet Bean. Reading her very own obituary in that morning's *Washington Journal*, she was losing the fight.

Shaneesa's tribute was so sweet and heartfelt. And there was something so stark, so *real* about the sight of her own photograph right there on page one. Amanda hated to cry. She especially hated to cry in public. *Oh, screw it,* she thought. She had the right to cry as hard as she wanted. In the past twelve hours she had discovered a murdered man in a refrigerator, watched everything she owned go up in flames, and spent the night on the road, sleepless, dodging police and federal agents. She was confused, frightened, and exhausted.

And now she was dead.

Fortunately, no one else in line took note of her behavior. Or of her. It helped that she had on a pair of sunglasses and the old rain hat that she'd dug out of the backseat of the Subaru—a "rolling closet" was what Carl had once called it. It also helped that it was still early in the morning and anyone who was here had been driving all night, just as she and Carl had.

The first story to hit all-news radio came over her car radio less than twenty minutes after they'd fled the scene of the fire. That's how they learned that Agent Shanahoff had been found dead in his car. That Carl was most likely his killer. That she was missing and believed to be part of the ashes. That the police were on the lookout for her car, which had vanished from her garage. They believed that Carl might have killed her for it. A spree killer, they were calling him now.

They were comparing him to famous serial killers throughout history.

"We have to go to the police," she had said when she'd rediscovered her ability to speak. They were frantically speeding away from her burning house, Carl keeping one eye on the rearview mirror to make sure they weren't being followed. "We have to tell them what we know."

"No," he had said.

"But Carl, they're wrong! I'm alive. I'm living, breathing proof that you didn't set fire to the house or shoot Shanahoff. I've been with you all night. I'm your alibi."

"And what about Maggie?" he argued. "What about Toni? What about Harry? They don't even *know* about Harry yet. When they find him, they're gonna think I'm Jack the fuckin' Ripper."

"If they see they're wrong about this, then they'll know that you're innocent of all the other things. Won't they?"

He didn't respond. They were both silent a moment.

"You have to turn yourself in, Carl."

"No, Amanda. It's not possible."

"Why do you have to be so goddamn stubborn?" she cried, her voice rising. He pressed his foot down on the accelerator, as if sudden speed would somehow convince her that he was right. "Where will we go? What will we do? We can't just stay out here in the street, driving around and around. You are a multiple-murder suspect. If you don't turn yourself in, they'll gun you down like an animal, don't you understand?"

"Believe me, I understand." He slowed down and reached for her hand in the darkness, gripping it tightly. "And I'm not disagreeing with you. Every word you've said is way too true. But the last time I tried calling the police, they did their best to kill me."

"It's your only choice, Carl. It's your *only* choice."

"When I have proof," he said quietly.

"Proof?" she said, not so quietly. "What kind of proof?"

"Real, concrete proof of what's really happening and who's behind all of it. Otherwise I'm going to prison for the rest of my life. Unless, that is, they decide to just go right ahead and execute me." He trailed off into bitter silence. It stayed there between them for a moment before he said, "Besides, there's another reason why we can't go to them."

"And what's that?" she asked curtly.

"You," he said. "We have to think about you."

She shook her head at him. "Come on, what's the worst they can do to me—accuse me of aiding and abetting a fugitive? I'll say I was reporting your story. My paper will back me up, no problem."

"*They?* You're still talking about the law. I'm talking about whoever is doing all this. You don't understand how powerful they are. Five minutes after I called the cops, they tried to kill me. If they control the police, Amanda, what else do they control? They've killed four people so far. As of this moment, they think you're the fifth. That means you're safe. But if you surface, they're going to come after you just like they're coming after me. You're dangerous to them now. You know too much. I don't know who *they* are, but I do know that the second we surface, they'll find a way to kill you. And I just don't think I can allow that to happen, if you don't mind."

She swallowed hard on this. "Of all the times for you to actually be right about something," she said, "you have to go and pick now." She tried to say it lightly, she tried to smile, but she just couldn't manage it. "Well, what are we going to do?"

"Find out what the hell is going on. That's what we're going to do."

He laid it out as they drove. It had all begun with the damned book. That was all they had to go on. They had to find out what had *really* happened down there. First they had to locate where "down there" was. Then they had to find out Danny's real identity. If they could find him, they could learn who was after them. Who was trying to kill them.

"It's my only chance," he said. "It's *our* only chance."

She had nodded silently, and so they had driven due south all night on Interstate 95, stopping only once for gas at a twenty-four-hour Mobil station outside of Richmond, Virginia. They paid with cash—he still had over $700 from his late-night stop at the cash machine on Broadway—so that the FBI couldn't trace them by their credit cards. She had taken over behind the wheel after that while Carl napped, shuddering fitfully in his sleep. Now it was morning and they found themselves approximately twenty miles east of Raleigh, North Carolina, pulling up at one of those alarming new enormous service stops that were cropping up on highways across the country. Each one was a self-contained twenty-four-hour monument to efficiency and bad nutrition erected in the highway's center divider so as to be accessible by traffic going in both directions. This one contained two gas stations—one for cars, the other for trucks and buses—a TCBY yogurt franchise, a Roy

Rogers, a Sbarro pizza, a Bob's Big Boy, a Nathan's, a Gourmet Bean coffee shop, ATM machines, fax machines, arcade games, rest rooms, a North Carolina tourist center, and a minimart where Amanda purchased the local newspaper and a copy of the *Herald*, as well as two boxes of animal crackers and a liter of mineral water.

Carl stayed in the car. He couldn't risk being recognized.

Amanda felt disoriented in this place. Her legs were rubbery after so many hours behind the wheel, and her senses felt positively assaulted by all the bright lights and grease fumes, the arcade noises, the screaming children, the busloads of jabbering foreign tourists. After so many hours on the road in the dark of night, she felt a little as though she'd parachuted into the middle of a theme park in hell. Satan World. This would make a good Sunday-magazine story for one of her babies, she reflected. Working behind a Roy's counter for a few overnight shifts, talking to the people, getting to know their— God, what was she thinking? She had no babies anymore. She had no job anymore.

Dear Diary, today I became an interstate fugitive. Otherwise, nothing new.

In the ladies' room she splashed some cold water on her face, staring long and hard at her image in the mirror. She appeared tired but otherwise unchanged. Amazingly, there was no discernible difference. She looked like the same person. She did not know how this was possible. She did not know how appearances could be so deceiving.

When she got to the front of the line at Gourmet Bean, she ordered two extra-large lattès and two cranberry muffins. The cashier, who seemed half asleep, barely glanced at her.

Outside, the sun was shining fairly brightly. It was already warm, the air noticeably softer now that they were farther south. She had parked as far away from the other cars in the lot as she could. Carl was hunched low in the front seat with the sun visor down. He rolled down his window so she could hand him her purchases.

"The good news," she reported, indicating the papers, "is that they think I'm dead. I don't know how long they'll think that, we've probably got a day, two at most. But when they do figure out I'm not urn material yet—"

"They'll figure you're either my prisoner or my accomplice."

"Either way, it means even more attention and a tighter net. From all concerned."

"What's the *bad* news?" he asked.

She looked at him as if she couldn't believe he didn't already know the answer to that one. "Everything else," she said. Then she watched as he started rustling through the paper, urgently flipping page after page. "What are you looking for?" she wanted to know.

"The Mets score. Don't they have a sports section in this paper?"

"The *Mets*, Carl? How can you possibly think about the Mets at a time like this?"

Carl had no response to this. He just gazed at her.

"It's in section two," she said finally. "At the back."

He turned to the sports section, scanned the column of box scores, and closed the paper back up. "They won," he said. "Bobby Jones pitched a three-hitter. I figured you really wanted to know."

"Do you feel better now?"

"I do," he confessed. "I know I shouldn't, but I do."

She got into the front seat beside him and they tore into their breakfast right there in the parking lot, grateful for the momentary stillness and quiet. Carl practically inhaled his muffin as he scanned the stories about himself on the front page: old girlfriends who professed to have seen into his dark side many years earlier, and the guy who ran his local Korean market, two blocks from his apartment, who told the waiting world that he went through a tremendous amount of Tropicana Homestyle orange juice, rarely spoke, was usually unshaven, often shopped in the wee hours of the morning, and had the furtive air of someone who had just done something illegal.

And then there was an interview with his father.

Some scuzzball reporter had actually tracked him down in Pompano Beach, Florida, gone to his house, and confronted him. Carl could see him now, standing in the front doorway, the one with the golf bag door knocker, peering suspiciously out at the eager reporter. His old man hated any kind of personal scrutiny, so the interview would have been painful for Alfred Granville, Carl knew. But not as painful as it was for Carl to read. His father said nothing to defend him. He talked about how difficult this whole experience was for him. *Him.* Not Carl. He talked as if Carl had changed, gone in another direction after his mother had died. *I did notice he'd become angry, kind of morose. He pushed me further away. No, I don't think he wanted help. I don't think he was aware that he needed help.* That was one of the quotes the reporter had elicited from his father. *It pains me to think that he's guilty of all this,* Alfred Granville had gone on to say, *but I'll have to deal with it, come to terms with my own culpability.* He was talking about Carl as if he were guilty as charged. As if no more questions needed to be asked. As if . . .

Carl ripped the page out of the newspaper, crumpled it up into a tight ball, held it against his chest, wished at that moment he could have driven it through his heart, and closed his eyes. Slowly his hand unclenched, and he let the wad of paper fall to the protective rubber mat on the car's carpeted floor. He was only torturing himself. Reading these stories was doing him no good. There was no information of any importance and even less truth. So, trying to pretend for just a few moments that he was a normal tourist taking a normal break from a normal drive, he began to read about something else. Anything else.

"What's the story with this priest?" he asked Amanda after reading the article on page three in the *Herald*.

"What do you mean?"

"Why would a priest just up and disappear?"

She shrugged, making it clear that a missing man of the cloth was not her number one concern at the moment. But then, after a brief silence, she said, "I met him once."

"The priest?"

She nodded. "We were doing a story on dealing with grief. One of my babies interviewed him, liked him a lot. Wound up having dinner with him and they became friends. Father Patrick, right? Patrick Jennings."

"Yeah. What was he grieving about?"

"His sister was killed in a car accident. A drunk driver. It sent him into a tailspin. What I remember most about him is that even though he was really handsome and he had this amazing voice—you could practically feel him preaching at you when he spoke—what really came through was how deeply depressed he was. He was the saddest guy I ever met. He was telling me all about his days at Marquette; he said they were the happiest days of his life. He was going on and on about how they were days of reflection and study, how he really *believed* in things then . . . and he still sounded so deeply sad."

"So what do you think happened to him?"

"It says they found his car down by the river, gas tank half-full. The paper makes it sound like he committed suicide."

"Sounds like you buy it."

She nodded. "He was unhappy enough, that's for sure." Scanning the paper, she made a face. "Still no mention of Harry's murder."

"And still not a thing on the radio. It's a little weird."

"Why?"

"Because someone has gone to so much trouble to construct this frame around me, that's why. Let's face it, I'm a living, breathing killing machine. And Harry's a slam-dunk to be one of my victims. I was in the man's house. My fingerprints are bound to be all over the place. He's a natural."

"A natural," she said softly, remembering the sight of Harry Wagner there in the refrigerator, the blood oozing from his unseeing eye.

"So why no mention of him?" Carl pressed.

"Maybe no one's found his body yet," she offered.

"Or maybe somebody's covering it up," he countered.

"Why would they do that?"

He shook his head. "I don't know. I really don't. Maybe I'm just being paranoid again."

"Maybe. But if you are, Carl, you have awfully good reason to be."

With that, Amanda started up the Subaru. Or tried to. It wouldn't kick over. Carl stiffened noticeably and closed his eyes. But she said a silent prayer and it did just fine on the second try, thumping and thudding valiantly.

They were back on the road.

Twenty minutes or so away from the service stop, Amanda reached for her map of the southeastern states and unfolded it. "I think it's time we get serious," she said. "We don't know the name of the town we're looking for, do we? We don't even know which state it's in."

"Correct," he affirmed. "We know it's a small town in Butthole, No-where, that it used to smell bad, and that Elvis once played there. Or very nearby. It could be in Arkansas, Alabama, Mississippi, Louisiana . . . we don't know."

"What we do know," Amanda said, studying the map, "is that if we stay on this interstate, we'll end up in Miami—and we don't want to do that. In about fifteen minutes we'll be intersecting with Highway Forty, which heads west across the Great Smoky Mountains in the direction of . . . Nashville. From there, all roads lead south. I suggest we take Forty. Agreed?"

"Agreed," he said. "And I suggest we make contact with your friend Shaneesa."

"Really?" she said, surprised and pleased. It pained her greatly that her friend and protégée thought she was dead.

"She helped us find Harry, didn't she? Maybe she can find out what the hell *bienvenue* means. Or be able to help us find our mystery town. At least she can narrow down the field. Otherwise we're looking for a needle in the world's largest haystack. Just as long as . . ." He trailed off, looking at her gravely. A lock of his blond hair had tumbled over his eyes, and she had to stop herself from reaching over and combing it back with her fingers. "What I mean is, can you trust her with your life? With both of our lives?"

"I can trust her," Amanda said confidently. "Just leave it to me."

When the dented little Subaru turned off Interstate 95 and onto Highway 40, heading west, the Closer immediately reached for the cell phone and dialed, keeping both eyes on the road.

The Subaru was much easier to lose now that it was daylight. In the middle of the night, cruising down that nearly deserted highway in the darkness, its taillights had served as twin red beacons. It was a no-brainer, like tailing another ship's lights at sea. A safe cushion of half a mile was permissible. Not anymore. Now there was morning traffic: trucks on the move, cars getting on and off. Plus the sun was low on the horizon behind them, sending glare off the oncoming windshields and chrome. And even the Closer's eyes were weary after so many hours behind the wheel.

Still, fatigue was not an option. If necessary, the Closer could tail them for forty-eight hours straight without sleep, thanks to proper mental and physical conditioning. In the Suburban's glove compartment there was also a generous supply of a new and powerful designer amphetamine known on the street as Seven-Eleven. The Closer preferred not to take drugs of any kind, but the uppers were effective in an emergency and vastly outweighed the alternative.

"Hello, wha' is it?" Lord Augmon's voice on the other end of the phone was hoarse and sounded disoriented. It amused the Closer that the man was so obviously still in bed. How many times had he bragged to interviewers that one of the secrets of his amazing success was that he always rose at five A.M., no matter where in the world he found himself? Which, right now, happened to be in Washington.

"You asked me to phone you if there was any change."

"Yes, yes," Augmon responded quickly. "By all means. What is it?" He was alert and focused now, his crisp accent back in place.

"I don't wish to alarm you, but they are heading in the direction of Nashville."

The only sound from the other end was the slightly raspy sound of the man's breathing. "I see."

The Closer wondered what it was that this billionaire saw, but said nothing. It wasn't the Closer's job to wonder about such things.

"Well . . . then I suppose it's time for us to take care of them. For *you* to take care of them."

"Is that what you want me to do?"

"One moment, if you please."

The Closer heard rapid-fire tapping noises now. Augmon was checking something out on his laptop computer, a device he reportedly took to bed with him every night—another one of his secrets to success. And when this one was revealed in a *60 Minutes* profile, millions of ambitious young executives all across America started imitating him. No doubt countless marriages had been ruined.

"By God," he said excitedly. "Have you seen the overnights for *Need to Know*?"

"No," the Closer answered. "Somehow I missed them."

"The ratings have gone through the proverbial roof! Up twenty-seven percent over last week."

"And that's good?" the Closer asked.

"Good? The only time they've been higher was the week of the O.J. verdict." There was the sound of more fervent tapping. "Lord, Lord, Lord," the man now breathed. "Circulation is up in New York and Washington, *advertising* is up . . ." He was making excited clucking sounds now. "ANN as a whole is up over ten percent for the week."

"In other words, leave them be for now?"

"In precisely those words, my young friend. Leave them be. My instincts were right. The public absolutely loves this boy, especially now that they think he's killed the only woman he's ever loved. I'm beginning to love him a little myself." He sounded downright jolly. "I'm afraid they remain vastly more valuable to us alive than dead. Until and unless they find out enough to be of serious danger. Is that understood?"

"Completely understood."

"Can I get you anything?" The way he said this made it sound like he was offering the Closer a cocktail.

"Such as?"

"I could arrange to fly Payton down, if you wish."

"I don't." Bringing Payton in as backup was the Closer's worst nightmare. The ex-cop was a slob, a fuck-up. Hence the supply of uppers.

"Suit yourself," the man said easily. "But whatever you do, don't lose them."

"You can count on me."

"If you ever get to know me better, and it is my sincere hope you never will, you will discover that I don't count on anyone. Good day."

The phone went dead at the other end.

The Closer pushed the power-off button and resumed driving.

Jeremiah Bickford had always thought he'd be president of the United States.

He'd thought so when he was captain of the debate club at Taft Junior High School in Athens, Ohio, in 1944. He'd thought so when he was voted president of the Lincoln High School graduating class of 1947. Everything after that seemed only to reinforce his belief and his ambition: second team All-American offensive guard on the football team and top of his class at the University of Miami, Ohio; rising to the rank of captain in the air force; in the top tenth at Ohio State Law School. He was wooed and hired by one of the Midwest's most prestigious law firms, was made a partner within five years, and when he was thirty-four years old he was elected to Congress with an astonishing 69 percent of the vote.

Jerry Bickford took to Washington, D.C., as he'd taken to everything else in his life: easily and successfully. When Bickford was a rookie congressman, Lyndon Johnson took a shine to him and placed him firmly under his wing. Soon he was not only standing before LBJ as the president sat on the toilet and talked about his gall bladder scar, but sitting with his shirtsleeves rolled up drinking bourbon with John Connally and breakfasting at the vice presidential mansion listening to Hubert Humphrey complain that no one paid any attention to him.

For the next twenty years Bickford did his job supremely well, stayed in touch with his roots back home, made new friends in Washington, kept his enemies few and far between, and became one of the most respected, fair-minded politicians in the country. He fought with Nixon, shook his head at McGovern's incompetence, pounded his head in frustration trying to cut through Carter's inexperienced and arrogant entourage, and made the best deals he could with Reagan, never 100 percent certain that Ronnie actually knew who Bickford was.

It was 1988 when he first realized that he would never become president himself, and the realization came as somewhat of a shock.

The country was not interested in hard work and good deeds and genuine midwestern values. The American people had become enamored with sound bites, flashy ad campaigns, and vicious mudslinging to which Jerry Bickford could never stoop. He reacted to this sudden and stunning knowledge the way he'd always reacted: He took a step back, assessed the situation, shrugged, and went back to work, becoming a mentor to the new breed of congressmen and senators, or at least those who wanted to bother learning the ropes.

One of those who did want to learn was Tom Adamson. They'd met when Adamson was a brilliant twenty-something and Bickford was a respected forty-something. Bickford admired brilliance, and Adamson was desperate for respect. Their relationship quickly turned into something far more than a political partnership. They became close friends, hunting together, going on vacations with their wives as couples, spending long evenings over dinners talking about the Middle East and Social Security and interest rates. Both Jerry and his wife, Melissa, grew close to Elizabeth Adamson, too. They admired Elizabeth's intellect and confidence, and they helped her to grow more comfortable with herself and more poised in the glare of the spotlight. Elizabeth was such a dominant member of Adamson's brain trust that Bickford spent almost as many evenings one-on-one with her as he did with her husband, tutoring her in the way things worked behind the scenes and showing her how to befriend the press and, in general, win friends and influence the people on the Hill.

It was Jerry Bickford who got Tom Adamson elected president. He was the first of the old guard to back the southern outsider. He made campaign speeches for him, raised money for him, and showed the party that Adamson could not only lead the party but win the country. It was no surprise to anyone in Washington when Adamson asked his mentor to become his vice president. Nor was it a surprise when Bickford accepted. They were the perfect pair: the older man with his balance and wisdom, the younger man with his dynamism and charisma.

They were a political match made in heaven.

It was only late at night that Jeremiah Drew Bickford would question the path he'd taken with his life, staring up at the ceiling, lost in his own thoughts. Thoughts that he had come so close to fulfilling his dreams and yet was an eternity away from fulfillment.

He was thinking such thoughts now, even though it was not late at night. It was midafternoon and he was walking into the White House, about to have an informal tea with the president and First Lady.

"I just want you to know," Tom Adamson said as Bickford strolled into the room, "that what you are requesting is totally unacceptable."

"Maybe you should hear me out, Mr. President."

"I'm not interested in hearing you out. And don't call me Mr. President, you old bastard. It means you're up to something. And since when don't you kiss my wife when you come into the room? Isn't she good-looking enough for you?"

Bickford glanced over at Elizabeth Adamson. She was wearing a red suit with a white silk blouse. Bickford thought she looked magnificent. She combined elegance with dignity as few women he'd ever seen.

"With all due respect, Mr. President, she's far too good-looking for you. And I'm not kissing her because I'm not very kissable right now."

"Let's take a look, Jerry," Elizabeth Adamson said softly.

That's when the vice president frowned and pulled the handkerchief, the one he'd been holding up to his mouth, down to his side.

"Pretty bad, huh?" he said.

"Not bad enough to resign, my friend," President Adamson said gently. "Not bad enough to stop doing what you love. And what your country needs you to do."

"I can't do what my country needs me to do any longer, Tom," the vice president said. "Look at me."

Tom Adamson stared at his closest friend and almost wept. The right side of Jerry Bickford's face, from the eyelid to the corner of his mouth, drooped, almost like the face of a basset hound. His speech was slurred, sounding as if he were drunk. His right eye was watering, and when he tried to smile reassuringly at the president and his wife, a little drop of spittle poured onto his lip and ran down his chin. Bickford immediately brought the handkerchief back up and wiped the saliva away.

It had been a little over a week since the vice president had developed Bell's palsy, a not uncommon paralysis of the facial muscles. It had come upon him suddenly, with no warning, and the doctors had no explanation. He simply woke up one morning with a drooping face and a perpetual drool. He also found out, soon afterward, that he couldn't taste his food. And sounds were disturbingly distorted, loud, and jarring.

The doctors said the disease would probably go away in a few months—if he was lucky, maybe six weeks. There was always the chance, of course, that it would never go away at all.

He looked like an old man who'd had a stroke—a drooling old man with slurred speech and slack muscles. Which was why he'd decided to resign as vice president. He would serve out his term, but he was there to tell Tom Adamson that three weeks hence, at the party's convention, he would have to announce a new running mate.

"Looks were never your strong point, you know, Jerry," President Adamson said quietly.

"It's not just the damn palsy, Tom. As far as I'm concerned, it's a sign, that's what it is. A sign that I'm too damn old to be playing a young man's game."

"You're the youngest man I know, Jerry," Elizabeth Adamson said.

"And you're the sweetest woman. But you're also a damn liar. And don't pour me any of that tea shit. I'll just slobber it down the front of my shirt. Give me a real drink, please."

The president poured out a highball glass half-full of scotch and handed it to Bickford. Then he poured some for himself. When he looked at Elizabeth, she said, "Why the hell not," and when she was handed her glass, she joined them in a silent toast.

"Can we at least discuss this, Jerry?" Adamson asked.

"We can do anything you'd like. I'm here to serve you, you know that, Tom."

"Oh, cut the crap. I want to know if I can talk you out of this. It's not just important to me personally, it's important to the country."

"I'd be a drain on the campaign. You know I'm right. Even if I could do the job, which I'm just not sure I can anymore, think of the field day the media'd have putting this mug all over the front page. It'd be a freak show. 'Next on CNN, listen to the vishe preshident try to shpeak!' "

Elizabeth Adamson stood up, went over to Bickford, and took his hand in hers. "Jerry," she said, "we wouldn't be here without you. We don't care what the media would do or say. We can deal with anything we need to deal with. You are the best friend either one of us will ever have, so the only thing that matters is what you want to do. If you'd like to run on the ticket, we want you to be there. And you will be. If you don't, we'll support you however you want to be supported. A cabinet job now or in six months, an ambassadorship, whatever you like."

He thought a long time before responding. Then, with a grateful, loving look at both the president and the First Lady, he said, "I want out. It's best for you and it's best for me."

There was an awkward silence. Elizabeth was ashen. Tom Adamson looked deeply shaken by the definitiveness of Bickford's words.

"I'd like to hold off on the announcement," the vice president said. "I'd like to make it as close to the convention as possible."

"Jerry," Elizabeth said quietly, "if your mind's made up, it's better if we announce it quickly. We don't want the voters going into the convention thinking that our choice for vice president was a last-minute one. We don't want any unnecessary surprises. If you still think you might change your mind, we'll wait until the last minute. But if—"

"My mind's made up. And you're right, of course. Any way you want to handle it is fine with me. It won't make much difference to my life. I'll be keeping a low profile until then, anyway, staying out of sight so I don't scare little children and small animals."

"What does Melissa think?" Elizabeth asked. "How terrified is she that you're going to be underfoot now?"

"She's excited. Thinks we can actually travel without having to plan the trips around a state funeral."

"Well," Adamson said, using gruffness to disguise his genuine sadness, "you'd better find me a replacement, you old coot. And try to find someone who'll actually do what I want him to do, will you? Not like you, you stubborn son of a bitch."

Bickford tried a smile but had to hide it behind his handkerchief. "I'll try," he said. "But I can't promise anything. Who the hell's going to want to work with you?"

The president drained the rest of his scotch and immediately poured himself another. As he raised the glass to his lips he saw Bickford staring at him. The vice president's eyes were narrowed, and Adamson thought, *My God, he really does look old. Old and frightened.* Then he thought, *Hell, maybe that's just what happens to you when you get old. You get frightened.*

"If I may," Bickford said slowly, "there is something else." Adamson nodded and waited. Bickford hesitated, then continued. "We now know that *I'm* falling apart," he said. "But it's you I'm worried about, Tom. Something's wrong."

"Hell, there are a lot of things wrong, Jerry. My budget proposal's shot to hell, the goddamn Iraqis are—"

"No. It's more than that."

"What then?"

"I don't know," the vice president said. "You seem preoccupied. Tense. I was watching you the other day when you were getting briefed for Netanyahu. You didn't hear a word they were saying. That's not like you, my friend."

"I have . . ." the president began ". . .a lot of things on my mind."

"When we were down at your mother's, for her birthday party, you looked as wonderful as I've ever seen you. I even said, 'You old son of a bitch, how can a president of the United States be so damned relaxed?' But something's happened since then. Something's strange."

"Tom hasn't been sleeping well," Elizabeth broke in. "For the last few weeks. His back's been acting up. That's all. Nothing stranger than that."

"For God's sake," Bickford said to his old friend, "why didn't you say anything? I know what kind of agony that can be."

"You know him," Elizabeth said with a grimace. "Still thinks he's sixteen years old. That he can just tough it out."

"Well, I have to say that's a relief," Bickford said. "I'm sorry you're in such pain, but still . . ." He smiled, dabbing at the fleck of saliva that came with the effort. "Now I can go back to feeling sorry for myself and not have to worry about you."

"You do know, Jerry," Elizabeth Adamson said, "that we love you very much."

"Yes," the soon-to-be ex–vice president said, "I do know that."

"Why are we getting off here?" Carl wondered when Amanda suddenly and without warning pulled off the highway.

"We're in Chapel Hill, that's why," she replied as she eased them through its leafy, prosperous outskirts into town.

Carl already knew this. He knew it because every store window on Franklin Street—from the Shrunken Head T-shirt shop to Sutton's Drug Store—was colored powder blue, the official Tar Heels color. He knew it because when he was a junior, Cornell had made the pilgrimage down here for an early-season nonconference game in the Dean Dome. It had been a real nail-biter—Dean Smith's nationally ranked team had edged out Big Red 90–44, although Carl had managed to dish out eight assists and hold Hubert Davis to thirty-two points. "So?"

"Have you by any chance watched the network news lately?" Amanda demanded. "Every single commercial is for denture adhesives, bladder control protection, Ensure, Cadillacs . . . are you with me?"

Carl gazed at her. When he was not in the best of moods—and for obvious reasons that was an understatement for his current state of mind—her leaps of logic could often elude him. Her charm, however, could not. How could anyone who had been driving all night look so delectable? He thought about asking her this question, then decided better of it. "Totally," he replied. "I just have no idea what you're talking about."

"College students don't watch TV news. They don't read daily newspapers, either. The *Journal*'s latest focus group showed that they're our toughest market. Current events bore them. They're vastly more interested in listening to music, drinking, and chasing down members of the opposite sex."

"I don't blame them."

"Be that as it may," she said disapprovingly, "the residents of a college town are much less likely to recognize either of us than the people in some hick town out in the middle of—"

"Are you *sure*?" Carl broke in.

"Especially during summer school," she added confidently, "when the only students who are here are football players or underachievers trying to make up classes they bailed on or flunked. And besides, what better place than a college town to find a store that rents out computer time?"

More and more delectable, he thought.

They spotted what they needed almost right away. There was a huge Kinko's right near campus that was open twenty-four hours a day. And Copy World was directly across the street. Both offered on-line rental time. Both were also hubs of morning activity, brightly lit, crowded with alert, fresh-faced students. Amanda idled out front a moment, peering at them warily. She did not appear especially anxious to put her theory about college students' media apathy to the test. Carl was in total agreement. So they kept going.

On a narrow side street, tucked in between a unisex haircutting parlor and a stereo repair shop, they found what they were looking for. Virtual Coffee, Chapel Hill's local cybercafe, was dimly lit, grungy, and nearly deserted at this hour. On-line rentals were ten dollars an hour, according to the hand-lettered sign in the smeared window.

She pulled over out front, parked, and opened her door. She saw Carl reach for his door handle and said, "Do you think that's a good idea?"

He hesitated, peering in at the coffeehouse's denizens. There were only two of them, and both appeared to have their foreheads glued to their terminals. "If I don't get out of this car soon, I'm going to turn into a pretzel. Not the soft kind, either. The hard, crunchy kind that you break your jaw on when you bite into them."

"Does that mean you're coming in?"

"I'm coming in," he said. He could tell that didn't sit well with her, so before she could get out of the car, he reached out for her. He was just going to explain, to make her understand that he had to do something, that he couldn't just passively sit still anymore. But it was a mistake. He shouldn't have touched her. He felt the charge, and he was sure she felt it, too. It was as if an electric current were running between the tips of his fingers and her skin. They sat facing each other, the silence overwhelming. It seemed like hours to him but must have been mere seconds. His eyes searched hers questioningly, but he received no answers—not unless slamming a car door counted as an answer. He watched her jerk away and practically run inside the storefront. He followed her, groaning from the stiffness in his lower back.

Virtual Coffee was a typical, no-frills campus coffeehouse where students could hang out and talk to each other. The only thing a bit unusual about it was that none of them were actually occupying the same physical space while they conversed. There were a dozen or so computer terminals of varying ages and brands, all of them well worn. There were mismatched tables and chairs that looked as though they'd been left out on the street for someone to haul away. Some were held together with silver duct tape. One appeared to have been a car seat in a previous life. There were flyers tacked to bulletin boards on the walls, which were covered with graffiti. There was a coffee bar with stools, behind which a cadaverous, goateed, neo-hepcat sat glued to a tube of his own. An old Dave Brubeck jazz album, *Time Out,* played softly in the background.

It was, Carl concluded, a most unusual clash of decades—Dobie Gillis meets the Jetsons.

Amanda arranged for the use of a terminal from the Maynard G. Krebs look-alike behind the bar while Carl sat in front of a scuffed, vintage Mac LC, keeping his face close to it as a shield from the other customers. Both were young men. One, dressed in a camouflage suit and unlaced running shoes, was locked into some form of on-line video combat. The other, with stringy hair down to his waist, was engaged in a furious, finger-flying cyberdebate. Neither appeared to be aware that he and Amanda had even walked in.

She joined him, carrying two espressos. She handed one to him and pulled up a chair. "Shaneesa should be in the newsroom by now." And then she went to work.

Carl read over her shoulder as Amanda sent Shaneesa Perryman the following instant message:

> [You fucked up the obit, girlfriend. I was NEVER head cheerleader—that was Devon Brown.]

Now they waited for a response, sipping their coffee anxiously. A minute passed. And then another. Amanda started tapping her finger impatiently. Carl started to walk away, but he heard Amanda's pleased little gasp of air and returned to look at the screen. The message was there, as plain as could be:

> [Whoever you are, this is a bad, mean joke.]

Amanda, nodding, a little smile on her face, let her fingers fly over the keyboard.

> [It's not a joke. And what do you MEAN I don't look good in purple?]

The response came back quicker this time, as if Shaneesa had recovered from the shock and was able to move at her usual warp speed.

> [This can't be happening . . . you're dead!]
> [Am not. Wasn't home. Thanks for the kind words, though.]

[Girl, where are you?]

[Whoa. First things first. Is your system safe?]

[The safest, you know that.]

[Who can access it?]

[Not a soul other than this little ol' cybergeek.]

[How certain are you?]

[Got my security so tight it'd be pointless for the good Lord himself—or even Steve Jobs—to try to crack it. Drives the suits here crazy. You talk to me on this machine, you're talkin' to me alone. So, I repeat, where are you?]

[You're better off not knowing. And we'll have to make this fast. And STRICTLY between us. Not a word to ANYONE. Cool?]

[Cool. You're not alone, am I right?]

[No comment.]

[God, am I digging this. It's love on the run. You two are freakin' it again, am I right? Please don't disappoint me.]

"I'm beginning to like this woman," Carl interjected.

"Shut up," Amanda snapped, her cheeks mottling. She answered:

[Get your mind out of the gutter. And now is not a good time for this discussion. We've got serious business.]

[Okay, okay, only, check, do I get the story?]

[This is a life-or-death situation. How can you think about the story at a time like this?]

[You trained me well.]

[It's yours.]

[Then use me, girl.]

[I need the biggest Elvis fan in the world.]

[Which Elvis?]

[Presley, duh.]

[Which one, duh? They have subspecies—young Elvis, Hollywood Elvis, Vegas Elvis, fat Elvis, dead Elvis . . .]

[The 1955 Elvis.]

[Gimme five. And your credit card numbers.]

[What for?]

[The Harry and David catalogue's been after me to join their Fruit of the Month Club. Now seems like a perfect time. Just give 'em to me, will ya? And don't ask why—unless you want me to start askin' some questions of my own.]

Amanda sent Shaneesa the numbers of her American Express and Visa cards. Then they waited for her to get back to them. Amanda sat stiffly, leaning forward, her hands locked around her knees, her eyes never leaving the screen. Carl sipped his espresso, glancing around. He did not like what he saw.

"Don't look now," he said to her under his breath, "but that guy behind the counter is staring at us."

"We're almost done."

"Time for the *Journal* to get a new focus group, because he also happens to have a newspaper in front of him. Let's get out of here."

"In a minute," she said tensely.

"He's looking over at the telephone. . . ."

"We've *got* to get her answer."

"Amanda, let's go."

"We need another minute!"

"Look, maybe he's thinking of calling his sainted mother, for all I know, but maybe he's not. And—"

"Here we go. She's back."

Carl looked at the screen. Sure enough, Shaneesa's new message was appearing.

[You want Duane and Cissy LaRue, Miller's Creek Road, Hohenwald, Tennessee. Fairly certain they fit your specs.]

[Are they on the Web?]

[No, for obvious reasons.]

[Why obvious?]

[You'll find out when you meet 'em. Anything else?]

[Now that you mention it . . . can you find out what *bien-venue* is?]

[I'm sure I can. But can you give a girl some kind of teeny clue?]

[Wish I could. It's a French word. Means "welcome."]

[What is it you need to know?]

[Why a man who's about to fly the coop would tattoo that word on his body.]

[By fly the coop, do you mean leave the country?]

Amanda looked back at Carl, who nodded.

[Affirmative.]

[I'll get right on it. Later, girl. Be good.]

[Too late for that, I'm afraid.]

[Well, then you sure as shit be careful. Love you.]

[Ditto.]

She disconnected the modem from the cybermail service and sat staring at the blank screen in front of her. She didn't sit long, however, because Carl was tugging at her arm, pulling her up.

"For God's sake, Amanda, let's get out of here," he said urgently.

She looked at the proprietor, who was staring at them, squinting. She looked at the two computer nerds, who now glanced up curiously at the strange sound of human conversation. And she looked longingly back at the computer screen, a tether to a much saner past.

They got out of there.

chapter 21

Partial transcript of the July 11 meeting of the Telecommunications, Trade, and Consumer Protection Subcommittee of the Senate Commerce Committee. Topic: international satellite and wireless communications. Transmitted on the Internet, http://www.anntranscripts.com.

Click Here for Today's Hearing	**Click Here for ANN Coverage**	**Click Here for Committee Members**

Click Here for Related Links	**Click Here for RealAudio Archives**

Watch Friday's hearing in its entirety on ANN-Span, ANN's new spin-off channel, devoted to coverage of the Senate and the House of Representatives.

Rely on ANN On-line for live coverage of all the Senate Commerce Committee hearings as well as the Senate Government Affairs Committee's hearings on campaign finance investigations. Listen to previous hearings with your free RealPlayer in our Senate Committee Archive.

The committee is tentatively scheduled to continue hearings on Tuesday, Wednesday, and Thursday next week. Each hearing is scheduled to begin at 10:00 A.M. Eastern time. Please note that the Congress will be in recess from Saturday, August 2, through Monday, September 1. Therefore no hearings will be held during the month of August. Hearings will resume in September.

On June 17, the Senate Commerce Committee began looking into complications arising from international business dealings and potential problems as to rights, monopolistic takeovers, and governmental restrictions relating to satellite and wireless communications. The House Committee on Commerce Reform is expected to begin similar hearings later this year.

Committee members: chairman, Senator Walter Chalmers (R-Wyoming); Senator Charles Benton (R-Rhode Island); Senator Molly Hearns (D-California); Senator Alexander Mayfield (D-Maryland); Senator Paul Maxwell (D-Texas).

Today the Committee's witness list includes
Lord Lindsay Augmon, chairman and CEO of Apex International.
Jeremiah D. Bickford, vice president of the United States of America,
has had his appearance canceled due to a scheduling conflict.

SENATOR WALTER CHALMERS: Good morning. I am Senator Walter Chalmers, chairman of the Senate Subcommittee on Telecommunications, Trade, and Consumer Protection. I would like to thank all of our committee members as well as our first witness, Lord Lindsay Augmon, for agreeing to testify and educate us all. Lord Augmon.

LINDSAY AUGMON: I am Lindsay Augmon, chairman and chief executive officer of Apex International. I would like to thank Chairman Chalmers and the entire committee for the opportunity to testify today.

SENATOR CHALMERS: Mr. Augmon . . . it *is* all right if I call you Mr. Augmon?

LINDSAY AUGMON: I'll even give you permission to call me Lindsay, Walter.

SENATOR CHALMERS: Thank you so much. Lindsay . . . you are aware that we had the president of Fairfield Aviation talking to us yesterday?

LINDSAY AUGMON: I am. I use Fairfield Aviation to build and launch my communications satellites.

SENATOR CHALMERS: And the cost of that building and launching?

LINDSAY AUGMON: Somewhere approximating a hundred million dollars.

SENATOR CHALMERS: That's per satellite?

LINDSAY AUGMON: Yes, per satellite.

SENATOR HEARNS: According to my figures, it's closer to a hundred and twenty-five million.

LINDSAY AUGMON: It can go that high.

SENATOR HEARNS: Then, for the record, can we say that the cost approximates a hundred and twenty-five million dollars?

LINDSAY AUGMON: It's a fair approximation.

SENATOR CHALMERS: Thank you, Senator Hearns. But I'd appreciate it if you would wait until it's your turn before questioning Mr. Augmon.

SENATOR HEARNS: You mean Lindsay, don't you?

SENATOR CHALMERS: Mr. Augmon, exactly what areas of communications do you use these satellites for?

LINDSAY AUGMON: All the areas Apex is involved with. Direct television broadcasting, radio, wireless communications.

SENATOR CHALMERS: Can you give us some idea of your holdings in these areas?

LINDSAY AUGMON: I can give you a very specific idea. Apex has satellite coverage on five continents. In Latin America we have Apex Entertainment Latin America and Channel Apex. In the United Kingdom we have Apex Star Broadcasting. In Germany we own ApexEin. In Australia, it's Aptel, and in India we have StateTV and Star India. And, as you know, Senator, we've just branched off into America with ApStarUS.

SENATOR CHALMERS: I wonder if you could give us a little more detail about some of these holdings. Would you mind elaborating on, oh, let's say India? This is strictly for our education, of course.

LINDSAY AUGMON: What, specifically, would you like to be educated about?

SENATOR CHALMERS: Let's start with the size of the audience.

LINDSAY AUGMON: Right now, not enormous. Only about forty-five million Indians have color TV sets. And I don't have exclusive satellite rights. I'm forced to share.

SENATOR HEARNS: I'm sorry to hear that. Sharing can be such a bitch.

SENATOR CHALMERS: Senator, please. Mr. Augmon, when you build and launch a satellite, then enlist your subscription base in a foreign country, are there any economic ramifications here in this country?

LINDSAY AUGMON: Wide-ranging ramifications.

SENATOR CHALMERS: Would you please elaborate?

LINDSAY AUGMON: We manufacture in southern California. That's where Fairfield is located. Obviously, we provide a substantial number of jobs. Every time we build a satellite, it brings tens of millions of dollars into the community. Then, of course, because so many of my entertainment holdings are American-based, most of the product that is supplied for overseas viewing brings money to those companies. Not only does that money keep those corporations going, which in turn provides tens of thousands of jobs and brings in money to the local communities, but quite a bit of it goes directly to your government.

SENATOR CHALMERS: You're talking about taxes?

LINDSAY AUGMON: I'm talking about hundreds of millions of dollars in taxes.

SENATOR CHALMERS: Where would you like to be that you're not, sir?

LINDSAY AUGMON: I'm afraid I don't understand the question.

SENATOR CHALMERS: What countries would you like to broadcast to but do not yet have a license for?

LINDSAY AUGMON: Ah. That's an easy one to answer. Every single country you could possibly name.

SENATOR HEARNS: You're in very good shape, Mr. Augmon, for someone with such a voracious appetite.

SENATOR CHALMERS: I've just about had it with your wisecracks, Senator. If you can't maintain the proper protocol, I suggest you leave for this portion of the testimony.

SENATOR HEARNS: I do apologize, Senator. And as hard as it may be, I'll do my best to bite my tongue for the rest of your grand inquisition.

SENATOR CHALMERS: Well, thank the good Lord above. Mr. Augmon, I am confused about something: Why *aren't* you broadcasting in more countries?

LINDSAY AUGMON: As you know, Senator, it's not that easy. There are rules and regulations. And I must follow them like everyone else.

SENATOR CHALMERS: Can you give us some examples?

LINDSAY AUGMON: Trade issues between governments, for one. That can cause quite a snafu.

SENATOR CHALMERS: Because we don't do business with Cuba, you can't get a license to broadcast to Cuba—that sort of thing?

LINDSAY AUGMON: Exactly that sort of thing.

SENATOR CHALMERS: Are there other examples?

LINDSAY AUGMON: Airspace. The FCC controls satellite airspace, the orbit slots.

SENATOR CHALMERS: It's hard to get those slots, is it?

LINDSAY AUGMON: Extremely difficult.

SENATOR CHALMERS: And why is that?

LINDSAY AUGMON: Many reasons. It's a very competitive business now. And there's a shortage of rockets at the moment. It takes up to two years to build one of these hundred-million-dollar toys. But a slot may not stay open for two years.

SENATOR CHALMERS: If you don't get a particular slot, what happens to it? Someone else gets it?

LINDSAY AUGMON: Yes. But that someone might not, by the time the slot opens, have the money to launch their missile. Or their satellite might not be ready. And since we—and by "we" I mean America, Senator—are not the only ones in this business, it is very possible for another country to then have the means to control the flow of communications to the country we were bidding for.

SENATOR CHALMERS: And when that happens?

LINDSAY AUGMON: Then all the money we've been discussing— the money that goes to the American communities, the jobs that go to American workers, the taxes that go to the American government—then it all goes somewhere else.

SENATOR CHALMERS: Now, we've agreed that a satellite launching costs about a hundred and twenty-five million dollars. And even for you, that's a lot of money to gamble with no guarantee of a launch slot.

LINDSAY AUGMON: Even for me. One would have to be crazy to take that kind of a gamble.

SENATOR CHALMERS: And yet unless you take that gamble, our gamble, the American gamble, is that we lose hundreds of millions of dollars in revenue.

LINDSAY AUGMON: That's correct.

SENATOR CHALMERS: Thank you, Lindsay. I greatly appreciate your participation today. It's with some trepidation I now turn the floor over to my esteemed colleague, Ms. Hearns.

SENATOR HEARNS: Thank you, Senator. I hope your trepidation is not wasted on me. Mr. Augmon, I'd like to go back to the discussion of your Indian holdings, the ones you're forced to share, if you don't mind. What is the cost, to the consumer, of that little nonexclusive service of yours? What was it, StateTV?

LINDSAY AUGMON: And Star India. The subscription cost is approximately twenty dollars per month.

SENATOR HEARNS: For both services combined?

LINDSAY AUGMON: No. Per service.

SENATOR HEARNS: Let's just say that half of those television owners subscribe to your service. Is that a fair estimate?

LINDSAY AUGMON: Ultimately, I certainly hope so. Right now it's much closer to twenty percent.

SENATOR HEARNS: Let's call it twenty-five percent, assuming a certain amount of growth. That's approximately eleven million subscribers. At forty dollars per subscriber, that comes to . . . let's see . . .

LINDSAY AUGMON: It comes to four hundred and forty million dollars, Senator.

SENATOR HEARNS: And that doesn't strike you as an enormous sum?

LINDSAY AUGMON: I was talking about the audience before, not the dollars. And no, considering the potential, I would not describe it as enormous.

SENATOR HEARNS: What *would* be enormous to you, Mr. Augmon?

LINDSAY AUGMON: It's a relative term. Hard to define.

SENATOR HEARNS: How about your own company, Mr. Augmon? How about Apex? Would you describe *that* as enormous?

LINDSAY AUGMON: It's a large company.

SENATOR HEARNS: I'm reading from a story in the *New York Times* from approximately two months ago. They list the holdings for Apex International. I'm going to read them, if you don't mind, and I'd like you to correct anything that might be inaccurate. In the area of film, it says that you own what used to be Crown International Films, now renamed the Apex Studio. Under that banner, you own Apex Films, Apex Century, Apex Independent, Apex Family Films, Apex Animation Studios, and Apex Television Productions. It also says that the Apex Studio was the second highest-grossing studio of the last three years. Does that about cover it?

LINDSAY AUGMON: I believe you left out our Apex Documentary division, but that's close enough.

SENATOR HEARNS: In the area of television, you own the Apex Broadcasting Network, the Apex News Network, fifteen Apex television stations, and, in England, Channel Nine. Your newspaper empire here in this country includes the *New York Herald*, the *Washington Journal*, and the *Chicago Daily Mirror*. In England, you own the four largest papers in the country—

LINDSAY AUGMON: Four of the five largest papers.

SENATOR HEARNS: Thank you for the correction. In Australia, you own one hundred and twenty-two newspapers. Can that possibly be correct?

LINDSAY AUGMON: It can.

SENATOR HEARNS: You own *TV Pathfinder* magazine and the Magazine Group, which includes scientific trade journals and four so-called women's magazines. You own Apex Books, the third largest book publishing company in the country. There are all your cable and satellite operations, which you've already enumerated. And then there are your various other companies— printing operations, paper manufacturing, record companies . . .

LINDSAY AUGMON: Yes, Senator, I concede your point. It's an enormous company.

SENATOR HEARNS: Can we focus just a moment longer on some of those satellite holdings?

LINDSAY AUGMON: It's the purpose of this little get-together, I believe.

SENATOR HEARNS: You said you'd like to be everywhere you're not yet, isn't that right?

LINDSAY AUGMON: I was being just a tad facetious.

SENATOR HEARNS: Were you? Well, then let's get specific, so we know when you're not just being facetious. Where would you like to be broadcasting to that you're not?

LINDSAY AUGMON: There are many—

SENATOR HEARNS: China?

LINDSAY AUGMON: Yes, of course, China. Plus—

SENATOR HEARNS: Would China qualify as an enormous market, in your opinion?

LINDSAY AUGMON: It would.

SENATOR HEARNS: And, as of this moment, how many people would you be forced to share that market with?

LINDSAY AUGMON: Well, it would be a bidding situation with the Chinese government running the—

SENATOR HEARNS: Yes, I understand that. I'm not asking who you'd be bidding against. I'm asking who you'd have to share with.

LINDSAY AUGMON: If you'd let me answer the question, I'd be happy to tell you what you want to know. As of the moment, there is no one to share it with.

SENATOR HEARNS: The bidding rights are up for grabs?

LINDSAY AUGMON: That's one way of putting it, I suppose. The Chinese government has not yet made its choices.

SENATOR HEARNS: And when they do, what would those rights be worth? More than the four hundred forty million dollars you stand to make in India?

LINDSAY AUGMON: It's not that black and white. There is a lot of technology that still has to be brought in, and we don't know exactly how prevalent television will—

SENATOR HEARNS: Mr. Augmon, would you like to know what the experts I've talked to estimate as the worth if someone could gain exclusive satellite broadcast rights to China?

LINDSAY AUGMON: I'm sure you're going to tell me.

SENATOR HEARNS: You're damn straight I'm going to tell you. Over the next ten to fifteen years, as much as a hundred billion dollars!

LINDSAY AUGMON: I'm sure that's a slight exaggeration.

SENATOR HEARNS: Only slight?

LINDSAY AUGMON: It's worth a great deal of money, Senator.

SENATOR HEARNS: Ah. So now we finally have an idea of what you consider a lot of money: a hundred billion dollars! I'm glad to hear it, because I also think it's a lot of money. And why aren't you bidding for China, Mr. Augmon?

LINDSAY AUGMON: I believe you know the answer to that.

SENATOR HEARNS: Because the president won't allow it.

LINDSAY AUGMON: Because the president's policies won't allow it.

SENATOR HEARNS: His human rights policies. Which I assume you disagree with.

LINDSAY AUGMON: I admire President Adamson's compassion. But I question his priorities.

SENATOR HEARNS: Yes, I'm sure you do.

LINDSAY AUGMON: I don't believe that a ban on trade with China is going to right the world's wrongs. I think, in fact, it will greatly exacerbate them.

SENATOR HEARNS: To get one of the satellite slots that open up, is there a lot of lobbying that goes on?

LINDSAY AUGMON: As I'm sure everyone in this room knows, Senator, when dealing with your government it never hurts to have deep pockets.

SENATOR HEARNS: An unfortunate but accurate observation. How deep do your pockets go when it comes to Senator Chalmers?

SENATOR CHALMERS: This is outrageous! How dare you! What the hell do you think you're doing? What the hell are you implying?

SENATOR HEARNS: Please calm down, Walter. I'm not implying anything. Please. It was an unfortunate transition. I was just trying to verify that Mr. Augmon is indeed one of the larger contributors to your presidential campaign.

SENATOR CHALMERS: And what the hell does that have to do with anything going on in here?

SENATOR HEARNS: I believe that now you're infringing on my time.

SENATOR CHALMERS: You are stepping on the wrong goddamn toes, Senator.

SENATOR MAXWELL: Senators, please, this is not the time for a down-home pissing contest. Why don't you sit down, Walter, and let Molly finish her damn questions?

SENATOR HEARNS: Thank you, Paul. Mr. Augmon . . . ?

LINDSAY AUGMON: I have given money to Senator Chalmers's campaign, yes. I find him a man of integrity and I support his political positions.

SENATOR HEARNS: Which do not include the same human rights policies and trade restrictions on China.

LINDSAY AUGMON: I'm not a hundred percent aware of the specifics in that area.

SENATOR HEARNS: You are aware, sir, that Vice President Bickford was supposed to be testifying before this committee later today.

LINDSAY AUGMON: I am. I understand he's quite ill.

SENATOR HEARNS: So your newspapers are implying. But we're not here to gossip about the supposed state of the vice president's health. Are you aware that Vice President Bickford has recently issued a statement in which he says, and I'm now quoting, "Modern communications empires like those owned by Lindsay Augmon are the new military-industrial complexes. One of the greatest dangers to American society and the world at large, possibly the greatest danger, is that Apex International already controls so much of what the world reads and watches. Lindsay Augmon, not the president, not any politician, is the most powerful man in the world because he has the insidious ability to make people think what he wants them to think." What do you think about that statement, Mr. Augmon?

LINDSAY AUGMON: I think two things. One is that I'm flattered that the vice president gives me so much credit. And two is that I look forward to finding out any plans for his political future so that I can use appropriately whatever power he thinks I have.

SENATOR HEARNS: Thank you, Mr. Augmon. I'd like to introduce you to your next inquisitor, the junior senator from the grand state of Maryland. Senator Mayfield?

SENATOR MAYFIELD: Good morning, Mr. Augmon. I'd like to go back to the subject of airspace, for a moment. There are four places in the world from which communications satellites are currently launched, if my information is correct.

LINDSAY AUGMON: I believe it has to do with weather conditions, Senator.

SENATOR MAYFIELD: And those places are, let me see, Cape Canaveral, Florida, in the United States; Xichang, China; Tanegashimi, Japan; and Kourou, French Guiana . . .

chapter 22

t was late-afternoon rush hour by the time Carl and Amanda reached the greater Nashville area. Blow-dried commuters in sparkling new cars were crawling home to the sparkling new suburban communities that seemed to sprawl in every direction. Carl and Amanda found themselves caught in the middle of honking, steaming, bumper-to-bumper traffic that brought them to a dead standstill. It made New York look like an easy city in which to navigate.

The thriving New South, Carl reflected impatiently. He could not imagine why a nice small city like Nashville had not learned from the mistakes that formerly nice places such as Atlanta and Houston had made. He could not understand why any city would purposely want to ruin itself in the name of so-called progress.

It was Carl's turn behind the wheel now. Amanda was working the map. Also the radio dial, in search of an all-news station. Which was no easy task. She found them a station that was All Country, no problem. Another that was New Country. She also found Classic Country, Soft Country, Rockin' Country, Best Country . . . Until finally, she found the latest headline news broadcast.

Carl's "spree killings" were far and away the top story. The station was even taking phone calls, soliciting theories as to where Carl was hiding and where and whom he'd strike next. In between calls they learned that after an exhaustive all-day search of the charred wreckage of the D.C. carriage house, authorities still had not located Amanda Mays's remains. Speculation was growing that she might not have been home at the time and was, in fact, missing rather than dead. The FBI would neither confirm nor deny this suspicion.

As to Carl Granville's whereabouts, authorities reported that they were still pursuing numerous very promising leads.

"Excellent," Amanda exclaimed, flicking off the radio. She hated country music—new, old, soft, loud, best, worst. It all depressed her.

"What's so excellent about it?" Carl asked.

"They have zippo, that's what. Zilch, nada, bupkes."

"What makes you so sure?"

"The phrase 'pursuing numerous very promising leads' is police-speak for 'We have no fucking idea where he is.' We got away clean," she assured him, patting his knee. "You can relax."

"I'd love to, Amanda, but I don't remember how."

After an hour of excruciating traffic they finally left Nashville's outskirts behind and were streaking south on Highway 65. She directed him to get off at a little town called Columbia, which boasted the birthplace of America's eleventh president, James K. Polk, as well as the largest, newest plant devoted solely to the manufacture of Saturn automobiles. Thanks to the Saturn plant, the modern world had caught up to Columbia. There were new housing tracts, new strip malls, new car dealerships. From there she had him get onto the Natchez Trace, an immaculate and lush green parkway that was utterly deserted except for them and the occasional family of deer. When they got off the Natchez Trace a few miles outside of Hohenwald, they found themselves in a place that progress had somehow managed to steer around. Here they were firmly rooted in the rural backwoods South of dirt farms, shotgun shacks, dog-eared trailer parks, and tiny whitewashed churches.

Hohenwald had a population of less than four thousand people and, seemingly, one church per resident—most of them devoted to fundamentalist faiths with which Carl was not familiar. There was a brief, run-down main street with parking on the slant, a Piggly Wiggly, a gas station, and a high school. There were a few stores, most of these devoted to the buying and selling of used clothing. As near as Carl could tell, Hohenwald seemed to be the used-clothing capital of Tennessee, if not the entire South.

At the stoplight, Amanda leaned out the window to ask directions from a bearded man who was getting out of his pickup truck. The man was somewhere between the ages of twenty and fifty and had more fingers than he did teeth. His accent was so thick Carl could not grasp one word he said. It sounded a lot like "Macrerosesenmisotowonthrow." Fortunately, Amanda was able to translate.

"Miller's Creek Road is seven miles south of town on this road," she informed him. "Take a left at the church."

Carl shook his head at her. "Jesus, how did you understand him?"

"You forget, I spent a summer down this way before I got out of school," she reminded him. "Working as a news intern at the paper in Birmingham, Alabama. My ear got used to it. Yours will, too, if you stay here long enough. It's a little like being in France, except the food's a lot greasier and they don't serve wine with their grits."

Miller's Creek Road was bumpy, twisting, and narrow. It was not paved, although the flinty, rust-colored native soil—known as chirt—was as unforgiving as stone. There was nothing but deep woods on either side of the road. As dusk approached, fat bugs smacked into the windshield, leaving behind their wet remains. The air was heavy with moisture and utterly still. The Subaru's wheezing air-conditioning system was no match for it. Perspiration streamed down Carl's face. The back of his neck felt slimy. He craved a shower and eight hours on a firm mattress. He was painfully aware it might be some time before he got either.

Every once in a while there would be a mailbox and a dirt driveway leading off into the woods. No homes that were visible from the road, not until they went over an old wooden bridge and around a bend. Here there was a clearing where a small grouping of spanking new reproduction log cabins had been erected, complete with satellite dishes and aboveground swimming pools.

The home of Duane and Cissy LaRue was not one of these.

Their place, a modest-sized brick bungalow with a screened-in porch, was located just beyond. Carl pulled over onto the shoulder of the road and they got out, stretching their legs, looking around. Carl had not been sure what to expect of a place belonging to the world's biggest fans of the young Elvis. It seemed surprisingly ordinary—all except for the two vehicles that were parked in their driveway. One was a 1955 Cadillac convertible. A *pink*

Cadillac convertible. The other was a battered green pickup truck, also of mid-fifties vintage, with a faded sign on its door that read Crown Electric.

"You do realize the significance of Crown Electric, don't you?" Amanda said, staring at it with just a touch of awe on her face.

"Refresh my memory, would you?"

"Crown Electric," she informed him, "was where Elvis was working in Memphis when he first started recording for Sam Phillips at Sun Records." She peered at the truck, then at Carl. "I wonder if this is going to be weird."

"Stop wondering," he said. "It will be."

He was right. The LaRues were quite friendly and pleasant, but they did take a little getting used to. A warning by Shaneesa would have been nice, Carl thought. Something, anything to prepare them for the sight of a 220-pound sixty-something grandmother dressed in pigtails, a plaid jumper, bobby socks, and saddle shoes. And of her stringy, elderly little husband with his jet black pomaded ducktail haircut and his shiny black shirt, black pants with a wide pink stripe running up and down, and white bucks.

Then again, Carl decided, maybe there was no way to prepare for the LaRues.

One thing most definitely in their favor: they were extremely gracious people, not in the least bit put out by two sweaty, desperate strangers showing up on their doorstep unannounced.

"Now you kids come right on in," Cissy chattered merrily. She had a high-pitched, singsong voice. She also had many, many chins, too many to count, and she wore a great deal of fruity, cloying perfume. She smelled, Carl thought, as if she bathed in large tubs of Hawaiian Punch.

"We're very sorry to intrude," Amanda started to say, but the LaRues immediately pooh-poohed her apology.

"It's a pure pleasure to welcome you," Cissy said. "We've gotten used to folks dropping in."

They stood expectantly, as if waiting for Carl and Amanda to say something in response. When they didn't, Duane snorted. "We do a weekly cable television show out of Columbia," he explained, his voice as low and rumbling as Cissy's was birdlike. His manner was much more reserved than his wife's, but also quite polite.

"Don't tell me you haven't seen it," Cissy chirped.

Carl shook his head. Amanda shrugged apologetically.

"How 'bout the newsletter?" Duane rumbled.

This time Amanda shook her head and Carl shrugged.

"Gracious," Cissy said. "It goes out monthly to some twenty-three thousand subscribers."

"Worldwide," Duane added, and there was no mistaking the pride buried in his deep monotone.

"All we try to do," Cissy said, "is share our pure, unadulterated love for Elvis with the people, and give them a chance to share their love with us. It's put all of us in closer touch with our humanity."

"Sounds very spiritual," Amanda said understandingly.

Cissy lit up, her smile spreading across her face. "It is. It really and truly is. All we're really doin' is spreading the gospel. The gospel according to Elvis."

"The Memphis *Commercial Appeal* did an article on us last month," Duane added. "Ever since, people've been dropping by all the time. Just like you."

"Sugar, you have the absolute prettiest hair," Cissy burbled at Amanda, who colored slightly. Compliments made Amanda uncomfortable. "Elvis was always partial to titian tresses, you know. Now, do tell, was it the house you wanted to see, or did y'all want to talk?"

"We want to talk," Amanda answered. "We're searching for something. A place. We thought maybe you'd be able to help us find it."

"We'll sure try," Cissy said warmly.

Carl glanced around at the house. He'd been expecting a kitschy shrine cluttered with Elvis memorabilia—black-velvet Elvis paintings with eyes that followed you around the room, bobble-headed Elvis dolls, that sort of thing. But this wasn't the case at all. True, the old portable record player over by the window was playing a scratchy forty-five of "That's All Right, Mama." True, there was a framed newspaper photo on the mantel of Elvis performing at the Louisiana Hayride with Scotty and Bill. Also a framed picture of Vernon and Gladys with Elvis when he was a little boy in overalls. Otherwise, the house was sparsely and rather humbly furnished. A table fan whirred weakly. There was no air conditioner.

"You mentioned the house," Carl said. "Is there something special about it?"

"Oh, my, yes," Cissy replied. "In March of fifty-five, when Elvis was twenty years old, he, Vernon, and Gladys moved into their first real Memphis home, the one on Lamar, partway between Katz Drug Store and the Rainbow Rink, where Elvis and Dixie first met." She trailed off, her round face dissolving into sadness. "Dixie was a good, church-going Christian girl who loved Elvis for himself, not his fame or his riches—unlike so many of the others who latched on to him through the years. But the strain was already there between them. She'd given him back his class ring once already, you know."

"I didn't realize that," Carl said, then winced as Amanda's elbow caught him in the small of his back.

"The Lamar house was a two-bedroom brick bungalow," Duane continued, "with a small, screened-in porch where Elvis, Scotty, and Bill would rehearse numbers for the neighborhood kids." He steered them over toward the kitchen doorway. It was a noticeably old-fashioned kitchen with fifties appliances and vintage yellow linoleum. "Our home is an exact replica," he revealed proudly, "accurate down to the slightest detail. We've compiled the plans and offer them to anyone who's interested. Free of charge."

"To date," said Cissy, "some seven hundred and ninety-seven people have already built replicas of their own, including one gentleman in Kyoto, Japan, who built his to nine-tenths scale."

Carl nodded. He did not dare look at Amanda or release the firm hold his teeth had on his lower lip, because this was a whole new level of weird. He was not sure he could handle this. Not now. Briefly he thought about waiting in the car, but he could not do that to Amanda—mostly because he was pretty sure she'd kill him.

"Have you been doing your show for a long time?" she asked them, her own voice quavering slightly. Asking questions was her way of maintaining a grip.

"Why, no, sugar," Cissy replied. "We both taught over at the high school until we took early retirement this past June. Duane was there thirty-six good years. I was there thirty-two. But we decided it was time to let some young people get started on their own careers. And for us, to, well, let it all hang out. Y'know, enjoy the time we have left."

"Which we have every intention of doing." Duane grinned at them crookedly, stroking his sideburns. "Where are you folks from?"

"Washington," Carl said. No point in pretending otherwise, since Amanda had a D.C. license plate.

"My, you've come a long way," Cissy said. "Sit and I'll fetch us some refreshments."

They sat on the sofa, which was of horsehair, and rather uncomfortable. Duane sat in the armchair. The record finished playing. The room was silent for a few moments except for the sound of the fan. Then a new forty-five dropped into place. This one was "Good Rockin' Tonight." Cissy returned a moment later with a tray loaded down with corn bread, a pitcher of milk, and glasses. "Elvis loved nothing better than to dip his corn bread in a glass of buttermilk," she declared, pouring them each a glass. "So you go right ahead."

Carl did. The corn bread was delicious, the buttermilk ice cold. And he was starving.

"Can I fix you a peanut butter and banana sandwich?" Cissy asked him, watching him wolf down the corn bread. "Take me only a second to fry one up. Elvis just plain adored them."

"No, no," Carl assured her. "This will be fine."

She sat. Carl tried not to stare at her bulging thighs.

"Now, do tell us what you're searching for," Duane said.

"Well, my parents both passed away when I was a little girl," Amanda began, lapsing into a bit of a drawl.

"Why, you poor thing," Cissy clucked.

"I'm trying to find the town down here where they grew up. You know, locate their birth records and so forth."

"Searching for your roots, huh?" suggested Duane.

"Exactly," Amanda said, nodding. "My roots. Trouble is, I have almost nothing to go on. Except for one thing—they met at an Elvis concert. That's one of the few things I can remember Mama telling me. And I know the approximate date of the concert. Because they got married one year later, almost to the day, up in Norfolk."

Carl nodded, wondering where on earth she'd come up with Norfolk. Where she'd come up with any of it, for that matter. He was beginning to realize that her nature was vastly more devious than his own.

"I just don't know the *where*," she went on. "Anyway, I thought if we could find out where Elvis was performing on that particular date—I mean, if you could look it up in your records . . ."

The LaRues both laughed hugely at this.

"Sugar, there *are* no records," Cissy roared.

"But," Amanda sputtered, "we were told you'd know. . . ."

"Oh, we'll know," Duane assured her.

Cissy, still laughing, tapped her own forehead. "But no records," she said. "It's all up here."

Duane peered at Amanda eagerly. "What was the date?"

"It was nineteen fifty-five," Amanda said. "And we think it was New Year's Eve."

Duane immediately shook his head. "Sorry. Not possible."

"What do you mean?" Carl objected. "Why not?"

"Elvis didn't perform on New Year's Eve that year, son," Duane said. "He was home with his family. In Memphis."

"Oh, dear," Amanda said, her voice heavy with disappointment.

"I'm sorry we couldn't help you, sugar," Cissy said sympathetically.

"Wait, hold on just a second. . . ." Carl racked his brain, trying to re- member what Rayette's diary had said. The exact words. *Damn, what were they? . . . "Three days before Danny's tenth birthday". . . What else? Shit! What else? . . . "A girl in class had a birthday of her own". . . Come on, come on, come on . . . yes! "As a present for her birthday and to welcome in the new year."*

"It doesn't have to be New Year's Eve," he blurted out. "What about over the next few days?" Amanda was staring at him. "What I'm thinking, dear"—Amanda raised an eyebrow at his use of the *d* word—"is that maybe the concert wasn't necessarily held on that exact date."

Amanda frowned at him, confused. "But I thought, *dear,* that Mama al- ways said—"

"I did, too. But she said 'to welcome in the new year.' "

"Are you sure?" Amanda said.

"How do *you* know what her mama said?" Duane asked.

"Well, I . . . I just think it's *possible* that's what she said. It's possible the show could have been a few nights later, isn't it?"

Amanda shrugged her shoulders at this. "I guess it's worth a try." Turning to Duane and Cissy, she said, "Would that be a problem? I mean, to cover the week or two after New Year's?"

"No problem at all," Duane said, scratching his chin. "No sirree. Elvis was with Scotty and Bill in west Texas the week of January the second on a Louisiana Hayride package tour."

Carl sighed inwardly. This was not looking promising. "And what about the week after that?"

"On January the twelfth he played the city auditorium in Clarksdale."

"What state is that in?" Carl asked.

"Why, Mississippi," Duane replied. "He was on a bill with Jim Ed and Maxine Brown. They were a brother-and-sister act. On the thirteenth he performed in Helena. That's Arkansas."

"What can you tell us about those places?" Carl asked, leaning forward.

"Couple of small towns straddling the Mississippi River," Duane said. "An hour or so south of Memphis. Clarksdale's in the delta. Don't know much beyond that about 'em. Don't know that there *is* much to know. On the fourteenth," he continued, sipping his buttermilk, "Elvis was in Corinth, Mississippi. Now, Corinth is just a hop, skip, and jump south of here. Right on the Tennessee-Mississippi border. From there he made his way over to Sikeston, Missouri, then on back to Texas for a five-day tour."

"After that," said Cissy, picking up the story, "poor Elvis's entire universe changed. And not for the better, mind you. Those were his last days of pure happiness, you see. Because it was soon after that, in February, that he joined a Hank Snow package tour under the stewardship of the devil's own instrument, Colonel Parker. That awful man robbed him of his blessed youth, his innocence, and his faith in people. But he could never take away his goodness. *No one* could ever take that away from Elvis."

Amanda turned back to Duane. "These towns that you mentioned— Clarksdale, Helena, Corinth—would any of them happen to have a big factory?"

"What kind?" he asked.

"We're not sure," Amanda replied. "We only know that it made the air smell pretty bad. That's something else Mama mentioned."

Duane pondered this a moment, tugging at a sideburn again. He seemed to enjoy doing that. "Well, you might find yourself a poultry works. You ever been downwind of one of them, you'd know it. Beyond that, I wouldn't say it's too likely you'd find yourself much of anything. Factory jobs are mighty scarce downriver of Memphis. Gone south of the border, most of 'em. Or all the way to Asia. That delta country, my oh my, there's not much there besides cotton fields and sugarcane. And, of course, all of those darn fool casinos they've been building. Not that I have the slightest use for those places. They don't *make* anything. All they do is suck what little money those poor people have right out of their pockets. Why, nine out of the top ten poorest counties in the entire nation are found right there. Poverty rate's three times the national average."

"Duane used to teach social studies," Cissy noted with girlish pride. "He still likes to keep up with current events."

Carl nodded, hoping the old man didn't like to keep up so well that he'd just watched the evening news. It appeared not. He didn't seem to recognize them. He wasn't acting at all nervous or suspicious.

"Are you sure this here plant is still in operation?" Duane pressed Amanda.

"We're not real sure of anything," Carl answered. "Why do you ask?"

"Could be it came and went, that's why," Duane replied. "River's littered with old mills that cleared out a long time ago and never came back. Gotta be a hundred of 'em." He took Carl's groan to be one of empathy for the unemployed. "What do those greedy so-and-so's care if they leave the folks with no food on their tables? They don't care, and that's the honest truth. Not that I mean to sound like some kind of Communist. I happen to be a big believer in the free-enterprise system. All it takes is for one big company to come in, like Saturn did over in Columbia, and wham, it brings the whole area back. You should have seen Hohenwald before Saturn got here. Man, this was *nowhere*."

Carl nodded. Near as he could tell, this still was nowhere. He signaled Amanda.

"You folks have been very kind," she said, getting to her feet.

"Nonsense," Cissy said. "I just hope we were a help."

"You were," Carl answered. "A huge help."

They made their way toward the hundred-percent-authentic replica of

Elvis's first front door. Outside, darkness was approaching. The mosquitoes and no-see-ums were out and biting. Carl and Amanda stood there on the front steps, waving hopelessly at the swarm. Carl had never been surrounded by so many insects in his life.

Duane and Cissy stood framed in the doorway, holding hands like a couple of decaying teenagers. "Just between us friends," Duane said cheerfully, "I'll tell you something that not many know about. That tour Elvis undertook for Colonel Parker in February of fifty-five? It started out in Roswell, New Mexico."

"*The* Roswell, New Mexico?" said Carl, smiling at them.

Duane nodded sagely. "And believe me, we have been contacted by more than our share of UFOlogists, every single one of them hoping to discover a link between Elvis and the Incident."

"And is there one?" Carl asked.

Duane let out a guffaw. "Shoot, no. Doesn't stop them, though. Why, they even have some fool theory regarding the colonel's true planet of origin, what with him always having been so secretive regarding the nationality on his birth certificate."

"I surely am glad you're not with those people," Cissy confided, lowering her voice discreetly. "Not that I like to be critical or judgmental about my fellow man. We're all God's creatures, after all. But, between us, them folks are just plain *weird*."

There was a gravel driveway a few hundred yards down Miller's Creek Road. It was where the Closer had chosen to sit behind the wheel of the Suburban and wait, shielded from the road by the dense brush and the darkness.

The Closer did not like this place. There were too many churches. Too much quiet. And the air was way too sticky and warm, especially with the windbreaker on.

They were inside the small brick house for nearly an hour. Not one car passed by the entire time. When they came back out and got in the Subaru, they turned around and headed back the way they had come—toward Hohenwald. The Closer watched them go. Waited precisely ten minutes. Eased the Suburban over onto the shoulder in front of the house, got out, walked up to the front door and knocked.

The door was answered by a grotesquely fat old woman done up like a bobby-soxer. She was positively ghastly to lay eyes on. Behind her was an old man with Grecian Formula black hair who was trying to look like a fifties schoolyard tough. If one didn't know better, it would be easy to jump to the conclusion that they were on their way to a costume party at the local senior center.

The Closer knew better. "I'm sorry to bother you folks, but I was supposed to meet my friends here." The Closer described Carl Granville and Amanda Mays. "We're on kind of an Elvis pilgrimage. Only I went the wrong way when I got off the Natchez Trace. I've been driving around in circles for the past hour and I was wondering if—"

"Dear, dear," the old lady clucked. "You just missed them."

"Oh, no," the Closer said.

"They left maybe ten minutes ago," the husband said.

"Such a lovely young couple," the fat Sandra Dee said. "Come in, come in, or the bugs will chew you to kingdom come."

"Well, maybe just for a second." It was very stuffy in the house, which reeked of cheap perfume. An old Elvis song, "Baby Let's Play House," was on the record player. "I don't suppose you have any idea which way they might be heading?"

"I'd say Corinth, if I had to guess," the old man replied, tugging at one of his long sideburns. "We gave 'em a few possible leads on her mama's hometown, but Corinth's the closest. Not more than an hour from here. Just over the line in Mississippi. If it were me, I'd start there."

Now the fat woman rattled off the names of two other towns they had given them—one of them a name that the Closer did not want to hear. Not in the least.

"You know, I was thinking," the old man added. "Y'all might go looking for a catfish farm."

The Closer frowned. "A catfish farm?"

"She was asking if we knew of any factories around there," the fat woman translated.

"And what I forgot to mention," the old man said, "is that they're starting to raise catfish down there. Big commercial operations. Of course, they don't taste the same as the real thing. Your catfish is a true bottom feeder—

that's what gives him his unique flavor. You can call a farm-raised catfish a catfish, but he isn't really a catfish—you know what I'm saying?"

"Yes, I think I see what you mean."

"Corinth," the old man said once more. "They'll probably find themselves a nice, clean motel down there tonight. Have a good look around in the morning. If you step on it, you just might catch up to them."

"You know, I think that's exactly what I'll do," the Closer said, pausing only to reach into the windbreaker and yank out the German-made SIG-Sauer 9 mm semiautomatic pistol.

The Closer pumped two shots directly into the old woman's face from point-blank range. She was dead several seconds before her body crumpled to the floor—slowly, like a big, bloated marionette.

Now the Closer took aim at the old man, who stood there wide-eyed and frozen, his hands up before him in an instinctive defensive posture. The first shot shattered his left hand and sent pieces of his fingers flying across the living room. The second shot went through his Adam's apple. He went down, gagging, an unpleasant sucking noise coming from the gaping hole in his throat. The noise got fainter and the old man's hand went up to his cheek. Almost imperceptibly, he tugged one last time at his sideburn. Standing directly over him now, the Closer fired once more, directly between his eyes. The tugging stopped.

Now all was quiet, except for the music that was coming from the record player. The Closer went over and shot the record.

The Closer had never been a big Elvis fan.

There was a black plastic garbage bag in the pocket of the windbreaker. Also a pair of disposable latex gloves. The Closer put these on. There was tidying up to do. Carl Granville could not, *must* not, be linked to this particular job. That was why the Closer had used the clean SIG-Sauer rather than the Smith & Wesson .357 Magnum that tied Granville to the murders of the FBI agent in D.C. and the blonde in New York. And that was why the Closer now had to remove any trace that Granville had ever been here.

There were four glasses on the kitchen counter, an empty plate with crumbs on it, and a wooden tray. The Closer dumped these things into the garbage bag. There was a dish towel hanging beside the kitchen sink. Humming cheerfully, the Closer used this to wipe any fingerprints off the kitchen faucet and the kitchen table and chairs. The Closer was thorough. Methodical. There were some photos of Elvis on the living room mantel. These went into the bag. So did the candy dish and ashtray that were on the coffee table, which were first wiped down with the dish towel. The Closer went back outside to the Suburban—stepping carefully around the bodies and puddled blood en route to the front door—and returned with a small, efficient Dirt Devil vacuum. This was put to good use on the upholstered sofa and armchair as well as the rug in front of them.

The Closer left the remains of the old man's fingers where they lay.

There was one bathroom. Granville might have used it. The Closer wiped down the surface of the door inside and out, both doorknobs, the toilet seat and handle, and the faucet controls. The Closer vacuumed the rim of the toilet bowl and the floor under and around it for any stray pubic hairs. There was a chance that Granville had opened the medicine chest in search of an aspirin, in search of whatever. So the Closer wiped the mirrored door clean and dumped the entire contents of the medicine chest into the trash bag, along with all the hairbrushes and toothbrushes. There was just no telling what people did in other people's bathrooms when the door was closed. And no point in taking chances.

The Closer had not gotten this far by taking chances.

It was hot, thirsty work. The Closer went back into the kitchen and opened the refrigerator. There was buttermilk and a six-pack of Coca-Cola. The Closer popped one of the cans open and drank it down, convinced as always that they used a sweeter formula down here than they did in the North. The empty can went into the trash bag.

Stepping carefully once again around the bodies, the Closer wiped off the front door, the doorknobs, the jamb, the doorbell, and the knocker. Shut every window in the house and locked the back door. Stuffed the dish towel in the trash bag, tied the bag shut, turned out the lights, and closed the front door, making certain that it too was locked. It was very dark outside. The Closer placed the trash bag and the Dirt Devil in the back of the Suburban and got in, pausing to remove the gloves and put them in the glove compartment along with the SIG-Sauer.

Satisfied, the Closer drove off into the night without looking back.

chapter 23

"It's a lovely street. Don't you think?"

"Oh, yes. Absolutely lovely."

"And the location . . ."

"It seems perfect."

"Easily accessible to Capitol Hill and Georgetown. Wonderful shopping nearby. It *is* perfect. Absolutely perfect."

Marsha Chernoff's crayony red lips curled into a smile. She smelled a sale. Well, a rental, to be absolutely accurate. But an excellent rental. The property was overpriced and unfurnished, not the best of combinations. Nonetheless, she was fairly certain she had this slightly out-of-their-element couple hooked and was now getting ready to reel them in.

Marsha worked for D.C. Realtors. Her specialty was finding suburban homes for government workers who'd be spending at least three months in the Washington area. The Hershes were the most easygoing clients she'd had in a long time. Marsha thought it was a combination of nerves and lack of sophistication. Also, D.C. could be a tad overwhelming to outsiders, and Mr. Leonard Hersh was as outside as an outsider could be.

Leonard Hersh was a lawyer, brought in from someplace in New Hampshire, coming to town to be part of the special prosecutor's attack-dog team investigating the latest senatorial scandal. This one had it all: sexual harassment, bribery, and obstruction of justice. Bad for the country, Marsha thought, good for the realty profession. In the old days, men like Leonard Hersh were in and out of the capital in two to three weeks. That was hotel time. Now they could be around for two or three years. That was unfurnished three-bedroom ranch house time. Marsha's motto, which she had needlepointed on a pillow on her office couch, was "Thank You, God, for

272

Giving Politicians Soft Brains, Fast Hands, Stiff Pricks, and Taxpayers' Money."

Donna Hersh, Leonard's wife, wasn't in the business. She was an elementary-school teacher. Marsha could see the entire scenario without being told a word: Donna wouldn't be working for at least a year, she'd get bored or frustrated, and presto, by Christmas she'd be preggers, ready to unleash yet another lawyer on the world. If this investigation lasted long enough, eventually she could populate her own school.

The house she was showing them had just been vacated. It was very curious: The previous tenant had disappeared without a word, forfeiting his security deposit and advance rent. But the property was in excellent shape. No damage. Clean as a whistle. Nothing stolen.

This was the third house she had taken the Hershes to, and Marsha could tell that Donna was anxious to find something she liked. She wanted to make a decision. This was a woman who needed roots.

"I know that the last tenant was wild about his neighbors," Marsha lied. She didn't know the last tenant from Adam. "It seems to be a real community here."

She let them in the front door and watched as Donna Hersh swept her eyes over the expanse of the house, ran her hand along the bland pale blue wallpaper of the entry hall, and said, "I like it. It *feels* right."

They went through each room, and Marsha could tell that with every passing minute they were talking themselves into renting a new home. In each of the two bedrooms they discussed which pieces of furniture they were shipping from New Hampshire and exactly what they would fit where. They both frowned at the size of the bathroom. They both nodded, pleased, at the half bath. She liked the half dining room; he thought the den would be perfect for a TV room and office.

By the time they got to the kitchen, they'd been inside for almost an hour. Donna swept her finger over the kitchen countertop, smiled at Marsha, and said, "We'll take it."

Marsha gave a brief glance to the heavens. Never one to press her luck, she thanked whoever might be up there. Then she started explaining a few necessities to the Hershes—the two months' advance rent, one month's security deposit, a minimum six-month guarantee . . . She looked up and Donna Hersh was frowning. Staring at the corner of the kitchen.

"Something wrong?" Marsha asked.

"In the brochure, I'm sure that it said a refrigerator was included. It specifically said a Sub-Zero refrigerator. I know because I wanted one back home and—"

"Of course. That's exactly what it says. A superb Sub-Zero. It's right over . . . right over . . ." Marsha turned and frowned herself. No refrigerator. "That's odd," she said.

"The appliances come with the house. That's in any rental contract," Leonard Hersh added.

"Absolutely," Marsha said slowly, still trying to figure out where the stainless-steel Sub-Zero had disappeared to. "And I guarantee you that when you move in, that same appliance or its exact equivalent will be here."

"Are you sure?"

"Absolutely sure."

Donna Hersh smiled broadly. "Well, then, as I said, we'll take it."

Marsha Chernoff finished explaining exactly what needed to be done before the Hershes could move in. She did not do her usual flawless job, forgetting to tell them about the utility payments, even forgetting to tell them about the three months' notice required when they eventually decided to leave the house. Her mind was elsewhere.

She was thinking: *Now who would come in here and steal a refrigerator?*

chapter 24

apientia. Pax. Deus.

The Latin words were carved into the dark mahogany archway over the door leading to the simple, rustic chapel.

Wisdom. Peace. God.

Father Patrick Jennings stared up at those three simple words and prayed with all his heart that one day he might work his way back to an understanding of what they truly meant. When his prayer ended, he raised his eyes higher to stare up at the cloudy sky. He smiled ruefully at one wisp of a cloud and thought, *Hell, right now I'll settle for one out of three.*

For a moment he turned his back on the chapel to look out over the luscious, wooded grounds of the Retreat of St. Catherine of Genoa, twenty-four acres cut into the Black Mountains of Yancey County, North Carolina. Father Patrick had been there once before. When he was offered the chance to go to Washington, he had packed up all his belongings into the back of his car, left Marquette, driven down south, and spent a week sleeping on a hard single bed in one of the sanctuary's three primitive dormitories, strolling the property, chopping wood, thinking, praying. He had walked miles and miles that week. Through old Cherokee burial grounds that had survived from the late 1700s. Into the town of Asheville to see Thomas Wolfe's grave. Halfway up Mt. Mitchell, the highest peak east of the Mississippi. It had been a glorious climb, but the footing was treacherous and he'd stumbled and sprained his ankle. He had sworn to himself that he'd return and get to the very top someday, where he would swim in the icy stream and spend hours listening to the rush of the legendary waterfall.

His mentor at school, Father Thaddeus Joyce, had been the one to tell him about this magical spot. Thad had come here when he was a young priest. Retired now from teaching, he was in charge of the retreat. He made the rules, provided guidance for those who needed it, spent his days in meditation. When Father Patrick needed a place to go, there was only one place he considered. Only one person he wanted to talk to.

He hadn't talked yet, though. He'd spent his days there in silence. He had craved nothing but silence since the chilling words of the confession that had sent him crashing into a roiling and tumultuous sea. It seemed so long ago. It was so distant as to feel like a dream. But Father Patrick knew it was no dream. He had thought of nothing else in the days since he'd stumbled, reeling, out of his beloved cathedral. He had barely slept, hardly eaten. His world had been turned upside down, and silence was the only thing strong enough to perhaps hold that world together.

It was a well-named retreat, he knew. In her time, St. Catherine had tried her best to avoid intimacy with God. She had plunged into a busy social life, only to feel empty and unfulfilled. So she removed herself from contact with all but other holy people and those with horrible and deadly diseases. The people who came to the retreat dedicated to her memory were there to rediscover their own sense of intimacy with God. Their sense of intimacy with their own selves.

Father Patrick didn't just need to rediscover God. He needed to know what to do.

He blew on his hands—even in the summer the mountain air was chilly and dank—and stepped inside the chapel. It was dark save for the light that came from the fifty or so white candles scattered throughout. For a moment he thought the room was empty; then he heard a rustling and a faint cough, and he saw his mentor rise from the front pew.

"Hello, Thad," Father Patrick said. "I didn't mean to interrupt your nap."

"For some reason," Father Thaddeus said, "the older I get, the more I like to sleep in church." He yawned and smiled at the younger man. "I'm glad you've come to talk. I miss our chats sometimes."

"I always thought they drove you a little crazy."

"Oh, they did, they did. No one could annoy me as much as you."

Father Patrick smiled. But it was only a flicker of a smile and didn't last long.

"If I may speak frankly, Pat," the older priest said, "you look like crap."

"I need you to speak frankly," Father Patrick said.

Father Thaddeus stretched out his arms and yawned. "You know," he said, "I've seen you angry, I've seen you depressed, and I've seen you extremely drunk. But I've never seen you frightened before."

"I don't think I've ever been this frightened before."

" 'Fear is a greater evil than the evil itself.' St. Francis de Sales. I believe that very strongly."

"I used to believe it. I don't think I do anymore."

"You've got a lot of people concerned," Father Thaddeus told him. And when Father Patrick looked startled, he said, "Your disappearance has been in the papers."

"I thought you didn't get the news up here."

"Times have changed," Father Thaddeus explained. "Those who want to avoid the world may certainly do so. I myself can't seem to stay off the Internet."

"I took a confession," Father Patrick began. "Before I left Washington. I heard something very bad from someone very powerful."

"And that's what's frightened you?"

"Somewhat. But not entirely. What frightens me most is that I think I need to do something about it. I think people have to know."

"Ah. So you're considering breaking a sacred covenant."

"I'm considering many things. But so far I've done nothing."

"Whatever it is you heard, whatever it is that will happen, you have nothing to fear from God. I know you well enough to know that."

Father Patrick laughed. A harsh burst of laughter. "It's not God I'm afraid of," he said.

"Pat," the older man said slowly, "I have always found you to be an extraordinarily intelligent man. And an equally moral one. Sometimes that is not a combination that goes hand in hand. It does not always provide for much peace."

"Well, that's what I want, Thad. Peace is exactly what I'm seeking."

"And who except God can give you that? Has the world ever been able to satisfy the heart?"

"No," Father Patrick breathed. "The world has never been able to do that."

"I've known you a long time now, son. Long enough to know something else about you. Peace is not what you're looking for. It never has been, and I'm sorry to say it probably never will be."

"Then tell me," Father Patrick whispered. "What am I looking for?"

"Strength," Father Thaddeus said. "Strength to do whatever it is you feel you have to do. But remember the words of St. Cyprian: 'No one is safe by his own strength, but he is only safe by the grace and mercy of God.' "

"Amen," Father Patrick said. He closed his eyes to shut out the light from the flickering candles. To shut out the world that was so distant and yet so horribly near. "Amen."

chapter 25

One of the most violent two-day battles of the entire Civil War was fought in Corinth, Mississippi, in October of 1862. Nearly seven thousand men lost their lives, two-thirds of them rebels under the command of General Earl Van Dorn, a native Mississippian who was forced to retreat, bloodied and defeated by the Union forces led by General William Rosencrans. Nearly a century and a half later, the town is dominated by its memory of the battle. There is a vast national cemetery, where the dead soldiers are buried—just under four thousand of them in unknown graves. There are monuments marking the battle sites. There is a reconstructed Union battery and a museum filled with remnants, artifacts, and papers documenting the devastation. Groups of reenacters converge there annually to re-create the battle in full costume and detail.

Corinth had been a strategic railroad hub then. Now, known as Mississippi's Gateway City, it is a town dependent on its charm for its survival. Its proud motto is "Big-Town Variety, Small-Town Atmosphere."

Carl Granville and Amanda Mays were not much interested in the town's variety or its atmosphere. They were interested in details. Details that would lead to proof, which would lead to the identity of Gideon. Which, in turn, they hoped, would keep them alive. That was why they headed for Corinth. They were looking for something, anything, that would match the description in Carl's head of the Mississippi town he had named Simms, the fictional town where the fictional eleven-year-old Danny had murdered his fictional unnamed baby brother.

All they had to do now was turn fiction into fact.

At least they'd gotten some sleep the night before. Finally.

On the road south of Hohenwald, after leaving the LaRues' shrine to the King and making a quick stop at a drugstore at Amanda's behest, they had agreed to spend the night in a motel. They chose a small, locally owned one in Chewalla, Tennessee, about ten miles outside of Corinth. By the look of it, the motel seemed to be distantly affiliated with the Bates Motel. Best Rest, it was called.

Amanda paid cash for the room while Carl waited outside in the car. The sleepy desk clerk did not bother to ask her for any ID but did ask for the license number of the car. She instinctively made one up on the spot, hoping he would not go outside to check it. He didn't. She gave him a fake name as well—Jeannette Alk, who had been her best friend all through elementary school. This was not a problem, either. The Best Rest was not the sort of motel where people gave their real names.

They were in the Bible Belt now, after all. Sin was taken seriously here. And with great pleasure.

The room was right off of the parking lot, next to the ice machine, which was out of order. All of the rooms were right off the parking lot, which had only two other cars in it. Their room was stuffy and smelled of mildew and Raid. There were a number of very large insects in the bathroom sink, some dead, but not all. A rackety window air conditioner hummed and did its best to cool the room. It was having moderate success. The temperature outside had to be over a hundred degrees. Inside it was probably only eighty-five.

In the midst of a vaguely Navaho motif, there was one straight-backed chair tucked under a Formica desk built into the wall, a television with cable, and a coin-operated queen-sized bed.

Amanda flopped down on the saggy bed, on her belly, and twisted her head to look over at him. "You can shower first," she said.

"No, no," Carl replied and swept his hand toward the tiny bathroom with a gentlemanly flourish. "I insist."

"No, *I* insist. I intend to use up every last bit of hot water in the complex, so take your shot while you can."

"Well, if you put it that way . . ."

"But first it's time for your new look." She pulled the chair out from under the desk, took it into the bathroom, and set it down in front of the sink. When she patted it firmly, he followed and sat in the chair. Amanda pulled a small paper bag out of her purse, and when he looked at her quizzically, she produced a pair of scissors and a bottle of Clairol hair coloring, mahogany, that she'd bought at the drugstore earlier that day.

"You're too recognizable," she said. Placing her hand on top of his head, holding it firmly in place, she began snipping away with the scissors.

"You *have* done this before, haven't you?" he asked.

"Do you think I'd mess around with your looks if I didn't know what I was doing? Of *course* I've done this before."

"You're lying, aren't you?"

"Sure." She flashed him a broad grin. "Now just face forward. And no sneaking peeks in the mirror."

As his hair began to fall away, he began to relax, to enjoy the light touch of her hands on his shoulder, on his neck, on the side of his head. He started drifting away, running through the list of what they had to do, of all the things they needed to remember. He felt as though it had been years since this whole thing had begun; he could barely recall when he'd last walked the streets of New York, carefree and easy. He thought about his apartment and the work he'd been doing before Maggie Peterson had come into his life. The friends he hadn't seen or talked to . . .

"Hey, watch it!" she said. Her words jolted him out of his reverie. "Sit still. You came very close to doing an excellent Van Gogh impersonation." She saw that he'd gone pale and the back of his neck was cold and clammy. "What's the matter?" she asked.

"I-I was just thinking"—he stammered over the words—"I needed to call . . ."

"Call who?" she asked incredulously.

Still rattled, Carl looked at her, embarrassed. And sad. "I'm sorry. I'm exhausted. I was sitting here thinking I needed to check my phone machine at home, to see if I had any business calls. As if I still had business. Or a phone machine. Or a *home*."

"I know," she said softly. "I keep thinking the same thing."

She finished cutting in silence. When she was done, she said, "Now remember that most of the hot water belongs to me." Tossing him the bottle of Clairol hair coloring, she added, "And don't forget this." She left the bathroom, closing the door behind her.

The shower revived him somewhat. The water was plenty hot, if a bit rusty at first and smelling vaguely of sulfur. The watery needles felt good on his sore muscles, and he let them rain down on his shoulders. When he stepped out of the shower, he dried himself off, then scrubbed the mahogany coloring into what was left of his hair. He stayed behind closed doors and forced himself to wait exactly half an hour—that was how long before the hair coloring took full effect—before moving to the mirror. He peered at the stranger staring back at him. The new Carl Granville had short hair, cut straight and close to the scalp. It was a dark brown color, one that didn't quite look as if it came from nature. But he had to admit it didn't look all that bad. And even he would have trouble recognizing himself at first glance.

He went into the room, the towel around his waist, and gasped aloud when he looked up at Amanda. He was not the only one who had just undergone a transformation. Her long, thick, beautiful red hair was a thing of the past, chopped off close to the scalp. She had also dyed it a dark, inky black. "They had my picture on TV, too," she said. "I thought, better safe than sorry." He still said nothing. "Well?" she asked. And as he stared at her with his mouth open, she burst into tears.

"Hey," he said, "come on. I was just surprised. It looks really good. Honest."

"Oh, God," she wailed. "After everything that's happened, what makes me cry? Cutting my hair! How can I be such a *girl*?"

He reached out to comfort her. It seemed like the right thing to do. But she brushed past him and marched into the bathroom. As he heard the water start to run, he ran his hand through his own new hair, plopped down on the bed, and with renewed energy began to study a map of the area, drawing circles around towns that were situated within a thirty-mile radius. He watched the latest headline news on the Apex News Network. The FBI was now receiving nearly three hundred calls per hour from people who were absolutely positive they had spotted him. Thus far, thirty-one of the fifty states had been heard from—including Hawaii and Alaska. The Bureau was, according to sources, attempting to check out the details of each and every lead.

Carl could not get used to seeing his picture flashed up there on the tube. Nor could he get used to the idea that every law enforcement official in the country was after him and would not hesitate to shoot him on sight. None of it seemed real. Unable to watch anymore, he flicked it off.

"Better?" he asked Amanda when she finally came padding barefoot out of the shower, flushed and pink, one towel wrapped around her, the other around her hair.

"Better," she said sheepishly. But her gaze was on the mound of red hair that filled up the wastebasket in the corner.

"Well, which do you want first? The good news or the bad news?"

"Let's have the bad first," she answered bleakly.

"They're now confirming that you did not die in the fire. You are officially missing and possibly under my spell."

"In your dreams," she sniffed. "I suppose this means my car isn't safe any longer."

"Amanda, your car was never safe."

She rolled her eyes at him, exasperated. "I mean, the state troopers will be seriously on the lookout for it now."

"Well, we're stuck with it," he said. "We can't rent one—we'd have to show a credit card, not to mention a driver's license. And I'm no car thief. A spree killer, yes, but not a car thief."

"Damn, damn, damn." Amanda considered the matter in grim silence a moment. Then she raised her eyebrows as if considering something, went to the window, and peeked out through the curtains. "Do you still carry that little pocketknife of yours?"

"What about it?"

"Hand it over."

He pulled the tiny Swiss Army knife out of his pocket and gave it to her. She stepped into her shoes, opened the door, and stood there in the doorway wrapped in her towel. "If I'm not back in two minutes, send for the cavalry."

"Amanda, where the hell are you going?"

It was no use. She had already gone out into the humid night. Carl tore over to the window and looked out into the parking lot. He saw nothing. Heard nothing. He paced the room until she returned a couple of minutes later, out of breath. "Here," she panted, handing his knife back to him. "I had to break the point off. Sorry."

"Amanda, what did you—"

"I unscrewed our license plates and switched them with one of the other cars in the lot. It'll be hard for them to ID us with Alabama plates." She smiled triumphantly—and a little smugly.

"Don't you think the guy from Alabama is going to notice?"

"Not a chance. People never look at their own license plates. I'll bet you seventy-five percent of the drivers in America don't even know what their license plate number is."

He stared at her a moment, admiringly. "You would have made a great criminal, you know that?"

"Carl, I *am* a criminal," she said. "You did say there was good news, too, didn't you?"

"I did."

"So what is it?"

"The editor of your paper is very concerned about you. He said you're like family."

"How touching. I wonder if he hits on all his other relatives after he's had one glass of cabernet sauvignon."

"That's not all. He said you have a history of getting trapped in one-sided, self-destructive relationships."

"Well, he had to say that." She shrugged. "Anytime you turn a guy down, he decides you must have a problem with men. That's the only way his ego can handle it."

"He also said you had a way of getting too involved in your work. That it leads you to make irresponsible, sometimes dangerous decisions."

She let out a long, pained sigh. "It's amazing," she said angrily. "They can turn everything you've ever done in your whole life—good, bad, or meaningless—against you when they want to. They can take something and turn it into something completely different. And no one has a clue. I've spent my whole career in the news business and I never really understood that before. Not really. No one can. Not until it's *you*. I'm going to make you a promise, Carl. I swear to you that when we come out of this crazy thing, when our lives return to normal, I am going to be a changed journalist."

Staring straight ahead, all he said was, "Amanda . . ."

She didn't say anything in return. Just shook her head slightly, as if she knew what he was going to say but didn't want him to say it aloud. But he felt that he had to say it.

"We're never going to come out of this thing, Amanda. Our lives are never going to return to normal."

She bit her lip and one hand rested on his shoulder, squeezing harder than she intended. "I know that," she said quietly. "But I have to keep talking or I'll start crying again. And I don't think I can handle crying twice in one day." She let out a strangled moan that fell somewhere between a sob and a laugh. And he could not help noticing the way her chest rose and fell under the towel. He watched her, feeling helpless, remembering other times he had watched her. Remembering when, after the watching, the towel had come off. Remembering it all . . .

"If I asked you to do me a small favor," she said quietly, "would you do it?"

"Under the circumstances, I don't see how I can refuse."

Slowly, tentatively, she went over to the bed and stretched herself out on it. "Would you hold me? Just . . . hold me?"

His mouth was suddenly dry. "I can do that."

He lay down beside her. She came into his arms and snuggled against him, warm and moist and smelling of Dial soap. Carl felt an overwhelming rush of animal responses as he lay there, cradling her in his arms: sensory memories awakening, bells going off, lights flashing, engines racing.

"I've missed you," she said drowsily. "I've missed being with you."

"I've missed you, too."

"Missed talking to you . . ."

She was fading now. Drifting.

"I'm here now," he said. "I'm here."

"No more complications," she murmured softly. "Just hold me. Don't need complications."

"No complications," he echoed.

"Just want to be held. Just need to be held . . ."

He watched her eyes close. Felt her breaths even out, saw her slide toward a gentle slumber.

"Me too," Carl whispered. "Just need to be held."

They fell asleep that way, joined together, with the lights on and the air conditioner cycling noisily on and off and the occasional car swooshing by on the dark road not far beyond their window.

They woke at dawn, still wrapped in each other's arms. No words were said. No words were needed. They cleared out within minutes, back in Amanda's car, heading toward Corinth.

They spent the morning combing the town. There were tree-lined streets of lovingly preserved antebellum homes, some of them now converted to bed-and-breakfast stops for tourists. There was a massive old courthouse, a thriving central business district on Fillmore Street. A banner suspended over the street read "Next Week: Annual Slugburger Festival. Come One, Come All and Eat Our Slugburgers."

Amanda would not even speculate on what a slugburger could possibly be. And she refused to let Carl ask anyone.

The sun was blinding, the heat was blistering, the air heavy and still and scented with honeysuckle. They pulled in at the Borroum Drug Store, the oldest drugstore in continuous operation in the state, and bought a couple of frosty cold Dr Peppers, which they drank down so quickly it made their throats ache. Carl also bought a Corinth Seed Company cap and a pair of dark shades. With his stubble, his rumpled jeans and T-shirt, and his new short, dark hair, he felt relatively safe. He looked no different from anyone else drifting along in this little town. He did not, he hoped, look like a deranged killer on the run from the police, the FBI, and the news divisions of every major network and cable operation.

A group of old-timers sat in the back of the store, passing the morning in a cloud of cigarette smoke. While Carl was trying on shades, Amanda bummed a Winston from one of the elderly ladies and struck up a conversation, steering it quickly to the subject of local factories. There was a big new Caterpillar diesel engine factory right on the outskirts of town, she learned. The most notable *old* factory was the Corinth Machinery Company, which had originally been built way back in 1869 as a cotton factory. In the early 1900s boilers and sawmill equipment had been produced there. During the 1950s it became the Alcorn Woolen Factory and did a thriving business. Presently it was set up for the fabrication of plywood.

They rushed back out to the car, eager to take a look. What had been the

Corinth Machinery Company was on Highway 72, right across from Dildy's Garage, which did full auto repairs and, Carl was willing to bet, sold more bottles of Coca-Cola than any other station in America. He bought three bottles and downed them immediately. Amanda had learned her lesson with the Dr Pepper and sipped her one bottle slowly and delicately. Standing in front of Dildy's gas pump, they stared across the street at the old brick factory.

"Well, does it strike a chord?" Amanda asked, feeling the sweat trickle down her neck.

Carl shook his head. "It's a factory. Like every other factory."

"That's it?"

"They lived about a mile away from it, I remember that."

She nodded, each nod sending another trickle of sweat down her long neck. They got back in the car and circled the area, two miles in each direction, looking for anything that would jog Carl's memory. But nothing did.

Corinth was picturesque. It was prosperous. It was not Simms.

So they headed on out, hitting the one-stoplight towns that surrounded it, Amanda behind the wheel, Carl working the map and trying to fight back the waves of frustration and desperation that kept washing over him with each fruitless stop: Jacinto, Kossuth, Glen, each and every one of them strictly a farming town. No help—although in Rienzi they did learn that General Nathan Bedford Forrest's beloved horse was named for this very town. Kendrick did have a big Kimberly-Clark plant, but it was brand-new, just like the Caterpillar plant had been.

So it was back to Highway 45 and south to Tupelo, where Elvis Presley was born and where they would pick up Route 6, which would take them west across Mississippi toward the delta. Old Mr. LaRue had been right, Carl reflected gloomily, peering out the window at the lush green countryside shimmering in the heat. They were investing in casino gambling big time down here. One giant roadside billboard after another promised unimaginable riches and glamour and fun in Helena Bridge, Tunica, Casino Center, Vicksburg, Philadelphia, Biloxi . . . The bright colors and loud boasts were a sharp and angry contrast to the country stillness.

"I've been thinking," Carl said, glancing over at Amanda. Her eyes were on the road, her chin raised with grim determination. "And I think we've got to narrow in on the factory. LaRue was probably wrong about it being a poultry works."

"Why is that?"

"We want a place that smelled *nasty*."

"Have you ever been near a slaughterhouse?" she asked challengingly. "They smell plenty nasty."

They passed by a sign for yet another casino. This one said: "Best Sports Book Outside of Vegas. Be the First to Pick Next Year's Super Bowl Winner. Great Odds."

Carl was silent a moment. Something was coming back to him, snaking into his brain, but in an instant it was gone. What was it? A detail he'd overlooked, something he'd forgotten. No, he couldn't dredge it up. *Damn.* There was something, some detail in Rayette's diary about the town he'd named Simms . . .

"They compost the manure for fertilizer, you know," Amanda went on. "It's very effective. And even smellier."

"But would it make people sick to live near it?"

"Maybe it was a paper mill," she offered. "There used to be a lot of those down here, I believe. Notorious chemical polluters, one and all. A garment factory is another possibility. I covered the State Department of Environmental Protection for a while when I worked in Albany. The state was trying to get the feds to declare this abandoned hat factory outside of Rochester a Superfund site. Would you believe they used to use *mercury* to make the dye? My God, this one old-timer told me you could tell the color of the hats they were making that day by the color the river was. They ended up contaminating not only the river but the soil on both sides of it. Absolutely nothing could be built there, and it was a total, toxic eyesore, so they—"

"I think you're on to something here," Carl broke in excitedly. "Your friend Shaneesa could do a computer search of the EPA's files to see if there are any Superfund sites around here. If we're talking about a big polluter, they'd be on record, right?"

"Well, no. You didn't let me finish the story. There's a sad part."

Carl groaned inwardly. "Okay, tell me the sad part."

"Superfund cleanups are so expensive it's mind-boggling. They literally have to take away freight-car loads of the riverbank soil to someplace like Nevada. It's prohibitively expensive. And there are thousands and thousands of sites that need to be cleaned up. Too many. So unless the site is near a heavily populated area, and that population happens to be white and affluent—and if you're keeping score at home, the place we're looking for flunks miserably on all three counts—then the feds can't be bothered."

"So what happens to the site?"

"Not a damn thing. Everyone just tiptoes around it and lets it fall into ruin and neglect. They call them brown fields, because nothing will ever grow there. If that's what we're dealing with, then the EPA would have no record of it whatsoever. The state of Mississippi *might* have something on it, but frankly I doubt it."

"Well, shit," he growled.

"My sentiments exactly."

They were nearing the town of Abbeville now, halfway between Holly Springs and Oxford, and they followed a sign that said "Business District." Abbeville's business district turned out to be one abandoned gas station, a savings and loan that looked as though it would be abandoned before long, a working gas station, and a general store called Frankie and Johnnie's, which had a sign boasting "Home Cooking."

"Are you hungry?" she asked him.

"Starved," he replied, gazing at the place through the car window.

"You think we can risk a take-out order?"

"No, I think we should sit down and eat like normal folks. If by some chance someone does recognize us, they'll figure it can't be us because we're sitting there eating like ordinary people. It's like when two people are cheating on their spouses. If they meet in some dark, out-of-the-way little restaurant, it's incriminating. Whereas if they meet out in the open, no one suspects a thing."

She shot a look at him. "Jesus, Carl, when it comes to thinking like a criminal, you're not too shabby yourself."

"Don't sound so horrified. It's a handy trait right now."

"I'm not horrified, just surprised. I thought I knew you."

"I thought I knew me, too," he reflected, his words hanging in the air between them. "Maybe I didn't. Maybe you never really know yourself at all until something like this happens to you." He glanced at her. "What do you say?"

"I say," she replied, "that you can forget the maybe." She pulled into a dirt parking area across the street from Frankie and Johnnie's, shut off the engine, and smiled at him tightly. "C'mon, Bubba—let's eat."

And like a normal couple, they strolled arm in arm into the country diner. Up front was a general store, its shelves loaded with cans of Green Giant vegetables and barrels of nails and sacks of flour. In the back was a twelve-stool counter, behind which were two women in hair nets slaving over an eight-burner cast-iron stove. Three men were sitting at the counter, one with his small daughter. Two of the men glanced up as Carl and Amanda walked in. They exchanged polite nods. The third man didn't budge. He was too engrossed in his newspaper. As Carl sat down next to him, he couldn't help but glance at the local headline. Carl tried to study the words without being too obvious. For a moment he felt a sense of relief when he saw that it had nothing to do with him. Then he realized what he was reading and what the ramifications were.

He read that Duane and Cissy LaRue had been murdered.

And he realized that meant that someone was following them.

chapter 26

" I don't wish to disturb your lunch," the Closer said into the cell phone, "but the path they are presently taking requires some serious attention on your part."

"Explain," Augmon commanded crisply. "Elaborate."

The Closer was sitting in the front seat of the Suburban, parked in the shuttered gas station catty-corner from Frankie and Johnnie's, less than fifty feet from Amanda's battered little Subaru. "Do you have your laptop in front of you?"

"Of course," Augmon shot back. He was back in New York now, in his corner office on the thirty-third floor of the Apex International building. He always took lunch in his corner office on the thirty-third floor.

"Log on to Maps Are Us."

"I assume you wish for me to pull up a map of Mississippi."

"You assume correctly." The Closer heard rapid tapping from the other end of the line as the man with the English accent accessed the Website and found what he wanted.

"Very well," he said. "I am looking at a map of Mississippi. Now explain to me why I am."

"They are heading west on Route Six. Toward the delta."

Augmon was silent a moment. "Oh, my. That is most unfortunate."

"Most."

"How did they—how much do you think they know?"

The Closer didn't respond. The Closer did not like to say the words "I have no idea."

"Bloody hell," Augmon cursed. "The story hasn't maxed out yet. I had been hoping to milk it for another day. Possibly two." He uttered something else under his breath, some British street doggerel involving various parts of the anatomy. The Closer couldn't quite make it out. "Tell me, how long have we got?"

"A couple of hours if they drive straight there. More if they don't."

"Do you have any reason to believe they know exactly where they are going?"

"No reason to believe they do. No reason to believe they don't."

"Ah, me. Such a disappointment. I don't suppose we can adopt a wait-and-see attitude?"

"In my opinion, you cannot. But it's not my decision to make."

"Quite so, my young friend. And we do have . . . what is the expression of yours? Bigger fish to fry?"

"It's not an expression of mine," growled the Closer, who had enjoyed this assignment. It had its challenges. It had its amusements. It would be missed.

"Can you take care of them before they get there?" he asked.

"Of course," the Closer said evenly.

"Then do so," he said briskly. "Make sure they're never found. They must never, ever be found." Then there was a click and the phone went dead.

Sitting in his office on the thirty-third floor of the Apex building, Lord Lindsay Augmon realized that his dream was about to be realized. He was poised for the greatest takeover of his career. One that would give him limitless power. People talked about Bill Gates, but Bill Gates simply provided the messenger. He, Lindsay Augmon, provided the message. Provided, hell. He *was* the message.

He had just made the biggest gamble of his entire life—and his was a life spent rolling the dice. He had committed nearly $150 million to the building and launching of a Fairfield FS601 satellite, the most expensive, well-equipped, latest state-of-the-art communications satellite in existence. Right now that beauty was circling the earth. Launched from French Guiana, it was up there now. All he had to do was push a button and it would be activated. And he had ordered four more to be built over the next two years. It was a total of $750 million. There was no guarantee that he'd ever be able to legally use them. No guarantee he could ever push that button. But there were other guarantees.

There were billions of them. A hundred billion, to be exact.

That was how much money there was to be made in China. And it was all so simple. So easy and available. One just had to be ready. One had to be first. One had to have the opportunity. And if there *was* no opportunity, then it became necessary to make one. So that the button could be pushed someday.

There was the potential to reach a hundred million television sets in China. Eventually more. Possibly a billion! It was more than potential. It was so close to being a reality that Augmon could touch it. Smell it. Squeeze it.

One hundred million TV sets. To start! At a subscription rate of, over a five-year period, one thousand dollars. Most reasonable.

And it added up to a most reasonable hundred billion dollars. And the quicker capitalism crept into and eventually took over the country—something that was certain to happen, just as it had happened in Russia, just as it was happening everywhere else thanks to the unstoppable flow of information that was circling the world—that hundred billion would turn into two hundred billion. Three hundred billion. There was no limit!

Put that together with his operations in South America, Latin America, India, the Middle East, and elsewhere, he would be reaching two-thirds of the world's population. Broadcasting to them, feeding them information, telling them whom to vote for, telling them what to think, telling them *how* to think.

Oh, it was glorious, glorious, glorious.

Augmon leaned back in his chair and closed his eyes. He thought about where he'd been in his sixty-four years and where he was going. He thought about the empire he was about to control and the mayhem he had caused—and was about to cause—in order to attain that control. He thought about the enemies he'd made, and the friends; he thought about the death and destruction that had surrounded him and would always surround him. Then he smiled. A broad, deep, satisfying smile.

Was it worth it?

Good Lord, yes. It was worth all he had done, all he would do, and much, much more.

Still smiling, his upper lip revealing glistening white teeth, he reached for the phone and dialed a number, a number that maybe twenty people in the world were privileged to know.

He heard the phone ring once, twice, and then it was answered. The voice he knew so well greeted him. The greeting was friendly but curt. Guarded. It was an efficient greeting.

Lord Augmon smiled again, his immaculate teeth practically glowing in the light that came from the bronze lamp on his desk.

And then he began talking to the person who would, once and for all, help make him the king.

The dynamite gave off a heavy, pungent, sweet odor as it lay there in the front seat of the Suburban.

Twelve eight-inch cylindrical sticks in all. Each one was exactly one and a half inches in diameter and wrapped in buff-colored wax paper. The Closer had bunched them into two bundles of six, wrapped silver duct tape around the two individual bundles, and then used more duct tape to join them together end to end, rather like a large salami.

Duct tape was the Closer's friend. There wasn't a plumber, furnace repairer, or bomb builder on earth who could live without duct tape.

Some assembly was required.

The Closer had brought along a supply of blasting caps. An old-fashioned kitchen-type timer was also needed, along with a small battery-powered hand drill, a simple electronic switch, two packages of nine-volt batteries (one to power the drill, the other for the device), a one-foot-by-two-foot sheet of tin chimney flashing, a ball of string, wire, and the duct tape. All of these things had been easily purchased at a hardware store in Corinth while Granville and the girl were madly combing the sleepy little place for clues.

They reminded the Closer of a pair of adventuresome socialites out on a charity treasure hunt.

And now they were going to win the grand prize.

The basic assembly was completed. A hole had been drilled into one of the sticks, and a blasting cap was inserted into the hole. The string was used to secure it in place. The timer was wired to the electronic switch, which was wired to the batteries. The batteries were wired to the blasting cap. When the timer went off, it would complete an electric circuit through the switch. The batteries would supply sufficient energy to the blasting cap to detonate it. This was known as the primary explosion. The resulting shock would then set off the dynamite. This was known as the secondary explosion.

Seated there, across the intersection from the general store, partially hidden but able to see who came in and out, the Closer finished the job. It was presently 12:17, according to the clock on the Suburban's dash—the timer was now set for one hour. The sheet of tin was bent around the underside of the bomb, so as to help direct the blast upward. Then the entire thing was wrapped in a plastic shopping bag and more duct tape tied around it, forming a tight, ticking silver bundle. Done. The Closer got out of the Suburban and strode over toward the little Subaru, pausing to glance around. There was nobody else outside. There was nobody looking. And even if they had been, what reason would they have to be suspicious? None. If folks did happen to notice someone fiddling around under a parked car, they automatically assumed it was that person's own. Moving swiftly and surely, the Closer knelt down under the rear bumper and taped the bundle directly against the fuel tank. The gasoline would provide more power to the explosion.

Way more power.

This was known as total and complete obliteration.

The Closer had planned to remove the Subaru's D.C. license plates and replace them with Mississippi plates, stolen two nights earlier from another Subaru. But this task was no longer necessary. They had already thought to switch the plates themselves. They were, the Closer reflected wryly, learning the ropes.

The Closer returned to the Suburban, got back in, and waited.

It was now 12:22.

In precisely fifty-five minutes, at 1:17 P.M., Carl Granville and Amanda Mays would cease to exist. Not one useful, detectable trace would be left of them for the forensic scientists to work with. No skin. No hair. No teeth— their jaws would be shattered into so many tiny, far-flung shards of bone that it would be impossible to identify them by their dental records. As for the car, the Alabama plates would confuse them. And sifting through the remains of the wrecked engine for the serial number would be painstaking and time-consuming. It would take weeks to identify it as the missing woman's, if indeed they even could. If indeed they even bothered.

And by then it wouldn't matter anymore.

The targets emerged from the restaurant at 12:36 P.M. He had on a cap and sunglasses. She also had on a hat—a rain hat, by the look of it. They both affected a laid-back, country demeanor that was belied only by the keen manner in which she was leafing through a newspaper.

Before they got into the car, Granville stopped and looked nervously up and down the road, as if looking for something. For one fleeting moment the Closer thought Granville was staring straight at the front end of the Suburban, but then dismissed that thought. And even if it was true, it no longer mattered. The clock on the Suburban's dashboard showed that it was 12:38. Carl Granville and Amanda Mays might be able to outrun the Closer—but only for another thirty-nine minutes.

They got into the car now, Granville behind the wheel. He put the keys in the Subaru's ignition and started it up. The engine didn't kick over on the first try. It didn't kick over on the second, either. Briefly the Closer's heart stopped. But it did just fine on the third try, so they backed out onto the street and headed out, the bomb clinging securely to the gas tank. It did not sag. It was not visible.

The Closer waited before starting up the Suburban. There was no rush. No need to follow on their heels. The Closer knew their destination. And knew they would never reach it.

The Closer glanced at the dashboard clock.

It was now 12:43.

It was 12:57 when Carl glanced at his watch.

The sign by the side of the road said they were twenty miles from Oxford. Judging by their present speed, they would reach the home of William Faulkner and Ole Miss at about one-thirty. From there, it was approximately one more hour to Clarksdale, the town where Elvis had, in January of 1955, played the city auditorium. With some luck, it would also turn out to be the town that would provide the answers they so desperately needed.

Carl momentarily shifted his gaze to his right. Amanda had been silent since reading the brief story about the LaRues' murder. He could practically see her reporter's brain whirring away, trying to make sense of it all. He was doing the very same thing, trying to put matters in rational order. Point one: Whoever their predator was, it was someone who seemed to know their every move. Two: It was someone who had no qualms about slaughtering innocent people. Three: Points one and two made for a bad combination. Who was this hunter? Why was he trailing them? More important, why was he letting them stay alive? Were they serving some awful purpose? *What* purpose?

"I can't make it fit," she said finally. *"Why?"*

"I don't even know which *why* to try to figure out first."

"Let's talk through it, okay?"

"Talk away."

"You were set up for the other murders, right? But in the story about the LaRues, nothing. No hint that you might be involved. And we'd be easy patsies. I mean, our fingerprints must be all over the place, we're still in the area . . ."

"Maybe there just hasn't been enough time."

"Maybe. But everything else broke instantly. They've been reporting suspicions and rumors all along, jumping to conclusions. It's just not consistent."

"There still hasn't been a thing in the news about Harry's murder, either," he pointed out. "Someone wants to keep that one secret, too."

"Add that to the list of whys."

"And here's another one," he said. "There hasn't been a car behind us since we left the restaurant. We could have turned off this road two or three times already and no one would have seen us. Which means no one's following us right now. Why would they follow us to the LaRues' and then stop there?"

"Maybe they don't *have* to follow us," she said after a long silence.

"Explain."

"Maybe they know where we're going."

"Amanda, *we* don't even know where we're going."

"*They* know what we're looking for," she said, starting to sound excited. "They've got to. And if they know *what* it is, they've got to know *where* it is."

"Okay, I'll buy that, but why kill the LaRues?"

"Because they knew where we were going. Don't you see what that means? We're getting close!"

"Well, if we're getting so close, why not just go ahead and kill *us*?"

She was quiet for a moment. Then she shook her head. "Add it to the list of whys," she said.

"I've got a new list now. A what list." Something on the dashboard had caught his eye and was making him nervous. "As in, what's this light for?"

"Which one?" She peered over at his side of the dashboard, at a red warning light that was flashing. "Forget about it. That's nothing—just the oil pressure."

"*Just* the oil pressure? That's a red light. Red means emergency, as in pull over and stop immediately."

"Trust me, Carl. It's not a big deal. Just keep going."

He shook his head at her. "Amanda, you aren't supposed to drive a car when the oil pressure light goes on. That's basic Car One-oh-one."

"I don't need one of your he-man lectures, okay? It does that all the time. It's just saying it wants a quart of oil."

"It could also be saying that it's *out* of oil."

"It's my car, for God's sake," she said peevishly. "It wants a quart of oil, period. It has a tendency to burn oil in hot weather, that's all."

Now he gaped at her, aghast. "That's *all*?"

"What's the big deal?"

"We've just driven over a thousand miles nonstop through blistering heat, that's what. We should have been checking it every time we filled up."

"We *have* had other things on our minds."

"I'm pulling over," he announced firmly. "We have to check the dipstick."

"Carl, you're overreacting. We'll hit a gas station soon, and we'll stop and get a quart of oil. We can't afford to stop now and—"

"Amanda," he warned, "if the engine seizes up, we'll have to hitchhike the rest of the way to Clarksdale. Which, considering our situation, is probably a really bad idea."

She rolled her eyes at him with weary resignation. "Fine. Do whatever you want."

So he did. Or at least he tried to. He started to ease the Subaru over onto the dirt shoulder of the road and bring it to a gradual stop. Only now the engine was starting to sound extremely unhappy—somewhat like a washing machine that had a load of boulders in it. He immediately shut it off and then coasted to a stop. But the clanking and rumbling under the hood did not cease right away. It was a gradual thing. And loud. And painful. Until, finally, Amanda's little gray Subaru putt-putted and shuddered and died there by the side of the road.

They sat there in brittle silence until Amanda snapped, "Don't say anything. Not one word."

He didn't. He popped the hood and got out, glancing distractedly at his watch.

It was 1:12.

They were in the middle of nowhere. To the left of the two-lane road were woods and farmland. To the right was the sprawling Sardis Lake, the water glistening in the sunlight. Straight ahead of them was scorching blacktop and, so it appeared, little else for at least ten or twelve miles, until they reached Oxford. He raised the hood, which provided some shade from the midday sun. Although the heat radiating from the engine more than compensated for it. He found the dipstick and pulled it out. Bone dry. He pushed it back down and pulled it out again. It was still dry. There was no oil in the Subaru's engine. Not one drop.

Amanda got out and stood next to him, looking warily down at the engine. "What do you think?"

"I think we're screwed."

"Even if we put oil in it?"

"Once it seizes up, it's too late," he replied. "At least I think so. But look, I'm not a mechanic. I don't know what the hell I am, but I know I'm not a mechanic." He looked back down the highway, where they had come from. "There's nothing back that way until Abbeville." Now he nodded in the direction of Oxford, straight ahead. "Let's hoof it this way and see if we can find a gas station. We'll see what happens." He smiled at her tightly. "Deal?"

She forced a smile back at him. "Deal."

It was 1:15.

They removed their scant few belongings from the backseat of the car and started to lock it. Then Amanda stopped and said, "Maybe I should wait here, stay with the car."

Carl considered this, thumbing his jaw thoughtfully. "What if someone stops to help?"

"Then we'll have help."

"What if it's a cop?"

That settled that. "Let's start walking," she said.

They were fifty feet from the car when she turned to say something to him. "Carl—" he heard, and then he saw her lips move and no sound come out. That was when the blast swept over them.

It was deafening. Carl flattened himself over Amanda as the Subaru was instantly transformed from a ton and a half of steel, rubber, and plastic into an exploding fireball. Pieces of metal went soaring into the air, landing in the trees and in the fields next to the highway, skittering and skimming along the road as if riding a monster wave.

The air in front of Carl was a blur of gasoline fumes, distorting everything around them. He looked up at what he thought was the sun, a bright, fiery ball, but as it came hurtling down toward them he grabbed Amanda, shoved her with all his might, and rolled after her into a ditch. The smoking chunk of twisted metal came crashing down right in front of them, embedding itself two feet into the ground. The dry brush along the side of the road immediately caught fire and began to crackle.

He tried shaking her. She didn't move. He screamed at her to wake up but couldn't hear his own voice. His ears were ringing and he pounded his head, trying to drive the ringing away. He saw a passing car swerve at the sight of the flaming wreck, then pull over to the road's shoulder. Amanda stirred now. She said something, but he still couldn't hear her. He pointed toward the woods and she nodded weakly. He stood up into a crouch; she lingered there on the ground, unable to make her body obey her mind's commands. He grabbed for her hand, pulled her to her feet.

Unsteadily at first, then quickly gathering speed, they hurried into the woods, farther and farther away from the approaching police siren and the cars that were now bunching up on the road. When their wobbly legs and the pain in their sides and their burning throats wouldn't let them go any farther, they fell back to the dry, caked ground.

Carl stared at Amanda's dirt-streaked face, at her scorched shirtsleeve, at her face, red from the heat of the explosion. He swallowed hard and suddenly realized he could hear again. Still breathing hard, he put his hand on Amanda's trembling shoulder.

"Carl," she gasped, "is that typical of what happens when an engine seizes up?"

"Next time maybe you'll listen to me about the oil."

She nodded and took a deep breath of air into her lungs. "I loved that car," she told him. "God*damn* them."

"Yeah," was all he said. It was all he had to say.

Then they struggled to their feet, dashed deeper into the woods, emerged into a cotton field, and ran as fast as their legs would take them.

There were three things in life that the Closer felt very negatively about— bottled salad dressing, the films of Meg Ryan, and failure.

The Closer could not tolerate failure. It was a product of poor planning and shoddy work habits. Failure was an unacceptable option in a business where the element of surprise was critical, second chances were scarce, and lethal rivals were forever waiting to get their hands around one's throat. It was not just that the Closer did not like to fail.

The Closer could not afford to fail.

It had all seemed to be going according to plan. Following the targets on Route 6 at a leisurely pace. There was no need to get within a mile of the rickety Subaru. The only need was to keep an eye on the dashboard clock. The Closer counted the minutes, savored the anticipation of the delicious explosion that was to come. There were but a scant few minutes left when suddenly, there was the dented little rust bucket, pulled over onto the shoulder of the road and stopped. The Closer couldn't stop, had to speed on by. When the Suburban was half a mile away, safely out of sight, the Closer slammed on the brakes, lunging for the high-powered binoculars in the glove compartment. Then watching as the two targets went rooting under the hood. Watching as they started to remove their things from the car . . .

pausing there . . . lingering there . . . the clock ticking . . . ticking . . . Watching as they—*Damn them,* damn *them*—started walking safely away.

When the explosion came, the Closer spun the Suburban around, sped back toward the targets.

There they were, sprinting away from the scene. Unharmed.

Failure such as this made the Closer physically ill. There was only one thing worse—having to admit such a failure out loud to a client. As it was now so painfully necessary to do.

"I assume you are calling me with good news," came Lord Lindsay Augmon's voice from the other end of the phone.

"I am not." The Closer could barely hear over the noise of the onrushing fire trucks, police cars, and ambulances. "There was . . ."

"There was *what?*" The voice was chilling. Even the Closer was startled and unsettled at the unforgiving tone.

"There was an unforeseen circumstance."

Now there was only silence from the other end. "Where are they?" he said, after a moment.

"They're on foot. Not an immediate threat. And they'll be dead by dawn, you have my word on that."

"I appreciate your professionalism, my young friend. Pride in one's work has gone the way of so many other warm, fuzzy American myths, has it not? But I'm removing you from this assignment."

The Closer's chest tightened. The pain reverberated as cramps in the stomach, electric stabs through the temples.

The Closer was never removed from a case. Never. This was incomprehensible. This was humiliating. This was intolerable.

"I don't feel comfortable with that at all," the Closer said, hoping the words came out calmly, hoping they didn't convey the agony.

"I'm not paying you to feel comfortable. I'm paying you to do what I tell you to do."

"I'm not done here," the Closer stated insistently. "I like to finish what I start."

"I'm sure you do," Augmon conceded. "Nonetheless, you are moving on—effective immediately. Something urgent has come up. Something that requires the degree of finesse and skill that you"—and here Augmon's voice bristled with sarcasm—"are *supposed* to bring to the table."

A white light went through the Closer's head. "I can't be pulled. I will not fail. Just give me twelve more hours here—"

"Not possible," Augmon said brusquely. "My jet will be landing at the Oxford airport in one hour and twenty minutes. Payton will be on it." *Payton.* Just the thought of that slob finishing the job filled the Closer with such anger and revulsion that it was almost impossible to speak. "He will get off, you will get on. Your instructions will be on board. Understood?"

Heart pounding, the Closer gripped the phone in tight silence.

"Understood?" he repeated, a hard edge creeping into his voice.

"Understood." The Closer bit off the word as if it hurt. Because it did hurt. Deeply and penetratingly.

"That's the spirit," Augmon said airily. "There's absolutely no need to let personal feelings enter into this. We're all team players, you know. We all pitch in. Your end of the job is over, that's all. It's a mop-up job now, nothing more. And if there's one thing Payton knows how to do, it's wield a mop."

When the phone clicked off, it took several long minutes for the rage to pass. The Closer had to stay parked by the side of the road, channeling it, breathing in and out, fists clenching and unclenching, visualizing something happy, something good and calming: Toby, the little stray kitten who had wandered into their yard on Christmas morning when the Closer was seven . . . Cabo, drifting on that raft out in the warm, clear, blue water last winter, the sun hot on tanned, hard shoulders, floating, floating . . . the blonde and how the slickness between her long, smooth, scrumptious legs had tasted and smelled and felt to the lips and tongue in those giddy, heady moments before the Closer had blown her face off . . .

The pain began to ease, the light stopped flashing. Feeling somewhat calmer now, the Closer started up the Suburban, made a U-turn, and eased out into the single lane that was crawling past the exploded car. A trooper was directing traffic. A fire truck was still hosing down the scene with foam.

The Oxford airport wasn't much. A small cinder-block terminal on the northern outskirts of town. A handful of airstrips. One of those cut-rate commuter airlines used it to connect the university town up with the state capital in Jackson, with Nashville, with Memphis and Atlanta. Private pilots flew in and out of there as well. The Closer parked the Suburban in the lot and got out, leaving everything behind with the exception of the SIG-Sauer and the Dick Dale tape. The Closer could not bear to leave that slob Payton the Dick Dale tape.

The private-plane offices and hangars were across the parking lot from the public terminal. There was no check-in or metal detector. The Challenger jet was due in thirty-seven minutes. The Closer chose to wait for it out on the tarmac in the broiling midday sun, as if serving some kind of penance.

It landed five minutes early, taxied smartly to a stop, and let its engines idle. The door opened and Payton descended, a hamlike hand shielding his eyes from the brightness. He wore a cheap, grease-spotted raincoat in spite of the heat, the better to conceal the friend he had brought along with him— a Mossberg pistol-grip pump action 12-gauge shotgun. The Mossberg could be concealed along the leg but whipped out like a pistol, which made it extremely popular with gangbangers. It cut an extremely intimidating profile. Personally, the Closer didn't care for the weapon. Or for intimidation. The Closer believed in quick, surgical execution, not in bullying. But a Mossberg was definitely Payton's style.

Smirking, he waddled across the tarmac toward the Closer, who handed him the keys to the Suburban without greeting or comment and got an unpleasant sneer in return. This was to be expected. Payton resented the Closer's youth, good looks, and tax bracket. He especially resented that the Closer had never pounded a beat.

"So you let 'em get away, huh, kid?" he jeered unpleasantly over the noise of the jet's engines. The man smelled like a barnyard animal—a pig or possibly a goat. And his breath was positively rancid. "Not gonna happen now, is it? Now that I'm on the job. When the Man needs it done right, he sends for a pro, you know what I mean?"

The Closer said nothing. There were too many thoughts about jabbing a length of piano wire into Payton's eyeball and driving it deep into his brain—such as it was.

"Don't let it get you down," Payton added nastily. "I'm happy to clean up your mess for you. In fact, I kinda like it." And with that he sniffed in a huge amount of air and snot, hitched up his trousers, and started across the tarmac to the parking lot, limping slightly.

The Closer watched him go, wondering why Augmon bothered with him. An utter failure as a street cop, he was angry, bitter, clueless. A racist. Most certainly an alcoholic. Why keep him on the payroll?

The Closer shook off the image of Payton lumbering across the airstrip and climbed on board. There was a flight attendant, a pretty young black woman who was in the process of tidying up. She seemed relieved to be rid of Payton. No doubt he had made a series of crude sexual advances toward her.

"Can I get you anything?" she asked, smiling brightly.

The Closer thought how nice it would be to sink into her arms, to have her clothes off, to make this black woman moan and groan in ecstasy. But now was not the time. So the Closer took a seat and said, "A tape player and headphones, please. And some mineral water."

The door was promptly shut now. The Challenger began to taxi back toward a runway.

The attendant returned a moment later with a Walkman and a tall glass of Perrier. Also the nine-by-twelve manila envelope that contained the details of the new assignment. The Closer popped the Dick Dale tape into the player and took a sip of the cold sparkling water. Then the Closer opened the envelope and began to read.

chapter 27

Carl and Amanda pulled into Clarksdale, Mississippi, in the early evening.

They had a new felony to add to their long list of crimes: car theft.

They had wandered, dazed but determined, for perhaps three miles after the Subaru had exploded. The delta countryside was flat and fertile farmland, the contour broken only by occasional unpaved roads, stands of old trees, and a few swampy bayous. Doing their best to keep heading south, they had passed through a grove of pecan trees. In the middle of the grove was a rickety old truck, used to drive amidst the grove to gather the nuts. The cab was sturdy enough; the back, which was still piled high with pecans, was dented and rusted and fenced in with chicken wire. It didn't look as if it had much more power than a golf cart, but it did have one absolute essential—a key dangling from the ignition.

"Carl," Amanda said, "this belongs to some poor farmer, some guy who probably can't even afford insurance."

"Amanda," he said, "here's the rule from now on. We can't stop and think about what we're doing. We've just got to think about what has to get done."

She sighed, nodded dubiously, but climbed into the dusty passenger seat. The shifting was heavy-handed, the shocks were basically gone, and there was a strong aroma of beer permeating every inch, but it started and it moved, and before long they were back on a real road heading toward Clarksdale.

Although neither of them had said so aloud, they were both counting on some kind of major revelation there. The LaRues had been killed because of what they told them. And one of the things they'd told them was to go to Clarksdale. It tied together; it seemed right. Nothing could bring that poor strange couple back to life. But maybe, if Clarksdale turned out to be the mystery town of Simms, their deaths would not have been in vain.

The downtown area was mostly old, the structures dating from the end of the nineteenth century and the beginning of the twentieth. The Sunflower River cut through the main business district, dividing it up clearly between rich and poor, black and white. They crossed the muddy, slow-moving river to explore the more upscale white neighborhoods first. There was no obvious main street. That seemed to have been usurped by Highway 49, the major thoroughfare that skirted downtown. On the highway were a string of businesses—mostly farm supplies—and fast-food restaurants, the Chamber of Commerce and an industrial park. The courthouse was an unimpressive new building with no personality of its own. It could have been a school or a factory or a prison. The residential areas were nice—neatly kept, quiet, and bland. The yards were landscaped with azaleas, magnolias, and assorted hardwood trees. The architecture ran the gamut from Victorian farmhouses to tile-roofed Italianate villas to reproductions of old southern plantations. None of the houses could be called grand. The word that came to mind was *clean.*

Crossing back across the Sunflower, they wandered through the black side of Clarksdale. They passed by the shanties and the Riverside Hotel— the hospital where Bessie Smith had died after a car accident because they refused to treat her. The stores were seedy, housed in two- to four-story brick houses. There was no particular style, even less ornamentation. They meandered in and out of the various blues bars and barbecue stands, too. The bars were dark and dingy, not meant to be viewed in the daytime. Some of them had small stages, platforms really, and a couple of ancient-looking music stands. They all smelled of stale beer and cigarette smoke and better days.

There were pieces of this town that could have been the town in which Danny and Rayette had lived. There were hints of what life must have been like half a century ago, elements that jarred Carl's memory and caused an exciting moment of recognition. But the town had been reshaped and redefined and moved into the present. The town had changed, and Carl realized they had no real way of knowing if what they were looking for still existed. Or had ever existed.

"I think we've been kidding ourselves," Carl admitted.

"Meaning?"

"Meaning we're trying to do the impossible."

"Oh," she said. "I didn't realize we ever thought otherwise."

But they knew they couldn't stop. They had to keep going. So, as twilight started tinting the sky above, they headed off in their rickety, stolen pickup truck to the next few small towns on their route through the delta. Hill House seemed to exist only because of the Buckshot Holler Restaurant and a hunting and fishing camp manned by sneering men in camouflage suits. Rena Lara was a tiny farming community with a country store, a Pentecostal church, and perhaps fifteen or twenty houses. Sherard had a defunct cotton gin, and Farrell had the first post office they'd seen in miles—built out of cinder blocks, with a permanent-looking sign out in front of it that said "Closed."

The last town they were going to hit that day was called Warren. Warren, Mississippi, seemed to be a town divided in two by the snaking, rusted railroad tracks. The black half was noticeably poorer. The houses were small, gray, and built on the cheap. The roads were not fully paved. There was a palpable sense of loss and defeat. The white half was almost Disneylandish in its orderliness and neatness. The lawns were all cut to the same length, and the houses were all freshly painted and shiny white. Basically it was a town like all the others. Near the river an old, abandoned factory had once produced tires and rubber products. Carl made a note of the existence of the factory. It fit the profile of the Simms factory. And Warren had a town square. The one in Clarksdale had long been replaced, covered over by an ugly new courthouse building. Some of the other town squares had retained some of their charm; the one in Warren was little more than a concrete slab, broken into thousands of cracks out of which grew clusters of grass and weeds. A rickety bench, its green paint cracked and dry, wobbled on the edge of the square. The rotted stump of a tree stood a foot to the right.

They stepped out of the pickup, knocked on the door of the town hall, but it was closed. Carl thought he heard a rustling noise from within, so he knocked a second time. The rustling noise stopped. Walking through town, they averted their eyes whenever they passed someone. They strolled for half an hour, looking, hoping to divine some sense of purpose, some miraculous answer—neither of which they found in the town of Warren, Mississippi.

They got back into the rickety pickup truck. Carl drove for five minutes, maybe ten. Then he saw something, an abandoned and overgrown field, and without knowing why, he slowed down. Out of the corner of his eye he saw Amanda turn her head and look at him curiously. He stopped the truck now. Didn't even pull over to the side of the road, just stopped and stared.

And started to remember.

It had been gnawing at him since they'd left Corinth. The signs. The casinos. The come-ons for the football betting. Football . . .

Now he was remembering.

"Carl?"

He barely heard her. Couldn't respond. Not when it was starting to come to him.

"Come on, Carl, what's going on?"

He didn't answer. He closed his eyes, blocking out the image off to his left, closing off everything except what he needed to find somewhere deep in his brain.

"Carl?" Amanda said again.

He opened the door and jumped onto the road. Leaving the door open, he started to cross to the other side, slowly at first, then faster, and then he started to run. The heat was forgotten; his exhaustion was irrelevant. He ran the couple of hundred yards to the splintered bleachers by the side of what had once been a high-school football field. And that's when he really poured it on, sprinting half the length of the field to the goalpost to his left. It was almost totally uprooted from the ground and barely standing. But when he reached it, he wanted to kiss it—it was the most beautiful object he'd ever seen.

He could hear Amanda now. She'd gotten out of the truck and raced after him.

"Carl, tell me what's going on. Please."

He took a deep breath, moved one step closer to the old goalpost, peered down at the base. Yes, there it was. Carved deeply into the side.

A heart. And inside the heart was carved a long-ago paean to teenage romance: *JD + SE = LOVE.*

Yes. Yes, he was remembering. Images were floating by. He could see the pages he had soaked up. The woman's near-illegible scrawl.

He could see Danny running . . .

"Carl!" Amanda was impatient now, frustrated. But when he turned to her, her eyes widened. She hadn't seen this kind of expression on his face in a long, long time. Maybe ever.

"We found it," he said. It came out quietly. Almost unemotionally. But then he threw his head back and laughed and screamed it as loud as he could. "We found it!" he yelled. And then yelled it again, and one more time for good measure.

"Wait," she said, confused, wanting to believe him, not quite able to. "How do you know? What are you looking at?"

He kept laughing and pointed to the carved heart.

"Amanda," he said, now gasping for air, "this was in the diary. A football field! Rayette wrote about how Danny used to run back and forth from goalpost to goalpost. He was obsessed with the carving, with this heart! With this goddamn heart that's right here. Right here in front of us!"

"Are you sure? I mean—"

He grabbed her now and shook her joyously.

"We found it! It was a throwaway, just a paragraph in the diary about this football field and the carving on the goalpost. The kid used to talk about it to his mother—it was some kind of romantic symbol to him. Jesus, I forgot all about it. Danny used to run here! Right here! Back and forth between the goalposts. We're standing right where he used to stand!"

He thrust his fist into the air and yelled again, not words this time, just a triumphant yell, and then he fell to his knees and took a deep breath, the first clear breath he'd taken in he couldn't remember how long. Amanda fell to her knees, too. She was smiling, a wonderful smile, a beautiful smile, and she started laughing along with him. And that's when he kissed her. Just grabbed her and kissed her. Hard and passionately. He didn't think about it, just did what felt right. And she kissed him back. They drew away from each other suddenly, as if a wall had instantly appeared between them. Then she yelped and flung herself at him and there they were, on their knees, kissing hungrily and holding each other tight, until they fell backward against the goalpost, knocking it over once and for all. They tumbled to the brown and brittle grass, holding each other, sweating and dusty, and kissing each other and laughing again.

"We found it," he said quietly, awe creeping into his voice.

He grinned at her, a full-fledged, wholehearted Granville grin. For a moment it was as if they were back in the past, as if they had never separated, as if the terrible events of this past week had never happened.

The grin made her heart soar, and she reached over to touch him, to cup her hand against his flushed cheek.

"Come on," she urged. "Let's go."

"Where to?"

She matched his grin, kissed him lightly on the lips. "You did your job," she said. "Now it's time to collect your reward."

chapter 28

He touched her cheek lightly. Ran the palm of his hand down toward her neck, just skimming the surface of her skin. Her neck was fine, very few lines. Tight and elegant and aristocratic. Her shoulders were silky smooth and white, as if they'd never been touched by the sun. His other hand came up now and he gripped her tightly, ran both hands down her bare arms. As thin as she was, the arms were soft, just a little too much flesh on them. He knew that she did not like her arms, never had, but she didn't flinch at his touch. Instead she moved closer to him, shifting her weight and the position of her legs on the bed, her mouth closer to his, her breasts grazing his chest.

Everything was spinning out of control. Everything was lost. Destroyed. For the first time in his life he felt completely and utterly alone. Abandoned. And it was that isolation that was eating away at him, paralyzing him, slicing through his insides and causing such suffering as he never even guessed existed.

He had many fears and just as many suspicions. He was not a stupid man. Nor did he live in a cocoon. There were things he knew, things he could only try to piece together. The one thing that was absolute was that every piece was adding to his pain.

The violence of their lovemaking jolted him from his reverie. They had made love so often over the years that there were no surprises. Yet this time their hunger for each other left them both a little breathless. Perhaps because they both sensed it would be the last time.

"Can you sleep?" she whispered when it was over, brushing his hair back off the top of his ear with her fingers.

"I think so," he answered.

"Do you want me to hold you?"

"If you'd like."

"I'd like," she said. "I'll hold you and you'll sleep, and for tonight the rest of the world doesn't exist."

She guided his body over so he was on his side, then she glided over the sheet so she fit against his back and his legs, wrapped her arms around his chest. He was sweating, even in the icy room. She brushed a trickle of his sweat from his collarbone and held him even tighter.

"Whatever you want to do," she said, "whatever you *have* to do, you know it's fine with me."

He nodded, but her words were muffled because he was already almost asleep. She waited until she was sure he was no longer awake, then she too closed her eyes. It took her a little longer to sleep because she had always been more of a realist than he was. She knew what was going to happen, where the future, such as it was, would lie. But eventually she too succumbed to the hour and her own exhaustion and finally drifted off.

They slept that way, Tom and Elizabeth Adamson, the president and First Lady of the United States, until it was nearly morning.

Until, once again, the dream came and the president woke up screaming.

It had never felt like this.

Not the first time, when they'd hungered for each other so fiercely. Not the last time, when every touch was tinged with sadness and the sense that things were ending. Not any of the times in between, when they'd laughed and lusted and experimented and felt that everything the rest of their lives was going to be perfect.

They had no barriers between them this time. They wanted each other, and they both realized they needed each other.

"Do you want me to hold you?" he'd asked when they got into the motel bed.

"No," she'd told him. "I want you to make love to me."

Carl realized that her body had changed. It had become harder, leaner. She'd been working out, and when she turned over, fluttering her hands to draw him closer, he could see the muscles ripple on her shoulders. Her body thrilled him, and he couldn't stop touching, stop kissing, every inch of her. He could tell that everything he did excited her, and that excited him even more. There was a certain strength to her now, and not just a physical strength. When he finally entered her, he felt as if she were swallowing him whole. As if they'd become one person.

Amanda had not expected this rush of joy. It began as a physical need. She had to hold someone, she had to connect with someone. Even after they kissed, it did not set off the electric sensations she was experiencing now. He had changed as a lover. He was far gentler, more sensitive, more concerned with her desires. When he began gently massaging her back, kissing the nape of her neck, running his nails through her now short hair, moving his tongue down her spine, she felt weak. She felt a sense of surrender. But she knew it was a mutual surrender.

They made love until early in the morning, until they were exhausted and drained. Until each of them knew they had nothing left to give, physically or emotionally. When they were done, no words were spoken. No promises were made as they clutched each other and held each other tight. But both Carl and Amanda vowed silently, separately, never to let the other go.

"We should talk," Elizabeth Adamson said. She was in bed, watching her husband stand by the window, partially hidden in the predawn shadows.

"There's no need," he said wearily. "I know what you want."

"Do you?"

"You want me to resign."

"Yes," she said, "that is what I want. It's the only way I think I can save you. Keep you whole."

"Whole?" His lip curled up in disdain. "What happens to my presidency? I just hand it over to Jerry Bickford?"

"He's earned it. He's loyal. He's honest."

"He's old, he's sick, he's weak."

"He's kind."

"In this town, kindness *is* weakness. He can't even handle being vice president anymore. You heard him. He wants out."

"He'll change his mind."

"Jerry Bickford hasn't changed his mind in thirty-five years."

"It's not so easy to turn this job down."

"No. And it's even harder to give it up. My God, Elizabeth, do you real-ize what would happen? What it would do to the party? The chaos . . . the damage it could cause . . ."

"Tommy, I don't want to talk politics. I just want you to do what's best."

"For the country?"

"No, my dear. For *you*."

"There *is* no best for me anymore." The words sounded bitter. Defeated.

"Then for *us*." When he looked at her blankly, she said, softly, almost to herself, "Perhaps the greatest tragedy in all of this is that we've forgotten there is an us."

"Elizabeth." Tom Adamson's voice was deep and clear. It resonated throughout the bedroom. "I'm the president of the United States. What I am aside from that, what *we* are, is of no consequence."

"No," she cried. "It's the *only* thing of consequence. What we are, what we mean to each other—"

"You're talking about what we *were*, not what we *are*."

"Then let's go back. Let's go back to when we could breathe again!" She saw him wince, as if her words were opening up some old wound in-side him. As if they were pulling him toward a place he could never really return to. "We can finish the farmhouse in the Ozarks. We can ride bareback at dawn and go skinny-dipping in the pond and not worry that some damn photographers are camped out on the rocks. You can fish and carve that mantel you've been saying you were going to carve for—what is it now, twenty years? You can go to a university and teach. Or if you miss the action, you can start a foundation, sit on a board. Tom," she pleaded, "we can start our lives all over again. We can make love in the daytime."

He turned around now, and his face emerged from the shadows.

"We can never go back," he whispered. "I told. I told someone about . . ." And now he said the word he hadn't uttered in so many years. "Gideon."

"Yes," she said. The word came out slowly and sadly. "Yes, you did. You told the priest."

"You know about that?" Then he shook his head in wonder. "Of course you do. You know everything."

"I know everything about *you*, my darling. I know when you're strong. And when you're hurting. And . . ."

"And when I'm weak?" Their eyes met across the room, through the shadows. "You *do* know everything about me. Which means you know I can't resign."

"It doesn't matter," she said. "Whatever you told him . . . whatever *any-one* knows . . . it doesn't matter."

"Nothing matters."

"That's not true, Tom. *We* matter." For the first time in many, many years she thought she was going to burst into tears. "Lord, how we matter."

"No," Tom Adamson said. "Someone knows about Gideon. So *nothing* matters."

The room was absolutely quiet now. No sounds intruded from outside the window. It was as if the real world had receded far into the distance. "Please come back to bed," she urged.

Tom Adamson nodded wearily. He took one last look out the window at her garden shimmering in the rising sun.

"I'm coming," he said.

But even as he spoke, even as he thought about all they had shared, all they had won and all they had lost, he knew he couldn't and wouldn't stay for very long.

They woke up in each other's arms. Amanda's eyes opened first, and for a minute or two she watched him sleep. The sun was doing its best to penetrate the thick motel curtain drawn across the window. It managed to sneak through just enough to cast a faint glow on a stained patch of brown carpet at the foot of the queen-sized bed.

Carl stirred now. She saw his eyes open, take in the room, and, for a moment, register confusion. Then he saw her. He smiled, but even before the smile, she could see in his eyes that his confusion had turned to warmth. He was comforted seeing her, and for that she was glad.

They had many things to say to each other, she knew. Things they *needed* to say to each other. But those things could wait. What was it Humphrey Bogart told Ingrid Bergman in *Casablanca*? The problems of two people in this world didn't amount to a hill of beans? A little much, maybe. But not so far off track. Their relationship could wait. They had bigger problems to solve. They were close to Gideon, she knew that. So close they could both feel him.

And thirty minutes after they'd awakened, they'd thrown on their clothes, quickly downed some strong, black coffee, and were back in their rickety, stolen pickup truck, getting even closer.

They drove slowly through the town of Warren, Mississippi, soaking in everything possible, doing their best to memorize the layout and any potentially important landmarks. Periodically Carl would mutter to himself as he thought he recognized something from the diary. Occasionally people looked up, but their interest didn't last long. Carl paid no attention to their curious glances. He was lost in the extraordinary experience of seeing the reality of a town he had created on paper.

Their first stop was at the local newspaper office, the *Gazette*. Amanda went in without Carl—if anyone was going to recognize him, it would be in the newspaper office—and told the clerk there that she was researching a book on the economic history of the South. It didn't take her long to latch on to the history of Warren's factory. It had been built in the midst of the Industrial Revolution, turning out rubber products. By the 1930s it was mostly producing tires. The salient point, as far as Amanda was concerned, was that the factory was flourishing in the mid-1950s. She struck gold when she discovered that in 1969 there was a lawsuit filed against the factory. Several people in the town claimed that the manufacturer was spewing toxic waste into the river. Between the years 1964 and 1969, seven children in this small town had been born with some type of physical deformity. One had been born with no arms, one with no right foot. Those were the two most extreme cases, but the others did not make for pleasant reading, either. In addition to those seven, two babies had been born severely retarded during the same period. Several ecologically aware citizens had enough sense to blame the rubber factory and take action. Amanda read until she came to the end of the suit, which was settled in 1977. The case had dragged on for so long, several of the families involved in the litigation had left town by then. The remaining filers settled for $12,500 each in exchange for dropping all charges. Two of the lawyers for the suing families went to work for the factory, which closed its doors in 1979.

Amanda rushed out of the newspaper building and filled Carl in on what she'd learned.

"We're definitely in the right place," he said. "The football field, the factory, the physical layout, just a few miles from the auditorium where Elvis played—it all fits." He lifted the cap and settled it farther back on his head.

"So let's go find us a witness," she said.

The town hall was half a mile away, and that was their next stop. It was near the ghostly railway station. They parked right in front of the two-story brick building, deciding that they should tackle this one together. As they walked through the front door, their hands sought each other out. Their fingers locked together and squeezed tightly. Then they were hit by a burst of cool air-conditioned air and were face-to-face with a tall, white-haired black man. He was perhaps six foot three, although he was stooped over several inches, as if he had a heavy weight on his back. His face looked as if it was carrying the same weight. There was a streak of pain and grief in his eyes and mouth that was quite startling and almost unbearable to look at.

"Hello," Amanda greeted him.

"May I help you?" the man wanted to know. His voice was deep and dignified and commanding. It seemed to echo throughout the room.

"Yes. We're reporters with the *New Orleans Times-Picayune*."

"That right?" He was neither believing nor disbelieving. Not interested in them, not uninterested.

"We're looking for someone," Carl said. It was his entry into the conversation, and he sounded just a little too eager. Amanda warned him off with her eyes.

The man tensed as soon as Carl spoke. Amanda could see his eyes narrow and the skin on his face tighten.

"Who might you be looking for?"

"Someone who lived here a long time ago. In the fifties. A woman."

"A black woman." It wasn't a question.

"That's right." Carl nodded.

"What's her name?"

"We don't know. All we have is a description."

"Lot of black women lived here over the years."

"Not too many like this one, I think. She had a very distinctive birth-mark. It covered one whole eye, like a ring around half of her face. She was a midwife."

"Is this for your book on southern economics?"

Amanda blushed. "Word travels pretty fast around here."

"Even faster than it used to."

"I'm not writing a book."

"No," the black man said. "And you're not from the *Times-Picayune*, either." Amanda started to protest, but he cut her off. "I'm the alderman here. Name's Luther Heller. That mean something to you?"

Amanda shook her head.

"You don't know who I am?"

"No."

"I read the papers," Luther Heller said. "I watch television. And I pay attention. So I know who you are. You mean something to me."

"You must have us confused with—"

"I don't have you confused with anyone. I know who you are, and I know why you're here. And I know that the police would be mighty sur-prised and mighty happy to find out that you're not in Portland, Oregon."

"Portland?" Carl asked. He looked at Amanda, confused and almost amused. He'd thought this man had recognized them. But Portland?

The alderman saw the look on Carl's face. He reached down, picked up a copy of that morning's newspaper off a nearby desk, and held it out for them to see.

"Might as well read it. I'm not about to call the police."

Amanda took the paper and buried her nose in the story. Moments later a harsh laugh burst out of her. She hesitated and glanced at the tall black man. He had them cold. There was no point in pretending any further.

"They think we're in Portland, Carl. They don't just think it, they know it. They have a positive ID. It's been confirmed."

"No way."

"We were sighted there, together, at a Gap," she affirmed. "You bought two pairs of khaki pants and a T-shirt. I bought a denim shirt and a pair of shorts. Our purchase totaled two hundred eleven dollars and eighteen cents. The clerk who waited on us recognized us."

"How?" he asked Amanda. "How could they—"

"Shaneesa! She hacked it into their computer—right down to which cash register it was and what time the purchase took place. That's why she wanted my credit card numbers. God, she's scary."

"But how could somebody have *recognized* us? We were never there."

"Only you and I—and Mr. Heller—know that," Amanda countered. "Credit card records don't lie. The credit card company says it happened, so it happened. The clerk *had* to say she waited on us. On *both* of us. The only other way it could have played out is if she'd accepted a stolen credit card, which would not only make her seem stupid and incompetent, it could have gotten her fired. Especially if she accepted it from *you*, someone on the Ten Most Wanted list. Instead she covered her butt and got her face on TV and her name in the papers." Amanda puffed out her cheeks with relief. "Shaneesa has bought us some serious breathing room."

They both turned toward Alderman Heller. He could choke off their breathing room with one phone call. But why hadn't he done that already? What was he waiting for?

The black man gave no indication of his motives. He merely nodded, a very quiet nod, as if he'd made up his mind about something. His hand slipped unobtrusively into his right pants pocket.

"Why are you looking for her? For Momma One-Eye?" he asked.

"That's her name?" Carl asked. It thrilled him to hear it. The woman he had read about, had half invented on the written page, was now real.

"It's what folks call her. It's what folks have called her for a long time."

Amanda and Carl exchanged a quick glance. Carl nodded, and Amanda went on. "We believe that she is privy to some very important information."

The man's voice deepened. To Carl it sounded like a clap of thunder. "Important to who?"

"To a lot of people," Amanda said.

"White people."

"All people."

He shook his head at her answer, not believing it. "How badly do you want this information?"

"Very badly."

"Enough to kill for it?" And before they could answer, "Enough to slit a little black girl's throat? Enough to burn down an old lady's house? Enough to take away any reason this old man you're looking at has to keep living?"

Carl stepped forward. He answered the black man's questions. "No, sir," he said quietly. "Not enough to do any of that."

"Mr. Heller," Amanda said, "you told us you weren't going to call the police."

"That's right."

"What *are* you going to do?"

The alderman's hand emerged now from his pocket, and with it came a pistol. The calm manner in which he waved it at them, the easy way it sat in his large, callused palm, made Carl and Amanda realize that he was a man who knew how to use the gun he was holding.

"Please," Carl said to the black man, "whatever you think you know, you don't."

"Don't you ever tell me what I know, young man. I know that too many people are dead for no reason. I know that whatever it is you think is so important, it got my baby girl killed. And *her* baby girl."

"We're sorry," Amanda said. "We're so sorry. But we had no idea."

"I've been waiting, knowing someone else had to come. Knowing it wasn't over yet."

"It's not over," Carl said. "But we're here to try to end it."

"Mr. Heller . . . Luther . . ." Amanda spoke softly, gently. "We don't know what happened here. But other people besides your daughter have gotten killed. If you don't help us find Momma One-Eye, there's a chance a lot more people will die, too." She waved her hand toward Carl. "Whatever you've read in the paper about him, or us, it's a lie. Somebody is setting us up. It sounds like the same person who killed your daughter. If you ever want to find out what happened, if you ever want some kind of justice, then you don't want to turn us over to the police. What you want to do is help us."

"I don't want justice," Alderman Heller said. "Black people don't get justice when things like this happen."

"Then what do you want?"

"I want revenge."

"Well," Amanda breathed, "then I don't know if we can help you. All we want to do is find the truth. And try to stay alive while we're doing that."

"I want the man who murdered my babies." Luther Heller held his stomach, as if the mere act of speaking those words were ripping up his insides.

"Did you see him?" Carl asked slowly.

The alderman closed his eyes. He took a deep breath and nodded. "He came into town, asking for Momma One-Eye, just like you."

"What did he look like?" Carl spoke gently. "Can you tell us what he looked like?"

Luther opened his eyes. "Can you give me one reason why I should trust you?"

Amanda took a long time before answering. "No," she said. "I can't think of a reason in the world."

Luther nodded again. He bit down on his lip until the blood drained from it. Then he stepped sideways and used the gun to motion them forward into the back room. Amanda went first. As she stepped through the door, Carl heard her gasp. He followed close behind her. As soon as he was in the alderman's office, he saw what had taken Amanda's breath away.

The walls of Luther Heller's office were covered with pencil and charcoal sketches. There must have been seventy-five of them. Every sketch was of a man's face. The *same* man's face. Some were profiles, some face-on views. Some were extraordinarily detailed, others focused only on certain features: hair, eyes, nose. Alderman Heller was a talented artist—and clearly obsessed with his subject. His portraits perfectly captured the man portrayed. The arrogance. The savagery. The thick, muscular good looks and the confident demeanor.

"Do you know him?" Alderman Heller asked.

"Yes," Carl said.

"Tell me."

"His name is Harry Wagner."

"Do you know where he is?"

Carl nodded. "He's dead."

"Did you kill him?"

"No."

"How did he die?"

"Very painfully," Carl said.

For the very first time Luther Heller's face relaxed. A small fraction of the grief faded. "Good," he said. Then he slowly placed the gun back in his pocket, sat down in his desk chair, and folded his hands in front of him. "Now," he said, "tell me more about this important information you say Momma One-Eye has."

Payton belched, and for a moment he was overwhelmed by the aftertaste of greasy fried chicken, jalapeño corn bread, and sweet, syrupy Coca-Cola that he'd gobbled down almost an hour earlier.

He couldn't risk being seen, not by the kid and the girl, so he'd eaten at some fried-food joint. A sign said it was a church. Yeah, right. What kind of fucking church sold fried chicken? A church way the hell down here, that's what kind. And the jigs who served there were so damn stupid that when he'd asked for a sandwich, they just gave him two pieces of white bread and a chicken leg. Like he was supposed to pick the thing apart himself. Or eat the goddamn bones! For a moment his rage had almost gotten the better of him. He flashed back to that night at the precinct: his choke hold on Yussef Gilliam, the savage beating, the fury. And the aftermath: his firing, his humiliation, the end of his dream. The end of his *life*. He almost grabbed the poor sap who'd handed him his bread and his chicken leg. He could have killed him, he realized. Would have *liked* to have killed him. And then he shook his head. Cleared his brain. What the hell was he doing? It was just a sandwich. So they were even stupider down South than they were in the New York projects. Big deal. Amazing, he thought. Hard to actually get your brain around. But not really that important in the scheme of things. You couldn't kill someone because he didn't even know how to make a chicken sandwich.

But it sure would be nice if you could.

They were still in there, the kid and the girl, still inside the town hall. What the hell were they talking about? Maybe he should just go in and find out. Barge in and shock the shit out of them. End it all now. Wouldn't be that hard . . .

No. No, better to wait. What was he thinking? Payton realized he was getting impatient. The last thing he needed was to cause a scene, have someone see him. He had to do this quietly, make sure no one knew a thing. He couldn't afford to screw up this time. This was a good gig. And if he did things right, it would lead to a helluva lot more.

He'd been out of New York too long, that was the problem. The pavement, the anger, the junkies, the pimps, the *action*—that's what relaxed him. That's what he needed. It's why he'd been a great cop. Put him in a subway station with some PR trying to stick a Jew for a pair of sneakers, that's where Payton belonged. It's where he was at his best. Not down here, where everything was so goddamn clean and green and slow and polite. He didn't like it here. He didn't like polite. He wanted out. Soon. But he couldn't let that affect the job.

Say what you want about him, Payton thought to himself, but he never left a job unfinished. You may not like the way he got the results, but he always got them. Always got the job done.

Always.

So he knew he'd wait. Wait until he could follow them someplace nice and quiet. Wait until he could do what he came here to do, and do it right.

They were coming out now. All three of them. Looking real friendly.

Payton turned the key in his ignition. His car started right up, another advantage of working for the Man. Everything always started right up.

They were pulling out of the parking lot now. Where were they going? And then Payton realized: What the hell difference did it make? He was going to get them in the end. Eventually.

Still, he hoped he could kill them all soon, go get a decent white man's meal, and get the hell home.

"Momma?"

The house was dark, and for a few moments Carl thought it was without electricity. But then Luther Heller reached to his right and flicked a switch, and a bare bulb hanging from a ceiling fixture in the center of the room, unprotected by any shade, came on. The room that was illuminated was shabby but spotlessly clean. It shone. As if the person who lived there had nothing to do except keep it polished. There was one couch, which had seen better days, and two straight-backed chairs. The floor was linoleum and the walls were covered in blue flowered wallpaper that, in spots, was water-stained and peeling. A small television sat on a metal cart right in the middle of the room.

"Momma?" Alderman Heller called out again. "Clarissa May? It's Luther." There was only silence as an answer. "I've brought two friends. *Real* friends. They think they can help end all this madness."

Still nothing but silence. Then Carl cocked his head. He thought he heard . . . no, it couldn't be . . . yes. He looked at Amanda, and he could tell she heard it, too. So did Heller.

Singing.

Low, gravelly. Almost tuneless, somehow delicate. Impossible to tell if it was a man's voice or a woman's. But definitely singing:

> *"I am poured out like water*
> *All my bones are out of joint*
> *My heart is become like wax*
> *Melted in my inmost parts."*

"Psalms," Luther Heller said, and smiled. "She loves to sing those psalms." Then he called out, "Momma?"

The singing continued, still soft and secretive and eerie.

> *"Dogs have encompassed me*
> *A company of evildoers have enclosed me*
> *Like a lion they are at my hands and feet."*

They moved toward a door at the back left of the room. Luther opened it, just a crack. Then a little wider. Then pushed it open all the way, the door creaking as it eased forward. They stepped through into a small bedroom, as bare and sparse as the room they'd just left. There was a single bed and a bentwood rocking chair. In the rocker was a tiny black woman, her entire body illuminated by the one lamp in the room. She couldn't have been much more than four foot eight or nine. And she was rail thin, almost skeletal. Her wrist bones jutted out well beyond the sides of her hands. Her elbows came practically to a point. And the skin covering her shoulders and collarbone was stretched so tight as to be practically clear.

But the most amazing thing about her appearance was her face. The woman had to be in her eighties. Yet there was not one line on her forehead. Her cheekbones were high and perfect. Her lips were thin slits and her mouth was small and narrow. She had the face of a beautiful young girl.

And then there was her eye.

The right one was unblemished. Its deep brown color had a penetrating brightness as she stared at them. But her left eye had a ring around it, perfectly round and dark black, darker than her deep brown skin. Carl remembered the description in the diary he had read, and it was exactly accurate. This ring on her face practically glowed as it circled her cheek and nose.

She rocked slowly back and forth, refused to look up at the intruders, and continued singing:

> *"The chords of death compassed me*
> *And the straits of the netherworld got hold upon me*
> *I found trouble and sorrow*
> *But I called upon the name of the Lord."*

"Clarissa May," Luther Heller said, "I'd like you to talk to these two people. I believe it's time to tell what it is you know."

"Don't talk to nobody," Momma One-Eye said. "Never talked to nobody." Her speaking voice was coarse. It whistled through her teeth. But there was great strength to it.

"Ms. Wynn . . . ," Amanda began.

"Shouldn'ta brought 'em here," Momma said. "Shouldn'ta brought 'em. When white people find me, I'll be a dead woman."

"Not these white people, Momma."

"I be a dead woman now." The tiny black woman now looked up for the first time. She was trembling, and a tear ran down her cheek.

"Momma," Amanda said, "we need your help."

"You wanna know what I seen. What I know."

"Yes."

"I seen the devil's work. I seen the devil come to earth and be killed by another devil."

"No, Momma," Carl told her. "There was no devil. All you saw was people doing what they do when they're at their worst."

"Nobody knows what I seen. Nobody knows what I know." She nodded at Luther Heller. "Not him. Not my children. Not my grandchildren or great-grandchildren. Nobody knows. And I'll never tell. Can't tell 'cause I'll be dead."

"*We* know," Carl said.

"Can't know. I'm the only one seen it."

"Would you like us to tell you?" The old woman said nothing, so Carl went on. "You were a midwife. And you helped deliver a baby a long time ago. Almost fifty years ago." The woman's face was impassive. Carl found himself staring at the magnificent eye as he spoke. "This baby we want to know about, you delivered him late at night, around midnight. You never saw the father, just the mother and her first son. That boy was nine years old. He's the one who went to get you when it was time for the baby. Do you want me to describe them for you?"

Momma One-Eye nodded, as if in a trance, so Carl told her everything he could remember. He described what the woman he'd named Rayette looked like, her hair, her body, her voice. Then he did the same for the boy, Danny. He described what the birth of Rayette's second child was like—the crying, the screaming—and he told about the baby's abnormal behavior in the weeks and months after he was born. When he was done, the woman known as Momma One-Eye was staring at him in amazement, her thin mouth agape.

"That baby, he was a devil-child."

"No, Momma. He was just severely retarded. We think it was caused by the pollution from the old factory, the rubber mill that used to be here."

She looked him in the eye now. And she was no longer trembling. "The one that smelled so bad?"

"That's the one."

"How much more you know?" Momma One-Eye demanded. "What you know after that?"

"We know just about everything."

"You know what that boy did? What he did to his baby brother?"

"Yes. We know what he did."

"Then what you need me for? You know everything. What you need from Momma? You need to kill her? You gonna take Momma and kill her to save that little white boy?"

Carl realized he was gripping his hands together. His upper body was tilted forward, and he was barely breathing. "We won't hurt you at all, Momma. We want to *stop* anyone from hurting you."

"How you gonna do that?"

"We know *what* happened, Momma. But we need to know where. We need to see that baby's grave. And we need to know who."

The old woman closed her eyes. Carl was certain she was remembering the events of years ago. He was sure she was picturing exactly what she had seen and heard.

"They didn't know I was there," she said. "But I was outside. I was worried about that child. Not the baby. The boy. That boy was smart. He was a special boy, he was. I liked that boy very much. So there I was. It was a hot night and I was outside, goin' to check up on that boy 'cause his momma, she wasn't never there. . . . He was such a smart boy. . . ."

Her eyes closed again and she seemed to be drifting away, lost in her memories. "I watched them. She carried that little baby in her arms. Her own little baby. Wrapped in a blanket, he was. A blue blanket. Sometimes I see that blue blanket in my dreams. She carried and he dug. Dug deep, but she kept tellin' him to go deeper. And then finally they put that baby in the ground. They put him in a box and covered him up with earth and then they left. They left right after that and never came back."

"Help them, Momma," Luther Heller said. "Help *us*."

"Nobody knows this. All these years, ain't nobody knows."

"It's time," Carl said. "People *have* to know."

Momma One-Eye closed her eyes, began rocking in her chair again, and the same tuneless song came out of her mouth:

> *"My soul is bowed down*
> *They have digged a pit before me*

They are fallen into the midst thereof themselves
My heart is setfast, O God, my heart is steadfast
I will sing, yea, I will sing praises
Thy glory be above all the earth."

The old black woman's eyes opened again. She waited until the rocking chair stopped moving of its own accord. Then she said, "I can show you." Her gravelly voice whistled through her teeth, but to Carl and Amanda it was the sweet voice of an angel. Especially when she stood up from the rocker and spoke her final sentence: "I can take you there."

chapter 29

"**M**other," he said softly, low enough so he couldn't be heard.

"Tommy. I'll be a son of a bitch if this isn't early even for you. Don't tell me they're keepin' you busy up there."

How long ago had he had that conversation? Months? Weeks? No, he remembered now. It was less than a week. Five days ago. Five days since he'd discovered that everything he thought he knew about life was an utter and complete lie.

"Have you looked in your safe lately, Mother?"

"My safe? Why in the world would I—"

But then she understood and had gone to look. Slowly, crippled by the arthritis that was the first thing ever in her life to slow her down, she had gone. And when she finally returned and picked up the receiver, she told him the diary was still there. Everything was still there. The tattered papers she'd saved from his childhood, the history she'd scrupulously and meticulously chronicled. The records. The proof . . .

"It's still there, son," she said. "But it's been moved."

He didn't say anything for a long, long time. When he did finally speak, his legendary glibness failed him. "Are you sure?" was all he could manage. "Are you positive, Mother?"

"I haven't been sure of too many things in this life, Lord knows. But I'm sure of this. Somebody had it, somebody saw it." And when he still said nothing, she said, "I'm sorry, Tommy. I'm sorrier than I could ever tell you."

"Mother," he said. And suddenly he was terrified that he was going to cry. He'd never let his mother see him cry, not even when he was a young boy. And he wouldn't allow it now, either. He closed his eyes and clenched his jaw until he was sure he could speak without weakness and fear permeating every word. "I'd like to ask you a question. Just one thing I've never asked you before. But I'd very much like an answer."

"What is it, Tommy?"

"Why?"

"I'm afraid I don't understand, son. Why what?"

"Why did you do it? Why did you write it all down? And dear God, why did you keep it?"

She didn't hesitate before answering. These were questions she'd asked herself a million times. And she knew the answer. "Because," she told him, "all these years, it's the only thing I had to let me know I was really alive."

Had it really been days since they'd spoken? He wanted to talk to her again. Now. To call her up and tell her that it was all right. That he understood, really and truly. Understood and forgave her, which, of course, he did, because he had never loved anyone, not even Elizabeth, the way he'd loved his mother. Wilhelmina Nora Adamson. He adored her. Always had. When he was young and she was weak, he'd let her lean on him. More than that, too. Much, much more. He'd done whatever she wanted. She never even had to speak about what she desired. He always knew. And he would do whatever it took to make her wishes come true. And when she got older and grew strong, when she'd finally used her beauty to marry well, she had reciprocated. She knew what *he'd* wanted, knew what he believed was his destiny. So she had made the ultimate sacrifice: She had reinvented herself so he could become president of the United States.

It wasn't hard, not really, was it, Mother? They'd had no roots. They had not lived in any one place long enough to be remembered. And those who did remember—her family, her husbands, her lovers—were dead or drunk or too stupid to ever understand what had happened. There were no official records, not really. There'd been enough name changes along the way to hide almost anything. All you had to do was give *enough* of the truth. The drunken father. The first husband. And the second. And the last one. The moving from town to town. The drinking. It made for a colorful tale: the southern beauty who'd pulled herself up from the mud to mold and shape the future president. She'd even written her autobiography. Gotten seven figures from the most prestigious publisher in the business. And when it was published, she became the adored heroine of millions of women around the world for having survived her past. No, much more than merely having survived. Having *triumphed* over her past.

Of course, it was a past that didn't really exist. Or rather, existed up to a point.

A rather important point, however.

Thank you, Mother, he thought. *Although it hasn't been too bad for you, has it? You've lived well as I've moved on. You shared the spotlight and found your niche and your fame. You could sit in the best box at the race-track, and you had heads of state fawn over you. But nonetheless I hope you know that I thank you. For what you gave up. And for staying silent. For loving me, deeply, in your own way.*

For letting me love you.

And so I forgive you. . . .

President Thomas Frederick Adamson opened his eyes and the roaring in his head stopped. For a moment he was bewildered. Where was he? Who was talking? Then he realized: *Oh, yes. Budget meeting.* It had been scheduled weeks in advance. They had to take a position on defense spending and the level of cuts being made. His secretary of defense was arguing now. He was angry. He thought the cuts were too deep. They would not only demoralize the military, they could cripple it.

The secretary was droning on, and Tom Adamson stopped listening.

He was thinking of the other love of his life.

Elizabeth.

There was a story about her in the paper yesterday. Front page of the *Washington Journal.* He had read it with such pride. The headline had been "The Most Admired Woman in the World." It was true. Elizabeth had become quite influential, even powerful. But it was not through any official means. It was through her compassion for other people, through her good deeds. She was the best speaker he had ever heard, far better than he was. She could stir a crowd's passions, could tap into their hearts and their souls. But then, she was smarter than he was. She always had been. He knew how much she had sacrificed to help him get to where he was. They had long ago decided to think of his career as *their* career, his goal as *their* goal. She'd been one of the best legal minds in the country, but she'd given up her practice long ago to oversee his campaigns and to make sure there was never any cry of conflict of interest. Like his mother, she had given up her life for him, he knew that.

He understood. He really did. He understood everything she had done and everything she would do from this point on.

Would she understand him as well? What he was about to do and why?

Tom Adamson couldn't stay in this meeting any longer. It was unbearable. Someone else was yelling now. His chief of staff. A total loser. That had been a mistake. He was too young for the job, too inexperienced. That was one of his flaws as chief executive, he knew. He'd valued loyalty over experience.

He should have realized there was no such thing as loyalty. There was only . . .

There was only oneself.

The president stood up from the table now and bolted. The rest of the people in the room were stunned. Tom Adamson didn't care. He ran down the hallway, turned toward the outer office that led to the Oval Office. His secretary said something as he staggered by. He didn't hear the words, didn't respond. Just went into the office he hated so much, the room that had always made him feel so inadequate, and sat down in the chair at his desk.

He knew that this was the moment. He had to decide now. He had to find the strength now or forever live with his weakness.

President Tom Adamson had crossed over into total despair and madness as he opened the top drawer to his desk and tried desperately to think of something he would miss after he left this world behind.

When it came to him, he smiled with great relief.

Her flowers, he thought. *Elizabeth's flowers.*

Then the despair was over.

The madness was just beginning.

The house was uninhabitable. There were gaping holes in the roof where the wood had rotted away. There was no foundation, so the front of the porch had sunk into the ground and was at an ominous tilt. The windows had been replaced by spiderwebs and any life that had once existed inside had been replaced by darkness, loneliness, and emptiness.

Nonetheless, Carl recognized it. It was the house that Danny and

Rayette had lived in. It was the house Rayette's second son was born in. It was the house in which Danny had murdered his baby brother.

They walked around the back of the house, the four of them—Carl, Amanda, Luther Heller, and the woman known as Momma One-Eye— through the overgrown weeds and the cracked, hardened mud. There was an ancient barn there, which seemed to have survived better than the house. The paint had long since cracked and the swinging door had rotted through, but it was standing. An overwhelming smell of manure emanated from within, and the buzzing from the swarm of flies that lived there was audible in the silence of the countryside. This was a property that time had forgotten. No, Carl thought, not forgotten. Time had cursed it. Had done its best to make it disappear.

Amanda clutched at Carl's arm. He covered her hand with his and squeezed as reassuringly as he could manage.

Momma led them to the back of the barn. Beyond it lay a forest, thick with oak and pine trees. She walked to the edge of the woods and stopped in front of a tall oak. Its leaves provided a large patch of shade on the burnt grass. Momma turned to face them; then she looked straight down at the ground.

She said nothing. Just stepped aside.

They had stopped off at the alderman's house to pick up a shovel. Carl now took a deep breath, grabbed the shaft of the shovel, hand over hand, and began digging. The sweat poured off him, but he dug ferociously and rhythmically. The ground was hard and rocky and filled with twisted roots. But in half an hour, there was a hole perhaps six feet long, three feet wide, and four feet deep. Carl stopped digging, ran a hand through his wet hair, then wiped it on his pants. He looked up at Momma One-Eye, who just nodded again impassively. Carl swung the shovel one more time, plunged it into the dirt. He pulled it back, lifted it to swing again, then stopped suddenly, holding the shovel steady in midair.

He was breathing hard but trying to keep the breaths even and under control.

"Amanda," he said quietly.

She took a step over to the hole, leaned over, and stared inside. Carl dug the shovel into the ground again, and then several more times, delicately now, carefully sweeping the dirt away from the center of the hole.

"Oh, my God," Amanda said. "Oh, my God."

They all stared into the hole. There was something there, a small wooden box wrapped in a faded and torn blue blanket. Pieces of the blanket were missing, dissolved by the passage of time, but stringy blue patches of cloth still clung tenaciously to the rotting wood. Carl brushed the remaining layer of dirt off the box, lifted it up, tossed the remains of the blue blanket off to the side, and pried open the lid.

Inside the box was a tiny human skeleton. It was absolutely intact, which made it all the sadder. The head, the arms, the legs were positioned so the body could have been asleep. The fingers were thin and fine, the skull small and perfectly formed. Carl felt as if he knew this child, as if the skeleton were a child still, capable of sitting up and walking and crying. The reality of what he was looking at sliced through Carl as vividly as a winter wind, making him shiver despite the southern summer heat. He picked up the top of the box—the makeshift coffin—and put it back where it belonged, covering back up the bones of a baby boy, murdered nearly half a century earlier.

He looked up at the old black woman, who was crying quietly.

Amanda was struggling not to cry herself as she asked Momma One-Eye, "Who is it?"

"You *know*, don't you?" Momma One-Eye said. "You know who his brother become."

"Tell us," Carl said slowly. "It's the only thing we don't know. So please, please tell us."

"That boy, the smart boy, that boy I loved when he was so little . . . he become the president of the United States."

Carl and Amanda stared at each other. Her hand reached out unsteadily for his and he took it, just as unsteadily. Luther Heller staggered one step backward and moaned a low, anguished moan.

"That's why I never told anybody," Momma said. "Who'll believe this nigger woman when I say the president killed a little child? Nobody gonna believe me. Like nobody gonna believe you. They ain't never gonna let you tell nobody, don't you know that? Never."

Carl turned toward the aged black woman. "What was the baby's name?" he asked.

"This baby?" Momma One-Eye said. "This devil-child buried here in this ground? It don't make no difference now."

"Yes, it does," Carl said. It was almost a whisper. "What did they call him?"

"This baby's name was Gideon. They called him the baby Gideon."

He had known that was coming. In a flash, he had known it as surely as he'd known anything in his entire life. Yet when she said the words, he reeled as if staggered by a heavy blow. Now it was all clear. There was no more doubt. As he looked at Amanda he knew that she too understood what was at stake: the very White House itself. Carl had seen the notes, studied the diaries, had just enough information fed to him, and been hired to write a book revealing that the president of the United States had cold-bloodedly killed his own brother. Somehow one of Tom Adamson's political enemies had discovered the truth—and had come up with the idea of using a book to destroy him. He'd used the code name Gideon to let the president know he had the whole story, to make sure he knew there would be no mercy. But Adamson had fought back. Refused to go away. He'd destroyed Maggie. Then Toni, taking no chances that she might have learned something by mistake. Then Harry, the messenger. And, Carl knew, Adamson was still using his considerable power to destroy *him*. That's what it was all about. Adamson's reelection. It's why all of this was happening. Politics. Control. Power.

"What are we going to do with . . . ?"

Amanda's question jarred him out of his reverie. He realized she was pointing at the skeleton.

"We can't just leave it here," she said.

"No," Carl agreed. "And we might need it. It's the only proof we've got right now."

"I can take it to the mortuary for safekeeping." Luther picked the box up, cradled it in his arms.

Carl started to issue a warning. "No one can—"

"No one will know," Heller cut him off. "People owe me favors in this town. It will be done quietly and discreetly. We'll hide it until you tell me the time for secrecy is—"

A tremendous boom shattered the silence of the deserted farmhouse and prevented Carl from hearing the last word of Luther's sentence. Carl momentarily thought a car had backfired. Or a thunderstorm had begun. For an instant no one realized what had happened. Then Carl saw the red spot on Luther Heller's shirt. There was no car. No thunder. A bullet had been fired. It had entered the alderman's back and exploded out his chest.

Heller fell to the ground, a stunned look on his face, as he finished the thought he'd begun: "—over."

Before he toppled, his hands flew straight out and he tossed the small coffin into the woods, behind the first line of small pine trees.

Carl flung himself at Amanda, threw her down just as another boom sounded and another bullet hissed by them. It cracked into the trunk of the oak tree to the right. The oak tree that had marked the grave of the baby Gideon.

Amanda scrambled on her hands and knees, lunged into the front line of the woods. Carl swung around, picked up Momma One-Eye and hurled her behind the oak, then jumped in after her. A bullet kicked up dirt six inches to his right. Carl rolled over to grab the box.

"Go, go, go!" he screamed, and all three of them dove farther back in the forest, gaining some protection from the thicker branches and clusters of trees.

They sprawled on the ground, waiting. There were no more booms. No more cracks. Only something much more frightening. Silence.

Luther Heller lay on the ground, maybe ten feet from them. The dirt to his right was stained a deep, dark red. With every passing second, the stain was spreading, growing. There was no other movement that they could see.

"Don't," Amanda said as Carl gathered his legs beneath him. She knew he was going back out into the open to pull Luther in with them.

"I have to," he told her.

"You can't."

"She's right, boy," Momma One-Eye said. "Luther be dead. No point in you followin'."

Carl stared at the motionless black man. He closed his eyes, a half second of tribute, then gathered himself and turned to face the two women. "All right," he breathed. "Momma, do you have the strength to run?"

"I can run," the old woman said, "but I sure can't run far."

"Then can you tell Amanda how to get through these woods and back to town?"

"Nobody knows these woods like Momma."

"Carl—" Amanda began.

"Just listen. Listen to me and do what I tell you. The shots had to come from over there. And I guarantee you whoever's doing the firing is moving closer and closer. So head that way. As fast as you can. Move quickly and keep zigzagging. Momma'll tell you how to circle back, but make sure you're far enough away before you come out in the open. Then head back toward town, someplace where there are people who can help you."

"Suzi's Café," Momma One-Eye said. "That's my niece. She lives right on top, on the second floor. Just tell her I sent you. She'll hide you." Then Momma told her how to cut through the woods and where to go when she came out the other side.

Carl said, "Okay. You go to the diner and we'll try to meet you there. Amanda, can you carry the box? It's not heavy, a few pounds."

"Yes, of course. But please"—Amanda spoke urgently—"just let's all go. What are you trying to do?"

"Look," he said. "We don't have a lot of time. Momma'll never make it at your pace. I want you to go. *Now.* She'll follow, go her own way, a different direction. I'll stay behind, try to keep them occupied. I'm the primary target. You'll have a better chance if we separate."

"No," Amanda said. Her voice was insistent. "I'm not going to leave you here."

"You have to," he said. And when she didn't budge, "You *have* to. Amanda, if one of us survives, it has to be you. You know everything now— and somebody might believe you. If I get out of here, it doesn't really matter. If I tell them what happened, it'll be the rantings of a desperate criminal. But you can tell people—you can make them understand." When she didn't answer, he said, "You know I'm right."

She nodded once, holding back her tears, and started to say something else. But he cut her off. "Just go. Please." He handed her the box with the small skeleton. "I'll meet you at the café as soon as I can."

Their eyes met, making it clear that neither one of them believed his last words. Then Amanda turned away, clutched Momma One-Eye by the hand, let go, and tore off into the woods.

He watched until she disappeared. Then he turned to the old woman. "Momma, now it's your turn. You do your best to get out of here. If you can't get far, just hide the best you can."

"What'll you be doin'?"

"I can take care of myself. But I promised you I'd stop people from hurting you, and I want to keep that promise. Go now, so you don't turn me into a liar." He watched the old woman turn and hobble off as quickly as she could. A bullet sprayed to the left, and Carl immediately sprinted in the opposite direction, getting about twenty yards before another shot rang out and he tumbled behind a thick pine for safety.

Carl peered around for some kind of weapon. Something, anything, he could use. He came up empty. Fallen branches were useless. He couldn't even spot a weighty-looking rock. And he had a hunch that a barrage of pinecones wasn't going to do the trick. There was nothing. He stayed crouched behind the tree for perhaps three or four minutes. Then he began to hear the crunching sound of footsteps. Carl remembered when he was a child, he used to think that if he closed his eyes, he could become invisible. No one could see him. He wondered if he should try it now; he had nothing to lose. But one more bullet kicked off just inches from him and he decided he'd be better off with his eyes wide open.

Eyes open, he sprinted another thirty yards into the woods and dove behind a tree, as two shots blew by. Okay, this was good. Whoever it was, he was keeping him busy. Amanda was getting farther away.

The footsteps rustled around him. Carl tried to see through the branches, thought he saw a blurred shape, but didn't want to risk further movement to get a better look. The footsteps stopped. The good news was that he could no longer hear the running steps of Amanda and Momma. Unfortunately, that was the only good news. Whoever was after him was close by. Very close by.

"Okay, asshole," Carl heard. "Come on out now and make it easy on yourself."

He said nothing. Tried to remain as still as possible.

"I hate the fuckin' woods," the voice said. "If I have to spend a lot of time lookin' for you, I'm gonna get pissed off. If I see a goddamn snake, I'm gonna get really pissed off. And if I get really pissed off, I'm gonna hurt you bad before I kill you. So why don't you come out now so I can just kill you nice and quick?"

Carl looked at his watch. Amanda had gotten a ten-minute head start. He hoped that was enough, because it didn't look as if she was going to get a helluva lot more time.

He tried moving, thought he could make it farther back into the woods. But a tree root spoiled his plans. He took three, maybe four steps before he tripped over it and went sprawling. He crawled on his knees to position himself behind another tree. But now he was really screwed. He was pretty sure his ankle was sprained. He tried putting his weight on it and almost cried out in pain.

"I'm comin' after you for real now, asshole," the voice now said. "I tried to be nice, but you had to go and fuck it up."

Carl heard footsteps off to his right. Then nothing. Then something off to his left. The cracking of a branch, the rustling of a few leaves. Then silence.

He thought about moving again and gritted his teeth in anticipation of the pain, taking a couple of deep breaths. He'd hurt himself before on the basketball court, and he'd always been able to play through pain. He could play through this. He could—

Something hard jammed into the back of his neck, right under the skull.

"All right, jerk-off," the voice said. It was directly behind him. The man it belonged to was holding a gun to Carl's head. "Stand up slow. Don't turn around, don't do nothin'. Try anything clever and I blow your brains out right here. Just stand up and walk where I point you."

Carl tried standing, but his ankle buckled. He started to fall back to the ground, caught himself with his hands. He lingered on the ground just a moment, then slowly, excruciatingly, pushed himself back up. The gun nudged at his head and Carl limped forward. After a few steps, the gun shifted to the right side of his head and pushed against him again, so Carl stepped to his left. It took about five minutes, and then Carl realized they were back where he had started. They were back at Gideon's grave. Back standing by Luther Heller's body.

"Okay, turn around now."

Carl pivoted on his good leg. What he saw was no surprise. He'd recognized the voice. Payton. The cop who'd come to his apartment, who'd tried to kill him then. Who was definitely going to kill him now.

Payton flicked his gun toward Luther's fallen body.

"Sorry about your friend," Payton said. He smiled almost kindly at Carl. Then, without any wasted motion, without any warning, he fired two more shots into Luther. The first one blew his back open. The second one took off most of his head.

"Well," Payton said, with no change in the friendly tone of voice, "I guess I'm not *that* sorry." Now he waved again with his rifle, vaguely pointing toward Carl's left. "Okay, pal, hop in."

Carl looked at the splotchy, pockmarked face in confusion. Then he realized what Payton meant. He realized why he'd bothered to walk him over to this spot. He wanted him to step into the hole he'd dug. It was meant to be his final resting place.

"Can I just—"

"No. Whatever it is, you can't. Just get into the hole so I can get the fuck outta here. Hop in, lie facedown, and make it easy on both of us."

Carl hesitated, then stepped forward and sideways. He teetered on the edge of the hole. The edge of Gideon's grave. This was not the way he'd pictured it all ending. Not here, in this overgrown field in the Mississippi delta. Not like this, bruised and defeated. On someone else's terms. Killed by a fat, smelly slob who probably didn't even know or care what the hell was going on. He would never live to clear his name now, Carl realized. He would never write the great American novel or see the Mets win another World Series or get to watch the next Michael Jordan. He'd never repair his broken relationship with his father. Or mourn his mother. Or spend that year in the south of France, sipping good wine. Smiling sadly to himself, he thought: *Well, at least I did one thing right. The last night with Amanda. It was perfect.* He sighed at the memory. His last and final memory.

"Can I just ask you one question?" He could still buy Amanda more time. That was all that mattered now. He was going to die, but if he could keep her alive, well . . . he could almost die happily.

"Sure, pal. Ask whatever you want. But make it quick. 'Cause your little girlfriend's next. The only way she's gonna get anywhere is on that road behind these woods, which she should be hittin' just about now. And you see that little hill over there? You know what's on the other side of that hill?" He reached into his pocket, pulled out a set of keys, and dangled them from his meaty hand. "My nice fast car. Unless she can run faster than anybody in the history of the world, I think I'm gonna catch up to her pretty quick. So sure, you got one question. Make it a good one."

Carl decided it was pretty good: "How'd you get so fuckin' fat?"

Payton's eyes practically bugged out of his head in surprise and fury. His first instinct was to hurt the kid. Then he thought, *Screw it, just get it over with,* but before he could do anything, before he could pull the trigger to kill this snotty asshole of a kid who'd been such a pain in the butt, the kid's hands flew up and two fistfuls of dirt went flying into Payton's face.

Christ, when he bent down in the woods, when his leg went out from under him. That's when he did it. Goddamn it. Payton thought the kid was just pushing himself back up, but that's when he'd grabbed the dirt. *Had to be . . . goddamn . . .*

Momentarily blinded, Payton scratched at his eyes, trying to get the dirt out. He saw the blur of a body come flying at him and he pulled the trigger, but he hit only air. The kid was strong, strong enough to knock Payton down, but now Payton could see. And it wasn't a fair fight. He had maybe fifty pounds on the kid. And he was a street fighter from way back. They wrestled for a few moments, the kid trying to get the gun, but when Payton's fist thudded into the side of the kid's head, he could feel him sag. And when Payton's knee came up and rammed into the kid's chin, it was all over. For good measure, Payton stood up and kicked him, kicked him as hard as he could, and the kid rolled over in agony. Payton kicked him again and the kid rolled again, closer to the open grave. Now it was a game for Payton. A kick and the kid was closer to the hole. Another kick, closer still. One more kick would do it. One more kick, one shot, then go get the girl.

And that's when he heard it. At first he thought he was going crazy. But he looked down at the kid and the kid, as beaten up as he was, had picked his head up, was straining to hear it, too . . .

Singing.

Tuneless, gravelly singing.

> *"O my God, rescue me out of the hand of the wicked*
> *Out of the grasp of the unrighteous and ruthless man."*

Carl groaned in despair. *Oh, Jesus,* he thought. *Psalms.*

It was Momma. Why hadn't she run? Why hadn't she gotten the hell out of there? What the hell was she doing?

"The old lady?" Payton asked incredulously. He looked down at Carl, who was sprawled in the dirt on the edge of the freshly dug-up grave, too weak to look up at him. "It's your lucky day, kid. You get to live long enough to watch me kill another one of your black friends." He turned to face the woods.

> *"In return for my love they are my adversaries*
> *But I am all prayer*
> *And they have laid upon me evil for good*
> *And hatred for my love."*

And with that Momma One-Eye stepped out of the woods into the clearing. Her hands were clasped behind her back and she seemed calm, at peace. She took two frail steps closer to Payton.

"Look at her," Payton said to Carl, his lips curled into a contemptuous sneer. "She's too dumb even to hide."

"You are not a good man," she said to Payton.

"A good man?" He snorted and turned to the old lady. "What do you think's goin' on, Momma? You think we're havin' a party? You think we're havin' a party for all the good men around here?" He laughed in Carl's direction. "She thinks we're havin' a party! Well, why don't you just go on singin', Momma? You just keep singin' for our party."

"I'm done singing," Momma One-Eye said.

"Aww, the time for singin's over?"

"Yes," she said. "The time for singing's over."

"Well, what's it time for, then? Maybe it's time for dying, huh?"

"Yes," Momma said. "It's time for dying."

Carl heard the shot. He didn't want to look up. Didn't want to see the strange old lady sprawled in the grass, didn't want to see her blood. He waited for Payton's words. And Payton's laugh. He waited for a second shot, the shot that would end his life. He wouldn't turn his head. Wouldn't give him the pleasure. He'd just wait, and then it would be over.

Nothing.

No words. No laugh. No shot.

Carl forced himself up to his knees. Waited to be knocked down as he rose, but no blow came. His ribs felt like they were broken, but he struggled to stand erect. And when he was on his feet, he turned and forced himself to face his tormentor.

Payton was pitched forward, dead as could be, blood pouring from the back of his head.

Momma One-Eye stood several feet away from him. Both hands were in front of her, held straight out, still pointing where Payton had been standing. In those hands she held a pistol.

Carl stumbled over to her. He put his hands on her arms and guided them down to her side. He said nothing to her, just stared in astonishment.

"He was a bad man," Momma One-Eye said.

"Yes," Carl told her. "A very bad man." And then he said, "How? How did you . . . ?"

"Luther carried a gun. Ever since his daughter was killed. Carried it with him wherever he went, case he ever met up with the man who did it."

"I know. I saw the gun in his office." He looked down at the gun in Momma's hand. "You took it off his body?"

"While you was in the woods. And the bad man went in after you."

Carl fell to his knees. For a moment he thought he might pass out. But after several deep breaths he struggled back up to his feet. He pulled Momma to him, hugged her tightly, then bent down and kissed her gently on her forehead.

"We can't leave Luther in the presence of a man like this," she said. "It just wouldn't be . . . dignified."

Carl nodded. He moved to stand behind Payton and started to roll him over, toward the grave. At the last second he stopped. Fighting to keep himself from gagging, he forced himself to reach into Payton's left front pants pocket and pull out the car key that was there. Then he shuddered, gave the big man one last push, and watched him disappear from sight.

"Now we can go," she said. Then she held the gun out, offering it to Carl.

"You should keep it," he said.

"I won't need it no more," she explained. "And I hope and pray Luther don't need it where *he's* going." Now Momma put her bony hand on Carl's cheek and caressed it. "But I'm pretty sure it'll come in handy for you," she said.

Carl took the gun, stuck it into his belt. Then he took Momma's hand, squeezing it tightly, and they headed back toward town.

For the first time in Amanda Mays's life, she felt paralyzed.

She was in Suzi's apartment, above the Warren café. Suzi and her husband and their three children were all gathered around the television, watching in stunned silence. They had closed the diner when they'd heard the news. Amanda was already in the apartment; Suzi had stashed her there without a word when she'd showed up and said that Momma had told her to come. But she hadn't turned on the TV or the radio, so she didn't know what had happened. Then someone had come into the café, spreading the word, so they all rushed up to watch, jabbering and screaming, and it took Amanda several seconds to understand what had occurred. They turned on ANN, their link to the unfurling tragedy. Amanda sat slumped in an easy chair in the corner while the others sat circled around the set. No one spoke. Even the commentator on TV was speaking only sporadically, letting the images stand on their own.

Amanda thought: *How could this be? How could this be happening? I'm losing my mind.*

The voice on the television was droning on now, talking about the tragedy, the global sadness, the words of sympathy that were pouring in from all over the world.

There was a knock on the door. One of Suzi's little girls went to answer it. Through her fog, something in Amanda's brain realized that that was a mistake. "No!" she yelled, jumping up. "Don't open the door!" But it was too late. The girl had yanked it open. Amanda recoiled, certain they had just let in their own destruction.

She had never been more wrong.

Carl stood there, covered in dirt, bleeding, and holding his arms against his chest as if he were hurt, leaning against the door frame for support. Next to him was Momma One-Eye.

It's a miracle! It's Carl! And Momma! But how? How?

She ran to him, hugged him to her, but he recoiled in pain. "What happened?" she asked. "Tell me what happened."

"Quiet," Suzi's husband thundered. "Come in and be welcome, but be quiet and be respectful."

Carl looked at the television. She could see his eyes focusing, see him trying to comprehend what was happening. As it began to dawn on him, he turned to face her and she nodded.

"President Adamson's dead," she said.

"Assassinated?" Carl asked.

"He killed hisself," Suzi's youngest girl said. "The president shot hisself in the head."

"Hush," the girl's mother said. "And watch."

Momma One-Eye stared at the television in fascination. Carl tried to imagine what she was thinking. She'd seen Tom Adamson practically from the very beginning. Had witnessed his act of ultimate evil. Had watched him go unpunished and rise to the top of the world. Now she was seeing the end. She was seeing it all catch up to him.

"It's Elizabeth. She's coming out to speak."

Everyone's head swiveled toward the set. Sure enough, it was Elizabeth Adamson. The First Lady of the United States was dressed in black. She moved slowly but steadily as she stepped toward a podium.

The camera never wavered from covering her walk as the ANN anchor murmured in hushed and respectful tones. "I've just been told that President Bickford has, moments ago, taken the oath of office in a hastily assembled ceremony in the White House. It is exceedingly difficult to keep anything in perspective right now, and we in the media must avoid jumping to any conclusions, but one conclusion that is inescapable is that the future of the presidency is in complete and utter turmoil. Standing next to me is Meredith Brock Moss, presidential historian. Meredith, do you have any insight into what's going to happen now? Will Jerry Bickford top the slate in November?"

"No one knows, Harry. The vice president—excuse me, *President* Bickford has been rather invisible as of late. His health problems were made public only recently, when he announced that he was going to step down as vice president for President Adamson's second term."

"Will today's events change his intent to step down?"

"It certainly might. But that's not the only thing that has to be considered. It's not merely a question of whether or not Jerry Bickford would like to be president. Does the party *want* him to be president? That's the real question. What makes these circumstances so extraordinary and so complex is that Tom Adamson swept the primaries. He had already won his party's nomination. He *is* their presidential candidate. Now, with no chance for any more primaries to be held, the delegates are going to have to choose a new candidate. Will they want to choose one who's seventy-one years old and has Bell's palsy, or will they feel that makes him unelectable? Let's not forget, the convention is in New Orleans in nine days—and it's going to be one of the few times since the eighteen-forties, when we went away from the concept of state political conventions and to open primary elections, that we will have seen a wide-open convention. In 1912 Theodore Roosevelt tried to wrest the Republican nomination away from William Howard Taft, but he failed in that effort and the delegates ultimately opted for Taft. The result was that Roosevelt started the Bull Moose Party, splitting the popular Republican vote, and the Democratic candidate, Woodrow Wilson, became president. We don't know if anything like that will happen in New Orleans. All we know is that the public will not be choosing the party's candidate. This is truly history in the making. A tragic and bewildering history, surely—one without any real context, in fact. We are in the middle of an almost unfathomable and unique moment that will alter and affect the future of America—"

"Meredith, excuse me," the anchor interrupted. "But I believe Mrs. Adamson is ready to speak. . . . Wait, there seems to be some sort of . . . I can't quite make out . . . it looks like . . . yes, President Bickford has just come out and is standing by Mrs. Adamson's side. He is escorting her up to the podium and is taking his place by her side. The chaos seems to be settling down just a bit, and it does indeed look as if Elizabeth Adamson is ready to speak."

"I can't believe she's going to do this," Amanda murmured, transfixed, eyes never leaving the TV screen.

"This is a brave woman," Suzi's husband said, awed.

No one said a word, in Suzi's living room or the room in the White House where Elizabeth Adamson now leaned in toward the microphone.

"This is a very difficult moment for me," the First Lady announced to the country. Her voice was shaky and she stopped speaking, waiting until she could continue without the quaver. "But it is a difficult moment for everyone in America and in the entire world." She looked up now, and the entire world could see the tears in her eyes. She did not let them escape down her cheeks, but they were there, being held inside. "At five-twenty P.M. today, Thomas Adamson, the president of the United States, my husband, shot himself. He died instantly."

Watching the television from the couch, Suzi burst into tears.

"My husband was a good man. I believe he was a great man, but greatness is usually decided by history, so that judgment will have to wait. What is certain and absolute is that he did many great things. He had strong beliefs and was willing to fight for them. President Adamson fought an enormous number of those battles and won more than his share. We can never know what kind of toll such battles take on a human being, on a human soul, just as we can never know, ultimately, why someone who had so much to live for, so much to contribute, would choose to end his life. What we can know, what I *do* know, is that President Adamson was exhausted. He was tired of the battles. Tom was not only frustrated by the wrongs he saw all around him, he was angry and depressed at the barriers set up that prevented him from righting those wrongs.

"This is a time of great turmoil. There is hunger in the world. And homelessness. There are wars and injustices. There are many battles still to be fought and won. Now is not the moment for politics, God knows. A tragedy like this tends to give us perspective on politics, allows us to see it for what it is: a game played by the powerful, all too often for the sole purpose of retaining that power. Too often it is played at the expense of the hungry and the homeless and the besieged. But the political ramifications cannot be ignored because they are too important.

"There are many questions that need to be answered and will be answered in the upcoming hours and days and weeks. I ask all of you, Republican or Democrat, friend or foe, powerful or besieged, to help answer these questions. Together. As human beings. It is a time to set aside differences, to lay down the swords, to do things simply because they are the right things to do. I ask you to stay calm and, yes, to grieve, but also to celebrate what my husband has done and what we're *all* going to do in the future. You will soon have to decide upon his successor. You will have to decide upon the future.

"That's really why I decided to speak today. To remind everyone that there *is* a future. One that must be filled with hope and joy and the promise of good things to come.

"I ask that we all pray. Pray for President Bickford, who is standing beside me, supporting me and keeping me standing, as he supported and kept my husband standing for many years. The president will need our prayers to keep up his strength for the battles he must now face. I ask that we also pray for my husband. Pray that he has finally achieved the peace he so richly deserves. And, finally, we should pray for ourselves. Pray that we have the strength and the courage to do what is right and what is best. Pray that we will heal. And pray that such tragedies never happen again."

As Elizabeth Adamson was led away from the podium, the people gathered around the television set in the small living room in Warren, Mississippi, were holding hands, hugging each other, and sobbing. The speech had overwhelmed them. As commentators were already beginning to acknowledge, the speech had overwhelmed *everybody*. The president's widow had managed to soothe, excite, comfort, and provide faith for the world.

Except for Carl Granville.

"She's amazing," Amanda said. "How can someone have the strength to do that?" She was sniffling, wiping away the copious tears that had flowed during the speech.

Carl's eyes were dry and cold. And he didn't answer her question. All he said was, *"Why?"*

"Why what?"

"Why did he do it? Adamson had us licked. He won. He got the disks from my computer. He got everyone who was in the way. He sure as hell thought he had us. Why would he kill himself?"

"I don't care," Amanda said. "All I care about is that it's finally over." When he didn't say anything, she wiped away the last of her tears with her sleeve. "It *is* over, isn't it, Carl?"

From the television, they heard the anchor announce that they were offering a tribute to Tom Adamson by honoring his greatest living legacy, Elizabeth Adamson. It had been prepared over the past few hours, documenting her speeches, her accomplishments, her life with the president. Carl and Amanda turned to watch. There, on the screen, was a tape of the former First Lady coming out of the White House. It was obviously an old tape, because she was on the arm of her husband. It was amazing, Carl thought. Her husband was dead only a few hours and, thanks to the miracle of modern television, there was already a documentary about her life. *Nothing stands still anymore. There's no time to mourn, no time to grieve. No time to think. There's only time to keep moving forward.*

"This is the last public appearance of Elizabeth Adamson with the president," the commentator was saying. "This extraordinary woman was accompanying her husband, several weeks ago, to Owens, Mississippi, where the president's mother, Wilhelmina Adamson, was celebrating her seventy-eighth birthday. After a private dinner at Mrs. Adamson's home, all three family members, along with then Vice President Bickford and his wife, went to a celebratory town hall meeting. Both the president and Mrs. Adamson spoke at the meeting. The president spoke about the need to legislate human rights. Mrs. Adamson talked about the need to change the way people perceived human rights. It was a perfect example of why they were an exemplary team. He went to the core of the political issue, she went to . . ."

Carl leaned forward to stare at the small TV screen. The tape showed Bickford and his wife, followed by the president and Elizabeth Adamson, walking into the Mississippi town hall.

"Amanda," he said.

"Please, Carl," she said. "I don't think I can absorb anything else right now."

"Amanda! Look at the TV!"

She peered at the images on the screen. "What?" she asked. The First Lady and the president had stopped to answer some questions being shouted by the media. "It's Elizabeth Adamson. I don't see what the—"

"To her right. Look to her right!"

"Secret Service."

"*Look,* goddamn it!"

Suzi's entire family spun around at Carl's harsh words. But he ignored them, as did Amanda. She was squinting now. Then she sat up straight, turned to Carl, and blinked, as if she couldn't believe her eyes.

"It's impossible," she said.

"It's not," Carl told her. "It's all too possible. And to answer your question: I don't think it's over."

On the tape, the Bickfords and their two Secret Service bodyguards disappeared through the doorway. The president and Mrs. Adamson were now stepping through the same doorway, accompanied by their two Secret Service men. Both men wore dark gray suits, white shirts, and sunglasses. One of them, clearly assigned to the president, was a stranger; they had never seen him before.

The other one, the First Lady's protector who hovered, shadowlike, at Elizabeth Adamson's elbow, was someone Carl knew well.

The other one was Harry Wagner.

book three

July 13–July 16

chapter 30

From a front-page story syndicated by Apex News Service, carried by the *New York Journal*, the *Washington Journal*, the *Chicago Press*, the *Los Angeles Post*, the *Denver Tribune*, and the *Miami Daily Breeze*:

BICKFORD SAYS NO TO PRESIDENTIAL BID
Cites Health and Age

Washington, July 14 (Apex News Service)—*A pale and shaken President Bickford announced at a dramatic White House news conference this morning that he will not seek or accept the Democratic Party's nomination for president in November.*

"I am seventy-one years old and my health will simply not allow it," said the president, his words slurred noticeably by the attack of Bell's palsy that has plagued him for several weeks. "Our nation needs someone of youth and vigor to lead it in the new century," he stated, adding in a choked voice, "I have lost a dear friend. We have all lost a dear friend. I wish I were in a position to carry on his important and compassionate policies, but reality dictates otherwise."

His stunning announcement, coming only one day after he was sworn in following President Adamson's devastating suicide—and a scant week before his party's convention in New Orleans—leaves the Democratic Party virtually without a primary-tested, nationally recognized candidate to run against Senator Walter Chalmers of Wyoming, the presumptive Republican nominee. Democratic Party leaders were caught totally by surprise. As the news spread on Capitol Hill, business in both halls of Congress came to a virtual standstill.

The response from senior legislators was quick and candid.

"This nation's government is now in disarray," reflected Senator Wallace Moon, the liberal Florida Democrat who is a longtime Chalmers foe. "I suggest we all get down on our knees and pray."

The fallout from President Bickford's announcement was felt immediately on Wall Street, where the Dow Jones Industrial Average fell 541 points after the press conference. It was the second largest one-day point drop in the Dow's history. The Dow would no doubt have tumbled even farther if the New York Stock Exchange had not shut down two hours early yesterday afternoon to prevent further panic sell-offs.

Wall Street analysts remain deeply concerned about how the financial markets will respond this morning. "We are sailing into uncharted political waters," advised Zig Halpern, a senior vice president for Merrill Lynch, the brokerage giant. "That frightens investors, both small and institutional."

Financial markets abroad were also sent reeling. The Nikkei Index in Tokyo fell 12 percent after the president's announcement, while the London market fell 8 percent.

The reaction from Senator Chalmers was measured. "My friends, this is why we have a two-party system in America," he said, aiming to calm the fears of both voters and world markets. "Not only so that there is a free and stimulating exchange of viewpoints but so that there can be an orderly transition of power. It is a painful time. A sad time. But we will prevail."

President Bickford, who answered no questions from reporters, gave no indication of whom he would recommend that the party now put forth as a candidate. But it is extremely doubtful, stated one senior White House aide, that anyone will emerge on such short notice who can match President Bickford's popularity with moderate voters of both parties, who consider him a steady, veteran hand with a strong track record on such social issues as abortion, health care, education, and Social Security. To those same voters, he is considered a viable alternative to the red-meat conservatism of Senator Chalmers, an ardent abortion and gun control foe who has vowed to privatize Social Security by the year 2010.

The latest Apex News Network–Washington Journal poll shows President Bickford favored to edge out Senator Chalmers in November, 46 percent to 42 percent. That number is closer than most political pundits had predicted following President Adamson's suicide and is seen as a result of public fear of and lack of knowledge about President Bickford's disease. A crucial 12 percent remained undecided.

According to White House spokesman Alexander Whitfield, President Bickford spent the morning with Elizabeth Cartwright Adamson discussing funeral plans for President Adamson. It is not known at this point whether a formal state funeral will take place. Since no sitting president in the history of the United States has ever taken his own life, no official White House protocol exists. Because of the nature of the president's death, there is also some question as to whether the Catholic Church will allow a religious funeral. The White House refused to comment on whether the Vatican was being consulted but, according to a spokesperson at Washington's St. Stephen's Cathedral, church doctrine would not prevent a funeral from being held there. "The dogma has changed considerably over the past decade," Sister Lucille Furia acknowledged. "The belief now is that only God is fit to judge the reason someone would choose to leave this life. It is not for the church to judge. It is for the church to serve."

"From this moment on, we are writing the rules as we go along," White House chief of staff Taylor Chapin conceded. "Mrs. Adamson, in consultation with the president and several religious advisors, is weighing the proper, dignified course of action. She very much wants to do what the voters would wish. My own view is that whatever she chooses to do will be the proper thing to do."

Phone calls and messages of condolence continue to pour in from the world's leaders to the White House, where Mrs. Adamson will remain in residence "for just as long as she wants," according to President Bickford. The president will maintain his residence at Blair House, the vice presidential home, for the foreseeable future.

President Bickford did not offer any new information on President

Adamson's suicide at this morning's news conference. Advisors close to the late president continue to maintain that they had no indication that he was unduly troubled or depressed. Chief of Staff Chapin did acknowledge that President Adamson seemed "preoccupied" at the cabinet meeting he attended moments before he shot himself in the Oval Office. But, Chapin insisted, this was nothing out of the ordinary. "He was the president of the United States, for God's sake," Chapin said. "The man had a lot on his mind."

President Bickford, a four-term senator from Ohio, was widely viewed as President Adamson's political mentor, first encountering the younger political hopeful when he served as a summer intern in his office while attending Harvard Law School. It was Senator Bickford who advised young Tom Adamson to return to his native Mississippi and seek office there, guiding him from the state legislature to the governorship, and eventually helping to throw national party support his way for a presidential bid.

Long considered the ultimate Washington insider, President Bickford was widely known to enjoy a father-son relationship with the late president, who never knew his own father. Advisors describe him as "devastated" by President Adamson's death and "concerned" about his own physical condition.

Among its other symptoms, Bell's palsy affects salivation, which required the president to dab frequently at the corner of his mouth with a folded white handkerchief during the news conference.

According to Dr. David Kaminsky, a neurologist on the staff of the Bethesda Naval Hospital who is treating the president, Bell's palsy, also known as facial palsy, is a paralysis of one side of the face that is brought on by an inflammation of a facial nerve. The cause is unknown, although stress is believed to play a part in it. The condition is usually temporary. Symptoms include the characteristic sagging of one side of the face, including drooping of the eyelid and one corner of the mouth. Ear pain, slurred speech, and changes in salivation are common. The president is currently receiving oral corticosteroid drugs to reduce the inflammation of the nerve and analgesics for the pain.

Dr. Kaminsky vigorously denied that the president had suffered a minor stroke, as had been previously speculated when the symptoms first appeared.

According to Dr. Kaminsky, Bell's palsy is an uncomfortable condition, especially for someone who is in the public eye. But it is not life-threatening, and a full recovery is expected within two to four months. President Bickford is otherwise in robust health for a man his age. His mind is alert and his reflexes are sharp. Until recently, he was known to swim one hour daily.

Still, prompted by his illness, he recently announced that he was going to relinquish his vice-presidential spot on the ticket to a younger candidate who could better withstand the rigors of the immediate presidential campaign as well as serve as a bridge to the party's future.

From a front-page story syndicated by Apex News Service, carried by the *New York Herald*, the *Washington Journal*, the *Chicago Press*, the *Los Angeles Post*, the *Denver Tribune*, and the *Miami Daily Breeze*:

POLL SHOWS STRONG SUPPORT FOR FIRST LADY

Washington, July 14 (Apex News Service)—*A new Apex News Network*–Washington Journal *poll of over 5,000 registered voters across America shows unexpectedly strong support by voters of both parties for Elizabeth Cartwright Adamson to carry on her husband's work in the White House next year by running for the presidency herself.*

The poll, in which voters gave the former First Lady an overall approval rating of 82 percent, showed Mrs. Adamson beating Republican Senator Walter Chalmers of Wyoming by a convincing 52 to 37 percent margin were she to face off against him as the Democratic challenger in November.

Her lead in the poll was even greater than the comfortable 10 percent margin enjoyed by her late husband in the days before his death, and substantially greater than that enjoyed by President Bickford. The poll has a margin of error of plus or minus 3 percentage points.

"What you are seeing here is a sympathy vote," Chalmers campaign coordinator F. Price Stingley said in response to the surprising poll numbers. *"The inherent kindness and decency of the American people are on full display. But believe me, when the time comes to pull the lever, they will vote with their pocketbooks, not their hankies. Besides, as much as they pay lip service to equality between the sexes, what they want at the helm is a strong hand, not a velvet glove."*

The polling numbers contradict his contention. When asked if they considered the matter of a woman serving in the White House a critical issue, only 18 percent of voters said they thought it was. Fifty-two percent said it was not an issue. Thirty percent had no opinion.

"The fact that she is a woman is a nonissue," countered Democratic pollster Eloise Marion. *"Margaret Thatcher ran Britain successfully for a number of years, and a woman can and will run this country as well. What these numbers tell me, more than anything else, is that Walter Chalmers scares people. Voters are more in tune with President Adamson's agenda. And much more comfortable with Lizzie."*

Mrs. Adamson's support was especially high among women voters, who preferred her to Chalmers by a 68 to 22 percent margin, with 10 percent undecided, and by African-American voters, who gave her a resounding 74 to 20 percent thumbs-up, with 6 percent undecided. Support among the young and the elderly was equally strong.

Even among white male Republicans, who are considered the backbone of Chalmers's support, Mrs. Adamson fared somewhat better than her late husband, losing to Chalmers by 58 to 34 percent. President Adamson trailed Chalmers for the so-called Joe Sixpack vote by a 59 to 32 percent margin.

Poll respondents cited Mrs. Adamson's stirring speech after her husband's death and her strong record as an advocate of social issues as reasons for their support. They also cited her "humanity" and "personal integrity."

A surprisingly low 11 percent of Democratic voters said they would prefer the party to run a different candidate.

Mrs. Adamson, who remains in seclusion at the White House, has not indicated that she has any interest in running or would consider doing so if drafted by the party. "She is a widow," said one staff aide. "People seem to forget that she wants to grieve, not think about running for office."

If she was to run, she would be the first woman to head a major party's presidential ticket in American history.

In response to questions, Democratic Party chairman Miguel Rodriguez continues to maintain that the Democrats will put forward a strong ticket capable of beating back the conservative Chalmers agenda. But behind closed doors, there is every indication that unless Mrs. Adamson takes the reins, the party's prospects will be bleak and that next week's wide-open convention will be "a no-holds-barred food fight," in the words of one White House aide.

Elizabeth Adamson has never been the prototypical First Lady, content to smile demurely at her husband's side and confine her activities to social events. A graduate of Duke Law School, she has long been outspoken on controversial policy issues such as federally insured health care for the poor and the use of land mines by the U.S. military. She has chaired international summits on global warming and family planning, and authored three best-selling books. White House insiders knew her to be President Adamson's most trusted advisor and sounding board.

If she was to run, her candidacy would revive a spirited and sometimes rancorous give-and-take between herself and Senator Chalmers, who once labeled her a "tree-hugging, bra-burning feminist extremist." In response, Mrs. Adamson called Senator Chalmers "the point man for the far right" and "a dinosaur determined to lead America back into the nineteenth century rather than ahead into the twenty-first, where we belong."

chapter 31

The thirteenth cardinal was in total agony.

Dear God, the pain, the throbbing. Not to mention the humiliation at being unable to perform so basic an animal function as taking a blessed pee. Cardinal O'Brien knew these symptoms only too well. And he had no one to blame but himself for how he felt right now. Because he was not supposed to drink anymore. Not with his enlarged prostate gland.

He was for certain not supposed to try to keep up with someone like young Father Patrick, who drank as if he were trying to put out a raging fire down below.

But Cardinal O'Brien had done exactly that. It was almost a week ago that he had sat up most of the night drinking Bushmills and beer chasers with the troubled young cleric, trying to soothe his tortured soul. And for several days now it was he who'd been the tortured one, filled with dread, the kind that came with knowing that first thing the next morning his urologist would be sticking his entire hamlike fist up the cardinal's rectum and attaching a catheter to his penis so as to drain his bladder for him.

Oh, the humiliation of old age, reflected the cardinal, who would be seventy-three in two weeks. *Oh, the loss of dignity.*

But he had done what he felt needed doing. When Father Patrick had phoned him, the young priest had been parked alongside the Potomac, sobbing hysterically and nearly incoherently into his car phone. The older man felt that suicide was a distinct possibility. Father Pat had studied with Cardinal O'Brien some years ago. He was a bright light, a highly promising individual who lately had been facing the gravest of troubles. His beloved sister had been killed by a drunk driver. Father Patrick had come to doubt God's very existence, putting the cardinal in mind of a favorite passage from the Book of James: "He who doubts is like a wave driven by the sea." The cardinal had counseled him and prayed with him at the time. And he had told young Father Pat to call him if ever he needed him.

Well, Father Patrick had called. And he had needed him.

Without hesitation, the cardinal had personally driven the forty miles into Washington from downtown Baltimore, picked him up, and brought him back to his private residence, the five-story neoclassical Archbishop's House, which was connected to the basilica by a sheltered walkway facing onto North Charles Street.

The two of them had sat up in his study drinking and talking for most of the night. Father Patrick had been in great torment. His hands shook and his teeth chattered. From time to time he wept uncontrollably, huge tears that wrenched his entire body. But the poor soul had been unable to tell the cardinal exactly what it was that preyed upon him. They had talked about church politics. They had talked about the cardinal's beloved Orioles and whether they had enough arms in the bullpen. But not about what tortured Father Patrick. He could not bring himself to put it into words.

He could not inflict that kind of knowledge upon the cardinal—that was what Father Pat had said.

In the morning the cardinal had phoned Father Thaddeus at his retreat in the Great Smoky Mountains and advised him that Father Patrick was on his way down there. Then the cardinal had handed the young priest the keys to his car and sent him on his way.

Father Patrick begged him to tell no one he had been to see him. No matter who came, no matter who was asking the questions. "Please trust me," Father Pat had said. The cardinal assured the younger priest that his faith in him was absolute, that he would not say a word. And he had kept his promise, even though the Washington police had phoned him that very afternoon to inquire if he knew anything about the priest's whereabouts.

The cardinal made a point of watching the news on television that evening while he ate his crab cakes and boiled new potatoes. Bad news and more bad news. And it kept getting worse. For the past week the broadcasts had been concerned with a serial killer who was still at large, a frustrated aspiring author. It was terrible, the cardinal reflected, what frustration could do to bright, creative young people. Father Patrick's disappearance had also received prominent mention. The authorities were considering his to be a missing-person case, and foul play was suspected. Now, of course, all other stories had been eclipsed by news of President Adamson's suicide and the ensuing political turmoil. A tragedy, the cardinal thought. A genuine tragedy. He had known Tom Adamson. Not well, but well enough; he had presided over two or three presidential masses and been to several teas and social functions. A clever man, the president was. And clearly a troubled one. But those two things so often went hand in hand. The cardinal himself often longed for the peace of being a student rather than a teacher, a follower rather than a leader. He remembered a particularly lively conversation he'd had, perhaps a year ago, with Father Patrick on that very topic. They had been talking about the president, as a matter of fact, about the extraordinary pressure he faced on a daily basis. Father Pat had known Adamson, too. Had taken his confession several times, on occasion had served as something of a spiritual advisor.

"Such troubles," the cardinal murmured under his breath. For the dead and for the living.

It was nearly midnight now. A warm, oily rain was falling. In the distance there was thunder and lightning, moving steadily closer. As he so often did before he retired for the night, the cardinal strolled across to the basilica, hunching slightly from the pain in his groin. He enjoyed walking through the basilica before he headed up to bed. There was a tremendous sense of coolness and peace inside its massive, unornamented granite-faced walls, the great dome looming overhead. Its quiet soothed him.

The Basilica of the Assumption of the Blessed Virgin Mary, which was situated across Cathedral Street from the Pratt Library, had the distinction of being the first Roman Catholic cathedral ever built in the United States. Construction had begun in 1806. Its architect, Benjamin LaTrobe, was the very same man who had designed the U.S. Capitol. A native Philadelphian, Cardinal O'Brien had presided here since 1987 and had come to love Baltimore in the process. It was a city of great grit and humor. A city that loved its past and embraced its future. And, of course, no other city had O'Brycki's Restaurant, which would specially deliver the world's best hardshell crabs right to the cardinal's door. He was the thirteenth prelate to preside at this see and, according to O'Brycki's manager, the one with the heartiest appetite.

Suspended from the arch above Our Lady's altar at the front of the sanctuary was the biretta of James Cardinal Gibbons, who had died in 1921. It would hang there until it crumbled. Just as his own would hang there when he passed on. Cardinal O'Brien stood there a moment, gazing at it thoughtfully, his hands clasped behind him.

Suddenly he heard a rustling nearby. And was startled to find that he was not alone.

A young man lurked by the wall in the semidarkness, wearing a black raincoat. Its collar was turned up, partly shielding his face. But not his eyes. His eyes were wide with fright.

"It is very late, my son," the cardinal said gently, moving a step closer to him.

The young man scurried deeper into the recesses. He seemed very skittish, like one of the stray cats they took in every autumn to keep the rodent population down. He was trembling.

"How did you get in here?" the cardinal asked.

Outside there was a clap of thunder. It felt far away here inside the basilica's massive stone walls.

"I hid," came the breathless whisper of reply. "I've been hiding for hours and hours. I must speak with you, Father. I simply *must*."

The lightning was directly overhead now, flashing brightly through the stained-glass windows. Briefly it illuminated the young man's face like a shaft of white-hot sunlight. It was a handsome face. The forehead was high and smooth, the features delicate, the mouth soft and vulnerable. It was a very young face. He did not yet need to shave.

"H-He's been here," the boy gasped at the cardinal. "I know he's b-been here."

"*Who* has, my son?"

"Father Patrick. You've seen him, haven't you?"

Cardinal O'Brien stiffened at the mention of his troubled friend's name. "What is it you want?" he said guardedly. And when the boy hesitated, he said, firmly but gently, "You had better tell me."

It was the thunder that rumbled first in response. The cardinal could feel it under his feet.

"Not here. Please," the boy hissed, his eyes flicking about wildly.

"Where, then?"

"I-I want to confess my sins. I need to. Take my confession," he pleaded desperately. "You must. You *must*."

"And I will," the cardinal replied. "Of course I will."

They went inside the polished rosewood booth. Cardinal O'Brien sat, wincing from the pain. He pressed his knees tightly together and waited.

"Forgive me, Father, for I have sinned," the young penitent began in a whisper. And then the whisper turned into a tortured wail. "Did he tell you, Father? Did Father Patrick *tell* you?"

Cardinal O'Brien hesitated. "I only know he was in great torment—as you appear to be."

"I *am* the torment, Father."

The cardinal sat in anxious silence. He was trying to stay calm, but he did not like where this was heading at all.

"I was an altar boy," the young man blurted out. "In service to Father Patrick. And . . . and we are in love, Father. Deep, passionate, beautiful love."

The cardinal tried to swallow, but his mouth was dry. There was a sour, bilious taste in the back of his throat and a burning in the pit of his stomach. Scandal! It was the last thing the Catholic Church needed now, when there were already so many doubters. When there was so much whispering and scrutiny. So much hurt. Countless good, decent young candidates were being scared off. Indeed, there were a third fewer parish priests in America than there had been a generation ago. Many of them were being forced to serve three or more communities at once, driving from parish to parish like traveling salesmen, their vestments stowed in overnight bags. All because of one or two bad eggs around the country who could not resist temptation. And who should never have been allowed in the priesthood in the first place. Those were the ones who got the publicity. Not the hundreds upon hundreds who worked tirelessly and selflessly in service to God and their communities. Was that what Father Patrick was—just another bad egg? It seemed so hard to believe. And yet . . . what else could have caused such torment the other night? Father O'Brien had thought he was seeing doubt and fear. But perhaps all he was seeing in his friend's eyes was a terrible guilt and shame.

This boy was handsome, to be sure, but how could such a fine priest abuse his privilege this way? The cardinal shuddered. The details were too horrifying to contemplate. But he had to know them. If he had learned anything over the years, it was that Father Patrick was wrong—knowledge was essential, no matter how painful. All solutions came only with knowledge.

Clearing his throat, he said, "And have you . . . consummated this passion?"

"I have knelt at his feet and swallowed his mortal seed, Father," the boy sobbed in reply. "I-I have gotten down on all fours on his office floor and received him from above."

The cardinal's head was spinning, and his anger at Father Patrick began to boil into full-fledged rage. But he needed to know the rest. "It was . . . consensual?"

"God, yes."

"Let us keep God out of this for the moment," the cardinal snapped. "How old were you when this . . . this . . . relationship began?"

The boy was silent a moment. "Is that so important?"

"I'm afraid it is."

"I was thirteen, Father . . ."

Cardinal O'Brien gulped. *Dear God—help me. Please help me. . . .* The boy was speaking again. The cardinal did his best to focus.

". . . and now my *parents* have found out! They want to go to the authorities. My father's a very powerful man. He has connections to the m-media. He can make this into a very bad thing!"

The cardinal's horror was increasing. It could not get any worse than this. He had harbored a sexual felon. He had helped him escape to North Carolina. And he had lied to the police about it. How would that look? How *could* it look? Like a church-orchestrated cover-up, that's how.

"Help me, Father," the boy pleaded. "Please, help me. We love each other. We really do. And we can help each other. I have some money. A passport. We can make a start together somewhere else. Somewhere far away. Amsterdam, maybe. We can be together. Otherwise . . ." The boy trailed off, breathing heavily. "Otherwise I don't know what will happen. I must see him, Father. *Please* take me to him."

"I can't," the rattled cardinal murmured. "I can't do that. I've sent him away."

"Where?" the boy pressed urgently.

Staggered, the cardinal felt his mind racing. He was ruined. His career was over. Surely they would ask him to step down. After all these years of service, he would simply be discarded. Where would he go? What would he do? How could Father Patrick have done this to him, used him and lied and run off to North Carolina? "What . . . what's that?" he finally said, rousing himself.

"*Where* in North Carolina?"

Dear God, had he said it aloud? What was wrong with him? How could he have just told him where Father Patrick was? He was in too much pain, that was it. He wasn't thinking clearly. Suddenly Cardinal O'Brien felt terribly old. *Where will I go? What will I do?*

"To the retreat?" the young boy asked. "To St. Catherine's?"

Had he said *that* aloud, too? No, he was sure he hadn't. A jolt of pain ran through his body, starting in his groin like before but now grabbing at his chest.

"How do you know about the retreat?" the cardinal managed to ask.

"I know everything about Father Patrick," the boy said, only now he sounded different. Less frightened.

"I'd like you to go now," the cardinal said as another blast of pain coursed through him. "Please . . . just go."

"I will, Father. But first I have to be sure that no one will know we've talked about this."

The cardinal raised his head and shook the fog away. "Young man, how dare you say such a thing to me?" he demanded. "Ours is a sacred confidence. I am God's right hand."

"And I am his left," said the Closer, shooting the elderly cardinal directly through the forehead.

For a brief instant, as he pitched forward onto the floor, Cardinal O'Brien felt an entirely new agony.

And then the thirteenth cardinal felt nothing at all.

chapter 32

C arl squinted out at the utter darkness of the country night as he steered them down the narrow, bumpy dirt road from Momma One-Eye's house back into Warren. Amanda rode next to him in grim, troubled silence. Payton's Suburban felt like a luxury condo on wheels after so many days bouncing along on the road in the little beer can of a Subaru. The air-conditioning worked. So did the shock absorbers. And the ignition. This would take some getting used to.

There was also a loaded Smith & Wesson .357 Magnum in the glove compartment. This too would take some getting used to.

Payton wouldn't be needing the big Chevy anymore. So they had ditched the old rickety pickup they had stolen, and now this road hog was theirs. That was the law of the jungle.

And the jungle was definitely where they were living right now. A jungle that was growing ever denser.

According to the vehicle registration form in the glove compartment, the Suburban was registered to none other than Astor Realty Management on Amsterdam Avenue in New York City. Astor Realty was the outfit that had managed Carl's apartment building. He had made his rent checks out to Astor Realty every month.

At one point in his life Carl used to believe in coincidence. But no longer. There was no way that this was a coincidence. He didn't know what it was or what it meant. Or where it would lead them. But, as he had quickly learned to do over the past week, he added this new bit of information to his mental checklist, then turned his focus away from the theoretical and back to the here and now. That meant getting back to Luther Heller's office in town without being seen.

Momma was taking care of Luther's body. And the little skeleton of the baby Gideon. "You two don't be worryin' none," she had assured them after she made sure they were properly stuffed with smothered pork chops, black-eyed peas, macaroni and cheese, mustard greens, and pecan pie. "Momma, she always takes care of what need doin'."

That she had, Carl reflected. No matter how long he lived, he would never, ever forget the sight of that frail little old black woman calmly blowing Payton away. The harshness and cruelty that she had endured in her long life had given her an inner strength, a toughness that Carl could barely even comprehend. It wasn't often that he met someone he desperately wanted to get to know better and to learn from. He felt that way about Momma One-Eye.

Warren's little Main Street was shut down, the handful of offices and stores dark and silent. On the side streets there were a few house lights on, here and there the insidious glow of a television set. But mostly the small delta town was asleep for the night. There were no other cars out on the road.

Carl pulled around in the parking lot behind the redbrick town hall and killed the engine. As they got out, a wave of heat and humidity instantly enveloped them. The smell of the river was strong here, yeasty and rank. He heard a dog barking somewhere and, off in the distance, a freight train. Amanda fumbled with the alderman's key until she found the one that unlocked the back door. They let themselves in and closed the door behind them. They flicked on a light.

If anyone happened to pass by, Momma had told them, they would just think that Luther was working late hours. He often had.

They found themselves in a storeroom stacked with office supplies. There were two doors. One led to a lavatory, the other to a hallway. The hallway led them up front to Luther's office, the one where the walls were lined with those ghostly drawings of Harry Wagner. Carl had been so overwhelmed by the alderman's artwork that he had observed nothing else about the office.

It was Amanda, ever the trained journalist, who had taken note of the computer.

It was not located on Luther's desk, which was very neat—every pencil in its place, every paper neatly filed. It was set up on a table in the corner of the room, under a bulletin board. There were hand-lettered signs tacked to

the board: *Please remember to turn off the machine. Please no food or bev-
erages.* Below those was a sign-up sheet for town hall workers who wanted
to reserve time on the computer. Latwanna Brisbee of the clerk's office had
it the next day from 9 to 10 A.M. There was another sign-up sheet for intro-
ductory lessons in computer skills, taught every Tuesday evening by Alderman Heller himself. Three people were signed up for next Tuesday's class.

"He was a good man," Carl said tightly as he gazed at the signs. "He
didn't deserve to die."

"No one deserves to die," Amanda said. "Certainly not that way."

Carl said nothing. But he remembered the pain of Payton's kicks to his
ribs. Remembered the son of a bitch's sheer animal delight at inflicting that
pain. And his own pure pleasure at seeing him go down and stay down. And
he thought: *Yes, some people do deserve it. They most definitely do.*

Amanda sat down at the computer and fired it up, her eyes flicking up at
the on-line access codes that were neatly printed on a piece of tape affixed
to the monitor. "The newsroom will be virtual insanity right about now,"
she said as she logged on. "A presidential suicide . . . it's almost incomprehensible. That is pure dope for action junkies."

"Sorry you're missing out on all the action," Carl said, stroking her hair
as he stood behind her.

She reached for his hand and squeezed it tightly. "The last time I
looked," she replied, "the action was all right here. . . . Ah, good. I got her."
Her fingers flew over the keyboard as she sent off an instant message:

[Hey, girl. What's up?]

Shaneesa's response came back right away:

[Some powerful white man named Tom something went and
offed hisself. Otherwise just the usual slow news day. And
you?]
[Just waiting for you to talk at me, sweet thing.]

Carl leaned forward anxiously as he stared at the screen, awaiting this
supremely gifted hacker's reply.

[Got two items for you. First, I've deciphered the aforementioned tat, *bienvenue.* Searched all over and the word itself led to one giant dead end. Started playing around and finally figured out it's a basic letter-number code. Each letter of the alphabet corresponds with its numeral value: A being 1, Z being 26. He then encrypted it by reversing it, so that instead of B being 2 it's 25, and so on. You told me he was flyin' the coop, so I concentrated on that. When they run, there's usually money involved. Turns out it's an account number for an offshore bank account in the Cayman Islands. Your computer-age version of ye olde Swiss bank account. Account was opened four days ago. And, check it out, five million dollars was just transferred in. Phat, no?]

"Looks like Harry set himself up with a nice little retirement fund," Carl said.

"Only somebody else had a different way of defining the word *retirement*," Amanda concurred.

"Damn!" Carl blurted out. "What did he *know*?"

"Too much," she replied. "Everything. Who hired you. Who was behind all this. He knew five million dollars' worth."

Their eyes met and then Amanda's fingers flew to the keyboard. Shaneesa's response to her typed-in question was instantaneous.

[Give me some credit, girl! Am already undertaking the highly difficult search for where/who the $$$ came from. I figured that would be of some interest to inquiring minds.]

[Take all the credit you want. But while you're at it, see who bankrolls Astor Realty Management on Amsterdam Ave. in NYC. What's item number two? Dish me.]

[Received a VERY strange e-mail. And believe me, it's only because I owe you my life that I haven't moved on this yet in a professional capacity. Decided I'd give you 24 hours. You've already used up 14 of 'em.]

[What did it say?]

[Am forwarding. Take care, girl. And best regards to Mr.
Right. He'd better be worth it.]

Amanda failed to respond, prompting Carl to nudge her on the shoulder. "Don't you think you should answer her back? Something like, 'He sure is' or 'Damned straight'?"

"I'm receiving now, big guy," Amanda said pointedly.

"What is this, ham radio? Since when can't you send and receive at the same time?"

"Oh, hush, will you? Here it is. . . ."

They read it together in rapt silence.

[Date: Wednesday, July 13 7:34 AM EDT
From: Fathathad@aol.com
Subject: This is not a prank
To: Sperryman@dcjournal.com
Dear Ms. Perryman—I have been reading the news on-line
since I have been here, with keener interest than you can
possibly imagine. I happened to read your extremely heartfelt article about your editor and friend, Amanda Mays.
After considerable deliberation I have decided to reach
out to you. You seem like a sincere and moral person, a
loving Christian person. I have to trust someone, so I am
trusting you. You will possibly think me to be some form
of lunatic or crank. I assure you that I am not. I may be
wrong with what I'm about to say, but please believe me, I
am deadly serious. And quite certainly at great risk.

Just as your friend and her companion Carl Granville are.

If you are not in touch with them, please ignore this
message. Do not attempt to contact me or find me. I will be
gone. But if by some chance, any chance, you know how to
reach Ms. Mays or Mr. Granville, you MUST get word to them
at once.

I have reason to believe that President Adamson's death

was brought about by a dangerous and high-reaching political conspiracy. There is more to his suicide than anyone
currently realizes. I am not even sure we should call his
death a suicide. Murder might be a more accurate way of
putting it. But that particular discussion will have to
wait for a later time, when we have the luxury of calm reflection. Right now, we have no such luxury.

I have been told some deeply disturbing things. Because
I was told them in sacred confidence I cannot share them
with you. I can only tell you that it is vital I make contact with Carl Granville.

You mentioned in your article that he has been ghostwriting a political memoir. A prominent New York editor is
suddenly murdered and the finger of blame is immediately
pointed at him. He flees to Washington, D.C., so as to seek
the help of Miss Mays, a journalist. Her home is promptly
destroyed and an FBI agent is found murdered. Once again
the finger of blame is immediately pointed at Carl Granville, a talented young author, an Ivy League basketball
star, a promising young man with no criminal record. Does
this not strike you as strange?

Believe me, it would if you knew what I know.

I know too much. And I believe that Carl Granville and
your friend Amanda Mays know too much as well. That is why
he has become a hunted animal. Because they cannot let him
stay alive. He is capable of ruining everything for them.

If I can see them, I can help them. And they can help
me. Possibly we can save each other from this awful predicament we face.

Possibly it is not too late.

Please, if you are in contact with them, tell them I am
at the Retreat of St. Catherine of Genoa, located near
Paint Gap in the mountains outside of Asheville, North
Carolina. I will be here for only one more day. I must
keep moving. And searching for answers.

If your friends need more convincing, please tell them these two things: I know about the manuscript he was writing. And I know about Gideon.

If those two statements mean nothing to them, this e-mail should be completely ignored. And erase it immediately from your computer, Ms. Perryman. It is not safe to leave in there. Not safe for me, not safe for your friends, and probably not even safe for you.

Thank you for your consideration. Sincerely yours, Father Patrick Jennings]

Amanda stared at the screen for a long moment. "It's the missing priest from St. Stephen's Cathedral," she said, her voice a hushed whisper. "The one whose car was found by the Potomac."

"He knows." Carl gripped her shoulders tightly. "He actually knows what's going on."

"How could he?" Amanda asked.

"How do priests know anything personal?" Carl said.

"Oh, my God." The words came out slowly. "He confessed." She turned in her chair to face him, her green eyes searching his face. "Adamson confessed! What should we do?"

"I think," he said slowly, "we should follow Luther's instructions and turn off the machine."

"And then?"

"And then we put the pedal to the metal all the way to Paint Gap, North Carolina."

It was just past four A.M. when the Challenger jet descended and made a smooth landing at the Asheville Regional Airport, situated on the southern outskirts of the lovely old North Carolina spa town.

The Closer had changed half an hour before the wheels touched the runway.

It was not a difficult change. Changing physically—clothes, hair, appearance—was never difficult for the Closer. Padding could be added or subtracted to alter weight. Hair could be colored, combed, and cut. Posture was easy to manipulate. Uniforms were easy to buy and so extraordinarily effective. People were definitely cowed by uniforms—police, military, even UPS. Voices were easy, too. Had been since childhood. It was *all* easy physically. The Closer could leave a conversation in a crowded room, go into any quiet room with a mirror, stay no more than fifteen minutes, return to the same room, and carry on the same conversation—completely unrecognizable.

It was a skill. Nothing to be particularly proud of. Just something useful.

Mentally, though, that was a different thing.

It was harder to change mentally. To *become* another person. To act differently, think differently. *Feel* differently. That was not a skill. That was an art. That was talent. That was, the Closer believed, genius. Part of that genius was understanding people. And understanding yourself. Not just the person you were but the person others wanted you to be. In the Closer's profession, it was a very useful realization: People saw what they wanted to see, believed what they wanted to believe. Particularly when they were in love, whenever their God was involved, or when they were about to die.

And so, once again transformed, the Closer strode down the steps of the plane into the coolness of the Smoky Mountain predawn, moving somewhat stiffly in the unfamiliar outfit. It was rather constricting, particularly at the throat. But there was no disputing its effectiveness. There were only a handful of people to be found in the terminal at this hour, but those who took note of the Closer were instantly respectful. The elderly redcap who was out front at the curb even went so far as to tip his hat and ask the Closer if he might be of any small service whatsoever. The Closer declined, treating him to a kindly smile.

The Closer felt sure it was kindly, having practiced it in the Challenger jet's lavatory mirror for several minutes while dressing.

A rental car, a white Toyota Celica sedan, was waiting for the Closer in the short-term parking lot, unlocked, the keys under the front seat. Lord Augmon's people had made the arrangements. That was one of the pluses of working for him. So was the peerless intelligence work. When the Closer had boarded the jet in Oxford, Mississippi, a file had already been prepared containing Father Patrick Jennings's detailed life story, a list of his closest confidantes, and, most significant, his cellular phone records, complete with the corresponding name and address of each party he had called in the twenty-four hours leading up to his disappearance. Lord Augmon happened to own a substantial interest in the cellular phone service that the priest sub- scribed to. Lord Augmon happened to own a substantial interest in all of the major cellular phone services—with the exception of one, which he owned outright.

The Closer had taken over from there. It was the Closer who had ze- roed in on Cardinal O'Brien. It was the Closer who had instructed the pi- lot to head for Baltimore's BWI airport. It was the Closer who had found out that the cardinal liked to take a walk in the basilica every night before bedtime. An extremely nervous, extremely bent young priest named Fa- ther Gary had been the Closer's confidential source. His body would be found later that morning not more than twenty feet from the cardinal's, the gun that had killed Cardinal O'Brien gripped in Father Gary's own lifeless right hand—the Closer having used that same gun to blow a hole through the roof of Father Gary's mouth. The autopsy would show that it had been fired at point-blank range. It would also show that Father Gary had expe- rienced an ejaculation shortly before his death. Traces of his semen would be found on the cardinal's tongue and lips, as well as smeared across the palm of the old man's right hand and several of his fingers. A small but critical sample of Father Gary's pubic hair would be found entwined in his sleeve.

God, as the Closer humbly believed, was indeed found in the details.

It would go down as a murder-suicide. The Closer felt quite certain of this, having used a similar technique two years before to eliminate a recalci- trant federal appeals court judge in St. Louis. Lord Augmon had felt that the judge was behaving in an unreasonable manner. Something to do with an antitrust case. The Closer did not recall the specifics or care about them.

The Closer climbed into the rented Toyota, adjusted the driver's seat for more legroom, and flicked on an interior light. After spending a long mo- ment studying the area road map, the Closer started up the engine and steered the white Celica out of the airport and onto Highway 26, heading north toward the Blue Ridge Parkway, the famously scenic mountain road that would twist and turn its way around Mt. Mitchell and eventually lead to someplace called Paint Gap.

It took them one hour to reach Memphis on Highway 61 and five more long hours before they hit Knoxville, streaking due east on Highway 40 in the moonless wee hours of the night. In addition to every other bell and whistle known to Detroit, the Suburban came equipped with a highly sophisticated radar detector. This was a good thing. They could not afford to be stopped for speeding.

Or for anything else.

They pulled in once at a rest stop not far from Nashville to fill the Suburban's not-quite-bottomless gas tank and themselves with hamburgers and coffee. At Knoxville, Highway 40 dipped south into North Carolina. Asheville, home to Thomas Wolfe and the colossal Vanderbilt mansion Biltmore, was another hour after that.

Thanks to the light traffic and Carl's heavy foot, they arrived shortly before 5 A.M. A sleepy young attendant at an all-night convenience store gave Amanda the directions to Paint Gap. It was just becoming light out as they got on the Blue Ridge Parkway. The climb to Mt. Mitchell, the highest point in the eastern United States at 6,684 feet, was breathtaking. The scenic road fell away sharply into deep ravines densely overgrown with laurel, azalea, myrtle, and rhododendron. Down below, where there were streams, an early morning mist hung in the still air. A red-tailed hawk circled slowly over the mist in search of its breakfast.

Amanda shut off the air-conditioning and rolled down the windows. The mountain air was cool and clean and mercifully dry after the Mississippi delta. It smelled of fresh pines. "This may be the most beautiful place I've ever seen," she said, her voice hushed with awe. "I'd like to come back and stay for about a year."

"I'd like to come with you," he said, smiling at her.

The momentary feeling of safety and solitude, as well as the dawn silence, was pierced by a shrill, high-pitched ringing. The sound was so unexpected, so jarring, that it took Carl a moment to realize what it was:

The Suburban's cell phone, ringing urgently in its cradle.

He shot a look down at it in disbelief. Amanda was staring at it, too, as if she had never heard such a noise in her entire life. Neither of them made any motion to respond.

It rang a second time.

They stared at each other.

It rang a third time.

Carl's hand reached forward now, grabbing for the compact black phone. He flicked it open with his thumb so as to receive the incoming call. He held it up to his ear, his heart racing. He swallowed, his throat suddenly dry and raw. And he said, "Yeah?"

"Is the job finished?" the voice on the other end demanded.

It was a man's voice. Impatient. Very self-important and British. It was a voice that sent icy shivers of terror down the back of Carl's neck. It was *him*. At long last Carl was speaking to the demon who was behind the deaths, the shattered lives, who was responsible for all of it.

"I am facing critical time restraints," the voice went on reproachfully. "Why haven't you reported in? I *need* to know: Are they dead or aren't they?"

Anger surged through Carl's body. The veins in his neck bulged, and he gripped the phone so tightly he thought he might crush it. He almost didn't recognize his own voice when he spoke, it was so full of quiet rage. "The party you're trying to reach isn't available," he said. "And I'm afraid it's going to take a *very* long distance call for you to get through to him."

There was no immediate response from the other end. Just heavy, raspy breathing. Then: "Bloody hell, it's *you*, isn't it? You've bested poor Payton. My, my . . . you're vastly more resourceful than I gave you credit for, my boy."

"Let's get something straight," Carl said through gritted teeth. "I am not your boy."

"It's a damn shame we didn't meet under different circumstances, Carl. It's so difficult to find a bright, independent young man who knows how to think on his feet. Most people your age require such constant supervision."

"Okay, so *you* know who *I* am." Carl was fuming. The knuckles on his hand were white with tension. "In the interest of fair play, why don't you tell me who *you* are?"

"Ah, you *are* young, aren't you? I'm terribly sorry, Carl, but you see, you've reached a level in our little game where I'm afraid there *is* no such thing as fair play."

"A game?" Carl roared into the phone. Amanda watched him wide-eyed as the fury poured out of him. "You've destroyed my career, my home, my *life*. What kind of fucking game is that? Why did you do this to me?! Why *me*?"

"It's nothing personal, I assure you, dear boy."

"Who are you?" Carl screamed. "*Tell* me, you evil bastard!"

"Alas, this conversation is deteriorating markedly. I'm going to ring off now, Carl."

"I'll get you!" Carl vowed. "I'll find you and I'll make you pay for this! I swear I will!"

But the phone was already dead in Carl's ear. Boiling over with frustration, he smashed it against the Suburban's steering wheel, once, twice, three times before Amanda wrenched it roughly from his grasp.

"Stop it!" she ordered. "We may need this phone."

He took a deep breath, let it out slowly. Then took the phone out of her hand and gently placed it back in its cradle.

"I want to kill him," he said very quietly. "I want to find out who he is and I want to kill him."

"Yes," she answered, just as quietly. "I know."

He resumed driving. They turned off of the parkway now onto Route 80, a narrow mountain road that meandered its way through the woods past a number of religious retreats and New Age hideaways. Quite a few were to be found here in the mountains outside of Asheville. This was a place where people came to find answers, to find peace, to find themselves. Paint Gap wasn't much more than a crossroads. The Retreat of St. Catherine of Genoa was located down a dirt road, behind a log gate, and up a long, steep private drive that climbed its way through the forest and passed over a rushing stream before it ended at a rambling lodge that seemed to grow right out of the side of the mountain. It was made of logs, with a great stone chimney in its center. Fragrant wood smoke wafted from the chimney.

One car, a white Toyota Celica, was parked there. Carl pulled up next to it and shut off the engine. As they stepped out they could hear the cool breeze wafting through the tall pines and birds calling to each other. Otherwise, it was so quiet after the endless hours on the highway that their ears rang.

Amanda's hand reached for Carl's and gripped it tightly. Together they walked up to the big house.

"And how may I be of service, Father Gary?" Father Thaddeus inquired politely.

"I hope I'm the one who may be of service," the Closer replied softly, shifting in the hard wooden chair. It wasn't so much the chair that was uncomfortable as it was the vestments—specifically the collar. It was stiff and constricting. But it would not do to draw attention to the discomfort. Father Gary would be used to wearing it. Father Gary had *chosen* to wear it.

"Please continue," Father Thaddeus urged, nodding. He was a large, powerfully built man in his fifties, deeply tanned from years of rugged outdoor work. His round, creased, brown face reminded the Closer very much of a baked apple.

They were in his private study. Its furnishings were rustic and spare to the point of ascetic. A small fire crackled in the fireplace to take the morning chill off the room.

"Father Patrick and I have been good friends for quite some time," the Closer explained, lapsing into a slight drawl. "I just happened to be visiting my folks for a few days in Murfreesboro when Cardinal O'Brien phoned to say that Pat was in residence here. He thought—we both thought—that it might make some good country sense for me to stop in and see how Pat was getting on before I headed back up to Baltimore. See if he needed anything. See if he felt like talking."

"That's very thoughtful of the cardinal," Father Thaddeus murmured, making a steeple of his index fingers to support his chin. "And of you."

"How is he, Father Thaddeus?"

Father Thaddeus sipped his coffee in heavy silence for a moment. It smelled strong and rich and good. The Closer wanted a cup desperately but had declined it when Father Thaddeus offered, not wishing to leave behind any fingerprints or trace of saliva.

"I wish I knew how to answer you," Father Thaddeus finally said, his voice laden with regret. "I can only tell you that Father Patrick is searching for strength. He is so preoccupied that he will scarcely respond to his name when I utter it. Occasionally I'll find him on the computer in our office.

Doing what, I can't imagine. Most of his time he spends alone, walking in the woods. Or up at Our Father's Rock."

"Our Father's Rock?" The Closer leaned forward. This sounded promising.

"There's a narrow foot trail out back that climbs to the top of this mountain," Father Thaddeus explained. "Ours is the tallest peak for miles around. There is a rock up there—Our Father's Rock—that enjoys commanding views for as far as the eye can see in every direction. It's a place of tremendous quiet and isolation. Ideal for contemplation. Many years ago a cabin was built up there."

" 'The wise man built his house on the rock,' " quoted the Closer. "The Book of Matthew."

"Precisely so," said Father Thaddeus, a pleased smile creasing his brown face. "It's quite primitive. And scarcely big enough for a cot and a table. Some choose to go there for reading and reflection. Some, like Father Pat, even choose to sleep up there. When the dawn comes, the sun feels so warm and near that you almost believe you can reach out and touch His hand." Now Father Thaddeus looked out of his study window at the early morning. "I suspect that's where Pat will be right now."

"May I see him?"

"Of course. If he wishes to see you." Father Thaddeus got up and went over to a door that opened out into the garden. "And there is only one way to find that out. By trying."

"Trying is all we can do in this life," the Closer said thoughtfully, staring out the door into the cool morning dampness. "And with God's help, occasionally we are allowed to succeed."

Once again he was unable to sleep. Once again Father Patrick Jennings spent the hours before dawn riffling feverishly through the worn pages of his Holy Bible by the flickering light of a small oil lamp, his teeth chattering from the mountain cold, the coarse wool blanket from the cot thrown over his shoulders.

Answers. Truth. Understanding.

These were the things he was searching for. These were the things he was desperate for.

But he could find no solace within those familiar pages. All he could find were mind-numbing platitudes. And more questions. As in Jeremiah 39:18: "You will be delivered because you trusted in me." *When, Lord? When will my trust be rewarded?* As in Corinthians 4:5: "God will bring to light the things hidden in darkness." *How, Lord? Please show me how, for I am lost in the darkness. Show me where the wisdom is to be found. And please—please, God—show me the way.*

Whiskey would be of tremendous help, he felt quite certain. It would warm him and calm him. It would erect soft, cushioned barricades in front of those dimly lit mental corridors down which there was only anguish and terror to be found. Whiskey would allow him to sleep.

But one of his purposes in being here at the retreat was to toss away that crutch. Learn how to walk on his own two legs again. Move forward by his own strength into the dawn.

If only that dawn would come.

No, he simply could not drink now. He needed to think clearly. So much was at stake. Too much for him to make a false step. Was that what it had been when he'd e-mailed the reporter in Washington—a false step? It was a risk, certainly. If he was wrong about these two people, about Granville and Mays, then his message was a disaster. It would bring the wrong people down upon him as surely as vultures swooping down on a rotting corpse. But he had thought it out carefully. Detail by detail. President Adamson had seen the beginning of a manuscript—a detailed account of his corrupt and tragic past. A young writer is hired to write a secret political memoir. His editor and others around him are killed, and he's accused of the murders. He seeks help from a Washington reporter; her house is burned down, an FBI agent is killed, and they flee together. The question was: Were they fleeing because they were guilty or because they were innocent? It made sense; he just *knew* it made sense. The young man, without knowing what he was getting into, had been hired by those trying to bring down the president. If they would destroy a man like Adamson, surely they wouldn't hesitate to crush young Granville. Adamson, in his confession, had said they would stop at nothing. And that they were powerful enough that nothing could stop them.

No, he didn't know if he'd done the right thing. But at the very bottom of it all, underneath all his suspicions and interpretations, was the one thing he knew to be true: A terrible crime had taken place, and he had to do something about it. But what?

If only the answer would come, Father Patrick reflected as he sat there in the tiny cabin atop Our Father's Rock. Perched there utterly alone in the darkness, vulnerable and exposed, shivering as he waited for the dawn. An apt parable of his present personal crisis, he concluded ruefully. In every direction but one there was a sheer drop of several hundred feet into the ravine below—certain disaster. Only one way led to the right path, the path back to safety.

Help me to choose the right path, Lord. Help me before I go inexorably, irretrievably mad.

At the purplish first light, when at long last he could begin to make out the shapes of the rocks around him, Father Patrick walked. Walking was his only escape from his demons. At first he stuck to the well-worn trail as it twisted its way around outcroppings of bare rock back down into the forest. But after a hundred yards or so he abruptly left the trail, breaking off into the wild brush. It was a densely overgrown primeval forest. Almost impenetrable. Branches and vines shredded his vestments and tore at his hands and face, inflicting deep, painful scratches. But he did not turn back. Rather, he went faster, ignoring the blood that trickled down his forehead into his eyes. And faster still. Until at last he broke into a mad gallop, crashing through the brush like a rampaging black bear, an animal roar coming from deep within his throat. He tripped and fell repeatedly on the downed tree limbs and rocks, turning his ankles, skinning his knees, his elbows, his palms. He came down heavily on his right shoulder and lost all feeling in his arm. But he would not stop. He would not be stopped. Not until exhaustion finally overtook him and he fell to his bloodied knees, quivering, sobbing, bathed in sweat. And so he prayed: *Lord God, I have reached my limit. You have always taught me that you would never give me more to handle than I was capable of withstanding. But I cannot go on, Lord. I am on my knees, bloodied and bowed. Deliver me, Lord, for I trust in you. Save me.*

Father Patrick remained on his knees for several minutes, his eyes tightly shut, before he finally shook himself and climbed unsteadily to his feet, gazing around blindly at the forest. Order. Priorities. He needed these things. He would go back up to his little cabin. Wipe his face clean. Don fresh clothing. Go down for breakfast. Eat. Father Patrick ran carefully through the list again, reciting the words out loud, collecting himself. And then, gingerly, he made his way back through the brush toward the path. When he reached it he climbed back up to Our Father's Rock.

The sun was breaking right over Mt. Pisgah now, bright and warm. It was directly in Father Patrick's eyes as he reached the uppermost outcropping. That was why it took him a moment to realize he was not alone up there.

Another priest stood perilously close to the edge of the rock, gazing out at the view. "Father Thaddeus was right," this priest said to him in a muted, awed voice. "You *can* almost reach out and touch His hand." Now the priest turned and smiled at Father Patrick. He was quite young and clear-eyed and uncommonly handsome, with sparkling white teeth, flawless skin, and lustrous dark hair. Goodness and kindness seemed to radiate from his thin but athletic frame as he stood in the morning light. "Good morning, Father Patrick."

"Wh-who are you?" he stammered hoarsely.

"I," the young priest replied gently, "am the answer to your prayers."

The trail was impossibly steep. And Amanda was quickly discovering that she was in no condition to make it all the way to the top. She was stressed out, worn down, and badly in need of sleep. Plus her body was not yet accustomed to this thin mountain air. She could not catch her breath. Her head felt light and her legs seemed as if they had lead weights strapped to them. Ahead of her on the narrow trail, Carl was breathing heavily, too. But they could not stop. They had to keep going. One foot in front of the other. They had to keep climbing.

Because someone else was looking for Father Patrick.

That's what Father Thaddeus had told them. A young priest, who had just preceded them up this very trail by a few precious minutes.

What young priest? Who was he? What did he want? Were they too late? After so many days and nights, so many miles of running, could they possibly be too late?

No, they couldn't be. They just *couldn't* be. Or it would all be over and they would be destroyed.

"I'm not going to make it, Carl," she panted.

"Yes, you are," he panted back at her, his own chest heaving. "We both are. We have to."

The last hundred yards to the top of the mountain were by far the most grueling: pure rock and very nearly vertical. She found herself climbing on all fours now, every muscle in her body quivering. She wondered if it was possible that her heart might hammer its way right out of her chest.

And then, at long last, the trail topped out at a flat, narrow outcropping of rock. There was bright sunlight here, a panoramic view, a tiny cabin perched like an eagle's nest. She could hear someone speaking. The blood was rushing so hard in her ears that she could barely make out the words.

But it sounded something like: "I am the answer to your prayers."

And then they found themselves face-to-face with two priests. They were standing at the edge of the cliff. Beyond them there was only a sheer drop down into oblivion.

One of the priests was Father Patrick. Amanda recognized him, although the poor man looked as if he had just been mauled by a tiger. He was covered with scratches. His vestments were badly shredded. And he seemed a bit glassy-eyed. But he was alive.

They were not too late.

The other priest, the young one, was tall and slender with dark, wavy hair and a high, smooth forehead. Eerily handsome. When he heard their heavy footsteps on the rocks, he turned and smiled at them. It was a reassuring smile. A kindly smile. Radiating calm and serenity.

He seemed to be expecting them.

"I wondered if you'd make it, Carl," the younger priest exclaimed pleasantly. His voice was soft and gentle. It seemed to caress the morning air. "Or may I still call you Granny?"

Amanda watched as virtually all of the color drained from Carl's face. What was going on? For some reason he seemed shocked. Jolted. His eyes narrowed and his breath was now coming in quick, desperate rasps. What was happening? Why did he look so stunned? So . . . wounded?

"I've wanted to see you," the young priest said to Carl now, a playful, tantalizing smile crossing his lips. In his eyes there was a triumphant gleam. "I've wanted you to see me."

Amanda's confusion deepened when the young priest turned and said, "Father Pat, let me introduce you to Carl Granville. I believe you know all about him."

How did he know the connection to Father Patrick? Who *was* this priest?

Father Patrick, eyes still glazed, turned to Carl and said hesitantly, "I'm so relieved that you've come. I can't tell you how relieved. I didn't know if you'd even get my message."

But Carl didn't respond to Father Patrick or so much as look at him. He could not take his eyes off this other priest. He was gaping at him with a look that was now beyond shock, beyond disbelief, beyond comprehension.

"Are *you* relieved, Carl?" the young priest was saying now.

But how was this possible? How did he know Carl? How did he know any of this? And what was it in his tone of voice? Familiarity? No, more than that. Friendship? More than that, too. Intimacy, Amanda realized. That was it. It was intimacy. But how? Why . . . ?

Carl was shaking his head back and forth, like someone in the midst of a horrible nightmare. And now he spoke, his words coming in short, harsh bursts. "No, this can't be happening. . . . No, no . . . it can't be. . . ."

She could not believe the look on his face. It had turned to horror. Pure and absolute horror.

"You're *dead*," Carl moaned, his eyes never leaving the priest's. "I *saw* you dead."

"You saw someone you *thought* was me," the young priest said. "Someone with no face."

"Carl, what's going on?" Amanda said pleadingly. "Tell me what's going on!"

"Who *are* you?" Carl screamed at the priest.

"I am whoever I need to be," the priest replied triumphantly. "I am *whatever* I need to be."

The priest's expression had already begun to change. The expression turned from one of peace and calm to one of fierce sensuality. Somehow the contours of the face softened; the posture hardened, with the back arching backward in a catlike, graceful manner. Even the voice was no longer so deep or throaty. It was much more melodious and seductive.

And he was not handsome. Not the way Amanda had first thought.
He was beautiful.

"It can't be," Carl breathed.

"Oh, but it is, Carl," the priest said. "Believe me, it is."

The priest turned now to face Father Patrick, who was standing, frozen, at the edge of the narrow cliff. "Do you accept that God saves those who believe?" the young priest asked the father. And when Father Patrick nodded, the priest said, "Then prepare to be saved."

The priest pulled out a semiautomatic handgun from under the folds of his clothing, but Carl was already in the air. And as he dove, his voice rose into a wild, guttural scream that stretched on and on, the noise of a savage beast, filled with hate and ferocity.

The word he screamed as he dove for the priest, for the gun, for their very lives, was:

"Toni."

Toooonnnnniiiiiiiiii.

Amanda watched the shot go wide, missing Father Patrick, and at first she thought that Carl had gone mad. But then she saw it, and it all made sense. The realization took her breath away as Carl and the person in the priest's vestments fell heavily to the hard ground, wrapped tightly in each other's arms like the lovers they had once been.

It was vicious and it was brutal, and it was a dead-even match. Toni was very nearly Carl's physical equal—six feet tall, wiry and strong. And she was a trained fighter. Every part of her body was in constant, slithering motion—leg whipping him, kneeing him in the groin, gouging at his eyes, biting down on his wrist like a rabid dog. Amanda could only stand helplessly next to Father Patrick as the two of them rolled around on the narrow cliff, grappling for the gun, snarling, cursing, spitting. All the while edging closer and closer to the sheer precipice. Right to its very edge.

Amanda cried out Carl's name, terrified that he and this evil woman would go over the side wrapped in one last embrace. Terrified that she would lose him.

Briefly he had a hand around Toni's throat. He was squeezing, choking the life out of her, but somehow she fought her way out of his grasp. Then she had both her legs wrapped around his neck like a deathly vise. He couldn't breathe. His face was turning purple. In a last, desperate move he pulled his arm back, launched it forward, and punched her in the nose with all of his strength. As bone broke and cartilage shattered, as blood spurted, she lost her hold on him. And she lost the gun as well. He jumped after it, both hands outstretched. So did Toni. It went skittering across the rocks.

It ended up right at Amanda's feet.

Swiftly she bent over and picked it up. She had never held a loaded handgun before. It was surprisingly cold and heavy. She stood there hefting it, transfixed by its feel and the blue glint it gave off in the sunlight. And now everything seemed to be happening in slow motion. Carl and Toni were realizing that she had possession of the gun . . . they were climbing to their feet, battered and bloodied, their chests heaving . . . and were standing there, watching her.

They weren't the only ones. She felt as if she were watching herself. Because this wasn't *her* standing on a mountain holding an instrument of death in her hand. None of this was happening. Not any of it.

Except it was.

"Shoot her, Amanda," Carl commanded. His voice was level. Emotionless. "Don't hesitate. Don't think. Just shoot her."

"The safety is off, Amanda," Toni pointed out helpfully, her gaze steady and unafraid. "All you have to do is point and squeeze."

"Shoot her now," Carl repeated urgently. "Do it."

Amanda raised the gun, pointing it at the woman, holding it in front of her as if fending off a wild animal. It wavered there in the air. Her hands were shaking. Her knees were shaking. She tried to speak. No sound came out.

Toni inched a step toward her now, blood streaming from her smashed nose. "Go on, Amanda." She was daring her, mocking her. She was a fearless, predatory cat. And even now, her face broken, her clothes torn and filthy, she exuded a sexual power that was commanding, hard to resist. Overpowering. "Give me your best shot. Show me what you've got."

At her elbow, Amanda heard a low murmur. It was Father Patrick saying a prayer. She had forgotten he was even there.

"Shoot her, Amanda!" Carl cried out desperately. "Shoot her or she'll kill all three of us. Just like she killed the LaRues and Shanahoff and Harry and Maggie and whoever that poor innocent girl was I found in her apartment."

"She was no innocent, Carl," Toni growled, running her tongue slowly over her lower lip.

"She's not a human being, Amanda." He too was edging nearer to the raised gun. "She's a professional killer. An assassin. An animal. Shoot her!"

Amanda's finger twitched on the trigger. It was starting to tingle. Her whole hand was getting numb. The gun shook from side to side.

Toni loomed directly in front of her now. Her sensuous lips curled up in a malevolent smirk. "Carl licked every pore of my body with his tongue," she said in a throaty voice. "He couldn't get enough of me. That's what he said to me. He was *starved* for me."

"For God's sake, shoot her!" Carl screamed.

But Amanda was starting to have trouble seeing now. Because the tears were starting to come, filling up her eyes, spilling out onto her cheeks. She could taste them on her lips.

And still Toni kept moving toward her, her voice low and seductive.

"When I went down on him, he told me nobody ever, ever sucked his dick like that before. Did he ever say that to you when *you* were doing him? Tell me, Amanda. I'm just *dying* to know."

Amanda choked back the tears, hating that she couldn't control them. Hating herself. Hating this sociopathic monster. Hating that Carl had been seduced into her bed. Hating everyone and everything. For the first time in her life, hating, hating . . .

"Shoot, Amanda!" Carl screamed one more time.

And then Toni charged her.

S he couldn't do it.

Amanda didn't have it in her to shoot Toni, and Carl knew it. He didn't blame her. He didn't think any less of her. He didn't think, period. There was no time to think. Only to act. To stay shoulder to shoulder with Toni as she inched ever closer to that gun. To stay ready. And alert. And focused.

Even though he was still reeling from the shock of seeing Toni alive again. He would never get over the shock of that. And not just the fact that she was risen from the dead. It was the extent of the web that had been spun around him. The levels of complexity, of deviousness and destruction, that had been put in motion . . .

But he had to shut it out of his mind for now. He had to shut everything out and focus on the plan in front of him. What was it his old high-school coach used to preach?

A champion doesn't think. A champion does.

"Shoot her, Amanda!" he screamed as he edged one precious step nearer to her and the gun.

And then Toni charged her. She was lithe and fierce and remarkably fast on her feet.

But Carl was faster. He got there first, wrenched the gun from Amanda's grasp, and with one quick movement pumped a bullet directly into Toni's body, stopping her in her tracks.

Toni let out a startled gasp. She stood motionless for a moment, her back to the cliff, her face contorted in pain. Then, ever so slowly, a remarkable transformation came over her. The expression on her face grew softer, her lips fuller. Her eyes began to gleam at Carl invitingly. She was gazing at him, seducing him the way she had when they had been joined in passion together. It was as if it were just the two of them alone up there, no one else. Not Amanda. Not Father Patrick. Not anyone.

"Oh, Jesus, I felt that one all the way down to my toes, Carl," she purred softly at him. Then, as if reveling in the exquisite pain, she yanked the priest's collar from her throat. Next came the vestment, which she pulled off over her head, hurling it out into space. She wore nothing underneath it. She stood there before him in the morning light, naked from the waist up, her bared breasts firm and beautiful, the nipples rosy and taut.

Carl stared at her, remembering how those nipples had felt under his tongue. Remembering how glorious she had tasted and felt, remembering the delicious smell of her.

The bullet had entered her flawless body just above the navel. It was a small wound, just beginning to ooze blood. She gazed down at it with frank curiosity, then slowly back up at him. "Do you love me, Carl?"

"Who do you work for?" he asked. His voice was quiet now, calm. "Who's paying you?"

Toni shook her head. It was the motion of a lover, as if he'd just asked her a favor and she was coyly refusing unless he'd come to her, give her another kiss.

"Do it to me again, Carl," she said, a wanton lover, hungry for him.

"Who's behind all this?" he whispered.

She took a step toward him. "Do it to me, baby. Do it to me *good*."

The second shot spun her halfway around.

Now she gazed out at the mountains and the valley and the sky beyond, a woodland nymph facing the dawn. She had a look of sheer childlike wonderment on her face.

She turned back toward him one last time, her bare arms held out to him beseechingly. "Love me, Carl . . . once more . . . if you love me . . ."

He fired at her once, twice, three more times. The force of the shots pitched her over backward and out into oblivion. Momentarily she was like a bird in flight, soaring on a current of air. But then she was just something heavy and dead that didn't belong up there, and she free fell for hundreds of feet before crashing into a million pieces on the rocks down below.

A shudder went through his body. It occurred to him that he was about to throw up. But the feeling passed quickly. He stared down at the thing that had been Toni. That wasn't really her name. He knew that. But it didn't matter. What mattered was that she was gone. Never to return.

Gradually he became aware of the others again. Amanda. His dear, sweet Amanda.

"I'm sorry," she was saying. "I'm sorry I couldn't—"

But he didn't even let her finish her words. He just grabbed her and they held each other tightly. Their lips met and lingered. And lingered for a little while longer. Hers tasted like salt. Then slowly, when it was time, he released her. Turned to Father Patrick, who was crossing himself, his lips moving in silent benediction.

"Father," Carl said, "I believe it's time for us to tell each other what we know."

chapter 33

The Ronald Reagan Airport in Washington, D.C., was a madhouse.

Dignitaries were flying in from all over the world for Tom Adamson's funeral. Traffic was bumper to bumper. Car horns were honking, limo and cab drivers were swearing. There were more security officers patrolling the gates, runways, and baggage claims than there were cups of Starbucks coffee being sold.

That's why Carl, Amanda, and Father Patrick were sitting in their car in the short-term parking lot across the street from the USAir terminal. That's why Shaneesa, good old unrecognizable, nonwanted, hungry-for-the-final-story Shaneesa was at Gate 9 right now, waiting to pick up the very special passenger they were flying into town.

Sitting in the car, there was no need for any more conversation. The three of them had talked for hours, sitting at a rough-hewn stone table, along with Father Thaddeus, at the retreat. Carl had gone first, telling his story from the beginning, leaving nothing out, including the gaps, the events that just didn't make sense, connections he and Amanda couldn't make or wouldn't believe.

Father Patrick had the connections. And as he spoke, they knew they had to believe.

Crossing himself, asking for forgiveness, he told them about the confession he had taken in Washington, D.C. He explained how President Adamson had previously used him as a confessor on occasion, but always with advance preparations and with security provided. But on this day, the early morning visit had come as a surprise. The president was accompanied by only one man. He looked to be Secret Service, the priest thought, he had that air, and when he described him in surprisingly vivid detail to Carl and

Amanda, they realized it was Harry Wagner who had driven the president to his final confession.

Harry Wagner knew that Tom Adamson had talked.

Father Patrick spoke precisely, recounting the story told to him by President Adamson. It was almost word for word the history Carl knew so well. It was the story of Gideon and how nine-year-old Tom Adamson had murdered him.

It was then that Carl learned exactly how he'd been used. The president told the priest about a partial manuscript that had been delivered to the White House. Carl's manuscript. It had come to the First Lady and she had shared it with her husband. The minutely detailed truth it contained was an extraordinary threat to their future, and it was an even more extraordinary shock to the president that it existed. As far as he knew, the only living people who could possibly know about the baby Gideon were his mother and his wife. His mother had lived it. His wife had been told. The night before their wedding he had fallen into her arms, weeping, and confessed his crime. He did not think the young woman he loved so very much, so absolutely, could enter into a lifelong union without knowing what was truly within his soul. So he told her, in all its graphic detail, about killing his only brother. She already knew of his great ambitions—she shared many of them herself—so all she did was hold him, letting him cry, and rocked him in her arms. *It's no longer your secret,* she'd said. *It's* our *secret now, and it will make us stronger. We'll keep it as long as we live. It will be* our *past. It will bind us in* our *future. And no one else will ever know. Ever.*

They rarely discussed their secret after that, the president told Father Patrick. Only twice. Once was when he'd discovered that his mother had been keeping a diary. She was getting older, a bit careless, and she'd let the fact slip in a conversation. He had panicked. The distant memory of his awful crime came roaring back into his mind with the force of a freight train. That night, for the first time in his life, Adamson woke up screaming. Once again Elizabeth held him and soothed him. She would talk to his mother, she said. She would make sure the diary was destroyed or safely locked away. She would, as always, protect him. And though he went back to bed that night, never again did he have a dreamless, peaceful sleep.

The second time was when Carl's manuscript had appeared at the White House.

Now, according to Father Patrick, Elizabeth was the one who was distraught. She could not explain the book's existence or its mysterious appearance. Someone had to have gotten hold of the diary. But who? They discussed every possible source. Walter Chalmers, the Republican presidential nominee. Their other political enemies on the religious right. The jackals in the media. They even considered Jerry Bickford. Could Adamson have unknowingly revealed his dark secret to the vice president after a night of drinking and camaraderie? Would Bickford descend to blackmail to realize his own lifelong dream of controlling the seat of absolute power?

Whoever it was had the upper hand, they both realized. More than just a hand—a fist that could come hurtling down upon them. Neither of them could let this secret come out, for it would destroy not only Tom Adamson's future but his past. Even if never proven in a court of law, it would make him a pariah. It would wipe out every one of his accomplishments and drive him not just from power but from society itself. He would become a leper, joining and even surpassing such historical outcasts as Benedict Arnold, Aaron Burr, and Richard Nixon.

At first President Adamson seriously considered giving in to the blackmail—resigning with his reputation and his legacy intact. *Retire,* she said. *Let the bastards win.* And why not? It would be quiet, peaceful, and safe. But his nature was to fight. He was, above all else, a political animal. He couldn't just slip away. Instead he went into overdrive, racking his brains, searching desperately for an answer—any answer but the one he gradually began to understand had to be the true one. And this time there was no avoiding it. He could not run from this as he had run from his childhood. So the president faced the truth and, on his knees in the cramped confessional of St. Stephen's Cathedral, had told Father Patrick the conclusions he had forced himself to accept. He told it all to the shaken priest: who had conceived the idea of the Gideon manuscript, who had manipulated all the pieces and brought the idea to fruition, who was now poised to become the world's most powerful politician.

"There's a partner," Tom Adamson had revealed. "It can't possibly work otherwise. Not without a very powerful partner. It can only be one of a small handful of people. I believe I know who it is. I believe I even know when it started. And if I'm right, God help you, Father. They'll know that I've talked to you. They'll come after you. You've got to disappear. *I'm* going to disappear—and as soon as I'm gone, there will be proof that what I'm telling you is true. It will be big and bold. It will be right in front of you in black and white."

But none of them knew what this meant. Not until Amanda had left the table and logged onto Father Thaddeus's computer, desperately searching the news services for headlines, for answers. And as she began to read, her eyes widened. "Carl!" she cried out.

He'd rushed to her and started reading over her shoulder. And now they knew.

They knew who the very powerful partner was. They knew who had organized the blackmail scheme. Who had manipulated the president into committing suicide. Who had been trying to kill them. They knew the name of the mysterious inside source, first mentioned by Maggie Peterson what seemed to Carl years and years ago. In another lifetime.

"It will be big and bold," President Adamson had told Father Pat. "It will be right in front of you in black and white."

It was.

Front-page editorial carried by the *New York Herald*, the *Washington Journal*, the *Chicago Press*, the *Los Angeles Post*, the *Denver Tribune*, and the *Miami Daily Breeze*:

WHY NOT LIZZIE?
By Lindsay Augmon
Chairman, Apex Communications Corporation

My friends, these are dangerous times in America. As we stand on the precipice, poised to take the leap into the unknown of the new century, our nation faces its gravest challenges since the end of World War II.

Never before in history has a nation enjoyed such unrivaled power and prestige. Never before has a nation enjoyed so much prosperity. And never before has a nation had so much responsibility. For I do not exaggerate when I say that the continued stability of the entire world is in our hands, my friends. We are the mighty captain of its armed forces and the master of its marketplaces. We are its peacemaker. We are its moral compass. We are its hope.

Meanwhile, here at home, the forces of government tyranny would tell us what to think and how to live, suppressing the very liberties that make this country the greatest in the history of the world.

Meanwhile, we are witnessing what can only be described as anarchy in the Oval Office. First, we have suffered the tragic loss of President Thomas Adamson, who somewhere along the winding trail lost his own faith in life. And now his mentor, President Bickford, has pronounced himself physically and mentally unfit for the challenge that lies ahead.

My friends, these are dangerous times indeed.

We have a choice to make in November. Possibly the most important choice we will ever make. That is why I am taking this unusual step of addressing you myself, of sharing with you, humbly and with great sincerity, my own personal view. It is a view tempered by years of firsthand experience in this, my adopted country, and shaped by my years in my native Great Britain.

My personal view can be summed up in three words:

Why not Lizzie?

Let us examine the alternative. Walter Chalmers of Wyoming is an able veteran of the congressional trenches, a loyal party man, an estimable scrapper. I admire his bedrock conservative principles and his impeccable personal character. But can Senator Chalmers lead this planet into the twenty-first century? Is he the leader to unite East and West, Muslim and Christian, Protestant and Catholic, Arab and Jew? Is he the leader to manage the complex, multinational economy of which I am living proof? I think not.

Why not Lizzie?

I freely admit that I have a long history of respectfully dissenting from her husband's views. I felt that the late president clung to his human rights agenda at the expense of the very progress and job growth that could bring to those same humans the rights of which he spoke. I felt he placed too much faith in the big hand of government control and not enough in the free hand of the marketplace. In that view, I was not alone. My views were and are consistent with those of the heads of the other Fortune 500 companies.

But in spite of our many disputes, I never doubted Tom Adamson's integrity or his intelligence. He was a good man and a great public servant. He deserves our gratitude and our respect. He deserves a funeral befitting the office and the man. He died from a loss of faith, and there is no shame in that. Just as there would be no shame if he had died from any other disease, such as cancer.

Why not Lizzie?

The two greatest political leaders of my adult life, I would submit, are Ronald Reagan and Margaret Thatcher. President Reagan was the Great Communicator, a man whose singular gift was the common touch. He was a figure of genuine warmth and humanity, a builder of bridges. Prime Minister Thatcher was a tower of indomitable strength, a determined free-marketeer who brought Britain back from the brink of economic collapse and made it into the lean and thriving modern powerhouse that it is today.

For me, Elizabeth Cartwright Adamson combines the very best of them both.

I know Lizzie. I spent several days with her at the World Conference on Emerging Nations in New Zealand last fall. I joined her for the Children's Literacy Crusade in Chicago last May, when I pledged—at her vigorous and irresistible urging—to make my newspapers more accessible to children. The weekly Kid's Page and monthly Kid's Edition, staffed entirely by local schoolchildren, are evidence of that commitment by each and every Apex newspaper across North America.

I found the former First Lady to be an individual of boundless vitality and enthusiasm, a vibrant and intelligent leader who understands that the needs of people and those of business are not

*two separate and distinct priorities but a single interlocking one.
When Elizabeth Cartwright Adamson views an issue, she sees it not
in simple black and white but as a broad spectrum of colors. I do
not pretend to agree with her on every issue, but I do agree with her
on most. And I have found her to be a uniter, a seeker of common
ground, a builder of consensus. She is capable. She is strong. She is
steady. She has the right stuff.*

*One look at the extraordinary results in today's Apex News
Network–Washington Journal polls will tell you that she is able to
reach out and touch voters of all ages and persuasions.*

So I ask you once again:

Why not Lizzie?

*No reason at all. That is why I am endorsing Elizabeth Cart-
wright Adamson to be the Democratic Party's candidate for president. And the person to lead us into the next century.*

Let us all join hands and ask her to take us there.

Lindsay Augmon and Elizabeth Adamson.

The entire pattern was suddenly laid out for all to see: the positive
news stories in all the Apex papers over the past few months focusing on the
First Lady's accomplishments, the reverential television news coverage on
ANN after Adamson's suicide, the adoring documentary that was ready moments after Adamson's death, the national polls—run by Augmon's own
polling services—showing her strength with the voters.

He was pushing her to be president—and no one could push with as
much force and effect as he could. The question was what he would receive
in return. What could the president give him? The answer seemed frighten-
ingly obvious: anything he wanted.

It was Lindsay Augmon whom Carl had spoken to on the phone. Lindsay Augmon who had wanted to know: *Are they dead yet?*

Okay, Carl thought, now they knew. Which made the next act simple.
All they had to do was bring down the most powerful media baron of the
twentieth century and the most beloved First Lady in history, who was now
a near shoo-in to become the next president of the United States.

So they got busy. That meant phone calls. Lots of phone calls. It meant reaching out to Shaneesa one more time, grouped around the speakerphone in Father Thaddeus's office.

"Can I actually hear Mr. Right's voice?" she said after Amanda had filled her in.

"You're hearing it," Carl told her.

"I can't wait for the face-to-face," she said.

"Believe me," he said, "that makes two of us."

"Make that three of us," Father Pat said.

"Sounds like I got the whole crew," Shaneesa said. "Which is good, 'cause I got some fresh meat for you. The five million dollars that was deposited into Harry Wagner's account . . . I know the name of the company that transferred it in."

"Quadrangle," Carl said. "The same company that paid me for writing *Gideon*."

Amanda looked up, surprised, and Shaneesa said, "Damn, what else do you already know?"

Carl said, "I'm only guessing. But it all adds up now. The same person who owns Quadrangle owns Astor Realty. He paid Harry off to lull him into thinking he was safe, then had him killed. He paid me to write the book, then made sure the woman who was supposed to kill me had prime access."

"Lindsay Augmon." Amanda nodded.

"Who also pays my salary," Shaneesa said. "It'll be so righteous to bring that motherfucker down. Oops—sorry, Father."

"Quite all right," Father Pat said. "And I just hope I'm there to see it."

"View you at the airport," Shaneesa said. "And put those seat belts on."

Their plan in place, they sped north on the highway toward the capital—Carl in the driver's seat, hands wrapped around the steering wheel; Father Patrick sitting next to him, his face white and drawn; Amanda in the backseat, hunched forward nervously. They barely spoke. There was no need. And now they were waiting for a plane to arrive.

The evil they were facing chilled Carl to the very bone; the power they were confronting filled him with a deep, all-consuming dread. And the idea that it was up to them to bring the whole thing tumbling down was both numbing and nearly incomprehensible. Yet that's what they were going to try to do. It's what they *had* to do. Their plan was precarious and ever-changing, risky as hell. Carl was beginning to think it would never work. And that he would never make it. His muscles ached. His entire being was screaming with exhaustion. But there was no time to rest or even slow down. He had to make it. They *all* had to make it.

Is the job finished? It's what Lindsay Augmon had first asked on the telephone.

The answer was no, the job *wasn't* finished. The job was just beginning.

chapter 34

Lord Lindsay Augmon was feeling quite pleased with himself. According to that morning's weigh-in, he had lost three pounds from the previous week. Weight had never been a particular problem, but he'd been feeling a bit puffy and had decided that some sort of disciplined regimen would not be the worst thing in his life. So he'd set a modest goal of shedding twelve pounds over the course of a month. The three this week left him a mere pound from his desired number, and he had to admit he felt particularly trim and vigorous. And that was just the beginning of his good fortune. His art broker had called; they'd stonewalled a Soho dealer and managed to buy a Picasso that Augmon particularly coveted. It was one of three in a sequence that the grand old man had painted called "Woman Before a Mirror." They had managed to buy it for a million and a half dollars. What the dealer hadn't known was that the other two paintings in the sequence were going up for auction at Sotheby's. So, after scrupulous research into the potential buyers, Augmon knew that within twenty-four hours of buying he could turn around and sell his new acquisition for nearly six million. For a fleeting moment on the phone with the broker, Augmon thought of keeping the beautiful canvas. He really did adore it. But the idea of quadrupling his money quickly pushed any such thoughts out of his head. Life was business, he knew. He would receive far more pleasure from selling the painting at such a profit than he would gazing at its splendor every morning.

Of course, the phone calls he'd been receiving all day did nothing to lessen his glow.

He thought of two with particular glee. The first had been from Walter Chalmers's campaign manager.

"I'm at a loss for words," the political hack told Augmon, picking his phrases carefully so as not to offend. The manager came from the press and would surely go back to the press. Which meant that one day he'd come to Augmon, hat in hand, looking for a job. "What I'm hoping is that this was meant to be an endorsement for the Democratic convention only and that once the real race begins, you'll still endorse our candidate, as we've been led to believe all along."

"I certainly don't want to dash your hopes," Augmon had responded, "but if that's what you're really thinking, then I'm afraid you've got shit for brains."

The second call was even more satisfying. It was from the Wyoming senator himself.

"Lindsay," Chalmers began, "may I speak with my usual candor?"

"Please do," Augmon said.

"Well, then, what the fuck do you think you're doing?"

"I'm backing a winner, Walter. As usual."

"You're backing a goddamn left-wing feminist whose tits are bigger than her brains!"

"If I were you, I should be careful what I say, Walter. I'm a journalist, after all, and I haven't agreed to speak off the record."

"Journalist, my ass. You're a rat-fucking, two-timing son of a bitch. What I don't understand is why."

"I admire you, Walter. Honestly. But you're a dinosaur, with all that implies. Your tiny brain can't comprehend that you're on the verge of extinction. You can't win. Not now, not ever. And Mrs. Adamson can. More than can. I'm going to make sure she will."

"You can't do that, goddamn it!"

"I'm sure we'll be speaking again, Walter. I wish you well. I really do."

It was soon after that that his secretary buzzed him, excitedly announcing that Mrs. Adamson was on the phone. He agreed to take the call and pushed down on a button connecting him to one of the four lines his desk phone was linked to.

"Good morning, my dear," he greeted her. "I hope you're pleased with what you read this morning."

"More than pleased, Lindsay," she told him. "Overwhelmed."

"Well, let me say your courage is an inspiration to us all."

"Thank you," she said. "Have you received much feedback?"

"I would say the general reaction has been one of shock and, from one or two obvious sources, even hostility. What about on your end?"

"Thrilled, for the most part. And, of course, surprised. I've just issued a statement—I'm sure it will be your lead story on the news tonight—that while my grief makes it almost impossible for me to consider running at this time, your editorial was not just flattering, it was inspiring. And that if the American people want me to carry on my husband's work, then it's something I will have to force myself to consider."

"So you've heard nothing negative?"

"Not really. Mostly extraordinary support. I got a strange call from Bickford, though."

"Ah. Saying what?"

"Nothing, really. It was his demeanor more than his words. Just a sense I got that he felt . . . manipulated."

"As well he should."

"He's quite smart, you know."

"And quite harmless now, as well."

"Yes. I suppose." And then she hesitated.

He sensed her discomfort and finally said, "Something? Please, you know there are no restrictions on what you can say to me."

"I would just like to be reassured that everything else is now under control. That there are no more loose ends."

"I'm expecting a phone call momentarily from one of my employees, giving me just such reassurance."

"Will you let me know when that call comes?"

"Most certainly."

She settled into another silence. This time he didn't rush her. And when she spoke again, her voice was wistful and distant. "I never believed he would do this. I thought he'd be logical. Resign."

"Yes, of course," Augmon said. "It was never our intention."

"We could have gone on. Quite successfully. In time he would have realized that all of this . . . our proposal . . . would have been for the best."

"It's still for the best, Elizabeth. You must never doubt that."

"He killed himself because he knew. I saw the way he looked at me that morning. He knew."

"He was a weak man. And he proved his ultimate weakness. Just as you are about to prove your ultimate strength."

"Thank you, Lindsay." She hesitated again. "For everything."

"No, my dear," he said, with absolutely no hesitation. "Or may I be the first to say, Madam President. Thank *you.*"

chapter 35

From ANN's all-day coverage of the state funeral of President Thomas Adamson:

John Burroughs, network anchor: *It's a sight both magisterial and sobering. It is an outpouring of love, and it is a collective cry of despair. It is an opportunity to say farewell and to try to deal with an almost unbearable loss, yet it is also an affirmation that not only people but institutions and governments and life itself will continue and thrive. Standing outside St. Stephen's Cathedral here in Washington, D.C., almost all emotions are mixed; what few smiles appear are stained with tears. Perhaps only two things are certain on this somber day. One is that over three-quarters of a million people are already here—some estimates go as high as one million—and they will be lining the streets from the steps of this church to Arlington National Cemetery to show their respect for and say a last goodbye to one of the most popular presidents of the century. The other is that there is an extraordinary political story emerging, a populist roar that harkens back more to a film by Frank Capra than to any real-life political scenario of the past.*

Elizabeth Adamson, the courageous—one must even say heroic— widow of the late president, is the object of an unprecedented outpouring of public affection. Because of the timing of the president's death, just days before the Democratic national convention, it looks as if that affection is going to translate into votes. Although resistant to the call at first, and, according to insiders, resistant still, nonetheless Mrs. Adamson is expected not only to announce her candidacy for president within twenty-four hours, but also to be the overwhelming choice of Democratic delegates when the convention begins two days from now.

According to the latest ANN polls— Excuse me, ladies and gentlemen, cars are beginning to arrive at the church for the president's final service. In case you're just tuning in, let me go over one more time the plans for the memorial. The church service, which will begin in approximately two hours, is private. Television cameras will be allowed in, but the doors are closed to the public. These were Mrs. Adamson's wishes, and they are being respected. When the funeral service is over, the president's closed coffin will be driven through the streets of Washington, allowing the public to pay their final respects. When that procession is over, President Adamson's final burial place will, of course, be Arlington National Cemetery. That burial will, again, be private, and the cemetery will be closed to anyone not in attendance at the church service.

Leaders from around the world began arriving in Washington last night. They have already been meeting with and expressing their condolences to President Bickford as well as the former First Lady. We have confirmed that President Boris Yeltsin of Russia will be attending the service today, and speaking, as will Chinese president Jiang Zemin, Israeli prime minister Benjamin Netanyahu, and PLO leader Yassir Arafat. President Bickford will also be speaking. It is not known yet if Mrs. Adamson will be addressing the crowd. The one thing we have had confirmed is that Nora Adamson, the late president's mother, has arrived at the church early, for a meeting with Bishop Moloney, who will be presiding at the service. Elizabeth Adamson is expected to arrive shortly. She will be accompanied by President Bickford and his wife, the new First Lady, Melissa Durant Bickford.

Heads of state from nearly every European nation will be here, of course. From Africa, the countries expected to send representatives are . . .

As Wilhelmina Nora Adamson was ushered into the bishop's comfortable office, she reached out to steady herself, placing her hand on the rock-hard

arm of the Secret Service man who was escorting her. She couldn't help herself: the old lady's thin, wrinkled lips curled ever so slightly over her yellow-
ish teeth as she smiled coyly at the young man and let her fingers rest on his
muscular bicep. Even at her advanced age, even in her painfully arthritic
state, even in the midst of the most overpowering grief of her long life, Nora
had to flirt. It was in her blood; it had been since she'd been such a luscious
young thing as a teenager. She felt that familiar thrill, the warmth and rush of
pleasure, when the handsome young agent smiled back at her politely and
patted her in return, his thick hand nearly covering her entire bony forearm.
But as he helped her into the bishop's cracked leather chair, she couldn't help
but once again burst into tears. This time she was crying not just for her dead
and beloved son—she had been sobbing over his death for nearly two days
straight—but for her own lost youth. For the errors she'd made and her lack
of regret over them. She cried because she knew she would never have another muscular young man or another pain-free moment, and she could no
longer think of a reason to keep on living.

Still, she had learned much over the years since her son Tommy had become a public figure. Perhaps the most important was to keep everyone at a
distance, never let anyone know exactly what you were thinking or feeling.
Once they knew what was inside you, they could destroy you. Just as they
had destroyed Tommy.

So Nora Adamson straightened herself up, arranged herself properly in
the leather chair, wiped the flow of tears from her deeply lined cheeks, and
turned to gaze at the bishop sitting before her. It was only then that she noticed the two other priests standing to the bishop's right. They were both
young, one particularly so. So boyish-looking and yet so drawn and hag-
gard. Tommy's death, she knew, had greatly affected everyone in the country. She was not alone in her mourning; she could tell that looking at the
expressions on the faces of these two men of God.

Comforted already, she nodded to the Secret Service man, dismissing
him from the room. She was here in this room to find solace. She did not
need protection.

"Thank you for seeing me, Bishop. I greatly appreciate your call. I am
in great need, as I'm sure you can tell."

"Mrs. Adamson," the bishop began.

"Please, Father, call me Nora. I'm still a down-home girl and I'm much more comfortable with Nora."

"All right . . . Nora," the bishop said, his voice solemn. He motioned to the priest immediately to his right. "Father Patrick here knew your son. Advised him on occasion, took his confession."

The old lady smiled. It warmed her to hear of someone who was spiritually intimate with Tommy. She nodded at the other priest, even younger, standing a few feet from Father Patrick. "Did you know my son, too, Father?"

The third priest in the room shook his head. "No, I didn't," he said. "But I feel like I did."

"The whole country feels that way," Nora said. "It's very gratifying."

"My case is a little different," this priest said. "I knew him better than most people in the country." The priest seemed to be struggling with his emotions. He was biting down on his lip, as if trying to control himself. "I know *you* better than you think, too."

"I believe that, Father. Young as you are, I can tell you seem to have great insight—"

"I know *all* about you, Mrs. Adamson."

The way he said it, somehow it didn't sound very priestlike. As Nora stared over at him she squirmed in her seat, which suddenly now felt uncomfortable.

"Did you bring your diary with you?" the young priest asked, his voice as steely as any she'd ever heard, and Nora Adamson turned even paler.

"My diary? I don't understand what you're talking about."

"I'm sure you don't. And I'm sure you don't want to. But there's someone who I think can convince you to listen."

She turned to the bishop. "I'd like to leave now," she said. "I'm in the midst of a terrible grieving. I don't think—"

"Bring her in," the younger priest said to the other one.

"Carl," the one whose name was Father Patrick said, "don't you think you should prepare her for—"

"No, I don't," Carl Granville said. "What I think is that you should bring her in now."

Nora watched as Father Patrick opened the door at the back left of the bishop's study. She breathed a barely discernible sigh of relief when the woman stepped through the doorway. She didn't know whom she was expecting, but this was not anyone she'd ever seen before. It was a young woman, twenty-five, maybe thirty—when they were that young, Nora couldn't tell anymore. Close-cropped black hair, quite attractive. But Nora was sure she didn't know this woman.

And then another woman was led in.

Wilhelmina Nora Adamson knew this woman.

"Oh, Lord," she said. She wanted to put her head in her hands, to hide and block this woman from her view. "Oh, Lord, oh, Lord, oh, Lord. It can't be. You're . . . you're a ghost."

"Ain't no ghost," this woman said. "Ain't no ghost a-tall."

The man they called Carl was saying something now. But Nora couldn't concentrate. She was having trouble breathing. "I believe you know Clarissa May Wynn," he was saying. "Or maybe you never knew her real name. Maybe you only knew her as Momma One-Eye."

No, it's not possible, Nora thought. *This cannot be happening. Cannot, cannot, cannot . . .*

But it *was* happening. This woman was standing right in front of her. The woman she'd thought of so many times, for so many years. The woman she'd loved for bringing her son into the world. And hated—for bringing her son into the world. And now the woman was talking. Telling her about long ago. What she had seen. What she knew. What she'd known and kept inside her all this time. What she was now ready to tell the world.

Nora was rocking back and forth now. Her bones were aching, her skin felt as if it would just crack and split, ripping her apart. And still this woman wouldn't stop talking.

"For years I been scared of you. Afraid you'd come back. Punish me for bringin' forth that tiny, sad little devil. But I ain't afraid no more. I'm stronger than you now. Maybe I been a ghost for too long, but I definitely ain't one now," Momma One-Eye was saying, looking down. "It's time to bury all them ghosts."

That's when Nora went to her and hugged her. The old black woman was tremendously frail, but she was strong. And when the tears came, she held Nora. And Nora held her. The years melted away, and it was that terrible night again. It was just the two of them there, sobbing in each other's arms. Remembering and regretting and forgiving.

After a long, long time, Nora gazed through her tears at the young woman standing next to Momma. Then over at the bishop, who was half turned away from her, facing the corner of the room, and at Father Patrick, who was shaking his head slowly and steadily. And then at the young man who was wearing a priest's collar but who didn't act or talk like a priest. It was to him she spoke her next words. "Why?" she said haltingly. "Why have you done this to me?"

It was to Carl Granville she spoke, and it was Carl who responded. "Because we need your help. Because there's something we know that you still don't."

"And what is that?" the old woman asked, blinking in confusion. "What could you possibly tell me that I would care to know on the very day my good boy Tommy is being buried?"

Carl reached down and touched her thin wrist with his hand. "Who killed him," he said. "And what you can do about it. It's too late to save him. But it's not too late to save the rest of us. That's what he would want—for you to avenge his murder."

"Murder?" Nora repeated, her voice quavering weakly. "Tommy took his own life."

"He was driven to it," Carl said insistently. "That makes it murder. But they haven't won yet, Mrs. Adamson. It's pretty damn close, but it's not over. Not if you do this one last thing for us. For *him*."

"No," she said, "this is crazy talk."

"You've protected him all these years. You've shielded him and been there for him. All we're asking is for you to be there for him one last time. Do that, and you just may save Tom Adamson's legacy in history. And maybe his soul, too." Carl gazed at her beseechingly. "Will you please listen to what we have to say?"

She considered his plea carefully. His words were so heartfelt. And he was such a blue-eyed handsome young thing. So serious and intelligent. If only she had met a man like that when she was a girl. She would have given him the moon and the stars.

Slowly and with some difficulty, Nora Adamson made her way over to the nearest chair and sat, pursing her dry lips thoughtfully. "Somebody get me three fingers of good Tennessee whiskey and one ice cube in a tall glass," she said. "Then I'll listen."

chapter 36

There was a famous story about Marilyn Monroe, a story Elizabeth Adamson had heard since she was a young girl, when she was just plain Lizzie Cartwright, but had never really understood. The blond star had appeared in public somewhere, in front of soldiers fighting the Korean War maybe, and she received a stupendous ovation. She was married to Joe DiMaggio then, and she excitedly told him all about it, how there were tens of thousands of people cheering her, screaming for her, loving her. "You can't imagine what it was like," she had said. And the great Yankee center fielder had quietly replied, "Yes, I can."

At long last Lizzie understood.

No one was screaming for her. No one was applauding. But today millions of people—tens, maybe hundreds of millions—were loving *her*.

The funeral was going to be magnificent. A triumph. The memory of Thomas Adamson would be secure, and her own future would be brighter than it had ever been. She knew that the strength she was showing in the face of his weakness somehow made them both seem better, more real, more accessible. Her courage nullified his cowardice. His sad end tempered her ambition. Even after his death, they were the perfect political partners.

The media was now officially in a feeding frenzy. They could not get enough of her. But she'd been holding them off, keeping both her distance and her dignity. That only fed the frenzy, which she knew would reach its peak of hysteria that night.

Lindsay was right. When it all began, he had said she was untouchable. Unbeatable.

Tonight, just a few hours after the funeral, she was going to announce her candidacy. By the end of the week she would have the Democratic nomination in hand.

Five months after that, she would be president of the United States. Untouchable.

She looked around the sitting room in the private residential section of the White House. Tommy had never liked this house, she knew. He had never felt comfortable here, never believed it belonged to him. She had loved it from the very moment she first set foot inside. She appreciated its beauty and its history. She loved its splendor and its many links to greatness. And now it was hers.

Elizabeth Adamson slipped on her shoes. She was ready. A simple black dress, a Valentino; it made her look elegant and somehow vulnerable and distinguished. And suddenly all she wanted was for the day to be over. She wanted to sleep. It had all been much more draining and exhausting than she had anticipated. So she slipped her shoes off again, sat, and leaned back on the overstuffed sofa, her head tilting backward to graze the pillow. Perhaps a quick nap, she thought. Two minutes. The briefest of rests, then she would regroup and clear her head. Then she would be ready to continue.

She didn't know how long her eyes were closed. What she knew was that there was someone else in the room. She could sense the presence, feel that someone was watching her. Elizabeth's eyes fluttered open. It took her a moment to focus. She glanced at her watch; she had been asleep less than five minutes. Then she smiled at the other face in the room and patted the sofa for the president of the United States to sit down beside her. But Jerry Bickford stood ramrod straight and unbending.

"I disapprove, Elizabeth. I just want you to know that."

"Yes, Jerry, you've made that quite clear."

"It's disrespectful to the office of the president. And to Tom," he said. "Most of all to Tom."

"I don't mean it to be. And I'm sorry if you feel that way."

"I don't know what kind of a hold Augmon has on you. I don't know quite what's happening between the two of you, but he doesn't belong here. Not now. Not today."

"There's no hold, Jerry. And there's nothing happening. It's just that, for some of us, the world is going to continue. You know better than anyone that it's all just business. And at our level, we can't allow death to interfere with business. Even Tom's death."

President Bickford said nothing, just looked at the woman who had been married to his closest friend. Looked at her as if he had never seen her before. And to her he said, "The car is waiting. Shall we go?"

The limousine idled before the front entrance to St. Stephen's Cathedral. There was a tap on the bulletproof window, and then the door was opened from the outside by a Secret Service agent. As Lindsay Augmon stepped out of the car and onto the street, he saw Elizabeth Adamson being ushered out of the long black car in front of him. Their eyes met, and she nodded solemnly. Properly. Thousands of people were already lined up along the streets. The whole city, it seemed, was out to catch a glimpse of her, and when she emerged from the limousine there was a sudden quiet. No one pointed her out; the normal buzzing of the crowd turned silent. Elizabeth raised her head and her eyes swept over her people. She smiled for them, a sad and mournful smile, sharing their pain, thanking them for sharing her pain. It was a magnificent smile, and it would be a wonderful front-page picture the next day, he knew, in every newspaper in the world.

She was brilliant, he realized. She really was. But ultimately she didn't have a clue. All she knew was that she was mere moments from an extraordinary opportunity. What she believed to be the ultimate power was just inches from her grasp.

She still didn't understand the real power, though. Then again, how could she? How could anyone? *Because the real power is me,* he thought.

Surprisingly, that thought did not bring him any particular exhilaration. Instead, he felt a subdued kind of tranquillity. The game was nearly over now. His most trusted employee had inexplicably failed—repeatedly. He had lost some key players. And he was up against a surprisingly strong adversary. Nonetheless, the end was close by. And he was prepared for it, so in the end, no matter what happened from here on in, he would win. As always, he would win.

The one thing no one ever understood, certainly not Elizabeth Adamson, was how exhausting it was to always win.

Elizabeth was next to him now. She held out her arm and he took it. He had asked to be in the presidential procession, he wanted that, and Elizabeth had arranged it. She had gone one step further and asked him to be her escort. Funnily enough, it pleased him to be with her at this moment. It was only fitting. They had arranged it all, seen everything come to fruition. It was only apt that they go in the door arm in arm, locked together, moving forward.

"Mrs. Adamson," a priest was saying quietly. "The bishop would like to see you in private before the service begins. To go over the final details. Mr. Adamson's mother is back there now."

Augmon began to remove his arm from hers, but the priest said, again in a hushed and reverential tone, "You're certainly welcome, Mr. Augmon." Elizabeth nodded, just once, and then he took her arm more firmly and led her behind the pulpit, following the priest. Together they would make the final arrangements.

The priest led them inside. Elizabeth expected him to leave, but he joined them in the room and closed the door behind him. She saw him nod to Nora, who was seated in a chair in the center of the bishop's office, stone-faced, her arms folded across her chest. Augmon walked up to her, kissed her gently on the top of the head, murmured his condolences.

Thomas Adamson's mother did not acknowledge his kiss or, for that matter, Augmon's presence. "Thank you, Father Patrick," she said to the priest, who retreated to the doorway, his hands clasped before him.

Elizabeth now stared over at the priest, startled. Shaken. She hadn't recognized him outside, hadn't paid attention. How had this priest gotten here? He wasn't supposed to be here. She turned to look at Augmon, who was looking down at the floor, unmoving.

"Where is the bishop?" Elizabeth asked. "Shouldn't he—"

"Bishop Moloney doesn't have to be here," Nora answered stiffly. "I'm the one who needs to make the final arrangements. A mother's job doesn't end just because her boy is . . . is . . ." She broke off and shook her head, her eyes filling with tears.

"There now, dear," Elizabeth said to her soothingly. She looked up at Father Patrick, then back at the old woman in the chair. "We're going to get through this awful thing, you and I. We're going to be fine. I promise."

One tear slid slowly down Nora's cheek. She wiped it away, struggling to hold on to her composure. Her cheeks were unusually flushed, Elizabeth noticed. She wondered if her mother-in-law had been drinking.

"I told him," Nora said slowly now, her gravelly voice trembling. "I told my Tommy when he first met you. You didn't have a heart. I could see it then, maybe because I was a woman—we're better at that than men. I'm telling you, Lizzie, it gave me a chill when you walked into a room. Froze my blood. But, Tommy didn't listen. How could he? He was in love. For the first time, too. And my boy deserved some happiness. Lord knows I didn't give him much. So, after a while, I kept my feelings to myself."

"Nora," Elizabeth said kindly, "would you like to lie down somewhere?"

The old woman pressed on, ignoring her question. "Somehow, over the years, I thought you changed. You got so . . . polished. Fancy and fine. And everybody just took to you, didn't they? Just like he did. Oh, Lord, he loved you so much."

"And *I* loved *him*. You and I both loved him. We've both lost him and we're both in pain. But what does this—"

"What does this have to do with anything?" Nora turned to Augmon. "*You* know, don't you, sir? You know what it has to do with."

"Madam, I assure you I do not," he responded quickly.

"Well, then sit down and listen," she barked at him, "because it so happens I'm in a talking mood."

Augmon nodded politely but made no move to sit. He stood where he was, his eyes flicking curiously over to Elizabeth, whose own eyes had not left the old woman.

Nora turned back to her daughter-in-law. "What is it you fear most in life, Lizzie? I know what it *used* to be. Tommy told me once. Tommy told me everything. Did as a child, did even when he was a grown man. He told me what you said to him. It was a long time ago, but I never forgot."

"What did I say to him, Nora?"

"That you were afraid he'd come back to me someday. That he'd lose an election, lose some ambition, decide that it was time to pack up and come home to Mississippi again. Home to his people. Home to his mama. And that you'd have to come home with him. No more fancy Elizabeth anymore. Just plain ol' Lizzie, the barefoot girl with the cow dung between her toes. You remember saying that, sugar?"

Elizabeth Adamson shifted her weight uncomfortably from one leg to the other. "I was very young. That was a long time ago."

"What about now? Do you still feel that way now?"

"I don't understand where you're going with this, Nora. But this hardly seems the appropriate time for your reminiscences. And they're causing me a great deal of pain. So why don't you just tell me what is it you want?"

"My first preference," the old woman responded, her words as cold and brittle as an icy winter storm, "would be for you to rot in a jail cell for the rest of your life. But I just don't know if we can afford to take our chances on that. You've been real careful, because one thing you're not is stupid. A lot of bodies are missing. So you'll hire yourself a baker's dozen of them real clever lawyers. The case'll drag on in the courts for years. And, hell, who knows what'll happen once a jury gets its hands on it. They just might take pity on you for being a poor widow woman. And we know they'll just plain love you. Everyone loves you. Everyone who doesn't *know* you." She let out a derisive chuckle. "Me, I'm sitting over here. And I do know you."

"Nora, you're under an incredible strain. I'm afraid you're not making any—"

"I'm making plenty of sense. I'm willing to be practical, Lizzie. That's what I'm trying to tell you. What I'll settle for, what I want, is for you to call a big ol' press conference this afternoon to announce that you don't want to be president after all. That you need time to recuperate from your tragic loss. And that you'll be going into seclusion down home in Mississippi with your beloved mother-in-law. That's what I want, Lizzie. To hear you say you're going to live under the same roof with me for the rest of my natural life. And I have to tell you, girl, that I am feeling mighty healthy. Yes, ma'am. I am feeling as if I won't be going nowhere for a long, long time."

Elizabeth stared at her in disbelief.

"I'm sorry for you, Nora. And I wish I could help. But the entire world is waiting for me to go through that door. To pay one final honor to my husband and your son. And that's where I'm going right now."

That was when the old woman motioned to the priest, who had moved to the back door of the office. He opened it and ushered in two young people, a man and a woman. Elizabeth stared at them, it took a moment for her to register the shock and horror she felt, and then she whirled to face Augmon. His own face was expressionless. The only thing Elizabeth knew for sure right then was that he was not surprised.

"I expect you know who these good people are," Nora drawled. "Carl Granville, Amanda Mays, say hello to Elizabeth Cartwright Adamson and Lindsay Augmon. *Lord* Lindsay Augmon."

"We've spoken," Carl said to Augmon, his eyes steely and hard. "Although not actually in person." Then he turned to Elizabeth. "You should have taken Nora's offer, Mrs. Adamson. I'm afraid we're not quite as practical."

Augmon's nostrils flared but he remained tightly silent, his posture ramrod straight.

Elizabeth's shoulders had slumped slightly. Her eyes had narrowed and her fists were clenched. For a moment she looked as if she was going to run. But she didn't move. And then she turned back to Nora, her shoulders raised again, tall and regal in the middle of the room.

Carl now spoke directly to the Englishman. "You need to hire a better brand of killer," he said. "The second one let you down, too. You'll find what's left of her at the bottom of a gorge just outside of Paint Gap."

"I have no idea what you're talking about," Augmon said to him brusquely.

"Don't you?" Carl demanded. "Would you like me to tell you?" He got only icy silence in response. "Okay, fine. I'll be happy to. You are the puppet master, Lord Augmon. You had Harry Wagner kill an innocent woman and her six-year-old daughter down in Warren, Mississippi. Then you turned around and had Harry killed—by the same woman, the same *assassin*, who killed Maggie Peterson. The same assassin who killed some poor innocent girl I found in the apartment above mine, and the FBI agent parked outside of Amanda's house, and the LaRues—"

"And Cardinal O'Brien in Baltimore." It was Father Patrick who now stepped forward and spoke, his resonant voice soaring with emotion. "And Father Gary."

"And Luther Heller." This was from Amanda. "You had Payton kill the alderman."

"Payton's dead, too," Carl went on. "And so is your assassin. That makes thirteen people dead."

"Fourteen," Nora Adamson said. "If we include my Tommy."

Carl nodded grimly. "We're most definitely including him."

"You can include whomever you'd like," Augmon said. His body was motionless, his hands and arms still. Only his eyes betrayed the slightest hint of nervousness. "However, I've had about as much of this as I'm going to take. There are federal agents and police sharpshooters all over the cathedral grounds, my young Mr. Granville. All that Elizabeth has to do is alert them that you're here and your life is over."

"They'll have to shoot me, too," Amanda said.

Father Patrick nodded. "And me."

"And *me,*" Nora Adamson added from her chair. "And I'm afraid, Lindsay, that even you would have some trouble explaining that one."

"This is preposterous," Augmon said, and despite the air-conditioning in the office, beads of perspiration were now beginning to form on his upper lip. "You have no proof for any of these wild allegations."

"Don't we?"

"No, Mr. Granville." Augmon allowed a tiny smile to cross his lips. "I don't believe that you do."

"We know for a fact that Payton was on your payroll. We got his Social Security number from his wallet and ran a computer trace on it. He was employed by Astor Realty Management. His car is also registered to Astor Realty. So is the rented Toyota that's parked outside the retreat in North Carolina. I'm sure you know whose car that is, Lord Augmon. And I'm sure you know that you happen to own Astor Realty Management."

"Allow me to assure you," Augmon scoffed at him, "that it is vastly more difficult to find companies I *don't* own than companies that I *do.*"

Carl plowed on, undeterred. "You also own a company called Quadrangle. That was a little difficult, because we thought it was publishing. But it's just a shell. You used it for only three purposes. One was to pay your assassin, the woman I knew as Toni. Two was to pay me to ghostwrite the novel *Gideon.* And three was to put five million dollars into Harry Wagner's account. Harry was the courier who brought me the pages for the memoir. He also worked for the Secret Service. And what a coincidence"—he turned now toward Elizabeth Adamson— "Harry was assigned to the First Lady."

Carl moved toward Elizabeth, stood face-to-face with her. "You couldn't publish the diary itself, because the president would have known instantly who was responsible—his own wife. By having me turn it into a work of fiction, you were able to prey upon his worst fears—that key elements of the true story had somehow, some way leaked out over the years. *You* had Harry steal Nora's diary and make a copy. *You* sent him to New York with the pages taped to his leg. *You* could allow for his periodic absences and turn him into little more than your errand boy."

"Harry was gay," Amanda took over. And when Elizabeth turned suddenly, when her eyes flickered questioningly, Amanda smiled triumphantly and said, "He left us a little clue. A matchbook. We traced it to a gay bar, Port of Entry. He would have been kicked out of the Secret Service if his superiors found out. So you blackmailed him."

The look on Elizabeth's face was a terrible thing to behold. The force of it made Amanda take a step backward.

"I *will* become president of the United States," Elizabeth Adamson said fiercely. "I was *born* to become president of the United States."

"Say nothing, Elizabeth!" Augmon ordered sharply.

But Elizabeth ignored him. Her eyes were flashing, her manner imperious. "If you try to stop me, I will fight you in the courts. I will fight you in the press. Anywhere. Anytime. I will fight you, and I will *win*."

"Elizabeth!" It was a command from Augmon, loud and absolute, and it stopped her. Then quieter, calmly, he said, "You will not have to fight them."

All eyes turned toward Augmon now. But his own eyes were focused directly on Carl Granville. "How rich would you like to be, Mr. Granville? In your wildest dreams. Because, you see, I can make you very, very rich."

Carl stared at him a moment, blankly. When he finally spoke, he was incredulous. "That's it? After all of this, *after everything,* that's what you think it comes down to? *Money?*"

"Why, of course," Augmon replied. "What else would it come down to?" He turned to face Amanda. "Would you like to run a newspaper? Tell me which one you fancy. If I don't own it, I'll buy it for you." And then to Father Patrick: "Would you like a church of your own? A charity? Perhaps a children's hospital?" And to Tom Adamson's mother: "Nora, do you really want to see your son's legacy destroyed? Simply for the sake of some cheap, hollow revenge? I can glorify his memory like no one else can. I can make

him live on as a hero in the mind of the entire world." Augmon turned back
to Carl now. "My reporters will uncover extraordinary new evidence proving your innocence. We will have confessions from the guilty parties within
days."

"What guilty parties?" Carl demanded.

"Don't concern yourself with that. I'll find them. And I'll condemn
them." He went over to the window and gazed out at the lilies standing tall
in the garden. Then, abruptly, he turned back to Carl. "You put me to a lot of
trouble, son. But I'm prepared to compromise, just as Nora was. I'm a reasonable man. You should accept this offer. It's the smart thing to do. And it's
as close as you will ever come to winning."

Carl didn't answer him for a long moment. When he did it was to say,
"You are responsible for the deaths of fourteen people. People are not
pieces of Kleenex. You can't just use them and throw them away."

"Of course you can," Augmon responded with a shrug. "That's entertainment, my boy. That's politics. That's *life.*" As Carl stared at him, Augmon said, "Take the offer. You cannot touch me. I control too many things
and too many people."

"If that's the case," Amanda spoke up, "why offer us anything at all?"

"Because it's easier," Augmon replied simply. "And because so much
else is at stake. I am on the verge of a truly extraordinary achievement.
When Elizabeth becomes president, she will do something her late husband
stubbornly and shortsightedly refused to do—lift the human rights ban on
China. When she does, I will be free to make my satellite communications
deal with the Chinese government, for which I will ultimately earn over one
hundred billion dollars." He began to pace back and forth in front of the
windows, caught up in the mounting excitement of his own words. "Can
you people even fathom the concept of a hundred billion dollars? I sincerely
doubt it. And would any of you believe me if I told you that the money, in
and of itself, is not even the point? I sincerely doubt that as well. How could
you? But the fact is that there is a new currency in today's world that matters much more than money. That currency is *information.* Who controls the
airwaves. Who decides what people know. That's where the true power lies.
I am about to become the most powerful man in the history of the world. I

will control what billions and billions of people watch and read and *think*. As a result, I will control what they do. I will control their governments. I will control *them*. And believe me, that is not science fiction. That is reality." He came to a stop now, running a hand distractedly through his hair. "That's why I'm prepared to make you this offer. And that's why you're going to say yes."

Carl glanced at Amanda. Then at Father Patrick and at Nora Adamson.

"Don't think too long, son," Augmon said. "You've done remarkably well. But the bottom line is that all you've got is guesswork and innuendo. No one will believe one word of it. Especially coming from a wanted and dangerous criminal such as yourself."

"Maybe not," Carl acknowledged. "But they *will* believe the results of the DNA test."

"What DNA test?" Augmon asked slowly. "On what?"

"On the remains," Nora Adamson said hoarsely, motioning to Father Patrick once more.

When he opened the door, in walked a frail, ancient black woman. Elizabeth drew in her breath sharply at the sight of her. Until this moment, she had felt quite certain it was all going to work out. That these people would be happy to take what they were being offered. That they were as greedy as everyone else and it would all be okay. But she knew instantly who this old woman was. She knew because her left eye had a perfectly round dark ring around it, as if she had once been branded.

And she knew what Momma One-Eye was carrying in that splintered and rotting wooden crate, its precious cargo partially covered by a worn, faded blue blanket.

Elizabeth knew. And this knowledge was like a severe body blow. It rocked her, and for a moment Elizabeth Adamson was barely able to breathe. She closed her eyes, struggling to regain her composure, her resolve. Telling herself that her lifelong dream was not melting away. Willing herself to believe this. *It cannot be. I will prevail. I am Elizabeth Cartwright Adamson, the most famous and beloved woman in the entire world. I have not come this far to be undone by these small, desperate people. I have worked too hard. And I am too close. So very close . . .*

Momma One-Eye was gently laying the crate down on the desk, a murmured prayer escaping from her lips. Then she opened the box. And they all stared at the tiny, fleshless skeleton inside.

"Say hello to my baby boy, Lizzie," Nora said, her voice choking with emotion. "Say hello to my poor baby Gideon."

"The DNA on his remains will match Tom Adamson's," Amanda said, her own voice low and steady. "Proving he was Adamson's brother. And Nora's son. Proving that this whole story is true."

"A grandstand play," Augmon said dismissively. "And a wholly implausible one at that. There can be no such test. In a few short hours Tom Adamson and his DNA will be buried for eternity. You can't stop that from happening. No one can. And there isn't a judge in the land who would agree to have the president of the United States exhumed on such flimsy evidence."

"They kept a supply of President Adamson's blood under lock and key at Bethesda Naval Hospital, for emergency purposes," Amanda told him. "They do that for every sitting president. And it's still there."

Augmon looked at Elizabeth. She met his gaze and nodded. And with that nod, it was as if she deflated, sagging as all hope escaped from her body.

"We can give Gideon a proper Christian burial," Momma One-Eye said to Nora. "In consecrated ground. So's your baby can finally rest in peace."

"Yes." Nora nodded. "So he can. And at long last, so can *I*."

With that, Nora slowly stood up. She undid the top button of her blouse to reveal a concealed microphone tucked inside her collar.

"Thanks to the computer skills of one of your brighter young *Journal* employees," Amanda told the stunned Englishman, "this mike is sending a wireless signal back to a Netphone. The Netphone is linked up to the Web. This entire conversation has been going out live over the Internet. Word for word."

"No . . . you didn't . . . " Elizabeth could barely force the words out of her body. She was overwhelmed by a tremendous feeling of emptiness. She was melting away. Becoming nothing. No one. "You didn't . . . you couldn't . . ."

"Every C-Span junkie inside the Beltway will be on to it by lunchtime," Amanda went on. "By tomorrow the whole world will know, thanks to the information revolution that you, Lord Augmon, are so proud to be in the forefront of."

"It means nothing," Augmon sputtered. "It's inadmissible in a court of law. You can't record us without our knowledge or consent. It's illegal."

"So sue us," Amanda said.

"We're not in a court of law," Carl pointed out. "We're in the court of public opinion. Rumor, innuendo, suspicion . . . it's *all* admissible. Hell," he said with a smile, "it's the *news.*"

The Englishman cried out now, an incomprehensible cry, the cry of a wounded animal, and whirled. He lunged at Nora and tried to wrench the microphone off her. Carl stepped between them and slammed the mogul roughly into a chair. Augmon gazed up at him, his face a mask of pained bewilderment. His voice seemed small now, and far away. "You can't even comprehend what I have achieved, can you? The sheer brilliance it took to engineer it. The clarity of vision. The unmitigated balls. No one did what I did. No one else *could* do it. Just *me.* If you've ruined it. . . ." For a brief instant Lord Lindsay Augmon, the most powerful media titan in the world, looked like nothing more than a little boy who had just found out he would not be getting the bicycle he wanted for Christmas. He slumped there in the chair, defeated, for a long moment before he said, "How could you do this to me?"

Carl crossed the room, his hands reaching for Augmon's throat. The mogul shrank from him in terror, positive he was about to be strangled. Carl's fingers briefly lingered on the Englishman's loose flesh; he could feel the heat emanating from the skin and the fear causing the pulse to throb. Then he gently and neatly straightened the knot in Lord Augmon's sober navy silk tie.

"How could I do this?" Carl repeated. He thought about how easy it would have been to have gone along with the billionaire's scheme, how he could have had everything he'd ever wanted, for himself and Amanda. Money. Luxury. Prestige. Power. Then he thought about the terror he'd lived through. The death and destruction he'd seen. And he thought about what would happen now to the people in the room who had caused it all. Then he smiled at Lindsay Augmon. A boyish, winning smile. The smile that first won over Amanda Mays. It had been a long while since Carl Granville had smiled that way. "Lord Augmon," Carl said, "it was my pleasure."

epilogue

July 16—August 24

Partial transcript from the July 15 ANN all-day coverage of the state funeral of President Thomas Adamson:

JOHN BURROUGHS, network anchor: *The sun is nearly setting and the president's final procession is nearly finished. In just a few moments, Thomas Adamson will be buried and his family, his countrymen, his mourners around the globe will begin their new lives without him. As we prepare to watch the president's coffin placed in the ground, my own feeling is that we should watch in silence, letting our own thoughts and emotions settle. I, for one, don't know how many more words I've got in me at this late hour. We have all heard many words spoken here today. Words that have elicited memories heroic and tragic, political and personal, and that have had enormous impact both immediate and historical. But of all the words we've heard on this sad day, of all the raw emotion we've witnessed, none have been quite so moving as the final eulogy delivered by Father Patrick Jennings, the pastor of St. Stephen's Cathedral, where the funeral service took place.*

Father Jennings, as many of you are aware, was the center of quite a bit of intrigue this past week when he disappeared suddenly and mysteriously. There are still many questions about his disappearance—as well as his unexpected reappearance—that need to be answered. And there are allusions in the eulogy to truths that will be revealed and guilt that must be expiated. Those allusions will also certainly be further illuminated as time goes on. But the gist of his words needs no further explanations. They need only to be repeated and heeded, as I am certain they will be.

As President Adamson's body is being brought into Arlington National Cemetery now, allow me to quote from the end of Father Jennings's magnificent oration: "Let us all understand that death is not an eraser. It does not remove the deeds or the meaning that existed in anyone's life. It does not make poor men rich or great men fallible. And when death comes, let us not romanticize its presence nor the person it takes from us. Let us see death for what it really is: a border that we all must cross, a border that, more than any other, defines the lives we are able to lead. Do not mourn for those who cross over. Rather, reflect on the definition they've left behind. It is the only truth we are able to know here on earth. When the definition is great, then celebrate it. When it is lacking, then learn from it and improve on it. And use it to make your own definition more truthful and loving and miraculous."

And now, let us watch and pray as we say farewell to President Thomas Adamson. . . .

Transcript of ANN's live broadcast of Elizabeth Adamson's July 17 press conference:

ELIZABETH ADAMSON, former First Lady of the United States: *What I have to say is probably going to surprise quite a few people. But it should surprise no one. The events of the past several days have been overwhelming, to me, to my country, to the entire world. The country has lost its leader, the world has lost a symbol and a voice of reason, but to me, the most overwhelming thing is that I have lost my husband. I find it rather extraordinary that so many people seem to think that I can replace Tom Adamson. But I'm here before you now to tell you that I cannot. That I will not. I'm not qualified, I'm not prepared, I'm not able in any way imaginable.*

To those of you who are disappointed, I am flattered. I appreciate your support and your love. But I will not be running for president of the United States. Not now, not tomorrow, not ever.

Thank you. Good night. God bless.

From page five of the *Washington Journal,* July 22:

SECRET BURIAL AT SEA

Washington, D.C.: *A Hollywood film crew, scouting underwater locations for the movie* Mission Impossible II, *discovered a body today at the bottom of the Potomac River. Divers on the crew came upon a strange sight—a nearly new Sub-Zero refrigerator lodged on the river bottom. Curious, the crew raised the refrigerator and, when it was opened, discovered the body of a man.*

Police have not released any information as to the state of the body nor ventured any theories as to how it came to be buried in its strange tomb, but say there are several leads and expect identification momentarily.

Front-page story in the *New York Times,* July 29:

AUGMON TO SELL U.S. HOLDINGS

by Amanda Mays, Special Correspondent to the *New York Times*
Amidst numerous rumors, allegations, and the threat of a developing scandal that threatens to bring down his empire, Lord Lindsay Augmon has confirmed that he will be selling off his vast media holdings in the United States. Expected to be included in the sale are the Apex Studio, which includes Apex Films, Apex Animation, and Apex Television Productions; the Apex Broadcasting Network, including ANN, the twenty-four-hour all-news network; and all of Apex's publishing holdings, including its book, newspaper, and magazine divisions.

Lord Augmon did not return phone calls for this story. In a statement released to the press, he blamed the sale on the restrictive business and economic policies of President Jeremiah Bickford, which he said "seem sure to continue now into the next century, thus making expansion and profit growth impossible. It is a tragic by-product of President Bickford's shortsightedness that businessmen with vision must now move their businesses to foreign soil if they are to prosper and thrive. I hope the president can live with the damage he is inflicting on the American economy and its workers."

Lord Augmon's statement made no mention of the explosive and controversial transcript of his "confession" that appeared on the Internet on July 15 and which prompted the ongoing investigation of his involvement, along with that of former First Lady Elizabeth Adamson, in various crimes, including the alleged murder of Secret Service agent H. Harrison Wagner. He has previously denied the veracity of the transcript, saying, "It is the ultimate recklessness, a hoax that proves the danger of communications tools when they are democratized to such an extent that any and all censorship is precluded."

The wide-ranging investigation is being led by Special Prosecutor Philip Arnold. Mr. Arnold, who was appointed by President Bickford soon after the transcript was transmitted on the World Wide Web and after this paper reported accusations made by novelist Carl Granville, himself recently cleared of any involvement in the allegations, declined comment.

Janice Morrison, media analyst for Merrill Lynch, speculated that "the Murdochs and Eisners of the world will be all over this sale like sharks at a shipwreck. While Augmon's legal problems are clearly weighing him down personally, his companies are quite sound with excellent management teams in place, and . . ."

From page one of the *New York Times* business section, August 4:

CHINA MAKES WORLDWIDE SATELLITE DEAL

Beijing, China: *Communications history was made today when the Chinese government concluded a multibillion-dollar deal partnering three separate international communications companies for partial rights to China's satellite, cable, and long-distance phone business.*

In an unprecedented arrangement, Rupert Murdoch's News Corp, Time Warner, and French Telecom will all be sharing, over the agreed-upon period of the next ten years . . .

The warm wave lapped gently up onto the shore, tickling the left foot of Amanda Mays and washing the coarse sand from between her toes. She was lying on her right side, squinting through her dark sunglasses at the un- stoppable glare, and smiling.

"What are you looking at?" Carl Granville asked her.

"I've never seen you tan before."

"I've been tan before."

"When?"

"Believe me, I've been tan."

"Give me a for-instance."

"Once I tried to light the stove in my old apartment—you know, the one with the pilot light—and I got a little too close and . . . well, it wasn't exactly tan, it was more of a burnt orange, now that I think about it."

"I'm happy," Amanda said. "Are you?"

"I'm happy," he said.

They had needed to get away. The media scrutiny and the legal pro- ceedings and the pressure that came with just walking down the street had become unbearable. Without knowing exactly where they were going to wind up, they flew down to St. Thomas and talked to various boaters and crew members and wound up in a tiny hotel—a series of lean-to shacks, really—on the south side of St. John. A hundred yards from their shack was a bar called the Soggy Dollar. It got its name from the days when a boat could get only so close and you had to swim ashore. All wet money was handed over to the management, who pinned it up on the wall while it dried and allowed those who wanted to to run up a tab. Calling it a bar was probably a misnomer; it was a stretch of white beach with a few tables and umbrellas and a black barman named Big Willie who made something delicious with rum called a Painkiller. But it served their purposes quite nicely. Carl and Amanda had done little the past two weeks but drink their rum drinks, lie on the sand, swim in the smooth wa- ter, and go back to their room and make love as often and as perfectly as they could.

"I'm extremely happy," Carl said again. "And you're asking because . . . ?"

"Because we can't stay here forever. Even Big Willie's going to want us to pay our bar bill eventually." Carl didn't say anything. He sat up, brushed a bit of sand off his chest, stared out over the blue-green water. "The *Times* wants me to come work there permanently," she told him.

"I'm not surprised," Carl said. "It was a hell of a series you wrote."

"And the *Journal* wants me back. Now that Augmon's selling, they want to make me city editor."

"I'm still not surprised," Carl said. "Anybody can tell you're the best. Even the people who run a newspaper."

"I think I want the *Journal* job. But it'd mean living in Washington."

"Oh," he said.

"Yeah," she told him, and she wasn't smiling anymore.

"Well . . ." He squirmed on his towel, uncomfortable. "I've got to get back to New York pretty soon. Finalize the book deal. Meet my new editor. That sort of thing."

"Uh-huh," she said.

"You know what I've been thinking?" he murmured. "I've been thinking that Washington might be a pretty good place to write a book." Now she took her sunglasses off to look at him. "For a little while."

"You mean for a month or so?" she asked.

"Maybe a month. Or two months . . . or six months . . . or six years . . ."

She reached over to put her hand on his shoulder and ran her fingernail slowly down his arm, scratching a thin white line all the way down to his hand. The smile was back.

They stopped kissing only when they heard the commotion at the bar. When they looked over, they saw Big Willie with a broad grin on his face. A workman was up on a ladder, attaching a small satellite dish to the top of the thatched roof.

"At last," Willie said. "Satellite TV. Mon, we get *everything* now."

The workman on the roof motioned for Big Willie to turn on the small TV that was positioned in the corner of the bar. He flicked the switch, then began fiddling with the most complicated-looking remote control imaginable. In quick succession, three baseball games appeared. And several old movies. Then a 1967 episode of *Password* and a rerun of *The Wonder Years*. Then Big Willie lifted his finger off the button and lingered on one channel. It was ANN. The breaking news. An ANN anchor was announcing: "The former First Lady of the United States, Elizabeth Cartwright Adamson, was indicted today in Owens, Mississippi. She's seen here being arrested at the home of her mother-in-law, Wilhelmina Nora Adamson, mother of the late president, Thomas Adamson. The former First Lady is being charged with four counts of obstruction of justice and three counts of conspiracy to commit murder.

"Mrs. Adamson's lawyer, T. Gene Monahan, called the charges unfounded. Mr. Monahan protested the treatment Mrs. Adamson was receiving." Then came a clip of Monahan, who was saying, "These wild charges are, as everyone knows, being made by irresponsible and highly dubious sources and will be shown to be without any merit whatsoever. Elizabeth Adamson is a patriot and a hero and—"

Big Willie clicked another button on the remote control. "Who wants to watch that shit?" he said, shaking his head. And then, after a few more clicks, his grin returned. "Now this be more like it."

Carl and Amanda watched the new program for a few seconds.

Wil-maaaa! Where's my brontosaurus burger?

The people at the bar laughed in delight.

Carl kissed her one more time, licking away a few grains of sand that had accumulated on her upper lip. Then they slipped into the water and swam, slowly at first, then faster, strong steady strokes pulling them farther and farther away from shore and the laughter and Big Willie and the satellite TV over his bar.

ABOUT THE AUTHORS

PETER GETHERS has written two previous novels, *The Dandy* and *Getting Blue*, and two best-selling nonfiction books, *The Cat Who Went to Paris* and *A Cat Abroad*, and is the coauthor of an annual, *Rotisserie League Baseball*, and *Historical Cats*. In addition, he is an editor and publisher and, with David Handler, has written numerous film scripts and television shows. Mr. Gethers lives in New York City and Sag Harbor, New York. This is the first collaboration between Mr. Gethers and Mr. Handler under the name Russell Andrews.

DAVID HANDLER began his career as a journalist and critic. He won widespread critical acclaim for his autobiographical first novel, *Kiddo*, and has gone on to win an Edgar and an American Mystery Award for his series of eight novels featuring the dapper amateur sleuth Stewart Hoag—a hero who, in the words of the *Detroit Free Press*, combines "the panache of James Bond, the in-your-face attitude of Sean Penn and the lethal wit of Gore Vidal." Mr. Handler has written many television and film scripts with his longtime partner, Peter Gethers. He makes his home in a two-hundred-year-old carriage house in Old Lyme, Connecticut.